LOST

Junctions Murder Mystery Series

Book One:

LOST

L. E. Fleury

The reader should be aware that the characters in the *Junctions Murder Mystery Series* are fictional. While most of the historical locations and events are accurate, the writer has taken artistic license on certain issues to enhance the plot or to paint a more beautiful mental picture. Enjoy the books!

Copyright © 2023 by L. E. Fleury.
All rights reserved.

First paperback edition November 2023.

Editing by Joyce M. Gilmour.

Cover design by Heylea, LLC.

Cover photo enhancements by
Kathy Rowe and Kelly Rainbow Butterfly.

Special thanks to BETA readers:
Louise Ginsberg and Patty Densmore.

Published by Heylea, LLC.
cabininthewoods2021@gmail.com

ISBN: 979-8-9890236-0-8 (paperback)

I dedicate this book

...to the Father: Thank you for giving us eternal life.

...to the Son: Thank you for your Blood Covering that gets us back Home.

...to the Holy Spirit: Thank you for enriching our earthly sojourn.

"Finally, brethren, whatsoever things are true, whatsoever things are honest, whatsoever things are pure, whatsoever things are lovely, whatsoever things are of good report, if there be any virtue and if there be any praise, think on these things."

Philippians 4:8 (KJV)

CHAPTER ONE

Thievery

Her mother's bright blue eyes were wide and glistening as she spoke: "Look at me, my girl." She gripped Lisa Marie's skinny shoulders, staring steadfastly at the one child who could put on a strong, brave front. The other three were going to be difficult, but Lisa could hold it together, for as long as she needed to. "It will only be for a few weeks," she promised, "and then I'll have a job and then I can come and take you all home again."

"Okay, Mama," came the shaky reply.

They hugged quickly and then a tall girl with long, black hair picked up the paper grocery bag containing all of Lisa's humble possessions and took the almost seven-year-old's hand.

"I'm Jenny," she said in a soft murmur. "I'm here to help you get settled. We need to go to the other building. It's pretty nice." Her tone was encouraging, and her smile friendly, so Lisa swallowed down the fear, down into the pit of her stomach and descended the curved cement steps into the large porte coshere, a brick and granite carriage porch, where Mr. Wilson's 1935 Ford sedan waited to take her mother away.

In front of her, her older brother, Sonny, was already walking toward a large building complex: two three-story brick structures connected in the middle by a low, single-story construction with a handsome, white-railed porch across its front. All three buildings had steep, wide stairs leading to their front doors. She saw her brother heading to the right-hand building — the Big Boys' quarters — and quickly concluded she was to go to the other big place at the left end of the porch. Sonny was being escorted by a sandy-haired teenager who was trying to make guy-talk. But the boy's head was bowed into his own paper bag bundle to hide his unmanly grief and his thin shoulders hunched forward under the burden of the moment… a weight far too great for this already fragile nine-year-old. She wanted to give him a goodbye hug but was pretty sure it was "boy" territory, so instead took another tremulous breath, and swallowed down the fear again.

And then she saw the girls. The six of them were sitting in a row on the edge of a low, flat, wooden platform, to the left of where she was walking along the cement driveway with Jenny. Long, flesh-colored cotton stockings covered the legs scrunched up under their jackets against the cold March wind. A seventh one dangled gently on the seat of a single playground swing… and they were all watching her, a knowing look in their eyes. She was about to become one of them.

Some people are gifted from birth, or maybe before, but nevertheless, gifted… and Lisa Marie happened to be a "born actress," much like Shirley Temple, without the dimples and the curls. So, Lisa let go of Jenny's hand, tugged her too-small navy blue dress-up coat into shape, and strolled boldly over to her little audience. Coming to as graceful a halt as possible, she put on her show-biz smile and sang out a big "Hel-lo, I'm Lisa Marie Dupree! What's your name?" The girls each piped up with an answer, but Lisa didn't hear those names… she was getting ready for her next line: "So-o-o… do you want to play Ring-Around-the-Rosy or something?"

The girls giggled at the silliness of such a suggestion, then paused to see what she would do next. To Lisa's great relief, the girl on the swing spoke up: "You wanna swing for a while?"

"Sure!" She slipped onto the seat and gripped the chains connecting the seat to the cast-iron pipes supporting the swing. With a push of her foot, she began to sway smoothly in an arc, back and forth. She smiled at the girls. "This is a pretty good swing," she said, trying to make conversation.

"We have four more at the other end of the playground," one of them replied as she pointed somewhere behind Lisa's back.

She turned her head to spot them but was suddenly stopped by the sounds coming from the main building where her mother had just said goodbye. She halted the swing to concentrate and sure enough, they were the cries of her two younger siblings. She had heard her three-year-old brother and her four-and-a-half-year-old sister cry many times. She knew those cries. But this time they were different... not the "fall down and go boom" toddler cries, not the coughing-choking cries of sick children. These were cries of innocents in shock, rising and shrieking in sheer terror.

Lisa stood up from the swing, her eyes riveted on the curved cement steps leading up to the office in that main building of the Children's Home. She could still see Mr. Wilson's car in the corner of her eye. It wasn't too late. They could all get back into the car and go... home... or someplace...

Suddenly, three shadowy figures descended the stairs and moved quickly into the car. Doors slammed, as the children's screams faded into the recesses of the building where toddlers and up to age six resided. The start of the Ford's engine drowned out the final echoes of the terrified children, as the car moved slowly forward, past the solemn sympathizers on the wooden platform and out toward Shelburne Road.

The Dupree children were officially residents of the Children's Home at 555 Shelburne Road, Burlington, Vermont.

It was 1946.

The rest of the day passed in a blur of activities for young Lisa Marie.

That night, she learned how to undress under a nightgown in the middle of a dormitory of twenty or so other girls, then brush her teeth with a mixture of salt and baking soda. The prayers to Jesus came next: The Lord's Prayer and The Lord is My Shepherd and some song and then, "God bless Mom and Dad and Uncle Whomever..." and finally falling asleep, knowing the very same Jesus she had trusted, back in Roman Catholic Catechism days, was right there in the Children's Home. It was a glimmer of hope in the middle of an unbelievably horrifying event. Still, she awoke in trembling and tears throughout the night. Jesus or no Jesus, it was still a real nightmare.

And so — no surprise — on that first night, she wet the bed.

Nobody condemned her. The bed was stripped and she was taken into the back part of the dormitory bathroom and allowed to do a sponge bath, with the quiet supervision of the upstairs housemother, Mrs. Hays. And by the very hour it was time to do morning chores, have breakfast, and get off to public school, Miss Dupree was professionally, promptly prepared.

But starting the very next day, she was awakened every night at eleven o'clock for a bathroom break. That went on for about a week. She never wet the bed again. It was a matter of somebody caring enough to get the job done, a fact that kept coming up concerning this little girl's upbringing before she was a resident... like so many others who had come to the Home before her.

She had to learn how to make a bed with hospital corners. She had to master braiding hair and polishing her shoes and doing her part in daily chores. Then there were table manners ("Tilt the soup bowl away from you and dip the soup spoon into the last bit of broth — again — in an away-from-you direction. Remember, it is impolite to slurp your food, so sip gently.") and rolling her white linen napkin so it could be slipped easily into the hole in the middle of a heavy napkin ring (hers was a pale green jasper-like material formed in the shape of a rabbit, with a small, gold stone for an eye, on both sides of its head). She had never had either one of those before, either.

There was much more, but the part of her day she looked forward to the most, was seeing her brother in the dining hall, that low building with the big, white porch railing, connecting the boys' and the girls' residences. He was always on the other side of the large room, seated at the boys' tables and even though his back was always toward her at his assigned chair, she could see him and love him and think about the time when they would — all four — be back in their own home with their mother and father.

"We're only here for a few weeks," she would remind herself.

But it would be a lot longer than that.

***

Nearly two years passed, as the four youngsters settled into the often-tedious routine of institutional life. Occasionally, however, young adults came to the Home and supervised special activities, especially over the holidays. These individuals were earning credits over the academic year toward degrees in social work, physical education, and the like. But all the children knew was those young adults showed up at every holiday, with decorations, goodies, and games. Other than that, there were hot, dusty, summertime walks to Queen City Park for swimming in Lake Champlain twice each week and the usual crafts to fill the empty hours of the long, school vacation afternoons. Nevertheless, the youngsters looked forward to these events, even though, most of the time, they were predictable.

5

There was one special occasion, however, that would bring the presence of the outside world chillingly close into that inner circle of innocence. A young college student, Dawn Somebody (The children never were told the last names of any of the volunteers.) took the Big Girls on a late-summer blackberry-picking adventure, across the street. Neither Miss Dawn, nor the children, were aware of the true nature of this popular berry-picking location. All Miss Dawn knew was that the country club and golf course were located across Shelburne Road from the Children's Home and there were wonderful blackberry bushes on the Swift Street side of the property. She had been alerted to this by one of her college classmates, the captain of the football team. "Check it out," he had said, with a wink.

And so, on a pleasant August afternoon, Miss Dawn gathered the Big Girls, all furnished with tin buckets to hold the luscious berries and led them along the heavily padded path into the depths of the blackberry bushes. There was a sense of adventure as the group moved along between the prickly greenery, enjoying a special romp outside of their ordinary routine. Indeed, the empty lard tins began to fill up as the foragers moved deeply into the bushes and the thought of blackberry pies and blackberry jam whetted the enthusiasm of the chattering young berry-pickers.

Suddenly, a little girl's voice called out in surprise: "Hey, look! It's a grass hut!"

All eyes went to the primitively constructed mound, with the little crawl-through opening of a door. Quickly, they ran and tried to peek into the hut, squatting and peering through the loosely packed portal.

"Oooo, this is so neat!"

"It has to be a secret meeting place... like a place where fairies meet and make special spells."

"No, it's not. It's a place where crooks hide out after they rob a bank, or something."

"Oh, grow up, will you? This is a Boy Scout project."

"Hey." One of the other girls had noticed something in the

tangled greenery around the perimeter of the hut. "What are all these balloons hanging on the bushes?" She bent forward. "They stink."

There was a sharp gasp.

"Don't touch those!" the college student shrieked.

Unfortunately, this ill-fated outing would cost her credits for the summer and take away her early graduation next spring. The Big Girls from the Home, however, would eventually enjoy the blackberries; they had no idea what that little grass hut was, nor of certain hidden activities taking place there on a regular basis. Indeed, they had no concept of that thorny shelter's dark link with what was going on, down the road, near the town of Shelburne, Vermont. They did not have the spiritual maturity to see it all, so of course, they did not, could not, see the predatory swarms of mysterious, menacing beings in the skies overheard, swooping and dropping down into the deepest corners of those Yankee hills and homes… darting and hovering, peering and watching… for the right opening… for the perfect, clueless, innocent target.

***

August passed and suddenly it was the start of the school year. It was a special time for the two older Dupree children, because all four of them attended public school together and got to see each other on a daily basis. Up until this year, the only time all four were together was during the occasional Saturday or Sunday when their mother would come for a visit. But this year, Richard "Dicky" Dupree was considered ready for kindergarten. This class ran from nine until noon each day, but all of the "Home kids" walked the twenty-minute route north along Shelburne Road, west on Flynn Avenue, and then north again on Pine Street, to Champlain Grade School. They also made that loop between school and the Home at noon. So, on the morning trek and the noon trip, the Duprees tried their best to walk together.

Although they were truly blood-related, only the boys looked somewhat alike. However, even with the same red hair and blue eyes, Sonny was a gaunt, sickly lad, while Dicky was a bouncing bundle of mischief. Lisa Marie also had the bright, blue eyes, but dishwater blonde hair; Clara Claudette ("Cee Cee") was the only one in the family who displayed the dark eyes and hair of the occasional American Indian ancestor. It was she who told on her little brother, during the noon sprint toward lunch at the Home.

"Dicky gots in trouble, Lisa Marie." She rolled her deep brown eyes upward to meet her sister's gaze.

"What do you mean?"

She took an extra step to keep up with the older girl. "He had the measles, I think." One more extra step. "Him and Joe Turner."

"Who's Joe Turner?"

"He's one of us Little Kids. He lives in our building." She noted the nod of Lisa Marie's head, then continued. "Anyways, him and Dicky climbed on top of the cupboards and hid there."

"What cupboards?"

"In the 'firmery."

"You mean the infirmary, where you go when you get sick? I've seen that room. Looks like a small hospital." She could picture the dark, polished cupboards lined up above the lengthy shelf on the long, back wall. "Yeah, I can see how they could hide up there. Those cupboards don't go all the way to the ceiling." She grinned at the mental picture of two little rascals lying flat in the sunken tops of the storage units, snickering while the housemothers panicked.

"Anyways, Miss Angela spanked Joe, but not Dicky. He had to sit in the corner." She took a couple more quick steps. "I don't think that's fair. Joe said it was Dicky's ideer, but Joe got the spanking and Dicky didn't... and the only time he gets punished is when Miss Teresa is watching us. I don't think that's fair, do you?"

"No, it's not fair." Suddenly she realized the Little Kids had two housemothers, like it was over in the Big Girls' building. "So, how come Dicky only had to sit in the corner?"

Cee Cee's hand reached out to catch her sister's arm and they came to a stop.

"Because Miss Angela never spanks Dicky, that's why. She spanks everybody else, but she doesn't ever even slap him on the hand, like she does to everybody else." A pause. "She likes him better than the rest of us."

The walking resumed. Lisa Marie lifted her gaze to the two red-headed brothers moving along ahead of them. She could certainly see how that happened. Dicky was not only cute — almost angelic in appearance — but quick and smart and spontaneous and fun to be around. She was sure, out of the four, the boy had adjusted to the Home better than the other three of them. And no wonder, with a doting housemother and a free hand to do pretty much what he wanted. But he was like that before they had landed in this place, she recalled.

"So, I told Mrs. Bushey."

"You what?" Big sister had come to a stop, again. Mrs. Bushey was the Home's director.

"She was walking down the hall and I was right there at the door and Miss Angela was taking the other Little Kids out to the playground." She got a twinkle in her eye. "So, I went like this": She crooked her pointer finger into a cute little *Come here*. Lisa Marie could almost see Mrs. Bushey's heart melting and then pictured her bending her portly body down to listen to this little sweetheart.

"So, what did you say to her?"

Cee Cee cupped both hands around her mouth and whispered loudly: "Miss Angela likes my brother, Dicky, better than the rest of us."

This time she could picture the amused look on the lady's face. "What did she say, Cee Cee?"

"She wanted to know why I was telling her this." She was

beginning to feel quite successful about taking care of the problem, so she spoke it out quite boldly: "Because it's not fair. He gets all the hugs and sits on her lap and everything and the rest of us gets left out and all the spankings." Her voice drifted off a bit. "I think I was crying or something."

"So, what happened then?"

"She patted me on the head and told me it would be all right and I should get on out there to the playground."

The conversation ended on that quiet note. Within minutes, they were walking up the half-circle driveway, where, at the carriage porch, Cee Cee entered into the main building with the other first graders and kindergartners. Lisa Marie hurried over to the dining room for a quick lunch.

She had a feeling Mrs. Bushey would handle things fine.

***

The first few school days seemed to be going well, but by the weekend, the Big Boys' two housemothers noticed a decline in Sonny's strength. He had been losing weight ever since arriving at the Home two years ago, which sometimes happened with children who grieved harder and longer, but there were new alarming signs he was not doing well: not eating, isolating himself at every opportunity, sleep-walking on a regular basis. No amount of cajoling or threatening broke the downward spiral. It was as though he had given up hope; two years was a long time to wait to "go back home." Then one morning he did not want to get out of bed. Mrs. Bushey was summoned and then the visiting nurse and the very next day, Sonny's mother was contacted at her job over there in New Hampshire.

"This boy has to get back home and soon," Mrs. Bushey told her.

"But this is the only job I could find. I live in a room with one of the other ladies from work. I don't know what to do."

"Surely there is an aunt or somebody who would take him. This is urgent. If he gets any worse, there could be terrible consequences." The director sighed. "And we can't take that responsibility. The board has already come to a decision; something needs to happen before the week is out."

By the third week in September, Sonny was enrolled in a Roman Catholic grade school in the same fifth grade class as his cousin, Annie. He was sleeping on the couch, but he was back within the folds of the Dupree family. Aunt Tony and Uncle Andy would keep watchful care until his mother could find a job somewhere in Burlington.

Meanwhile, Sonny would be welcomed with the Sicilian brand of hospitality so typical of the Italian neighborhood in which these relatives resided. He was hugged and loved and there was a glimmer of hope.

But the other three Dupree kids felt the blow. Even though it was carefully explained that Sonny was so sick, the fact remained he was gone.

The girls got it right away: Sonny could die if he didn't get better. But Dicky was dismayed. He was abandoned again and tears welled up into those beautiful eyes. Lisa Marie tried to encourage him as they walked to school one morning. "But Mama is going to come and see us more often, because she's getting a job right near us and pretty soon we'll all be going home. Isn't that great?"

His grubby hand wiped the drip from the little pug nose and he nodded. She grabbed his other hand and brought him alongside his buddy, Joe Turner. "In the meantime, you and Joe can walk to school together, okay?" She put her face down close to the Abenaki lad, looking closely into the deep, dark wells of his eyes and whispered, "Dicky and you need to be blood brothers, like in the movies. You need to stick together and help each other, okay?"

"Okay," the Indian boy replied. "But what's a bwud bwudder?"

She laughed. "Well, you each prick your finger with a pin and then you rub them together so your blood mixes up together... like red paint. That's all."

That morning there was a finger-painting craft in the kindergarten class.

Both boys had to be scrubbed down before heading back to the Home. They figured if a little red paint on a finger was good, smearing it from head to toe would probably be a lot better. The pact was sealed, in no uncertain terms. From that point, the blood brothers wreaked havoc everywhere they went.

That night, they stole candy from a jar in the Little Kids' dayroom. When Miss Angela caught them, she spanked Joe Turner and sent Dicky into the usual corner. The redhead felt sorry for his Indian friend, so he heisted a few more pieces and sneaked them into the dorm, slipping them under his buddy's pillow. When Joe got caught eating the sloppy sweets under the sheet, he got spanked again.

He yelled so loudly, Mrs. Bushey came up from her apartment on the first floor, standing there in her ruffled robe, much to the other kids' wonderment and had a private word with Miss Angela, out on the landing of the beautiful, spiraled staircase.

Things settled down for a couple of weeks, since Miss Angela had had her own private word with her little carrot-topped darling: "If you two don't stop all this, I may not be here anymore. Then there might be a mean lady who would spank you and everything. You wouldn't want me to leave, would you, Pumpkin?"

But kindergarteners can forget important stuff, especially when presented with more intriguing adventures... like the canning kitchen in the basement of that building.

The two of them sneaked away during playground time, having discovered an open cellar door, out of sight of Miss Angela. When their eyes adjusted from the sunlight to the darkened depths of this cavernous facility, they stood there with their little mouths open. Huge metal bowls and row upon row of shiny canning jars lined a shelf beside two large, flat sinks. Two long, narrow tables stood end-to-end in the center of the room, making a wonderfully inviting tunneled fort. They stood there, marveling.

"We should build a castle," Dicky said.

And so they did.

When they got caught, there were eight huge, metal pans tilted on their sides for walls, tucked precariously under the tables. Reinforcing those, a row of tilting paring knives stuck into the linoleum floor on each side. The two builders were standing on top of the tables, canning jars in hand, ready to create a glass shard barricade surrounding the entire structure. It could have been the best-defended fortress ever constructed, anytime, anywhere, bar none.

This time, Miss Angela spanked Joe Turner and gave Darling Dicky a swat on his behind before she put him in the corner. She spent the next day cleaning up the mess, with the help of the blood brothers. It took most of Saturday, but at four in the afternoon, she felt they had all learned their lessons: the boys would not do this again and she, herself, would be more alert.

When Mrs. Bushey came back from her afternoon at the beauty parlor before the supper hour, Miss Angela presented the two boys at the director's apartment door. There, the two wide-eyed kindergarteners said some soft apologies. Mrs. Bushey shot a meaningful look to the housemother and said, "I trust this will never happen again."

"Yes, ma'am." Miss Angela tilted her head toward the two youngsters. "Right, boys?"

The duo responded with tight smiles and then all three went back toward the Little Kids' dining area.

What this housemother didn't know, was during the kitchen clean-up that day, Dicky Dupree had slipped a bundle of stick matches into his pants pocket.

The fire was an accident. All they wanted to do was to see how matches worked. It wasn't like a couple of bad boys would plan to burn up a whole mattress. It was more like crawling under the bed in the middle of the night was logically the safest place to hide from the housemother.

But the fire alarm went off and the Little Kids were bawling and the two housemothers were trying to get them all down the spiral stairway and Mrs. Bushey was bustling around in her ruffled robe, snatching fire extinguishers off the walls and then everybody was sitting on the wet grass outside, while the firemen yelled and kept checking on this, that, and the other thing.

Meanwhile, the exhausted pyromaniacs fell fast asleep in the playground sandbox.

The next day, Miss Angela was nowhere to be found. It was as though it had all been planned, because the new housemother came into the room and took over as though she had been there for a hundred years. Miss Bertha's words were sharp, her decisions precise, and if anyone moved without her permission, they would get a sharp snap of her finger against the temple. When things got busy, she would wield an eighteen-inch ruler like a lethal weapon, slapping it against her own hand so smartly, it made even young Master Dupree cringe. Little wonder Miss Teresa stepped carefully around this new housemother. Further, the Halloween festivities were different this year. No candy (only popcorn), no walks around the block in the dark, no masks. Things were pretty much limited to costumes and cupcakes with licorice stuck into the bright orange frosting. The routine was different without Miss Angela around... especially for Dicky Dupree. Oddly, several times over the next few weeks, the indistinct figure of what looked vaguely like Miss Angela was spotted by Cee Cee and Lisa Marie, along the school route. They wondered if they were seeing things.

Otherwise, the school year went on as usual. The children continued to walk back and forth, even as the weather got past the Vermont fall season. They waded through the yellow elm leaves covering the sidewalks along Shelburne Road and

Flynn Avenue. They bent into the new winterish winds signaling upcoming weather. They looked up at bare tree branches against a grayer sky. Still, an ever-rebounding youthful spirit kept them looking ahead to the next special occasion. Then suddenly it was the third week of November... Thanksgiving, 1948.

The Thanksgiving Day parade was a special outing, because everybody got out of school at noon on Wednesday and went to Church Street in downtown Burlington, where there were marching bands and Scout Troops and fine horses with girls in shiny shirts and cowboy hats and some guy with a shovel and a little wagon who came along behind them to pick up what Mrs. Bushey explained were "horse muffins." She, herself, always attended the event with all of the Home kids and it was she who also gave the strict order that those school children had better get right back to the Home on time for lunch, so the whole group could take the Burlington transit bus that would transport them close to their special place at the top of Church Street. The local police always expected this little crowd from 555 Shelburne Road and so that spot right in front of Sears and Roebuck was always ready and waiting. This bus, Mrs. Bushey emphasized, was the last one on the scheduled runs that could get them there on time and they should be especially careful not to disappoint all those nice police officers. "In fact," she said sternly, "if anyone is late, they will not be allowed to go to the parade."

So, when the bell rang for dismissal, the Home kids hit the path full speed. Even Cee Cee did not wait for her older sister, who had to make a stop at the girls' restroom in the basement of the school building. By the time Lisa Marie was finally running up the slight slope of the Flynn Avenue sidewalk, she was already far behind the hurrying stream of youngsters. She pressed forward to catch up to the last one, knowing if she made it that far, she was going to be on time. But even as she neared her goal, that last child walked quickly past another smaller one... a little boy, who was limping.

Suddenly, she realized it was her little brother.

"Dicky, for Pete's sake," she exclaimed as she grabbed his hand. "Move along!"

"I can't!" He pulled his hand back and started to cry. "My feets hurt."

"What do you mean?" She looked down to see what was wrong with the little brown oxfords poking out from under his pant legs.

The boy opened his mouth and let out a pitiful wail, the drool falling from the sides of his mouth. She could see something was wrong, so she squatted down to pull the heavy cotton legs up in order to see what was what.

"Oh, for Pete's sake," she said again. "You don't have any socks on."

Dicky scrunched his eyes shut to squeeze the tears out and let out another howl and then Lisa could see why: He had raw blisters on both heels.

She took his hand gently. "Okay, we'll have to go as good as you can, Dicky. We'll have to go slow, okay?"

At one point she thought about having him go barefoot, but decided it was way too cold. She didn't want him to get sick like Sonny did. They kept moving along until she delivered him at the door of the Little Kids' quarters in the main building.

Then she ran.

"Why are you late, young lady?" Mrs. Bushey was dismissing the kids from the dining room.

"I was helping my brother." She hesitated, then decided to tell on the housemother, whoever she was. "He has blisters on his heels. Somebody sent him to school with no socks. He can hardly walk. I stayed with him."

Her director-face went hard and she looked over at the main building. "Well, you're too late to make the parade."

"I could skip my lunch... I don't mind."

"No child at the Home is ever going to go without a meal," she said as she turned to go. "Sit down and eat," she called over her shoulder. "When you are finished, go to your dayroom and sit at the window seat and stay there until we get back." Then she headed for the Little Kids' quarters.

Twenty minutes later, Lisa Marie settled onto the window seat. She knew she wasn't alone; there was a housemother somewhere nearby, but that old feeling of abandonment suddenly came flooding over her. She gazed out at the playground swings, the big lawn, the half-circle driveway, and back over at the carriage porch where her mother had slipped into a car and left. It had been so long. It had been so lonely.

A movement to the left brought her back to the present. It was the group from the Big Boys' and Girls' quarters meeting and walking toward the carriage porch. They stopped under its covering and watched as the Little Kids came down the stairs. Each of the little ones took the hand of one of the big ones and the small crowd walked down the driveway toward the corner bus stop. It was when they were about halfway to that mark she spotted her brother. He was happily hopping and skipping along and he was wearing bright red socks.

It was a sight she would remember for the rest of her life.

CHAPTER TWO

Parades

"I think you're obsessed with that kid," Martha Donaldson murmured through a mouthful of cigarette smoke. She tapped the ashes off into a large ashtray on the coffee table as she watched her daughter tucking long locks of ebony hair under the edges of a white knitted cap. When Angela didn't answer, she pushed it farther. "So, why do you think you have to take pictures of him? He's not even any of your business anymore."

The young woman shrugged. "Just something I want to do, Mother." She bent closer to the mirror because it was a dark, old apartment. "Could we turn a light on for a minute?"

"No lights during the day. Can't afford it." She drew deeply on the cigarette. "Which brings up another thing: you need to get another job." Again, the former housemother remained silent. "Or, you could go back to the farm. Your father would be happy to have you back doing hard labor, like before." She rubbed a hand over her deeply wrinkled face. "God knows, he drove us like a couple of mules." She let her head fall forward, staring down at nothing in particular.

Angela studied that drooping mop of tangled gray hair for a moment. Then she moved closer. "It's going to be okay, Mother." She clapped her hands twice and the older woman looked up, curious. "I have an idea. Trust me." She pulled on a warm, gray coat, slung the strap of her Canon camera over a shoulder, and was out the door before Martha could ask another question.

Outside, the cool wind bathed her face as she stepped carefully down the old steps to the sidewalk. King Street was a couple of blocks south of the corner where Main Street and the south end of Church Street met. As she crossed over to the Church Street side, her steps quickened. Folks were already lining the sidewalks. The Thanksgiving parade would be starting soon and she knew exactly where the Home kids would be.

***

Two priests sat silently in a small room, out of sight of the sanctuary of the Cathedral of Immaculate Conception, awaiting the arrival of another one — this cleric being from St. John Vianney Church in South Burlington, out there on Hinesburg Road. The older one tapped a soundless cadence on his knee, revealing the great pressure of his position: leading the Diocese of Burlington — a responsibility which also included the whole state of Vermont. His auxiliary bishop sat beside him, lips pressed tightly, as though to keep any unseemly remarks from escaping. The bishop checked his pocket watch and sure enough, at the precise hour, there came a sharp rap on the hand-carved wooden door.

"Enter," the bishop commanded.

The South Burlington priest already knew he was in trouble before he arrived, but when he entered the room, the color drained from his face. The fear was so great he only caught snatches of the conversation that followed: "We've had another complaint from the parents of one of your altar boys... same as what happened in New York State... How many times must we cover for you? At this point, we can only assign you to office duty... better if you resigned from the priesthood... by the end of the month... and stay away from the orphanage; we've got enough trouble over there, already."

He had no defense, knowing he was fully guilty... again.

When he finally stepped outside into the crisp November air, he paused at the top of the grand stairs leading down to the sidewalk of the northernmost end of Pine Street. Right there in that moment, he realized his life as a priest was over. He could not help himself. There was no hope, for he was what he was.

A few blocks away, a curious mixture of music was playing. Visiting school bands were tuning up for the parade. Slowly, he descended the steps to the street.

"Might as well enjoy one last day of fellowship with the Queen City of Burlington, Vermont," he mused, as he headed for Cherry Street... which would lead him to the corner of Church Street, right in front of Sears and Roebuck.

***

"I hate that damned squirrel," Mr. Turner declared, as he descended the drop-down attic ladder.

"Oh, you don't mean that," his soft-spoken wife replied. She steadied the wobbly structure until his feet finally stood firmly on the hallway floor. "It's being who God made it to be... a squirrel."

He reached down to lift the ladder back into place. "Yeah, well, it's that there are so damned many of them." He slammed the ladder into place above his head. "They've spread all over the neighborhood." He turned to head down to the kitchen. "I should have plugged up that lightning hole a long time ago. That's where they started out."

"Well, they were fun, with cute little babies, remember?" She was following him down the stairs.

He strode into the tiny kitchen and dropped his electric drill down on the table. "That was before they started making nests in my attic!" He leaned forward, both hands flat on the table. "I should go ahead and seal up the hole in that tree. The guy from the University of Vermont said it would prolong the life of the tree, anyway." He looked at his wife. "What do you think? Should we finally do that?"

"Yes, but not to get rid of the squirrels — they're already all over the neighborhood — but to preserve the tree. After all, it has been a landmark on Hinesburg Road, for a long time." She smiled. "Yes, Joe, I think that would be a good idea."

Happy to have that decision in place, the harassed repairman headed out the back door to return his tools to their place in the barn. "I'll have a sandwich when I come back in, Ava."

"Oh, it's already made, dear. Remember, we have to leave in half an hour, or we will miss the Thanksgiving parade."

He stopped in his tracks. "Oh hell, I forgot about that. Do we have to go?"

"Yes, we do," she replied sweetly. "We promised Little Joe we would be there."

***

Sixteen-year-old Bobby Nelson was assigned as Dicky Dupree's partner for the day. When he realized he was watching over the most notorious of the Little Kids, he was glad he had stashed a pocketful of jellybeans deep into the lint-lined recesses of his corduroy pants, in case he got hungry. About the third time he pulled the little guy out from under the bus seat, he decided to take action. This time he grabbed the wiggling lad by the back of his jacket and drew him close to whisper into his ear: "Here's the deal, kid. If you keep doing this, I'm going to open the window and throw you out, head-first. Got that?"

The large blue eyes got larger. For a couple of seconds, Dicky sat still. Then he spoke up defiantly: "If you do, I'll tell."

Bobby's sandy-haired head tilted back as he laughed. "No,

you won't, 'cause you'll be dead!"

"Will not."

"Will to."

For a couple more seconds, the little redhead was silent, but then he rallied, "Then I'll tell God and you will go to H-E-double-toothpicks!"

This time the laughter was even longer. As he drew a breath, he reached into his pants pocket. "Tell you what. You can be dead and tattle on me, or..." He paused dramatically as he drew out a bright red jellybean. He picked a little fluff off it before waving it in front of the Little Kid. "You could get some of these, for being good all afternoon." Again, the blue eyes widened. "Tell you what," the Big Kid repeated for emphasis, "you be good and you'll get one of these every half-hour." The little one was definitely interested. "We got a deal, Mr. Dupree?"

He held out his hand for a handshake. Very slowly, his eyes on the candy, Dicky reached out to shake Bobby's hand... even though he didn't have any concept of how long a half-hour was and every delicious treat would have to be licked clean before he could eat it.

***

The tops of Mt. Mansfield and Camel's Hump were already white, but the snow had barely touched Burlington on this cold November afternoon. Local parade organizers were grateful for that blessing, since the logistics of getting this annual parade together were overwhelming, to begin with. They scurried in and out of side streets, checking on school bus loads and floats, easing each group into place at the start-up point. Last-minute repairs were feverishly implemented, including the Miss Vermont float, which had lost power to run the heater inside the clear plastic box where the lovely lady would appear in her bathing suit, a sash which bore her title draped carefully across her bosom.

People from all over the state were beginning to line the streets, the biggest number being on Church Street, itself. But the real place of honor was on the steps of City Hall, which sat on the northwest corner of Church and Main Streets. Here was the greatest view of the whole event. The mayor and his entourage would sit at the top of the front stairs, ready for the local newspapers to snap happy shots for their constituents. Special patriotic decorations, mixed with holiday wreaths, draped the front of the building, both behind and either side of the smiling gentlemen and their wives. When the parading enclaves passed by, there would always be that benevolent, royal wave and the cameras would click away. It was always a great time for everybody.

Because of the celebration, however, the Burlington transit routes had to be altered for the whole afternoon. That was why the bus which was transporting the little crowd from the Children's Home had to drop them off a whole block away from their destination. They walked past the State Movie Theater, the Little Kids being tugged along by the older partners, until reaching the parade route. There, an alert Burlington police officer escorted them across the street to their reserved space in front of the Sears store, ahead of the oncoming police vehicle, whoop-whooping its siren for final clearance of the parade's path. The mayor's vehicle followed that of the parade marshal, which got them both back to their City Hall seats of honor in time to see the majority of the parade. Photographers walked along beside these two shiny cars, doing what newspaper people do and then they were gone and the crowd's attention was turned to the rattling beat of the first high school band.

Once more, Mrs. Bushey issued a warning to her group, addressing the three housemothers and the Big Kids: "Keep an eye on the little ones. We don't want anybody getting run over." Then she leaned forward with the crowd. The festivities had begun.

For most of the one-hour-long Thanksgiving parade, Bobby and his little charge got along fine. But before it was over, Dicky grabbed the front of his pants and yelled, "I gotta go! I gotta go!"

Mrs. Bushey wearily instructed Bobby to take the little guy inside to the Sears restroom. "And stay with him," she cautioned.

As they turned to go into the store, the Big Kid peered down the parade route and hesitated. The Miss Vermont float was a half-block away. He could see the light glistening off the plastic box and his head went to that place where healthy teenage boys often go, at the thought of seeing something they did not often get to see in the long, Vermont winters — a beautiful girl in a bathing suit. Further, living for the last few years in the Children's Home had certainly restricted any access to magazines or the like. The most he got to see was long-legged dancers in the movies and then only on rare occasions. So, Bobby Nelson wanted to see Miss Vermont.

He thought quickly and before Dicky knew what hit him, the door on the restroom was slamming and Bobby was saying, "Now you stay right here and don't move! I'll be right back."

It took longer than Bobby figured for the float to pass where he was watching, inside the front door of that department store. When the Big Kid came back, the restroom door was open and the Little Kid was gone. "Oh, no."

Angrily, he started up and down the aisles of the store, calling in a loud whisper, "Dicky! Dicky, you little brat! Get out here!" He repeated his search over the entire one-and-half-story layout of the inside of the store, but there was no giggling, no patter of hide-and-seek. A couple of clerks saw the teenager frantically bounding through the store and tried to help. Finally, one of them asked if he was with the children's group out front. The boy nodded and kept searching. Then Mrs. Bushey was standing in front of him, her jaw slack in disbelief.

"What happened? Where is the boy?"

"He's just being a brat." Bobby wanted to believe it.

"How did he get away?"

"I told him to stay in there until I came back."

Within minutes, a policeman showed up. "I've put in a call for back-up, but we have a real traffic mess out there. The parade is finishing up." They all glanced out through the big front windows, where Santa's ornate float was jing-jingling by, officially opening the Christmas shopping season for all the local merchants. "Ho-ho-hooo! Me-e-erry Christmas, boys and girls!"

"Wait!" Mrs. Bushey suddenly had an idea. Going to see Santa was exactly what that precocious youngster would do. Surely, that was where he had to be.

***

The downstairs housemother opened the door of her private room adjacent to the dayroom where Lisa Marie was still sitting on the window seat. She approached the girl in a nonchalant manner. "Mrs. Bushey has called and let us know our group has missed their bus. They will be a bit later than we thought." She wiped her hands across the front of her apron. "Why don't you go ahead into the dining room and start setting tables, so we aren't late having supper." It was not a suggestion.

"Yes, Mrs. Ferndale." She was glad to get out of that corner, whatever the reason. As she crossed the dayroom toward the sturdy double doors, the woman seemed to have a sudden thought.

"Don't be lollygagging around about it, talking with the kitchen help and all that. You're pretty much going to have to get it all done by yourself."

Setting out plates, napkin rings, flatware and glassware for the whole dining room took her a while. She was putting the salt and pepper shakers on the last table when the children came walking quickly up the sidewalk. Jealousy stirred up inside her, until she saw their faces.

"Somebody got in trouble," she whispered, as she headed back into the dayroom.

Mrs. Ferndale was actually coming across the room to meet her. She stopped, a grim look on her face. "You need to come into my room for a minute."

"Now? It's time to line up for supper."

"The other girls still need to put away coats and get washed." She put her hand gently, but firmly, between the girl's shoulder blades and ushered her across the linoleum floor toward the room.

"What have I done this time?" she wondered.

Fifteen minutes later, Lisa was standing in line to go in for supper. Two of the older girls held the double doors open for the rest of them to file into the dining room. Lisa stepped forward, but she kept her head down, because the rest of the kids would be watching her, with that knowing look in their eyes and she didn't want to see that look again.

But still, her little brother was gone, and nobody knew where.

When they passed her plate of food down to her from where it was dished up at the head of the table, she could only sit and look at it. Mrs. Ferndale took a moment to give Lisa Marie a stern look, even though she was filling the next plate. Food was not wasted in this facility. Fortunately, the girl was let off the hook when a teenager at one of the boys' tables threw up into his own lap. When they excused him from the table, she saw it was Bobby Nelson.

"Please may I be excused?" she asked softly, without looking up. A nod from Mrs. Bushey, seated at the head of the next table, allowed her to leave.

The search went into full swing, as soon as the parade duty ended. All departments in the local police precinct went on overtime. The restroom, which had been roped off by the first officer who showed up at the store, was thoroughly examined for every bit of evidence. A few drops of blood were scraped off the floor surface and the whole area was checked for fingerprints... but then, it was a public restroom. Sears was shut down until further notice, while every nook and cranny was checked — even every piece of cargo in the shipping and receiving departments.

From there, the search spread out to the parking lots and alleys, to no avail. Then all adjacent stores were scoured, including rooftops. And so it went, hour after hour, then the next day and then more days, with no leads.

By the end of the week, the ever-elusive Mrs. Dupree had finally left her job in New Hampshire and was staying with friends in Essex Junction. This was a wake-up call no decent mother could ignore. In fact, she was actually trying to reach the children's father. A phone contact with her former mother-in-law revealed he was hospitalized someplace in New York State. Grandma Dupree promised to try and track him down.

Still more days passed and no sign of Dicky.

Meantime, Cee Cee, who was close to seven by then, was moved over into the Big Girls' building to be near her sister. The little girl was suffering from nightmares and panic attacks. She needed all the hugs she could get, so it was a good thing she was assigned to the upstairs housemother, like her sister. Mrs. Hays was a woman who loved children. Between her and Lisa Marie, daily life became more bearable. In addition, for both girls, it was comforting to have their mother nearby, even though she was limited by cash and transportation as to how often she could visit.

Nevertheless, five weeks passed and Dicky was nowhere to be found. By that time, Mr. Leroy "Roy" Dupree had made it to his mother's home in Burlington, still weak, but angry. He had been encouraged by a lawyer to sue the Children's Home for every last cent he could get. "Just plain neglect!" he quoted the barrister, over and over, even though he wasn't quite sure what it all meant.

The threat of a lawsuit put the already dazed board into a tailspin. A better plan of action had to be implemented, to save the integrity of the institution, and certainly to find this child. The government agencies were not getting anywhere. So, on a freezing January morning, Mrs. Bushey paid a visit to the Burlington Savings and Loan. On that very day, a private detective was hired to solve the case of the disappearance of Dicky Dupree.

***

John Courtney was an Air Force Captain, working to set up the JAG office at Fort Ethan Allen. The Air Force was scheduled to take over the historic facility sometime soon. Because the young lawyer was from Burlington, he had some vital connections, so he was on temporary duty, living in a rundown barracks while he put together the physical office. The task was relatively uncomplicated for this gifted, intelligent officer and his team of enlisted airmen was right on the job. Other than visiting with his mother, he had plenty of time to spare. The challenge of finding a missing child was right up his alley; it was both necessary and rewarding. Further, the Courtneys and the Busheys were longtime friends and Leona Bushey had no problem with hiring the man... after all, she had plenty of resources. She was working because she liked what she was doing. John understood the feeling well. Further, the entertaining notion of becoming a private investigator was too much to pass up.

It wasn't long before, on a cold winter afternoon, he arrived at the director's office in the main building of the Children's Home. Dressed in civvies, the likeable young man sat on a stiff wooden chair and listened intently as Leona gave him all the details she could remember. Her bluish-white hair glinted under the small chandelier above her desk as she bent forward to make a point: "Mind you, the authorities have gone above and beyond to get some solid leads. They have photos taken by the press — you know — of the mayor and other dignitaries in their parade cars. You can see who was standing on that corner, in the background and even across the street. They have sorted out a couple of suspects, but have no hard evidence, so no arrests, just interrogations, if you will." She wiped one hand across an imaginary blackboard. "Those poor guys interviewed almost everybody in those pictures. People were parading in and out of police headquarters for weeks."

"I'll be able to access most of what the police department has on file," he spoke thoughtfully. "Thank God, my dad was a cop." He gazed out the window behind her, into the shadow of the carriage porch. "Of course, I'll have to use a great deal of discretion." His grayish eyes went back to her. "But let's start at the beginning. Do you have any suspicions? What about those two people you just mentioned?"

"One is a priest. I don't know much about him, but…" She shook her head slowly. "The other one is a young woman who used to work here." Seeing the spark of interest in his eyes, she continued describing Angela Donaldson and her unusual attachment to the missing boy. "Had to let her go. It was not pretty — I really thought she was going to hit me."

"Hmm. Interesting." His eyebrows arched as she went on.

"I keep my car under cover at the old nurses' quarters. This all was built as a hospital complex for World War I troops. Did you know that?" A negative nod got her back on subject. "Well, anyway, there's a garage with that cottage. Unfortunately, there is no door." She nodded toward the out-of-view structure standing a couple hundred feet back from the Little Kids' playground. "Anyway, not long after I fired her, I had to deal with two flat tires before I could get the car out of the garage. But I couldn't prove she did it."

"Ay-yuh. That's probably a lost cause, so... any reason why Miss Donaldson would kidnap the kid?"

"It's like... like she was fixated on him. Never disciplined him. Favored him over the other children. That sort of thing."

"Do you think she would, you know, hurt him?"

"It wouldn't make much sense, would it?"

He was reaching into his ski jacket pocket. "Do we know where she is?"

"The police detectives indicated she was moving back to her father's farm, just outside of Shelburne." She tilted her head to one side. "I don't know about you, but I'm thinking you can hide a lot of things on a big old farm."

At that point, John Courtney started taking notes.

CHAPTER THREE

Snoops

"It works like this: you find out whatever you can and then you report it back to this office." The detective leaned back in his desk chair and clasped his hands together over his round tummy. "I've known you since you were a tyke, Johnny, and I'm sure you'll be a big help." The gentleman was head honcho in the department that one of the wives had lovingly labeled the "Snoop Squad."

"Thanks for the vote of confidence, sir."

Detective Smith's unique smile was divided neatly with a slight space between the two front teeth. "You're welcome. Let's get you started." He reached over and drew a large manila envelope from the top of a wooden file cabinet. "Let me introduce you to some 'persons of interest.'" He pulled out a pile of photos, spreading them side-by-side in front of the aspiring PI. Slowly, he pointed out various people whom he and his team had interviewed. "So, most of them remembered the kid. Guess he was pretty rambunctious, in a charming way. At least, that's how they described him." He lifted up one photo. "Here's a good one of the group from the Home... and here is the missing boy."

John took the black-and-white picture and peered closely. "Hmm." He reached for his notebook to jot down details. "Do you know what color the jacket was? And the rest of his clothes?"

"I have that all written down."

Minutes later, he had most of the information he needed on that issue, so he turned his attention to the rest of the group. "What about the rest of the kids? Anybody I need to know about?"

"Probably ought to know about this one." He was pointing to an older teenager. "That's Bobby Nelson, the one who was supposed to be watching him."

"Wow... that has to be a hard one... a terrible consequence to live with." He dropped the picture and picked up another one. "What's this?"

"The other side of the street from Sears, in front of the jewelry store and one of our top 'persons-of-interest.'" He pointed once more. "That's Angela Donaldson."

"Mrs. Bushey told me about her." He moved closer. "Is that a clock in the store window?"

"Good. You spotted that."

"Is it on time? It says two-forty-five."

"We think so. As far as we can tell, the kid disappeared about ten minutes later."

John studied the photo. The young woman was standing with her hands behind her back, staring at someone across the street. There was something odd about her coat, but he couldn't quite put his finger on it. He went to the next picture, which was the same group from the Home in front of Sears, taken from farther away. "I see we have a shot showing more of the Cherry Street sidewalk." He tilted the sheet. "Is that our priest suspect leaning against the wall of the store?"

"Ay-yuh, that's him." He grimaced. "One of those 'problems' in the Roman Catholic Church. Of course, we didn't get our information from the diocese; they keep that stuff under wraps. But we happen to know at least two families took their sons off altar boy duties because of him."

"Why isn't he behind bars, for Pete's sake?"

"We can't touch him without formal charges. Nobody

wants to speak up."

He waggled his head in unbelief. "And so there he is, just a few feet behind those kids."

A moment of silence passed before John thought he had better not take any more of the police detective's time. "I guess I need to get going." He rose halfway out of his seat before Smith raised a staying hand.

"We have one more suspect, Johnny." The photo was placed in front of him. "This gentleman and his wife are aunt and uncle to Dicky Dupree's best buddy, one Joe Turner." He leaned back into his chair again. "Little Joe is full-blooded Abenaki Indian. He was adopted at six months, but the new parents were killed in a car accident two years thereafter. These two people in the picture are his only legal relatives. You're looking at Uncle Joe Turner and his wife, Ava."

"So we have Big Joe and Little Joe. Must have been named after his uncle for a reason. But they didn't take him into their home…?"

"Told us Snoops they were too old, but they would go visit him at the Home, like once a month or so."

"So, why are they suspects?"

"More him, than her. She looks pretty clean."

"Okay, so then…?"

"Caught him in a lie." He tapped his fingers on the arm of the chair. "We talked to them separately, of course and Ava let us know they were neighbors with the Dupree family, a few years ago, when Dicky was about two, two-and-a-half; but when they asked Big Joe if he knew the kid, his reply was, 'Not really.' The fingers stopped drumming. "Trouble is, Ava was in this other room, telling me what sweet a little neighbor he was, right from the time he was born and what a shame he was missing and how she felt sorry for his mom, what with the divorce and all this on top of that." The hands clasped across the belly once more. "And all Joe Turner can say is 'Not really.' I think there has to be a lot more to it. A gut feeling."

Johnny waited politely.

"So, I think you have your work cut out for you, Johnny."

As he left police headquarters at the north end of City Hall, his head was chock-full. It was going to be a challenge, but overall, this had been a good meeting with the head of the Snoop Squad.

***

Early the next morning, the captain assigned duties to his crew. Just as he was leaving for the rest of the day, Staff Sergeant Bill Flannigan caught up with him on the path leading to the parking lot. His movie-star face was amused.

"Have you heard the latest scoop from the group, Captain?" John stood still. It was always interesting how men gossiped as much as women and probably got the facts more twisted up than those same women. The sergeant was grinning. "You going to become a private investigator, sir?" The officer snorted incredulously, then turned to walk away. The forty-something enlisted leader got bold. "Kind of a come-down from being a lawyer, don't you think?" he chuckled.

"Just helping somebody out," the captain sang out as he walked down the snow-covered path. Suddenly, he stopped. "You might haul out some snow shovels and get a couple of your men to clear this mess, Sergeant."

"But, sir, I'm an airplane mechanic."

"I know," came the reply from the car window. "Kind of a come-down, wouldn't you say?"

Both men laughed out loud. They both knew the captain loved making justice happen and the sergeant loved making anything mechanical come to life. In fact, they were both underground heroes, each in their own way and that was what made them so compatible. In the next few months of working together, they would become good friends.

In the meantime, there was evidence to be studied and

theories to pursue.

***

John had another friend, an actual childhood buddy, who lived on Shelburne Bay, a few miles south of the Children's Home, a little way off Vermont State Route 7, which was also called Shelburne Road. On this February day, he would be visiting Tommy Ladue at the big brick house where the Ladues grew up. The two youngsters had spent many hours at a fishing hole a few hundred feet behind it, on the shore of Lake Champlain. But today, they would be sitting in front of the fireplace in the colonial-style house's living room. Johnny Courtney needed to ask some important questions of his pal, now known as Father Tom.

Leaning back into the dark green wingback chair, he came right to the point: "Tell me about this priest from St. John's over there in South Burlington. I know you have been 'shadowing' him for the last seven or eight months, as you've been completing your training." The captain understood what on-the-job training was in the service, so he felt somewhat familiar with this final phase of the process in becoming a priest.

The clergyman ran a hand through his auburn hair, his deeply freckled brow furrowing. "Johnny, let me say this: the folks out there on Hinesburg Road and all around that area... they are wonderful, loving people. They are faithful. They give to the poor. They volunteer at the church. They try so hard. They love Jesus." He took a sip from his hot toddy. "I am so dismayed this thing ever even happened to them. They don't deserve it. That man should never have been assigned to any church, let alone, St. John's." He shook his head. "But maybe that's why God had me intern there."

"So, you knew what was going on?"

"Not at first. It took a while. The guy is a real charmer. Everybody loved him." He looked at Johnny's cup. "Your toddy okay?" When his buddy nodded in approval, he continued: "Anyway, he's always been like that. We never had a close relationship, but I have been acquainted with the family for years. I'm surprised you never met him. Anyway, they live on a farm a little ways out of the actual town of Shelburne. So, I was willing to give the guy the benefit of the doubt, you know?"

John was thumbing through his notebook. "Just never ran in that particular circle, I guess." He looked up. "I know I have his name here, but help me out."

Father Tom fixed his eyes on the mirror above the mantle. "His formal name is J. Canon Johnson, but he's called 'Father Jeff.'"

"So, what can you tell me about him? Is he an only child?"

"No." He held up a wait-a-minute pointer finger. "Actually, he was raised by his single mom, until he was eighteen, or so. Then she married Arnold, who was divorced, with one daughter living at home." He shrugged his shoulders. "The boy never took his stepfather's name, though. Who knows what a young kid is thinking?"

The air sucked out of the room as the front door swung open. Emerging from the early dark of the winter evening, the slender figure of a woman slipped quickly inside, slamming the door behind her. As she pulled the blue scarf off the shining auburn hair, Johnny's mouth dropped open.

"Sarah?" He stood up, holding the toddy precariously in both hands.

She stopped midway from slipping the heavy coat off her shoulders. A quick breath of surprise escaped before she could check it. She was speechless for a moment, then the words came out: "Hey... Johnny... Johnny Courtney." A little laugh. "I thought you'd be on the Supreme Court by now." Another soft laugh escaped.

He smiled and placed the cup on the small table between the chairs. As he watched her slip the coat off and lay it on the bench by the door, he saw her petite body wrapped in a soiled white apron. "Well," he responded, "I'm afraid that probably won't happen for at least a couple of years, if I'm lucky."

She suddenly became aware of the apron and reached back to pull the ties loose. The garment dropped forward into her waiting hand and she laid it over her other arm. A soft, flannel shirt was tucked into the top of her dungarees, the denim pant legs skimming the top of her little leather high-tops.

"This is Sarah's day to volunteer at the church kitchen," Tom said.

"Oh yes," Johnny suddenly remembered. "I forgot. That's great. We need more people like you, Sarah." He bowed politely. "And that's not all you do. You take care of the Ladue house, whereby you keep your cousin, Tommy, grounded in his earthly roots." He motioned around the room. "It looks great and feels like a real home, young lady. You have been doing a good job, obviously." His voice trailed off. He was talking too much.

She seemed a bit surprised. "So, what brings you back to Vermont?" She tilted her head to one side but did not approach the two men.

"The Air Force is taking over Fort Ethan Allen."

At that, she moved closer toward the uniformed captain. "What?" One small hand pushed the loose strands of gleaming hair back from her temple. "In what way?"

She was close enough for him to see her golden-brown eyes. As he looked down into them, he knew there was something up, so he answered carefully. "Don't worry, Sarah. This is not going to destroy the historical value of the fort. In fact, it will only add to that history."

She took one more step toward him, holding her shoulders back like a soldier at attention. "It had better not, mister. It had better not. Otherwise, I will spend every last bit of energy and influence I have to halt the destruction of yet another Vermont historical landmark."

"Don't worry, that's not going to happen."

She eyed him up and down, a little smile on her face. "Better not be lying to me, Johnny Courtney."

And then she swayed a distinctly feminine exit into the kitchen.

The man was still staring in that direction when Father Tom removed a hand from his soft grin and spoke, "She's grown up, don't you think?"

"Yup," the lawyer replied. "In fact, that would be an understatement."

The two men laughed and John got back to business. "So, what can you tell me about this Father Jeff?"

"This could take some time, my friend." The priest stood up and moved toward Sarah's exit, calling through the doorway. "Johnny's staying for supper, Sarah." He turned to wink at his buddy before using his theatrical whisper to her: "Be sure to hide the silverware!"

***

"So, Tom tells me Arnold and his wife have a pretty diversified farm operation there... some dairy, some sheep, and even a maple sugar operation every year." He cut another bite of ham and popped it into his mouth.

"Ay-yuh," she murmured through a mouthful of mashed potatoes. "They seem to be doing all right." She held her fork upright, handle-down on the checkered oil cloth table covering, tapping it lightly in place. "But..." A thoughtful look covered her countenance. "But, I have to say, there is just something about that place, the whole farm is... downright creepy." She stabbed the fork into the home-canned string beans on her plate. "Always has been."

Her cousin seemed surprised. "What does that mean, Sarah? I don't remember anything in particular."

"You were older. But us younger kids saw and heard

stuff... we didn't even know it wasn't right." She leaned forward toward Tom. "Jeff was older than most of us. He had this commanding influence, like he was Superman, or something. He would talk us into all kinds of weird things... like tickling each other in weird places." She took a small sip of the raw dairy milk in her glass.

The lawyer zoned in on this immediately. "Sarah, how many other kids were there with you and can you still get in touch with them and would they be willing to testify to this stuff, if we asked?"

She wiped the white mustache off her mouth with the cotton napkin. "I... would have to think about that."

Father Tom started to reach out to her in sympathy, but Johnny raised his hand to stop the words, then he leaned back in his chair before asking: "I'm so sorry, Sarah, but I have to ask this question." He bent forward to look into her eyes. "Please know I will do everything I can to protect your privacy... please know that, Sarah." The vulnerability in her gaze made him phrase the questions even more carefully. "I need to know if... whether... this guy ever did you any harm." He swallowed hard. "Did he... ever...?"

Her head bowed slightly. After a big breath, she spoke in a whisper: "He tried... in the barn... but his stepsister came along." She sniffed a quick breath. "She was furious with him." She shook her head. "That was the first time I ever heard so much foul language in my whole life." She closed her eyes and leaned back in her chair. "I got up and ran for my life and I never went back there, again, as long as he was living there."

"Lord God," Father Tom whispered. "Lord God... Lord God." He wiped his forehead with his hand. "I never knew this."

But the lawyer was right on it, again. "He has a stepsister?"

"Yes. Angela."

"Okay, another Angela." He frowned. "Or... not. What's her last name?"

"Umm, Donaldson, just like her dad's."

"Well, that's one for the books. My first two suspects are related."

"Related!" Sarah exclaimed. "They're not only related, they're a team." She lifted the glass of milk. "In fact, they are the original 'Team from hell!'" The two gentlemen waited for her to take a sip. "When I think back on how she would bring these little kids home." The glass was firmly set upon the oil cloth. "She told us she was babysitting. They would get off the school bus and who knows what happened after that?"

"What do you think happened?" the captain asked.

"Don't really know, but once I asked the bus driver if their mom knew about this. He just laughed and said he had a note from their folks and that's all that mattered to him."

There was a long pause in the conversation. All three continued with the meal and finally their plates were clean. It was Johnny who spoke up first.

"You thinking what I'm thinking?" He looked at Tom. The priest wiped his mouth with his napkin, then leaned forward on his elbows.

"I'm afraid so."

"The guy is a known predator. That's a fact. But the girl was cleared to work with children, so... she doesn't fit that role."

"Unless something slipped through the cracks," Tom said.

"Oh, she's not interested in molesting little children — not that one." Sarah was definite. "She had the hots for her stepbrother." Her chin jutted toward her cousin. "Why do you think she was so mad he was making the moves on me? Remember, I was almost sixteen at the time... not a little kid."

"So... she was bringing little kids home... for him?"

"Yes, Thomas. She was... and winning a certain kind of attention from him, for doing that." She glanced at Johnny. "I told you... it was just plain creepy." She stood and started to clear the table. Both men helped, but they were quiet.

When they retired to the living room, Tom and Johnny sat in front of the smoldering fireplace, nursing nice cups of coffee. Sarah spoke from the hearth where she had flopped tummy-down on a large pillow.

"Do you think they took that little boy — what's his name? Dicky?"

"They could have." The captain was staring into the coals.

"He must be very frightened," Father Tom said.

"If he's still alive," came the soft comment from the floor.

"We need to find a way to search the whole farm." The legal mind was into planning mode. "It can be done. There's always a way. But it would be easier if somebody had a birthday party on the premises, or even an open house."

She swung her body around and sat up. "What about a sugaring-off party? They have one every year, somewhere near the end of February, when the nights are still cold, but days are warm enough for the sap to run. In fact, they make a lot of money doing that. It's like a seasonal business."

"That's right." Tom fixed a hopeful look on his buddy. "It's open to the public for a whole week. They do tours through the sugarhouse and everything. We just need to show up."

"And maybe 'get lost' and have to wander around to find our way back, or whatever." He looked to Sarah for her take. "And before we go, I'll need a map of the whole place — the home, the barn, any outbuildings. Would you do that for me, Sarah?"

"Sure. But just be aware they don't let you wander away from the walking tour. You would have to invent some reason for deliberately getting away from the crowd."

"Okay. Thank you for setting me straight on that." He looked back and forth between the other two. "So, why would anybody want to get away from the crowd at a sugaring-off party?" Before they could answer, he had another thought. "We need to be there every day, so it has to be something we can do, at least a couple of times, without creating suspicion."

"Wait a moment, sir." She held up a pointer finger to stop the conversation's path. "Would you please clarify what you mean when you speak of 'we'?"

It caught him by surprise. "Oh, uh... well, maybe I'm being presumptuous, here." He smiled broadly. "I was thinking we three were being partners-in-crime, I guess. That's probably a bit over the top. Sorry."

There was a gleeful chuckle and she scooted over to sit cross-legged in front of his chair. "Not at all." She wiggled her shoulders once. "Tell me more."

"Sarah-Sarah-Sarah! You need to talk to your dad... or somebody, before you get involved in something like this." Her cousin was genuinely concerned. "What interest do you have in something like this, anyway?"

The family bond between the two closed that part of the discussion. "Daddy may be old, but he's not stupid. I know he would want to protect me, but he would also never want a little boy to go through what this one is going through... or has... You know that, Thomas." She turned back to the serviceman. "So, let me make this very clear: other than God, Himself, there are two things I am passionate about: number one, that the best of Vermont history be preserved, as accurately as possible, for generations to come. Number two, that the worst parts of Vermont history be made right... and including the garbage that has occurred at the farm of one Arnold Donaldson, which, if it turns out to be what we think, will become part of Vermont underground history... the part we need to make right by justice, so it will show the resilience and honorable character of the citizens of this state." Her little pointer finger was still waggling as she finished.

For a moment, Captain John Courtney thought he was in a courtroom, listening to some super-patriotic female shaming the jury into submission. He lowered his head to hide the amusement on his lips.

"Sarah, you don't know what you're getting into," her

cousin admonished.

"I need you to help, wherever you can, Thomas, okay?" She turned back to the lawyer. "So... what did you have in mind?"

"I have in mind, that... that you take twenty-four hours to think this thing through... and I mean, both of you." He nodded hopefully. "We could possibly do this. Or, at the least, help the authorities to solve this case... to find this little guy." As he rose to leave, he reached down to grasp Sarah's hand, lifting her gently to her feet. She kept her eyes lowered as she thanked him and he turned to his good buddy. "Walk me out to the car?"

Before his slid into the car seat, he looked the priest in the eye. "You know I wouldn't do anything to hurt her, don't you?"

Father Tom clasped his friend's shoulder in a solid grip. "I know that, Johnny... and I will be in prayer about this, for sure." As Johnny slipped into the driver's seat, the priest made the sign of the cross over him. The Air Force officer turned the key in the ignition and was back at Fort Ethan Allen well before taps sounded.

The next night, again just before taps, Captain John Courtney received a phone call in the officers' barracks. It was Father Tom Ladue.

"We're in, Johnny and we need to get a plan in place right away. Time is passing quickly."

CHAPTER FOUR

Plans

The two cousins were walking home from school, when a ruffian fifth grader overtook them, jerking Sonny's arm hard enough to stop the boy.

"Hey! You related to that Dupree kid who got kidnapped?"

The slender face tightened with confusion.

Annie shoved herself between the two of them. "Shut up, you pitiful puddle of puke!"

The bully sneered and slapped his hand into the bent elbow of his other arm, in a disrespectful gesture unique to the Italian community.

She swung her arm down in a fast, little arc, landing her fist under that elbow with such force it drove his own knuckles into his face. He staggered backward, shocked.

"Get lost," she said.

"I'll get you for this."

"No you won't, stupid. I have too many friends looking to do a chop job on guys like you." She grabbed her cousin's arm and moved forward.

"What the heck is he talking about?" The slender kid knew he could depend on an answer from Annie.

"Just wait a couple of minutes, Sonny. Mama will tell you what is going on."

From the top of her wavy, black hair framing the golden-skinned face with an aquiline nose, on down past her nicely rounded body to her little square feet, Aunt Tony was Italian. Her parents were from Italy and she was their first born in America, so she retained many of the old ways, including Mediterranean cooking and wine-making. At any time of the week, one could enter their small home, a block and a half from Battery Park in that northwest Burlington neighborhood and there would be a mixture of delicious fragrances... often morning toast, mixed with spaghetti sauce simmering on the stove. But she was not so much into wine-making as was her widowed father, who lived just over the fence. No, she was into homebrewed beer. In fact, there was a barrel fermenting in her kitchen, a few feet from the back door. When folks came for a visit, she would lift the wooden top off the barrel and scoop up a dripping glass of refreshment. The odor would remain for hours. But everybody would have spaghetti and there would be bonding and listening to Peggy Lee singing about not leaving the jungle, on the portable record-player in the compact living room and all would be well. On this day, however, there was no such thing going on. Indeed, it was not easy for Aunt Tony to tell Sonny about his brother's disappearance.

The saving grace in that situation was she could give the good news: his mother had landed a job as a housekeeper/babysitter for a divorced man with one child. She would start next week and Sonny could go and live there. He would be with his mother and that was a good thing. In the meantime, Aunt Tony kept the grieving brother at home for a week. The nuns sent homework with Annie and it all limped along. Uncle Andy shook his head a lot but was hopeful it would all work out. "At least we have a plan."

***

Lisa Marie joined the other girls in prayer. They knelt by their own beds and recited the Lord's Prayer, then sang the song they called "The Doxology," where they praised God from Whom all blessings flow, all creatures here below, all heavenly hosts praise Father, Son, and Holy Ghost. It concluded with a long, drawn out "Ahh-mennn." A couple of minutes were allowed for individually petitioned blessings for Mom and Dad, or whomever. Lisa always took this time to ask God to protect Dicky and bring him back real soon. Early on, she thought it would probably be a more powerful prayer if she could pray the rosary, but she had decided these people didn't do that because they went to a different church... but that was all right, because it was the same Jesus who was hearing her prayers. Mrs. Hays had told her so and she had reassured Cee Cee of this important fact.

But as the girls rose and slipped into bed, she secretly kept on praying, her head under the covers, the lips moving to form words having no sound: "Dear Jesus, thank you for being here a little longer to hear my thing I need to ask you. Please let me just ask you this one thing and if it doesn't turn out like I want, I promise to never ask you for this again, okay?" She did a quick mental check, trying to remember how she had rehearsed it in her head, all day. "Please could you get my mama and daddy back together again? I promise that if they don't stay together this time, I will never ask you to do this again. I won't be mad, either. I promise. I will just know it is better if they don't. I promise. Amen." As she pulled the covers down under her chin, a little warmth stirred inside. Her mother had a new job, starting the next day, in a house on Main Street in Burlington. It was a block up and across the street from the old Strong Theater, where the Home kids often went to the movies on a Saturday afternoon. Things were working out.

Now, if only God would bring Dicky back home.

***

It had been a long-distance divorce, with him signing the

papers in Plattsburg, New York, then mailing them back to her lawyer in Burlington. She had charged him with desertion, even though it was she who kicked him out to go find work. He had walked from the house on Maple Street all the way into Essex Junction, taken the bus and not come back. After all, she had made him quit working on the Wilson dairy farm, taken all of their savings, and nagged him into buying the home of her dreams. There had been four babies, with four miscarriages in between and too long without indoor plumbing and enough was enough for this city girl.

Meanwhile, over in Plattsburg, he was lost and tired and developed stomach ulcers, going on a diet of milk for months and still ending up in the hospital. No one told him the house was repossessed and the four kids were in the Children's Home. Further, he failed to send twenty dollars a week child support, because his seventh-grade education barely enabled him to understand the legal paperwork. Besides, he was trying to do part-time carpentry, to keep a roof over his own head. The once "tall and handsome" farm boy arrived at the front door where she was the housekeeper, a gaunt facsimile of that former body, stooped under the heaviness of this latest tragedy.

When she opened the door, she saw it in his eyes and he saw it in hers.

"We still don't know..." Doreen whispered.

Roy stepped forward and wrapped his arms around her. The door was wide open, but they stood there hugging for a long time, sobbing deeply.

***

Mrs. Bushey did not like what she saw happening with Little Joe Turner. It had been almost three months since the disappearance of his "blood brother" and the boy was acting out in alarming ways — dancing in wild circles while hooting and yipping like a wild animal until he scared the rest of the

Little Kids and more seriously, gashing his arm with whatever he could find, until the blood oozed and dribbled off his wrist. A social worker visited with him a few times, then recommended medicine to calm him down. When he began to sit and stare too much, they took the medicine away, which made matters worse.

It was time to take a strong stance with his only relatives, Joe and Ava Turner. She skipped her Saturday hair appointment and detoured them into her office for a frank discussion. "This boy needs family right now and I do mean now!" she told the couple. "You have to visit more often and stay more than twenty minutes." Her hands spread palms-up in front of her. "Why is it you don't stay long enough to get a good, healthy bonding with this wonderful little guy? Don't you care about him?"

"Of course we do," Ava replied. Her husband broke in before she could go on.

"Look. Ava has a heart condition. She can't do too much. Otherwise, we would take him to live with us. But we can't. It could be fatal for her."

"I have that information, Mr. Turner, and I do understand the risk... but why couldn't he go home for an all-day visit, or even a whole weekend? Surely, this would help a great deal with his spiritual and physical health... and still not be too much for either one of you." She pulled a calendar from the corner of her desk. "All we need is a couple of weekends a month and you must know someone who could come in to help you." She caught the glimmer of hope in the woman's eye.

"How about we try an all-day visit, first?" Ignoring the aggravated look on Joe Turner's face, she pointed out two Saturdays. "Look. He could come this week, or the next. Although," she looked firmly into the man's eyes, "it would be much better if you could do both of them."

They had the boy on his way for a home visit in ten minutes. As he climbed into the Turners' car, he could hardly contain his excitement. "I want to see the cow, Uncle Joe. Can I see the cow?"

"Ay-yuh," the man answered. "But remember, we have to get you back here by four o'clock so's you can have supper with the rest of the kids."

And they did. Little Joe was a different child when they brought him back into the building. Mrs. Bushey was there, again and very pleased. "See you next Saturday."

Mr. Turner lowered his head, but Ava's face was glowing. "We made cookies," she said. "And he got to see the cow!"

***

The last of the sugaring-off tours were only weeks away, so John, Sarah, and Father Tom had to pull a viable plan into place, quickly.

"We probably all should go to it on different days," Sarah suggested. "Although that would limit us to only three visits and each time we each have to 'get lost' on the property." She wrinkled her nose. "That doesn't work. Doesn't give us each enough time and probably they would start taking measures to keep people from wandering around their property." She sighed impatiently. "That won't work."

"It has to look accidental, I think." The lawyer approached the problem from years of perusing law books. "Otherwise, we could break the law somehow and suffer the consequences." He sat back in the kitchen chair, sipping hot chocolate left over from the early supper. "I sure don't want to blow my career as a lawyer."

She noted the deep concentration on her cousin's face and asked, "What do you think, Thomas?"

Father Tom stood slowly to his feet. "I think I may have a plan. Let's go sit by the fire and talk about it." He cast a reassuring glance toward her. "The dishes have been cleared, Sarah. I can help you wash them, later."

When they came to the stone hearth, the priest motioned

the others to sit in the two wing-backed chairs and he took a standing position in front of the fireplace. The soles of his leather slippers squeaked over the warm stones as he came to a halt, facing the two of them as though they were part of his congregation. He folded his hands behind his back, looking back and forth between the two.

"This is only a suggestion," he began, "but I really think this would work... at least for a couple, maybe three days." He looked up at the ceiling. "Actually, four days, if we work it right."

The other two listened intently.

"Now, Sarah, whether or not you like them, you have an 'in' with that family and so do I." He was looking directly at her. "What if we had some reason to want to participate in their next year's sugaring-off party, in a special way... a way to allow us to check out every last location on the farm?" He smiled. "What if you wanted to get married next year, at that farm, during their annual celebration?" He was grinning. "Not that you would really be doing that, but I think it would get their attention. This would be a real money maker for them. Think of the publicity." He brought his hands around to a loud clap in front. "And what if we wanted to check out this special Maple Sugar Wedding venue right now, this year, to see if such a celebration would even be viable? You know... pretending to see whether such a wedding could happen."

She was intrigued. "Ay – yu-uh...?"

"Don't you see it? We could go all over the place, deciding where to have the ceremony, the reception, the photo shoots, the music accommodations, the caterer's access... make them think they have a real possibility of even a year-round wedding and anniversary and even birthday party facility."

John leaned forward. "Tom! That's genius. It could work." He turned to Sarah. "That could work! The two of you would have complete access to the farm. I think you should go for it."

"Well," Father Tom said as he shifted his weight a bit.

"There's one thing we still need, my friend." He pursed his lips. "We need a fiancé... a real life on-the-scene fella who she's going to marry... and it needs to be somebody we trust. The fewer of us involved in this, the less the risk of being discovered." He put forth his best freckle-faced smile. "That means you, mister."

The young man glanced sideways at Sarah. "You want us to pose as an engaged couple?"

"Uh-huh." Tom slid his hands into his pants pockets before he delivered the last part of the plan. "That means you have to be very, very convincing. These people are slick. They will spot a phony in a split second, especially if they have something to hide." He took a big breath. "Sooo-oh, you will have to convince these folks you are both head-over-heels in love. That means, holding hands, pretending to gaze into each other's eyes, whispering private endearments, 'wandering off to be alone,' and — if you get caught snooping around — pretending to be making out." He took another big breath. "Okay, I don't mean, you know, actually making out to the extreme... just look like there is some serious smooching going on." His brow furrowed with the question. "Think you two can pull that off?"

The only sound in the room was the crackling fire.

***

Sonny Dupree was glad to be living with his mother over there on Main Street, but while it wasn't all that much farther to walk home from the Catholic grade school, the problem was Annie went in the opposite direction. So, when dismissal came, he dashed out the door and started dodging little snow piles left over from shoveled sidewalks. His marathon took the shortest direction to St. Paul Street, where he headed south past St. Paul's Baptist Church and then the Harvest restaurant and the busy Burlington transit bus station, where there were lots of people who could see if any bullies were after him. Once to the corner of St. Paul and Main, he crossed over and hurried past City Hall Park and across Church Street, arriving at his new home a half-block later. All this happened without stopping to use the restrooms along the route, for fear of being cornered and beaten, or whatever else he could imagine. So, when he burst through the door of the house, he was ready to hit the bathroom, in no uncertain terms.

But his father was sitting there, waiting for him... like a frail ghost from the past, a visage so intense the young man immediately stopped in his tracks.

"Daddy?"

He heard his mother's voice: "Yes, Sonny. It's Daddy."

The man stood and reached for him and the boy started to cry and then the worst thing happened: he felt the warmth trickling down the inside of his thighs. The poor youngster was completely undone, pushing away from the embrace and running for the bathroom.

"Sonny!" she called.

"Wait, Doreen," the father cautioned. "Bring him some dry clothes."

Fifteen minutes later, father and son were reunited, their heads resting against each other in a long-delayed embrace.

Suddenly, the thirteen-year-old daughter of Doreen's employer burst in through the front door. "What's this?" she inquired. "This your daddy, little man?"

"Yes, I am," came the answer. "I'm Roy Dupree. And who might you be?"

"The house princess, that's who." She addressed Doreen: "You allowed to have visitors while you're working?"

"I think you have homework to finish before supper, young lady."

"That so?" She stuck a rude finger into the air. "Make me." She trounced toward the back bedroom where she liked to stay to herself.

Roy waggled his head in disbelief. "Looks like you have your hands full with that one."

"Yeah, well, we do what we have to do."

Roy left shortly thereafter, with a promise to come back at noon the next day. "We need to get things straightened out. We need to find Dicky. We need to talk."

And they did. She had done more than her obligated amount of cleaning and fixed tuna sandwiches, before he got there. They walked back into the kitchen which was adjacent to the two back bedrooms — one for the house princess, a much smaller one for Sonny — and sat down at the modest table with the mismatched chairs.

He bit into the sandwich like she remembered for the whole sixteen years they had been married. But after the first bite, he laid it down, at the direction of his injured stomach. "Sorry," he apologized, "can't quite do that yet."

"I'm sorry, Roy." She offered him a glass of milk.

"No," he said and bowed his head. "I've had all of that stuff I can take."

She raised her eyes to meet his. "Will you ever get well from this? I feel so guilty."

He stopped all movement for a few seconds. "No… no. We just got off-track, I think. And there were… are… some things that should not have happened." He looked up. "I am so sorry, Doreen, but I didn't know what else to do. We couldn't afford that house."

She burst into tears. "I know that. I know that now, Roy, and I am so sorry."

He held her close for a long while… and then it was time for the children to come home from school.

Before he left, they had determined that since he would see Sonny almost every day for the next week, the two girls would get to go visit their daddy in Plattsburg for the whole spring-break week. Meanwhile, he would go back to work in New York, because after all, they needed to build their savings for a new beginning. Arrangements for the girls' visit could be completed by then. When Roy got on the Greyhound bus at the end of this first visit, all three of the children were there. They saw their mama and daddy exchange a tender goodbye.

It was going to be all right.

***

"A couple of things I would add to this scheme," Detective Smith said to John Courtney. "I would ask to take pictures, so you could make decisions on where to have the different activities... without unnecessarily bothering the Donaldsons. That would be a legitimate reason... shouldn't cause any suspicion and would give us investigators something to go on. You never know what can show up in a snapshot." His hands were, as usual, clasped over his stomach. "The other thing is your story is more believable if you keep your identity as close to the truth as possible. Like, you have known each other for a long time and you're in the Air Force and she's a history buff, or whatever. That way you won't give conflicting facts. Of course, if they have nothing to hide, they won't be so suspicious, but if there is something going on... you get the drift."

"I do."

"As for the rest of the story... you should rehearse and rehearse. How did you finally fall for each other? Where did that happen? What's her favorite color?"

"We've been working on that already." He tapped his notebook gently on his knee. "Her favorite color is aqua." He raised one eyebrow. "And that's the actual truth. So, yes, it is a lot easier to fool people when you put a lot of truth into a lie."

"Ha!" The wry, spaced-out smile emphasized his agreement. "Didn't Hitler operate from that angle?"

"We could add Karl Marx and Lenin to that list, I think, but..." The captain decided to change the subject. "So, we will be contacting the Donaldsons on the next weekend of their sugaring-off thing. We'll act like we just got the idea and take it from there."

"So, you'll be at the farm on Sunday?"

"Right after noon Mass. We have to wait for Father Tom. All three of us agreed he would be the one to approach that family with this idea. I mean, everybody believes a priest, right?"

"Mmmmm... not everybody. And that reminds me. You may run into either one of those two. We are not quite sure where Johnson or Angela are. Keep an eye out, would you?"

The young man stood up. "Anything else, sir?"

"Yeah. Don't come back here anymore. City Hall is just the other side of this wall and you never know who might see you coming in and out." He pulled a pen out of his pocket and scribbled a phone number on a scrap of paper. "This is my dry cleaner's number. Call and tell them what time you want to pick up your shirts. I'll meet you at Colodny's Market over on the corner of North Street and North Avenue. You know where that is?"

"Yes, but how will they know it's me when I call this place?"

"My cleaner doesn't do shirts."

"What if the market is closed?"

"Not a factor." He stood up, handing over the slip of paper. "Don't worry, Johnny. I have lots of friends."

Nevertheless, Johnny pulled the ski jacket's hood up over his head before stepping out onto Church Street.

CHAPTER FIVE

Hiding

Thirteen people stood in the parking lot below the sugarhouse on the Donaldson farm, listening, as a tall lady in a long, black winter coat introduced herself. Granny-style glasses failed to hide the dark circles under her troubled eyes as she spoke: "Greetings and welcome to Donaldson farm's sugaring-off party. I am Delores Donaldson and I will be your guide for this afternoon." It was as though she had made the same speech a hundred times and her mind was somewhere else, entirely. "We have a couple of rules you need to know before we start. We need to stay together at all times and we need to avoid getting too close to the evaporator, where the sap is boiling… especially the children, because it is very, very hot." She nodded at the couple standing to her right, who were trying to keep three young boys in tow. "We will start by walking through part of the maple grove, then proceed past some family history, to the sugarhouse, where you will also enjoy our delightful gift shop. We will then serve hot chocolate and sugar-on-snow at the outdoor seating area. You may take pictures, if you wish." She turned to start up the hill, but stopped to say what she almost forgot. "There are no actual restrooms, but an outhouse is available and yes, you are in rural Vermont." It was supposed to be amusing, but the tone of her voice squelched that in a hurry, leaving most of the adults rolling their eyes. The boys, however, were delighted.

The small crowd followed single file, the rear being brought up by a priest in a warm hat with flaps tied upward over the top of his head, and a couple who were holding hands. The three had arrived together and were chatting as they walked carefully through the plowed driveway.

"We get to take pictures!" Father Tom said softly.

John pulled Sarah's arm through his, drawing her close as if to keep her from falling. He bent nearer to her face to whisper the question: "Is that Father Jeff's mother?"

"Uh-huh," she replied sweetly, tilting her head toward his as though she was flirting.

"O-o-kay, then." He patted her mittened hand there in the crook of his arm. "Here we go then… 'darling.'"

The priest looked back, wondering what they were chuckling about, almost missing the sharp turn to the left. "Hey, you two! We have to go this way."

It was only a short walk upward before the line of visitors broke out into another drive, this one marked with unfamiliar ruts. Delores climbed steadily forward toward a large grove of trees, finally bringing the group to a stop in front of a particularly large maple.

"This is a sugar maple," she announced. "We actually have thirty-one of them here and a few more on the back side of the property. But what you need to see, is all right here in front of you." Her hand patted the trunk. "You can tell it's a maple tree by the scaly bark. Please notice there is no pattern to it… it is a completely random collection of scales."

"How come you put two buckets on each tree?" one of the boys asked.

It was a question she had heard many times, but the woman answered politely, "This is common practice. In fact, some farms put three or four, depending on how big the tree is." She went on quickly, to avoid any more interruptions, reaching for one of the tin buckets, each of which had a peaked "house roof" cover on top. She lifted the tin cover to expose a small, metal object which had been driven into the bark. "This is a spile, or a spigot. You can see the sap dripping from it."

"It looks like a leaky faucet," somebody said.

"Can I taste it?" one of the boys asked.

"Me, too!" the other two called out in unison.

She nodded and all three ran a finger under the spigot and licked the watery sweetness. They were disappointed in the taste, but Father Tom got a great shot of them with Delores Donaldson.

The sound of hoofs and jangling harnesses turned the group's attention farther up the road into the grove. A black horse came plodding along toward them, steam blowing forth from his nostrils. Behind him, a low sled's runners cut furrows into the snow. The ruts were deep since the barrels of sap were full. As this horse and sleigh slowly passed the sightseers, they were surprised to see the driver walking alongside the sled, holding the reins. He wore a red plaid cap with the earflaps turned down to keep warm and his coat collar was turned up around his chin. The booted feet were slipping and sliding as he moved to keep up with the steed. There was obviously no time for a friendly wave or nod, but Father Tom took several quick shots of that rather unique sight, anyway.

"He's bringing in sap pretty late in the day," the solemn woman remarked. "We'll have to boil it down. Can't just store the stuff because it gets bacteria and turns to vinegar." She pressed her lips tightly. "That means we'll be up half the night, but it all comes out even... an early sugaring season like this, is usually pretty short."

They moved along through the tapped trees to a fork in the sled road, taking the one to the right. In a moment, the sugarbush grove was left behind and they were standing in front of a large gazebo which was perched at the edge of a ridge overlooking the valley below. Delores continued her rehearsed litany: "The steps have been shoveled, so feel free to enter this unique viewing point of the Donaldson farm."

As the group entered the structure, they could see the sugarhouse directly below. Steam billowed from its roof and large stacks of wood leaned against the shed wall just behind it. Father Tom stepped forward to snap a couple of shots of the quaint scene below. As he did, the young hand-holding couple went forward to take in the view. She looked up at him and slid closer. "This would be the perfect place for a wedding," she exclaimed out loud.

Her adoring escort drew her tightly to his side. "Yeah," he whispered.

"Are you two engaged?" asked the mother of the three boys.

Johnny kissed the top of Sarah's head. "You bet."

"Oh, that is the sweetest thing I've heard in a long time. My husband and I got married in a gazebo in my grandmother's backyard." She turned to her husband. "Remember, honey?"

"Absolutely," the man replied as he yanked his youngest son off the circular front rail.

The woman turned to Mrs. Donaldson. "Have you ever thought of doing weddings up here?" Delores's eyes betrayed her disapproval, but the young mother went on: "You really should. It's the newest thing… theme weddings. In fact, they are doing theme anniversaries and theme birthdays and theme parties of all kinds these days." She swooped a hand across the front panorama of the little building. "You have the perfect…" She had another thought. "Do you have any more unused buildings?"

Delores's long coat flared as she turned to lead them on. "We do, but I doubt they would be usable anymore." A few more feet down the road, she pointed to a large house with a veranda across the front. "This is the old farmhouse," she said, as she kept walking. "And down there," she pointed forward along the descending drive, "…is the old barn. It's big, but pretty dilapidated."

"Well, you never know." The young mother let it go and turned her attention to the view as the group made its way down to the sugarhouse.

Despite the large vent in the roof, the inside of the house was filled with a sweet, sappy steam. It rose from a long, rectangular stove in the center of the room. Underneath this evaporator pan, a wood fire raged behind closed metal doors. The visitors removed hats and loosened coats as the woman introduced her husband.

Arnold "Arnie" Donaldson picked up a split log from a pile against the wall, clanged wide the metal opening and gingerly inserted more fuel. Quickly closing the double-hinged doors, he stood up and grinned. He looked like the famous movie star, Humphrey Bogart, even talking out of the side of his mouth the same way.

"All right." The left corner of his mouth drew back as he spoke through his upper bicuspids. "Just one more warning: Keep back from the heat." He picked up a skimming paddle and strode to the far end of the stove. "As you can see, the evaporator pan is divided into three sections. This first one is just getting the sap hot; the second one is starting to boil, and the one on the other end is nearly syrup. You can tell by the foam, see?" He pointed to the slight froth in the center compartment. "We take this skimming paddle and scoop it off at this point, but when it comes to the final stage..." He moved to the rapidly boiling last batch. "You usually have to tame it down." Leaning the paddle against the wood pile, he reached for a long, thin branch with a piece of salt pork on the end. "We use grease," he said. With one swift pass over the top of the roiling foam, the brownish suds suddenly dropped away into the pan.

An appreciative hum came from the audience.

"In the old days, folks sometimes used a small branch of evergreen. Some still do." For the first time, he looked at the small group. "A couple more things you might like to know."

He looked hard at the priest for a moment, then went on. "It takes about forty-three gallons of sap to make one gallon of maple syrup. And it takes hours and hours of working the sugarbush and sugarhouse chores to make this whole operation successful. We hope you will keep that in mind as you stop and look around in our gift shop for a few minutes, while Delores gets the hot chocolate and packed snow ready for the candy treat." He dismissed them with a curt, "Thanks for coming by."

As the others moved into the gift shop, the last three approached the man.

"Nice to see you again, Arnie."

He acknowledged the greeting with a nod. "Tommy Ladue, right?"

"Right." He extended his hand. "Been a long time, for sure." As they shook hands, he looked over Arnie's shoulder. "Quite an operation you have here, mister."

The corner of his mouth seemed to stretch farther. "We try."

"Do you remember my cousin, Sarah?" He touched her shoulder and she smiled shyly. "And this is her fiancé, John Courtney."

"Nice to meet you." John made a polite bow of the head as he spoke but couldn't help noticing the man eyeing the large "diamond" on Sarah's finger. He stifled a smirk, since the stone was really a zircon and a cheap one, at that.

"Why don't you two lovebirds check out the gift shop while I catch up with Arnie for a couple of minutes?"

The small gift shop was crowded, so Sarah didn't spot Angela until she and John stepped up to pay. The two ladies recognized each other instantly. Sarah squeezed John's arm as he laid the little boxes of maple sugar candy and a gallon of Grade B syrup on the counter.

"Angela!" she exclaimed with a big smile. "How nice to see you again."

"Hi." It was a hollow greeting, accompanied by a curious glance at John.

"We sure enjoyed this tour." No response seemed forthcoming, so Sarah went to the next step. "Oh, this is my fiancé, Johnny." The two "lovers" exchanged an endearing look, but Angela chose not to pursue the subject. She grabbed the items, shoved them into a bag, and announced they owed thirty-two dollars. By that time the priest caught up with them. They pressed through the crowd and took seats well away from the others.

"Well? Was he interested in letting us have a wedding here?" the two wanted to know.

"I think so. I have his phone number, to call him back tomorrow. So, I guess he might go for it."

The hot chocolate was a welcome treat, but when Delores brought a large pan of packed snow to the table, they all gathered around, eager to watch the magic.

She disappeared into the sugarhouse for a moment, emerging carefully with a pot of steaming syrup. "Step back, so's I don't splash you," she cautioned and then started pouring a thin dribble of syrup, up and down, around and around, making lacey patterns that melted into the snow, finally hardening into candy. As each person picked up a strip, it crackled off into a separate piece of delicate deliciousness. Ooohs and aaahs followed in sequence around the table. John was licking his fingers when he looked up and saw a deep, purple dusk on the horizon. He looked at his watch.

"Omigosh, honey," the fiancé cooed to his fiancée. "It's almost five o'clock. I have to get back to the base."

As the three of them pulled out of the parking lot and headed north, the "engaged" couple sat close together in the back seat, still playing the role, in case somebody saw them get into the car. The sky was dark by then and she was looking up through the side window at the stars, when she suddenly moved over to press her nose against the glass.

"Well, well… now isn't that interesting."

The young man moved in closer for a look. "What?"

"Isn't that the old, abandoned Donaldson farmhouse we walked by?"

He looked up to the ridge. "Ye-a-h." His long breath made a cloud on the window and they both swiftly wiped it off, his hand over hers. Quickly, the two faces peered out, nearly cheek-to-cheek.

"There's a light in the top story window," she murmured. "See it?" But it flickered out before he could. They stared hard for a couple of seconds longer, then slipped back into the seat, side by side.

"I wonder if that's where they're hiding him." She sounded worried.

"We're not even sure they have him," John reminded her, as he patted her hand. That touch lasted just a little too long.

Suddenly, the young man leaned forward to talk to the driver.

"What's your take on this thing, so far? Think they have him, Tom?"

***

Mrs. Bushey descended the beautiful spiral staircase and crossed the hall to her office. "Thanks for waiting," she said to her private investigator. John nodded. "I had some arrangements to take care of up in the small auditorium on the third floor. I swear, every time I go up and down that whole stairway, I feel like royalty." She sat down at her desk. "So, what do you have for me, Johnny?"

He filled her in on his contacts with the Snoop Squad, but left out the part about Colodny's Market, thinking that was more than she needed to know. She was especially impressed with the scheme to scour the farm by posing as an engaged couple, although she did wave a cautious finger as she gave approval. Then he told her about the visit to the Donaldson farm.

"Angela is definitely there. We met her waiting on customers in the gift shop. Of course, she's known Sarah since childhood and Father Tom, as well."

He shifted his weight in the hard chair. "The good news is Tom called back and Arnold, her father, is interested in finding out about this theme wedding business plan. In reality, it's a lucrative investment and this man is no fool when it comes to making a buck."

"So, what's the bad news?"

"Like you said, there are lots of places to hide stuff on a big, old farm. If they have the boy, it could take a while to find him and then... who knows what we will find?"

"When do you think you'll even get the chance to start snooping?"

"Hopefully, by this Saturday." He sighed impatiently. "It's frustrating, because every day that passes..." Suddenly he remembered to ask about the other suspect. "Anything new on Joe Turner?"

She gave a glowing report on the home visit and reassured him all was going well. "That little boy is in seventh heaven," she cooed.

***

Like the sugaring-off season, the school spring vacation had come early this year. The warmer days dictated that. An early sap run also meant an early thaw of the dirt roads in rural Chittenden County, which, in turn, dictated the spring break in the city schools. Things had to be coordinated. "Mud vacation" was just around the corner. It was the first time in a long time it occurred in February.

Roy and Doreen Dupree, though divorced for two years, showed up together for an appointment with Mrs. Bushey. After an hour's discussion, it was agreed the board of the

Children's Home would not sue Roy for back child support, if he would agree to not sue them. The Duprees were impressed the director was using her own funds to get to the bottom of Dicky's disappearance. This meant people *really were* trying to find their boy. Doreen cried again, Mrs. Bushey's eyes filled with tears and that was reassurance enough for Roy.

"But there is something else," he said. "We want to take the girls on a week's visit with me over there in Plattsburg, during this next week's spring vacation."

Mrs. Bushey's white eyebrows moved. "Is that all right with you?" she asked their mother.

"Yes. I think it would be a good thing." She looked at Roy. "We're trying to make a new start and they need to get to know their daddy, again."

So, it was on the next Saturday morning, they all took off in Roy's mother's car. There was one stipulation on the borrowing of the car: his mother, Ellen, who didn't drive, wanted to go with them. Doreen was unhappy about that, because she was well aware Ellen did not like her. It was something the rest of the Dupree family had had to bear at every family event in the whole sixteen years Roy and Doreen were married. Indeed, she wasn't looking forward to the return trip to Burlington, because she had to drive the car back leaving her and Ellen alone for the whole time. But that was the deal and she had to go along with it.

The two girls sat on either side of their plump little grandmother in the back seat; Doreen sat in front and watched adoringly as Roy drove the half-day trip looping north around the tip of Lake Champlain and back down to their destination in upper New York State. They sang and chatted and laughed a lot and then suddenly, Roy pulled the car up to the curb in front of a row of tightly jammed houses.

"The apartment is on the first floor," he announced, as they unloaded. In a moment, he was unlocking the door and the little family entered together. Grandma Ellen, however, lingered behind, a grim look on her face.

The girls were excited beyond containment, the questions coming forth in a continuous cacophony. "Is this the living room?" "Is this where we eat, at this table?" "Is this where you do dishes?" "Where's the bathroom, Daddy?" "Where do we sleep, Daddy?"

But Doreen was standing still in the center of the living room, her eyes taking in photos on the wall, crocheted doilies on the end tables, and through the doorway of one of the two bedrooms, a pink chenille bedspread and flowered wallpaper. The color drained from her face.

Roy looked up from his chattering daughters and saw the storm about to hit. Gently, he pointed the girls toward the flowery bedroom.

"I thought you knew." He moved closer. "I have a roommate. You have to do this here, or you can't even afford to get an apartment."

Her lips were tight. "A woman???" She could hardly speak.

"I thought you knew. I thought Ma told you..." He looked over at his mother, whose eyes were focused on the floor. "It's my cousin, Laura. You know Laura."

Doreen's mouth dropped open in unbelief. Laura was known as the man-eater in the family. She went through boyfriends like there was no tomorrow and she didn't care who knew it, or who got hurt in the process.

"H-how could you... do that?"

"You kicked me out, Doreen. I was staying with Ma. Laura offered me a place over here, where there was work."

"You mean to tell me you have been shacking up with that... slut... for the whole two-plus years we've been separated?"

He didn't want to address that. "I thought you knew. I thought it was something you had forgiven me for." Hoping for support from his mother, he whispered, "Ma..."

"She had to see for herself."

"Well, I'm not leaving the girls here while that's going on," Doreen snapped.

"No, Laura is staying with her daughter for the whole week. They won't even see her." He noted the girls still checking out the bedroom. "We don't want to upset the girls. We can still do this. We can still work things out."

"He's right. The girls should have this time with their father. What harm can it do?" The grandmother tapped her purse against her knees.

Doreen walked slowly toward the door, then stopped. "Call them out to say goodbye." He did, but before they got all the way out there, she warned him: "I expect them to be on a bus next Saturday morning."

Lisa Marie and Cee Cee got their hugs and kisses, then retreated happily to their new bedroom. The grandmother embraced her son and went to the car, leaving the two alone.

Lisa Marie had one more thing to tell her mother. She had reached the doorway into the hall where the two were standing, when she saw her mother's face, wet with tears. She stopped and slipped quietly behind the doorjamb. Her father tried to embrace her mother, but Doreen pushed him away.

"I wouldn't marry you again if you were the last man in the world," the woman cried. The door slammed hard behind her.

LeRoy Dupree went to the sofa and sat down, his head in his hands. Lisa peeked at this sad sight, then decided to sit down right where she was and wait.

But Cee Cee appeared in the bedroom doorway, saw them both, and whispered to her sister: "What's wrong with Daddy?"

CHAPTER SIX

Searching

"We were especially interested in the gazebo, Mr. Donaldson," Sarah called out as the three of them followed him up the hill. The man was moving quickly.

"Thomas! Thomas, slow down, will you?" The priest turned to look back from his position of second-fastest climber, hesitating before following the rugged Vermonter.

Arnie reached that lookout point, climbing up the stone steps ahead of them. "So, what happens here?" he asked.

"Sarah tells me this is the perfect spot for the actual wedding vows." He flashed that freckled smile as his pretty cousin was escorted up the steps by her fiancé. "And she's a girl... so, she probably has that right."

She drew a recovering breath before she went into the spiel. "Oh my gosh, I have always loved this place. Look at the stone foundation and the beautiful detail in the railings and the roof... not to mention the fantastic view." She turned to John. "When we were kids in high school, we would throw snowballs down at the sugarhouse. Of course, it was too far down, but we did it anyway."

"I suppose we'll have to do some painting," Mr. Donaldson mused.

"Oh no, sir," she admonished. "Please don't touch a thing, not for us. We want the vintage look, the Vermont history look."

"That's right," John interjected. "We don't want you to change this spot at all. Maybe the next event you have will want you to do that, but I bet the income from our wedding will provide for improvements."

His eyes glinted and his lopsided grin grew wider. "Now, that's a thought."

"Here's another thought, Arnie," Father Tom said. "These kids want a fairly small wedding, so there won't be any need for a sound system... especially out here in the gazebo. Most of the guests will be able to hear the whole thing quite well." He looked at the couple. "Of course, I can't speak for what you'll need for the reception."

"The reception should be in the barn," Sarah piped up. "I remember there was an open space as you came in through the double doors in the front. Am I right?"

"Ay-yuh-h-h-h," the farmer replied slowly. "Course, the floor there is old."

"Perfect!" she chirped. "Rustic! Rustic is what we want. And we'll be having square dancing. Right, hon?" Her face glowed as she spoke to him.

"Right." He looked at his host. "But we probably should take a look, just in case."

In a few minutes, they were down the hill a bit, opening the front doors of the unused dairy barn. The three of them were surprised when Arnie reached over and turned on some overhead lights. The soft glow revealed a wide space between two long rows of empty stalls. On the outer walls behind the stalls, long rows of dusty windows framed the facility.

"Oh, wow..." she whispered. "Just a little sprucing up is all it needs. The tables can go in the stall spaces on each side of the dance floor."

A few minutes later, they were closing the doors. Sarah twirled around to look up the road.

"We'll need a place to have the rehearsal dinner and for the wedding party to change clothes. I think we passed the old farmhouse on the way down here." She turned to Mr. Donaldson once more. "I know you have to get back to the sugarhouse. But would it be all right if John and I took a look while you two discuss business? We'll only be a few minutes, then we'll join you down there." When the man nodded his consent, she asked for the house key.

"Just don't touch stuff," he muttered, as he slipped the key off the ring.

As soon as the two of them were inside the front door, she was all business. "You start in the basement, and I'll start with the upstairs." She was unbuttoning her coat. "If that little boy is on this farm, I'm betting there is evidence right here in this house." With that she disappeared up the stairway.

John found the cellar door leading off the kitchen. A yank on a long string looped against the stairway wall brought light from a single bulb, halfway down. He descended, found another string and this bulb illuminated the whole open basement. Carefully, he checked the walls and floor for any recent disturbances, opening dusty cupboards and wooden boxes as he proceeded. Finally, he climbed back up the stairs, satisfied there was nothing to find down there. Almost an hour had passed without his noticing. He was carefully rummaging through the kitchen's broom closet when he heard her scrambling down the stairs.

"Johnny!" she called in a loud whisper. "Angela is on the front walk! Get in here, quick."

She was standing in front of the sofa, holding her coat wide open. "Pretend we're making out, quick." He came to her, not quite knowing what to do. As Angela's footsteps hit the porch, Sarah pulled his arms around her, then wrapped her coat around them like a blanket. The storm door squeaked as she pulled his head down into her shoulder and when Angela opened the inside door into the living room, she saw the embracing couple. Sarah was stroking the back of his head and making little kitten noises.

"Oh, for gawd's sake," she snorted. "No wonder you two were taking so long."

On the way back to the Ladue house, the two sat in the back seat, not talking. Father Tom looked at them from the rearview mirror. "You two okay? Awfully quiet back there." His eyes went back to the road. "I think we're doing well at our undercover work. But did you find anything at the house?"

"Nothing in the basement or the kitchen," John said, looking out the window.

"I didn't get to look at all the rooms upstairs," Sarah said. "But I'm positive somebody is living in that one room where we saw the light from the road last time." She slipped her hand over and tapped John's knuckles gently. "Remember?"

"Ay-yuh." He glanced at her quickly, then back out the window.

"But no evidence so far...?" the priest asked.

"We have a lot of work to do, Thomas."

At the house, Johnny said a quiet goodbye. But when he got into his car, he found himself sitting there, staring at Sarah's car which was parked in front of his. A tap on the window jarred him back to reality. He rolled the window down for her.

"I can't move my car until you get out of the way, handsome."

He half-laughed as the words came out. "Sarah Ladue, are you flirting with me?!"

She smiled as she bent closer. "Well," she said with a slow wink, "maybe just a little."

Things were hectic back at the base. The usual partying in the enlisted barracks was especially loud on this particular

Saturday night. Captain John Courtney tossed and turned on his cot, but it wasn't just the noise. He had a lot on his mind, not the least of which was how Sarah had made those little mewing sounds in his ear.

***

Mrs. Hays, the upstairs housemother for the Big Girls, knew a lot about God. Her late husband had been a minister in the First Methodist Church for many years and that made a big impression on Lisa Marie. The same Saturday they got back from Plattsburg, both girls asked to talk with her. At six o'clock the two of them curled up on the floor in front of the rocking chair where this gray-haired lady sat, her crooked fingers folded together on her lap. Her room was warm and smelled like lilac water.

"So, you made a promise to God, Lisa Marie?"

"Yes, ma'am. I promised Him I wouldn't get mad if our mama and daddy got back together and then got apart again. I told Him I would take that as a sign that they shouldn't be together, ever again." Cee Cee saw her sister's chin quiver and slid over closer to her. "Only... only, I guess I am really, really sad and so is Cee Cee."

"Of course you are. That's perfectly all right." She stopped rocking and leaned forward. "You never promised you wouldn't be sad, did you?"

"No," they answered in unison.

"Well then, I think we should go ahead and have a good cry, don't you?" She stretched her hands down and pulled gently. "Come here and let me cry with you." The tears were released in little-girl sobs, as the housemother spoke words of comfort: "There, there, there. It's hard, but we can make it through this. Nobody wants this to happen, but sometimes it just does." The mournful flood wore itself out in a few minutes. As the weeping subsided, she kissed their little, red faces and leaned back. "There. That's better. Now let's have a little talk."

The girls slipped back down onto the hardwood floor. "I... I want to go home," Cee Cee choked out the words, her shoulders still heaving from grief.

"We can't, Cee Cee." Her sister wiped her nose on her sleeve. "We don't have any place to go."

"Do, too! We gots Gramma's house."

"No, we don't. It's too small for three kids and a mother."

"Aunt Tony's house?"

"That's even smaller and there aren't even any beds for us. Sonny had to sleep on the couch until he moved in where Mama works."

"We could go there!" she said with a sudden brightness in her voice.

"I already asked Mama. She said her boss can't afford to feed all of us."

The tears welled up once again. "I... want... to go home..."

"We can't, Cee Cee! We don't have one!"

"Oh, but you do," said Mrs. Hays as she handed each of them a tissue. "Here. Blow your noses." When the two stared at her in wonderment, she said it again. "Blow, please. You don't want to soil your sleeves, do you?" Two little noses rattled in compliance. "Wipe-wipe-wipe!" She fluttered her hands in front of her own nose, then pretended to put the soiled tissue into a nearby wastepaper basket. That task completed, she proceeded to answer the question in their eyes.

"You both have a lovely home just waiting for you. It is exactly like what you want. You have your own bedroom and everything." She definitely had their attention. "And your own closet and all the clothes you could ever want and all of the best food and the nicest people will be your neighbors and you will have picnics and go to music festivals as often as you like... which will be all the time, I'm guessing." She smiled softly. "You look surprised. I guess nobody ever told you about this. Am I right?"

"Right." Lisa Marie was curious. "Is it a house, or a department?"

"Definitely a house… in fact, it's a big house."

The eyes widened. "A big house? How big? What color is it?" The questions came tumbling out too quickly for her to answer them all.

"What's your favorite color?"

"Pink!" Cee Cee said, immediately.

"Um… blue. Why?" Lisa Marie asked.

"Your house will be whatever color you want."

"But she wants pink and I want blue. What about that?"

"It will all work out, don't worry." The gray head tilted to one side. "I would think you'd be too busy looking at all the flowers, anyway… and especially at the golden street in front of your house."

Two quick gasps filled the room. "Golden street? We have a golden street?"

She nodded, the soft smile still on her face.

Lisa Marie's quick mind did a fast check on the facts. "I don't think we have a golden street in Burlin'ton. Is this house somewhere else in Vermont? What's the name of that place, anyway?"

"It's referred to as The Kingdom."

"Okay, so where's The Kingdom, Vermont? I hope it's not too far from Burlin'ton."

The woman chuckled. "It's closer than you might think, Lisa Marie."

Because she would turn ten in a couple of months, the reasoning naturally became more persistent. "So, when are we going home to this place?"

"Whenever God says it's time."

"What does that mean?" Her backbone straightened. Cee Cee saw the suspicious look come across her sister's face. "Is He going to make us stay here even longer than this? Why is He doing that?" The little sister's brown eyes turned toward the housemother, waiting for reassurance.

"Because He wants the best for you. He knows you have to be ready. He doesn't want anything to keep you from getting home, so He is making sure everything is exactly right."

"But we don't like it here. We want to go home now."

"Oh my goodness! You don't like it here? Does that mean you don't like me, either?" She was speaking softly. "I hope that's not what you mean."

They were looking at the floor, so she continued carefully: "I know it's hard to live someplace where you don't want to be, but I'm trying diligently to show all of you girls something good about it. Surely, you can find something good in all of this." Her bumpy fingers entwined again upon her lap. "Tell you what... Answer a couple of questions for me, okay?" There was a thoughtful pause. "Tell me, Lisa Marie, have you been without any food, or a place to sleep in a clean bed, or without shoes, or snow boots, or mittens...?"

"Mittens," Lisa Marie suddenly remembered. *"Walking home from first grade at the Park School in Essex Junction. Cold, so cold. Both Sonny and I had to hold our hands over the open oven door when we got home. It hurt. It hurt a lot. The next day, Mama pulled socks over our hands before sending us back to school in the freezing winter morning. But we still had no boots. It was cold, so cold."* She wondered how Mrs. Hays would know all that.

The upstairs housemother looked tenderly at Cee Cee. "Remember the beautiful Christmas tree we had in the dayroom this year? Weren't the lights wonderful... all glowing in amongst the branches? And how we made ringed garlands out of colored paper? And the popcorn strings looped along all the boughs? And the presents under the tree on Christmas morning... what did you girls get this year? Oh yes, the nice little partitioned boxes to go inside your dayroom lockers." She suddenly remembered a real winner. "And what about the goldfish bowl on top of the dresser at the foot of your bed, Cee Cee? Didn't you win the contest to name him "Leroy," after your daddy?" She smiled broadly as the girl responded. "Wasn't that fun?" She looked at them both for a second. "So, it hasn't been *all* bad, *has it*?" Her eyebrows twitched as she asked the question.

"Well, it was fun doing the popcorn strings," Cee Cee admitted.

"There you go, Cee Cee. Try to remember the popcorn."

But Lisa Marie needed to have some answers. "So, we still have to stay here, huh? Even though we have this great, big house and everything." Her head stayed bowed as she spoke, but her eyes rolled upward to fix firmly on Mrs. Hays' face. "I don't want to get into trouble… but it sounds like a fairytale… you know, big house on a golden street." Her gaze did not move. "You just trying to make us feel better? Or do we really have a place to go home?"

"You really have a place to go home, girls. You just have to get ready, first." She reached into her knitting basket which sat to her right on the floor and pulled a black book up onto her lap. "I can prove it, if you will give me a few minutes." She looked at her wristwatch. "We don't have much time before getting the whole dormitory ready for bed, so please pay attention." She opened the book and smoothed back the pages.

"Let me tell you about your new home," she said.

***

March came on the next morning. Angela Donaldson was making her way up the sled road to talk to her stepbrother. She was uncomfortable about this new wedding venue idea. Not that the farm couldn't use the four thousand dollars. She still couldn't believe people spent that kind of money on a wedding. And then there was Sarah, who had not been around the place for years, all of a sudden wanting to get married there. It just wasn't adding up.

She hurried along, dodging puddles of melting snow. *"At least we don't have any more tours,"* she thought. When she spotted the horse and sled headed down the hill toward her, she waved for them to stop. The former Father Jeff pulled the reins to bring the horse to a halt.

"What do you want, Angela?" he asked wearily.

"We need to talk."

"About what?"

"These damned wedding plans. Something's rotten in Denmark."

"You're not kidding." He pulled out a large handkerchief and blew into it. "Soon as I get this load in, I'm going to find out what those tracks are, out in the field." He motioned toward the barn. "They go from the house down to the barn, then disappear. As soon as I'm done, I need to check it out."

"What tracks? You mean footprints in the snow?" She peered more closely at the hillside. "Oh… yup, I see them." She looked back at him. "I'll go check them, myself."

"Just don't walk in them. We need to match somebody's boots to those prints." He slapped the reins and the horse dug in to move the loaded sled slowly downward through the slush.

Angela decided to take the easiest route to where the footprints seemed to end. The barn's driveway was flooded right up to the double doors, but she was able to wade through to the field, where she turned to step into the foot-deep snow blanketing the shady side of the slope. A few steps in, she stood still to observe the path which came downward from the front porch of the old farmhouse, wobbling as though it was hard to find the next step, to a place behind the back corner of the barn.

"This had to have happened last night, or very, very early this morning," she conjectured. "Somebody couldn't see very well."

The morning sun was glinting off the flat space where the

footprints disappeared, so Angela was half-blinded until she got almost on top of the spot. Suddenly she gasped and froze. Her feet were only a yard from a collapsed hole in the ground.

"The old well." She stepped back, terrified. "It's... caved in." She stared in disbelief, then suddenly realized the trespasser had stepped onto the rotten wood of the dilapidated cover. "Somebody's down there. Oh, my gawd...!" She cupped her mittened hands around her mouth and yelled as loudly as she could. "Hey! Hey! Can you hear me?" There was silence. She tried again. "Hey! Are you down there?" Again, there was no answer. She looked around at the edges of the shaggy opening. Seeing no continuing trail of footprints, the frightened woman could only conclude there was, indeed, somebody down there.

Deputy Maxwell Duncan was running for sheriff this year, so he was trying to do everything well. He made it from his home in Colchester in record time, even beating the current sheriff to the Donaldson farm by ten minutes. He was at the scene, keeping the Donaldsons as far back as he could get them. After the sheriff got there, the rescue team assembled and went to work. This was a new team, but they knew what they were doing. Still, it took them almost two hours to haul the body up out of the hole. They slipped it into a bag, leaving the opening unsecured, waiting for permission from the authorities before moving it into the ambulance.

As officers were photographing the footprints and anything else that might matter, another deputy came up to where Max Duncan was standing. "Hey, Max, we spotted a car pulled off the road, about a half-mile away."

Max saw that the sheriff was busy. "Did you run a check on it?"

"Yeah. Registered to one Sarah J. Ladue." He handed the information to Deputy Duncan.

"Thanks, Smitty. I'll remember you if I get elected." He gripped the slip of paper like it was an apple for the teacher, then strode confidently over to his boss.

"Got something you might be interested in, Sheriff."

Reading it quickly, the man walked over to show the information to Arnie Donaldson. "You know this person?" Arnie nodded his yes. "Come with me, please." The sheriff led the man over to the bag, where he pulled the corner down to reveal the victim's face.

"That her?"

There was a Humphrey Bogart grimace. "Ay-yuh, that's her."

CHAPTER SEVEN

Death

"The only thing about going home to Heaven," Jenny Roth was saying to the Dupree sisters, "is that you have to be dead, first."

The teenager had taken to Lisa Marie from the first day she had escorted the girl from Mrs. Bushey's office. Her heart had gone out to this new kid as she tugged her ragged coat and introduced herself like she was some kind of celebrity. Such spunk was rare at the Children's Home. She had watched the poor thing bravely hold back the tears as the car carrying her mother pulled slowly away down the half-circle driveway and right then and there, she had decided to keep watch over her, like a big sister. Today she was getting the facts straight about "going home."

"Only dead people go to Heaven."

"But you don't gots to stay dead," Cee Cee averred.

"You don't *have* to stay dead," her sister corrected the grammar. She turned back to Jenny. "But she's right; you don't ever stay dead. You slip into a new body that never gets tired and is never hungry and never gets warts, or anything."

Her little sister held up a roller skate. "I can't get this over my shoe."

"Here." Jenny inserted the skate key and loosened the clamp that was to slip over the side edges of the shoe's toe. As they slid the shoe into place, Jenny tried one more time to get her point across. "Look, you still have to die first. That's the part I don't like." She tightened the clamp. "Dying is scary because it hurts like heck."

Lisa saw Cee Cee's eyes going wide again, so she thought quickly. Her eyes went to the sidewalk, now being warmed by the sun. Something was moving on it. "See that ant?" All three looked down from where they sat on the bottom step of the front entrance to their building. The insect was scurrying across the cracked cement surface. Lisa stood up and stomped it with one wheel of her skate. "There," she said, "that didn't take long, now, did it?"

"Lisa!" Jenny was incredulous.

Cee Cee patted the older girl's hand. "It's in Heaven, right this very minute," she reassured her friend. And with that, she wobbled away to skate around the spots of snow on the driveway.

"You're my friend, Jenny, but please don't make things too comp'cated for my little sister. At least she can feel like she's going home. And," her voice softened, "she's hopeful we'll see Dicky again. You know, he might already be in Heaven."

Jenny stood up, testing her own skates. "Okay." She reached over and hugged her younger friend. "Sorry." Sitting back down to tighten the strap over her left ankle, she still aimed to make her point. "But, I don't want to die yet; I still want to go home right here in Vermont, first."

"How old are you, Jenny?"

"Fourteen." The girl's long, black hair hid her face.

Lisa spoke up quickly. "Wow! You're probably going home really soon."

"Yeah," came the subdued reply.

Suddenly, Lisa changed the subject. "Hey, I'll race ya!"

They were off like two gangly fawns racing across a bumpy meadow. For a while, there would be no thoughts of going home, or of a little brother who might already be there.

Meanwhile, across the lawn edging the sand of the Big

Girls' playground, Little Joe Turner sat on Aunt Ava's lap, watching the girls roller skating up and down between the carriage porch and the steep driveway exit onto Shelburne Road. In a bit of a pout that they had to come on a Tuesday instead of a Saturday, Big Joe Turner was leaned back in one of the two Adirondack chairs, his eyes hidden from the light by the bill of the cap he had pulled down over the bridge of his nose. The first day of March was still nippy.

"Did you enjoy our visit today?" Aunt Ava asked in her whispery voice.

The boy's head leaned back onto her bosom. "Yup."

"That's good." She looked toward her husband. "Uncle Joe says he's going to show you how to milk the cow, before too much longer."

The uncle looked at the peeling white paint on the flat arm of the chair. "They should scrape these things down and repaint them."

"I understand they only have one handyman for the whole place," she said.

"Is that right...?" He seemed distracted.

"I imagine it's all he can do, just to keep the place working right... all that plumbing and repairs." She stroked the boy's coppery face. "At least we know our Little Joe is safe."

"Yup, well, we probably better get going. It's almost his suppertime."

The boy let out a moan.

"Oh-oh!" she cautioned him. "Remember the rule. No crying when it's time for us to leave. Otherwise, they won't let us come, because it upsets you too much." She kissed the top of his stiff, ebony haircut. "That's my big boy."

Uncle Joe slid the boy off her lap before gently pulling her to her feet. Then they slowly walked him back to Mrs. Bushey's office. Pleased by what she saw, the director took the boy's hand, turning to speak before leading him down the hall to the Little Kids' dayroom. "See you next week." She wasn't just asking. Not at all. The way she saw it, it was a matter of life or... bloody little arms.

***

The call came from Sarah's father that same Tuesday night. Thomas Ladue fell to his knees in shock and grief. There were no words to express what he was feeling... to the very core of his being.

"Sarah, Sarah, Sarah... what have I done?" The tears streamed so heavily, there was no way to wipe them away. He dropped to her favorite sitting place on the stone hearth, weeping until he fell into a fitful sleep.

It was the banging on the door that awakened him. He lifted his face up off the wet stones and made his way toward the noise, weaving like a drunken sailor. As he opened the door, he started to cry again.

It was John. His face was white with shock and he was trembling as he reached out to hug his dear friend. "Oh, our sweet, sweet Sarah," he kept saying.

The priest finally stepped back, pulling the collar from around his neck.

"What did I do to my beautiful little cousin?" He held up the collar. "I don't deserve to wear this. I don't."

John grabbed that hand and held it steady. "I am as much to blame as you are... maybe more. Don't blame yourself, entirely. We both agreed to do this. In fact, Sarah, herself..." The collar remained in Tom's hand as they lowered it together. "Okay... okay, Tom." He breathed in slowly. "We need to get a second wind, here. We need to draw back and think more clearly." He took his friend's arm and steered him toward the wing-backed chairs. "We are not going to get over this, probably for a very, very long time." He seated his buddy in one chair and took the other one. "God, I am so sorry." The tears came again, as both men leaned forward, elbows upon their knees, hands hiding their faces.

It was John who interrupted the quiet grieving. "We have

to get a handle on this, if for no other reason, than to honor her memory. We need to know what happened." He looked up. "What was she doing, going back there all by herself?"

"I'm wondering the same thing. Do you think she may have found something, after all?"

"Maybe. Or maybe she realized it later... something right there in front of her nose... something she needed to go back to get."

"But why didn't she tell us?" The priest shook his head. "I don't get it."

Neither one spoke for a few seconds. Again, it was John who took the lead.

"I guess you heard the news from her father." Tom nodded in agreement. "That poor old guy. He doesn't deserve this, for sure."

Tom cleared his throat. "So, who notified you?"

"Detective Smith. He met with me just before I came here. He feels there is more to the story, but his Snoop Squad is pretty much reduced to overseeing the forensic work — get this — under the supervision of the Chittenden Country Sheriff's Department." He drew a handkerchief from his back pocket and wiped his nose. "He feels there might be a connection to the Dicky Dupree case."

"No kidding. That's what we were doing... trying to find the kid."

"Oh Lord." John leaned back in his chair, his hand on his forehead. "We need to get real, here."

"What?"

"We are going to be questioned by the authorities, probably more than once, about what we were doing at the Donaldson farm." He rubbed the stubble on his chin. "And we have to tell the truth."

Father Tom sat up straight in his chair. "Yes. Yes, we will," he said.

They were careful to do exactly that.

The questioning took place over a three-day period. In every setting, the two of them were open and honest and all about finding this missing child. They apologized to the Donaldsons for their undercover activities. They gave all their theories and researched materials to whatever government agency wanted the stuff... not that there was any great amount. They even surrendered their time off, to help whenever called upon. Most of the questions they could answer, but one they could not: What was Sarah doing, walking through the field between the old house and barn, at that particular time of day?

Then suddenly, everybody backed off. The authorities appeared to dismiss any connection between this unfortunate death and a kid who disappeared way last November. The more-experienced lawmen thought it odd, but decided to play it cool. They would sit back and wait.

Except for Deputy Maxwell Duncan. He had an election to win and this could be his ticket. The current sheriff was retiring, so there was no danger of offending his boss. In fact, the man could be credited with training this new, younger candidate for sheriff. It was a great set-up. So, the young man determined to launch his own assault on rotten kidnappers of innocent children.

His first interview was with Captain John Courtney. It took place at the American Legion Hall in Burlington. It was a busy Saturday night and so the two of them retreated to the back side of the parking lot, each holding a paper cup of beer. They squatted down to sit on the cement curb edging the perimeter of the lot, safely hidden from prying gossips and whatever else might come along.

"So, Captain Courtney... tell me why you are so swept up in finding this little kid." He took a small sip from the cup. "What's in it for you?"

The captain looked surprised. "Actually, I could lose my

commission because of my involvement with this case."

"What do you mean...?"

"This could be the end of my military career, Deputy. That's what I mean."

Maxwell Duncan sat up straighter. "Um... I had no idea." He slowly spun the paper cup a couple of times before he went on. "So, the Air Force could can you for your involvement in this case?"

"They could."

"Oh-h-kay. So, I repeat my question: What's in this for you?"

The weary captain took one more sip, then tossed the rest of the beer into the bushes behind them. As he stood up, he told it like it was: "Some piece of lowlife scum has taken this little kid and done to him — God only knows what — and he is getting away with it." He crushed the paper cup with his two fists. "I want that son-of-a-bitch sliced up and barbecued, before I die."

He was halfway across the parking lot before Max caught up with him, catching him by the elbow.

"Stop! Stop, man!" He put his face in front of the lawyer's. "I'm with you, mister. I really am." He put both hands against the officer's chest. "We need to get to the bottom of this. It needs to stop. It really needs to stop." He stepped back, because he could see that the officer was listening. "We can get to the bottom of this. I know we can. Work with me. Just work with me, okay?"

"I could lose my commission."

"I will fight for you, to the very last inch."

***

They were having breakfast at Connie's Diner, the restaurant snuggled near the first floor of Abernethy's Department Store. Traffic was moving steadily along Pearl Street to the Monday morning beginning of Burlington's workweek. The cops who frequented this small diner had mostly been in and now were off to their assigned duties. The deputy purposely chose a booth to the far end, where the conversation would not be overheard.

"So, I appreciate that you and Father Thomas have been really open and honest about everything concerning this case. It means I can trust you and believe me, that is a rare and valued thing, in my business." He sipped from the cup of black coffee. "But there is something that just sticks in my craw... like a lump in my throat. I hope we can address this openly and without any condemnation. We all make mistakes, right?"

The young captain's eyebrows raised in question.

"I need to know... how involved was this relationship between you and Sarah Ladue?"

"Not very... although we seemed to be headed in that direction."

"So, she wasn't confiding in you — you know, like her past association with the defrocked priest?"

"What do you mean?" John asked cautiously.

"Well," the deputy waved a dismissive hand, "according to the stepsister, Angela, the two of them were pretty thick." He caught the surprise in John's eyes. "So, I guess you weren't aware of that, huh?"

"Angela told you that?" A derisive laugh escaped the captain's lips. "Why anybody would believe what that woman says, is beyond me. I really think she did not like Sarah."

"Oh, she hated her... still does. She admitted it several times in her interviews. So, she makes no bones about it. Even said Sarah was providing little boys for him, while she was still in high school."

"*What*?!" John's face flushed in anger. "That's not true. It was just the opposite. Sarah told both Tom and me that night during supper..." He paused, then decided to tell the rest of it. "It was during that same conversation she said Jeff tried to rape her. She said Angela stumbled upon the two of them and flew into a cursing rage, allowing Sarah to escape. Sarah said she never went back there because she was afraid of him, because he was too big and strong and she wouldn't be able to protect herself."

Deputy Duncan picked a toothpick out of its little glass container and slowly stuck it inside the corner of his mouth. "Hmm," he mused, "seems like we have a real contradiction here." He looked directly into the man's eyes. "Angela spoke of that incident, also. Only she says Sarah was the instigator of that little tryst and more than just that one time." He did not lower the steady gaze. "What do you get from all that?"

"I get that this woman is one hell of a liar, mister." He leaned back in his seat. "Let's look at this Angela. She was — what do you call it? She was grooming little Dicky Dupree for her pedophile stepbrother. All the signs were there."

"Yeah, we have her being fired and all that, all on record. She was very open about it."

"She admitted she was prepping the kid for Jeff?" He stared as Max affirmed this with a nod. "So, why isn't she in jail?"

"She never really did anything illegal. You can't prosecute a non-crime."

"But that's despicable!"

"But not a crime."

"But she had to be an accomplice."

"To what? The encounter never even came close to happening."

"But what about all the other times she brought little kids to him, right off the school bus? She's guilty as hell."

"She says it was Sarah who was doing that, not her."

"Wait a minute." John leaned forward. "What does Jeff, himself, say about this?"

"Mister Nasty-pants refused to discuss that subject, in every single one of his interviews. Said it would be tantamount to a confession and he wasn't about to do that."

He moved the toothpick to the other side of his mouth. "Also wouldn't say anything about Angela or Sarah, other than one was his stepsister and the other an acquaintance."

"He's protecting his backside. I understand that. But we're trying to find a little boy, and all we have is Angela lying and Jeff refusing to cooperate."

"By the way, John, have you ever met Jeff Johnson?"

"Nope."

"I was hoping you would say that." He took the toothpick out of his mouth and tapped it lightly on the edge of his cup. "I have an idea that could get us some answers, if we play this right."

"You think we can find the boy?"

"Maybe." He dropped the pick onto the table. "But you'll have to stop working for Mrs. Bushey. We need to keep this between the three of us."

"Three?"

The deputy stood up. "You and me and Father Tom. I still have to talk to him, but I believe he will want in on this. I think the two of you also need some answers... like why Sarah went to the old farmhouse all by herself." He picked up his hat. "I'll be in touch."

***

John Courtney wasn't at all sure he would be working with Deputy Duncan, but he was sure about the fact that the director of the Children's Home didn't need to get personally involved any further in the investigation of this missing child. The level of federal investigation involved procedures and policies that were way over her head.

"So, I won't be on your payroll any longer," he explained to the blue-haired lady.

"Well, I will pay you what I owe you, then," Mrs. Bushey said.

"Actually," he held up a hand. "That would probably not be in my best interest. I need to keep my nose very, very clean, so I don't get any more warnings from my superiors."

"Oh, you're such a nice young man; I can't imagine them being too harsh on you." She held up her checkbook. "Are you sure?"

"Yes, ma'am."

"Well, all right," she said as she put it away. Then she leaned forward, placing her folded hands on the desk. "Captain, I am so sorry about your friend's passing. It especially moves me, because I know she was trying to find our Dicky. That is so sad. How is Father Tom doing?"

"Good days and bad days, but he's a man of strong faith."

"I understand." Her eyes foretold a change of subject. "So, you will still be looking for our boy, right? Only not as a private detective." He nodded. "Good, because I trust you. And Father Tom?"

"They want him to finish his OJT and get on with being a full member of the priesthood. I do know he wouldn't want Sarah's death to be for nothing, however, so I can see where he might stay somewhat involved." Once again, the less she knew, the better.

"I must confess, I am losing faith that we will find Dicky alive and well. It has been almost four months." She sighed heavily. "It's getting harder and harder to answer questions from the family. Mostly I refer them to the Burlington Police Department... but now, suddenly, this whole thing has mushroomed to an investigation by the Chittenden County Sheriff's people and I hear the federal investigators are interested. It's hard to know who's in charge, you know?"

"I'm sure they are all cooperating," he said, hiding his surprise. "After all, we all want the little guy back." He looked at the hallway door. "Will he come right back here, or go to some relative?"

"Depends on what shape he's in. We just don't know."

"Speaking of his family, any more threats to sue the

Home?"

"No, but that household is permanently dissolved. It looks like the mother is on her own." She clucked her tongue. "The father blew that one, for sure." Suddenly, her face brightened. "But you should see Little Joe Turner, Dicky's best buddy. His aunt and uncle have taken him most every Saturday for the last month. He's the happiest I have ever seen him." She smiled broadly. "Now that's the kind of thing we love to see."

Captain John Courtney drove slowly down the half-circle driveway, the roller-skaters slipping off into the soggy grass on either side, to let him pass. It was a cool spring day, perfect for young people to be out playing.

He hoped Dicky Dupree was somewhere out there, doing that very thing. But something else was bothering him. He wondered why all the different law agencies were suddenly so interested.

He had no idea these things were being conducted on more than a worldly level... that there were other powers at work and they had been at work for too many centuries to count. The United States of America's agencies were not in charge of anything; John Courtney was also in... way over his head.

***

Doreen Dupree changed a lot after she came back from that trip to Plattsburg. Everybody could see it. She started smoking and when she could afford it, drinking. She wore different clothes and dyed her fading red hair a blazing shade of orange. She also started dating. On her days off, she had friends over to play cards. She made deviled eggs and popcorn and they always brought the beer. Most of the time it would be other ladies, but sometimes it would be couples, including a fellow for her. This was the case on one particular overnight visit of her girls.

Lisa Marie and Cee Cee arrived via the local bus line. They

got off a block from the house, toting canvas bags with extra underwear and toothbrushes, amongst other necessities. When they reached the house, they politely knocked on the door and waited. Sonny opened it, his arms reaching for hugs. Noisily, they gathered in the living room, all three talking at once, until Mama came in from the kitchen. The girls stared at their mother.

"Mama, you look like a movie star," Lisa exclaimed as she hugged the painted lady.

"Lipstick," was all Cee Cee could say as she held out her arms for her hug. For a while the three females sat together on the sofa, the young ones adoring her with little-girl eyes. Cee Cee reached up to touch the glowing curls.

"You look like a dolly," she cooed.

Sonny sat in the armchair, grinning at the stupid girls. Finally, he cut into the conversation. "We're having company tonight."

The girls looked to their mother for verification. She stood up and smoothed the black rayon dress's skirt. "Yes. Some friends are coming over to play cards."

"We only know 'Go Fish' and 'Solitaire,'" Lisa said.

"Oh, that doesn't matter. You will probably be in bed by the time they get here. Don't worry about it." She started toward the kitchen. "It's time for some lunch. I fixed tomato soup and crackers."

"Where's that girl who lives here?" Lisa whispered to Sonny.

"Who, Sassy-mouth?" The two didn't respond to his snicker. Calling names was not allowed in their world. "She's with her mother for the weekend."

"What about Mama's boss?" Lisa wanted to know.

"He ain't here. He don't come home until two in the morning, from his job." He pointed to a room that brought the front of the house right out to the sidewalk. "That's his room. He comes home and sleeps until noon. Then he gets up and goes to work. We hardly ever see him."

The three of them followed Doreen into the back of the house, where they sat together around a kitchen table. It wasn't fancy; there were no napkins or napkin rings. But it was wonderful. It was their family all together, except Daddy and Dicky, of course. But nobody was talking about that.

After lunch, the three children took a walk up Church Street to roam around in the dime stores and the shoe department in Sears. They got penny candy in a small drugstore at the corner of Church and Pearl Streets, then crossed over to look at the window dressing in Abernethy's. When they had had enough wandering, they returned to the house, where Doreen had already set up two card tables in the living room.

"Can we play cards, Mama?" Cee Cee asked.

"Oh, I was hoping you would help me make popcorn," came the reply.

The girls were thrilled at the prospect; they never got to make popcorn at the Home, so they hurried back to the kitchen.

"Well, it's almost five-thirty. You must be hungry. Let's eat something, first."

They watched her getting out the pans and oil and a large package of popcorn kernels, as they ate peanut butter and jelly sandwiches. The gooey feast stuck to their teeth, making their words sound funny and that kept them entertained for another half-hour.

"Okay, wash up the mess and make sure your hands are nice and clean," their mother admonished.

Ten minutes later, the popcorn chefs stood ready.

Doreen supervised the hot oil and made sure the lids were held tightly in place so no fluffy, white puffs would go flying into the air. She helped Cee Cee shake a pot, holding her hand over the little one's. Cee Cee held the holder against the handle, for dear life, her lips pursed in great concentration. The older two enjoyed watching her, just as much as pouring out their own snowy treats into the big bowls. Spirits were high and the room was filled with a delicious aroma.

At last, Doreen was pouring warm streams of butter over the cloud-filled bowls. She used a spoon to scrape out the last drop, then stood back.

"Good job!" she told the children. "Now, Sonny, you get three cereal bowls out and you can each have one bowl before you go to bed."

They ate slowly, licking the butter off their fingers and then it was suddenly seven o'clock.

"You girls will take my room," she said, pointing to a door just off the living room. The bathroom is right next door, okay?" Lisa Marie noted the bathroom was in between her mother's room and the boss's room. Maybe she could stay up late enough to see what the boss looked like. She made a mental note to keep her mother's door opened, just a small crack. Satisfied this was a good plan, she proceeded to get ready for bed and at about eight-thirty, she crawled into the double bed beside her sister.

She was asleep by nine.

It was adult laughter that woke her. Lisa took a minute to realize where she was. An electric alarm clock on the dresser across the room told her it was eleven o'clock. She had rolled over to go back to sleep, when she remembered she needed to stay awake, if she wanted to see what the boss looked like. She took another minute to decide whether she really wanted to do that.

Another roar of laughter cut into her thoughts. Curious, she slipped out of the bed and peeked around the tiny cracked opening she had so carefully prepared a few hours before.

The room was hazy with cigarette smoke, making it difficult to discern the card players. Lisa pushed the door a tiny bit, so she could see with both eyes and saw four couples seated around one of the tables. All of the ladies were sitting on the men's laps and there was a lot of giggling going on.

One of the men made a remark and the others laughed again. That was when she realized her mother was one of those ladies and she was sitting on some man's lap. Her arm was around his neck and he was hugging her close to him.

"What are you looking at?" Cee Cee said, as she pushed the door wide open.

All heads turned toward the two little girls in cotton nightgowns.

"We need to use the b-bathroom," Lisa squeaked. The littlest one pulled her hand back so her sister could not tug her along.

"No, I don't," Cee Cee said as she walked over to her mother. "What are you doing?"

Doreen jumped up and grabbed her daughter's hand. "Taking you to the bathroom," she said.

"But I..."

"No buts about it. It's eleven o'clock. You know the rules. They told me to make sure we did this." By that time, they were all in the bathroom and she pulled the door shut. They could hear the laughter on the other side, but their mother was not happy. "You get on there and do your thing, young lady." Seeing the deep brown eyes puddling up, she put a stop to it in a hurry. "If you start bawling on me, you won't ever come back here for a visit, Cee Cee. So, stop it. I want to hear a tinkle, understand?"

Once back in bed, the two lay there for a long time, being careful not to cry. Eventually, they slept. There were just some things more important than seeing what the boss looked like.

The next morning, Doreen got the girls ready and walked them to the bus stop. As the vehicle moaned to a stop in front of them, she bent down and kissed them on the head. "See you soon."

Mrs. Hays was in the dayroom when they walked in. She looked up with a smile. "Did you have a nice time?" The girls looked at the floor, so the housemother beckoned them to come closer. When they did, she took a short breath. "Oh my," she said. "You need to have a nice bath, right after lunch."

Setting the dining room tables was done with her friend, Jenny Roth. They were standing in the pantry when Jenny handed a pile of plates to her. She sniffed. "You stink, Lisa. Where have you been?"

"Overnight with my mother."

"Home?"

"Nope," she whispered. "At least, it didn't feel like it."

Mrs. Hays saw that the girls were troubled, so she talked to them as they shared one of the large bathtubs in the downstairs bathrooms. Lifting a dripping washcloth over Cee Cee's head, she began the gentle inquiry.

"So, what fun things did you do at your mom's?"

"Um, we got to go look in the stores on Church Street," Lisa answered as she watched the lady pour a dab of shampoo on her sister's hair.

"Did you enjoy that, Cee Cee?" She stroked the wet hair to make the suds appear.

"Ye-es," the little one said through the dry washcloth she was holding over her face.

"And what did you buy?"

"Just some penny candy." Lisa Marie was studying the Ivory soap bar in her hands. "It was kind of sticky. I didn't like it all that much."

"Oh, that's too bad." The housemother put her hand under Cee Cee's neck. "Lie back, honey, so we can rinse the suds off." Gentle splashes rinsed the soap from the sides of the little girl's face. "Well then, what was the most fun thing you did at your mom's?"

Cee Cee pulled the washcloth away from her face as she was swept back up from the bath water. "The popcorn!"

Mrs. Hays leaned back from the tub to rest her back. "The popcorn!"

"Yeah, the popcorn. We got to pop it, ourselves." Lisa jettisoned the soap into the far end of the tub.

"Oh, my-my-my! So, you had a fun visit!"

"Not really," Lisa murmured.

"Want to tell me about it?"

By the time the Dupree sisters were dried and dressed in fresh clothing, they had told her the whole story. The woman nodded wisely before she spoke. "You need to remember something very important: Your mama has a broken heart." The two of them stared at her. "And when people have a broken heart, they can do some silly things."

"But she wouldn't even let us cry," Lisa objected.

"We didn't get a goodbye hug, either," her little sister moaned. "I don't like her anymore, so there!"

"Oh, you don't mean that, Cee Cee." She gave her a side-embrace. "You will always love your mama, you know that. Sometimes we have to forgive each other and not be mad anymore."

"Aw, Mrs. Hays, how can we do that?"

The lady tilted Lisa's chin upward, looking into her eyes.

"Remember the popcorn," she whispered.

That night, after the long "Ahh-mennn!" of "The Doxology," Lisa Marie had a few words to say to the Father.

"What happened to Mama, God? I promised I wouldn't get mad, but You didn't tell me about this part." The tears burned. "Mama was acting silly with that man. I don't even know who he is. He just laughed and laughed. It was awful in that room. It made us smell stinky. And do you know what the worst part was?" Her breath was loud and noisy, but she couldn't help it, so she pulled the sheet tighter over her face. "The worst part," she mouthed the words slowly, "the whole time we were there nobody even talked about Dicky." A sob escaped. "I'm afraid he might be dead and nobody even cares." She snuffled up the wetness for the last time that night. "He was so... alive... and he would have loved the popcorn."

That night she dreamed of Dicky and making popcorn and he was happy and funny and hugging everybody.

CHAPTER EIGHT

Images

Captain John Courtney called the cleaners from the barracks phone and asked if his shirts could be ready "by this evening." The girl said they would call him back. Detective Smith returned the call, identifying himself as manager of the captain's dry cleaner. John answered the call and they agreed the shirts would be ready around seven. He thanked them for their patience concerning the late hour.

Wearing civilian clothes, the young man parked his car in front of Colodny's Market. It was nearly dusk on this cool April evening. As he got out of the car, he spotted Smith crossing the street from Battery Park. The detective waved and pointed toward the back of the store, then turned left, disappearing behind the front corner of the building. John hurried to join the man, who was standing in the shadows at the northernmost end of the parapet, a low wall which separated the park from the view of Lake Champlain.

"I take it, this is important, Johnny. Otherwise, we shouldn't be here."

"It is. Thanks for coming."

"Be aware those are apartment windows above the store, so if you ever need to meet me here again, it's best to park over here, right near these trees, okay?"

"Right. Hopefully, it won't have to happen again." He jammed his hands into the pockets of his slacks. "It's just that the whole search for Dicky Dupree has taken on another dimension, what with the death of my — our — friend, Sarah. I have so many questions and so does her cousin, Tom. We want to know why she went back to the farm that night, or morning. We are no longer involved in the search for the boy — that's your job and the sheriff department's job — but we need to have some closure to this death."

"Sure, kid. I understand." He brushed his hair back with a hand. "Just exactly what do you think it would take to do that?"

"I… Tom and I would like to talk to somebody else who knew Sarah when she was younger. We thought we could figure out why she was, you know, trying to get something done about the boy, you know, all by herself. After all, it cost her her life."

"Yeah." He pushed the hair back again, then cleared his throat. "I was wondering how you were taking it and I can see it's pretty much how I thought it would be with you. So, I've been thinking about this." He looked over into the darkness behind the store, then back at the man. "I think I could do you a favor and you could do me a favor."

"Really?"

"Yeah. The person you need to talk to is Angela Donaldson's mother." John looked surprised. "Yeah. She lives on King Street in a rundown apartment and she feels very much abandoned by her daughter." He shook his head confidently. "I interviewed this lady, myself. Her weakness is self-pity. If you play up to that, you can learn anything you want… and you can probably get what I want, as well."

"And that would be…?"

"Pictures, my friend, lots of pictures, taken with Angela's own Canon camera, of the Thanksgiving parade and who knows what else?"

Johnny suddenly remembered that strange thing about Angela's coat in the one snapshot. *"It was the strap to her camera case,"* he thought. He was surprised he had missed that.

***

He arrived at the King Street address at noon the next Saturday. It was going to be touchy, because the lady had no phone. All he could do was to knock and wait.

A puff of smoke streamed through the narrowly opened door as she greeted him with a hoarse, "What do you want?"

"Hello, ma'am. I am Johnny Courtney, an acquaintance of your daughter, Angela. You are Martha Donaldson, aren't you?"

"You know Angela?" The door opened wider. "What do you want?"

"Has she told you yet… about the accident on the farm?"

The door opened all the way, revealing a forlorn figure in a wrinkled cotton robe and sloppy slippers. Her heavy gray hair fell in snarls to frame the furrowed face. "What do you mean, 'accident'?" The hand holding the cigarette trembled. "Did something happen to my Angela?"

"Oh, ma'am, I am so sorry. I didn't mean to frighten you. Are you all right?" He moved forward enough to tenderly touch the bluish cheek with the very tips of his fingers. "You aren't going to faint, are you?" He tried to look beyond her into the room. "Can I help you to a chair?"

She looked surprised, but rose to the moment. "I… do feel a little woozy."

"Oh no." He took charge like the white knight she needed. "No-no, don't you dare faint on me, young lady." He stepped in and took her arm. "Let's get you down where you can get your legs back." He looked lost. "Where do you want to sit?"

"I usually sit over there in the Early American by the front window… if I can make it." She swayed and he quickly steadied her with a side-hug. "Oh, thank you," she whispered sweetly. They scuffed across the room, where he held her shoulders until she was properly seated on the tattered cushion. She reached shakily over the flat, wooden arm of the chair and placed the cigarette carefully on the edge of an ashtray full of crushed Lucky Strike butts. He could see thick dust on the turned spindles of the chair from top to bottom, even though the place was quite dark. Then the young man stood in front of her, hands folded at his waist, trying to look solicitous. "My Angela?"

"Oh! Oh, of course. She's not hurt, but it was..." He looked at the torn sofa beside her. "May I sit down? This could take some time." She motioned for him to sit, which he did, gingerly perching on the front edge. "So, she was not hurt, but it was an ugly accident. In fact, it was a fatal accident."

"Fatal? Somebody died?" She leaned forward. "Who? What happened?"

"A young lady fell into the old well by the dairy barn. You probably remember that well..." He waited for her acknowledging nod. "Yes, well, we don't really know how it happened and we don't know why she was out there in the wee hours of the morning, but... well... she was coming from the old farmhouse... the one where you... probably lived... while you were there." Another quick acknowledgment. "So, we needed to tell you. I'm surprised Angela hasn't told you already."

"Don't be. Don't be surprised. She thinks I'm a loser. Why should anybody want a loser for a mother, huh?" He lowered his head. "Yeah, that's right. That's what she thinks. Hasn't she ever talked about me?"

"Uh, we're just acquaintances."

"Well, I can tell you for a fact." Her voice was cracking. "She... she..."

"You're not going to fall apart on me, are you? I don't want to be responsible for your being overcome by all this. Do you feel faint?" He looked up toward the kitchen in the back. "Tell you what, do you have some spirits? You probably could use a little jolt right now."

Leaning back in her chair, she closed her eyes. "No, sir, I

can't afford such a luxury. If I pass out, I pass out. That's just how it is."

"But you could fall. You could get hurt." He hoped he sounded like a panicky schoolboy. "Maybe you should put your head down, you know, between your knees."

It was a scornful look. "You've never been old, mister. People with hernias don't put their heads between their knees." She sighed. "A little spirits would help a lot, though." She smiled a pitiful smile. "Such is my lot in life, hon."

He knew he had her at "hon."

"Mrs. Donaldson, I have a lot to talk to you about, so I am about to break a code of conduct I rarely break." He stood up. "I have in my car, two bottles of brandy. One is for my buddy at the base and the other was for a bachelor party for tomorrow afternoon." He strode toward the door. "I am going to see to it that we have a safe and comfortable conversation over the next hour." He opened the door and turned for her approval.

She was positively wistful. "This is the sweetest thing anybody has ever done for me... ever, ever, ever."

It was half an hour later before she remembered to ask who was actually killed. They had discussed the ugly divorce and how the farm had gone downhill since she left it and how they had all abandoned her and she was almost destitute. As he leaned over to refill her little juice glass, she suddenly seemed alert.

"Okay, I am so glad to know that Angela, the brat that she is, is not hurt. So, what happened? Some girl fell into that frickin' old well?"

"Yes, Mrs. Donaldson..."

"Hey, stop calling me that, would you? You make me feel like an old broad, for gawd's sake. My name is Martha." She gave him a punch on the arm. Fortunately, the bottle was being held upright.

He bowed courteously. "Thank you. I would be delighted

to call you Martha." The brandy was placed on the dusty table, where she could see it. He carefully leaned back into the sofa, leading her to the next question. "You were asking, Martha, who the girl was... who fell into the well?"

"Right. What a shame. Who was she?"

"I think you may have known her. It was the cousin of a friend of mine, Thomas Ladue...?"

"Thomas... Ladue." A light went on. "You talking about Tommy Ladue, that young man who grew up to be a priest?"

"Well, he's almost a priest. Still has to complete the final phase. But yes, that's the guy. He's a friend of mine."

"No kidding!" She almost laughed, but was waiting for the rest of the news.

"So... it was his little cousin, Sarah Ladue, who accidentally walked into that well."

It got quiet in the shadowy room.

Martha lifted the juice glass and took a long, slow sip. She was definitely not in a hurry. When she set the glass down, she reached into the pocket of her threadbare robe and drew out her pack of Lucky Strikes. A book of matches was tucked into the outer cellophane wrapping. She pulled it out slowly. Before she lit up, she shook her head in disbelief.

"Talk about justice," she finally said.

He waited.

The flame touched the end of the cigarette and she drew it into the tobacco. As the plume of smoke exited from her mouth, she said it, loudly and clearly: "Out of respect for your friend, Tommy, I won't tell you what I think of that... little cousin."

"*Here we go,*" he thought.

"There was a lot of stuff going on out there on that place." Her eyebrows went up. "Bad stuff." She shook her head before repeating her sad story, only this time she added more to it. "I never shoulda married that guy, you know. He was ten years older than me. Then Angela came along and I figured I had to stay on board." She puffed the cigarette. "He just wanted to make money. Drove me like hired help. Angela, too. But by the time she was twelve, I couldn't take it anymore." She tapped the ashes lightly into the tray. "Angela wouldn't come with me. I figured she was afraid to leave, but that wasn't it. Seems she knew about Arnie's affair with a widow-lady from in town and that lady had a handsome son and Angela had eyes for him." Her gaze went downward. "So, Arnie divorced me and got remarried right away. I never got a cent. Had to work, so I did, as long as I could."

"I can't imagine what you went through, Martha."

"Ay-yuh. It was hell, for sure, but at least I wasn't there for the weird stuff those kids were up to."

"What kids?"

"Well, it was him — the boy — Jeff... and Angela was involved, but she wasn't the ringleader. It was..." She winced as she spoke it out. "The Ladue girl. Sorry, but she was the one bringing in those kids off the school bus."

He feigned ignorance. "I'm not following you."

"Sara said she was 'babysitting,'" Martha smirked. "Only, there was something else going on, she told me. But all she would say is it was weird stuff and somebody was going to get into trouble if they didn't put a stop to it. So, I guess it's still going on, or something." She took another slow sip. "I suppose it had to do with her and Jeff, because she caught him 'in the hay' with Sarah and she kicked Sarah off the farm." She drew smoke, again. "Told her if she ever showed up there again, she would call the cops on her."

"This was when they were teenagers, right?"

"Ay-yuh. Except Jeff was about twenty-one, I think." She shrugged. "Who knows what kids are thinking? And what a shame, too, because the three of them were all taking photography classes together. Until Angela caught the two of them, it had been a close friendship."

"I'm surprised you didn't step in and get your girl out of there. You were certainly a good mother, Martha."

"Oh, I never knew all that until last year. She lost her job at the Home and moved in with me. That's when she told me this stuff."

"I see." He took a big breath. "I am so sorry to hear she went through all that. She seems to be a great gal... and a talented photographer, from what I hear." He smiled. "You must be proud of her. The word is, she's good enough to go professional. Those people make a lot of money, if they do it right."

"Oh?"

"You know, I would love to see some of her work. Do you happen to have any of her pictures?"

"Well, she keeps them hidden, but I know where they are."

"Trust me. We have a photo lab at the base. I have connections, if you know what I mean."

She leaned forward. "What kind of connections, hon?"

"The kind who buy pictures for postcards, calendars, and greeting cards. It's a gold mine, Martha."

Fifteen minutes later, John Courtney exited the King Street apartment with a shoebox full of Angela Donaldson's photos tucked under his arm.

He left the bottle.

***

Deputy Max Duncan was sitting in the same back booth at Connie's Diner, but this time he was looking across at Detective Smith, leader of the Snoop Squad. The detective smiled his spacious grin.

"How's my boy doing?"

"Smitty is doing great, Ed. If I get this election, he'll be my first right-hand man." He leaned closer. "Of course, I'll have to start calling him 'Smith' instead of 'Smitty,' so's he can look more professional." The two laughed softly. "But I am proud of that guy. He's sharp, Ed, no doubt about it."

"You're a real politician, Max... you got all the right answers."

"Let's hope so. That election is coming up soon. It's already April."

"You won't have any problem, mister. You always know what to say."

"Ay-yuh, and you know what else I know, Ed? I know who my real friends are, buddy. I do know that." He glanced around, then picked up his coffee cup. "I also know when I see the lowest kind of filth going on in our county." He looked up at his friend. "We see a lot of crap in our line of work. A lot of it. But when it comes to a little kid disappearing and who knows what." He set the cup down without drinking from it. "This Dupree kid is only the tip of the iceberg." He raised his gaze. "Unless we stop it." He leaned back. "And we can't do that by competing, Ed. We can't."

Ed looked up at the ceiling. "Oh, man... we could open a whole bucket of worms, here."

"And we might save some little lives, here."

"I have to answer to people, Max."

"I know. So do I." He set the cup down. "But if we pull this off, we could make a difference." He went in for the kill. "Listen... would you please just think about the mother... that little kid's mother, for god's sake! What kind of hell do you think she's been going through for the last year?"

Seeing Detective Smith did not want to answer the question, Deputy Duncan offered the gentleman's way out: "We need to share information... be a wonderful example to our community and when we get the whole thing figured out... find the culprits and bring them to justice... we need to share the credit. No Superman syndrome at work here, Ed. No department or figurehead taking all the glory. We need to do the honorable thing and I think we can do this, if we all pull together." Max shrugged his shoulders as if in massive disbelief. "Don't you see the picture? Can't you see how this could work?"

The leader of the Snoop Squad slid out of the seat. "Tell you what," he said. "I'll think about it." As he walked toward the cash register, he pulled a dollar out of his wallet and placed it on the counter. The fresh-faced waitress smiled. "Keep the change," he murmured.

Outside, he paused for a moment, thinking how great it would be, if only these different departments would make a massive effort, together, to find that little boy. It presented a great public image of law enforcement at its best.

And then he remembered what a slick politician his friend was. This would be a great platform for the next candidate for sheriff to run on.

"Aw, hell... I get the picture, Max."

***

"Thanks for coming by," Father Tom said to his friend. "I know it's been rough for you going through all this and still on duty at the base."

"Well, you've been carrying quite a load, yourself." He patted the man on the shoulder. "So, you're all done with the on-the-job-training and you're a real priest, now. Congratulations."

"Thanks. I have opted for no celebration dinners or any of that, though. Too much grief." He motioned for John to sit down in the usual fireside chair. "It's still too raw." He slid heavily into the other seat and stared for a moment at the empty fireplace.

"Got to forgive yourself, Tom. We both have to do that."

"I think we are both working on that one, Johnny."

The captain sought to change the subject. "So, any news about your first church?"

Tom's face brightened. "Yeah! They want me to go up to Holy Family in Essex Junction. Father Joe is getting along in years and they want me to move into that spot. He's pretty good though, and I'll probably have plenty of time to fit in."

"Hey! That's great." There was a thumbs-up. "We can still hang out."

"We can." He took note of the uniform. "You made any decisions about staying in yet?"

"Still up in the air about that. I do have an offer from my uncle in Montpelier."

"With his law firm. Great." He drew a couple of fingers across the freckles on his forehead before he finally got to the real business at hand. "Got a couple of things to tell you, my friend."

"Okay."

"That sheriff's helper, Deputy Duncan, was here this morning. Told me a couple of things, then asked if I would talk with Father... uh... Jeff Johnson. They think he'll be arrested shortly. The deputy asked if I would work with you and him and go talk to him there in jail... guess he thought, me being a priest, I could get him to come clean."

"Probably so. Are you open for that?"

"Nah." He shook his head emphatically. "It's a case where these guys who do this stuff need help. Jail is only to keep them away from kids. It sure doesn't stop them from doing it with grown men."

John leaned forward, a curious expression on his face. "I just don't get it, you know? What makes a guy like that, anyway? Don't you have something in your training...?"

"Yeah. We think it has something to do with imprinting."

"What's that mean?"

The priest leaned back. "I guess I'll tell it like they explained it in class." He went into teaching mode. "You know how, when a little foal is born, a little horse, how, from the first day of life, the trainer starts stroking its body, ears, mouth, and even gently tapping its hooves? Well, all that rubbing, scratching, and tapping prepares the little guy for grooming and even horseshoes being nailed on later. He grows up thinking all that is normal. He doesn't ever remember when it did not happen, on a daily basis. All that stimulus is normal to him.'

"But, in fact, all that would never have happened to him if he were born in the wild, in a natural setting. As a grown stallion, he would not put up with that, if he was raised in a normal, wild horse environment.'

"Bottom line is the imprinted horse is not behaving in his natural behavior; he is behaving in an abnormal, unnatural manner, for a horse."

The student was paying attention.

"Johnny, do you remember your first birthday cake?"

"No-ooh," came the amused answer.

"Your first step?" A negative nod. "Your first word?" A negative shrug. "Most men don't and they don't remember being stimulated unnaturally by some sick predator, either." He sighed. "All they remember is they have had these feelings as long as they *could* remember." His hands went palms-up. "How many times have you heard these guys make that statement?" The palms stayed upward.

"How many times have you heard the claim, 'I was born this way!'?"

"Oh my dear God... Tom... All that time in law school, all those cases we studied... I never heard this imprinting thing. Never. Never." He was standing on his feet. "It... it... changes everything. No, not everything. But it explains a whole lot."

"It really does, John." The teacher was finished, replaced by the priest. "So, you can see why it seems so futile to try and help. These poor guys don't think they even *need* help."

John paced across to the kitchen door and back again, stopping in front of his friend's chair. "Do you think... this happens to baby girls, as well?" He watched the sad nod of confirmation. "My God... my God. If I were a more religious man, I would call this... pure evil."

"Oh, and you would be so right, John Courtney, because it is all based on repeated, depraved behavior. The predator was once the victim. And the predator before that one? He was also a victim. In fact, the whole victim-predator-victim-predator cycle is pure, unadulterated evil. It originated in the depths of Hell and it is as old as the disembodied spirits."

"The what?"

"Disembodied spirits... also known — amongst other things — as 'demons.'"

Father Tom caught the bewildered look. "Okay, briefly, because I have something else to tell you." He took a couple of seconds to get his thoughts together. "Demons are disembodied spirits, okay? They have no bodies, so they can't feel things like we do and that ticks them off. So, they try to get inside real human bodies so they can get... their kicks, so to speak."

"Whoa, Tom. In all the time I have known you, you've never spoken of this before." He thought for a moment. "Where do these things come from? Are they aliens?"

"The theory is they are from a previous time... a time between the first two verses of Genesis one, verse one and verse two. It speaks of a time when the earth was void and without form. Well, we know God would not create a world void and without form. So, there is some... thought... there may have been a civilization before Genesis one, verses one and two." He looked a bit apologetic.

"And so, there may have been other beings before us?"

"Well, I've been studying for the priesthood. This came up along the way. We're not even sure how it all works yet."

"No kidding! So, what do you know? I mean, um, how do these creatures with no bodies, how do these... demons get inside of human bodies, anyway? Can you tell me that?"

Father Tom paused again. "As far as we can tell from Scripture, we open ourselves up to them.

"You got actual Scriptures?" the lawyer asked.

"Quite a few, in fact." He looked at his watch. "But you don't have time to get into that, right now. You need to get back to your Air Force duties." The concern showed in his eyes. "But please remember all this, as you deal with Jeff... if you decide to deal with him, at all."

"So, Tom, even though you know all this, you don't think you should talk with him?"

"I can't... until I forgive him." His mouth formed a straight line. "I feel he was somehow involved in our Sarah's death. I don't know how, I really don't... but I need some space here."

The captain was overwhelmed, himself. Demons, evil beings, and all of them hanging around, making trouble... was more than he could deal with and he was sure Thomas was dealing with the same stuff.

"That's okay, buddy." He tapped a reassurance on the man's shoulder. "All in good time, right?"

They hurried quietly out to the captain's car. A cool breeze off Lake Champlain's nearby shores carried the fragrance of fresh foliage on this early spring night. Tom laid a hand against the car door, signaling to his friend there was something else.

"The other things that the deputy told me? Um, Sarah died suddenly, so she didn't suffer."

The Air Force officer sighed in relief.

"The other thing," Tom said, as he moved to open the door, "was they measured her footprints... the depth of them... and she was definitely carrying something."

John slid slowly into the driver's seat as he spoke. "Does he know what it was?"

"No... but he thinks — whatever it was... is at the bottom of that well."

CHAPTER NINE

Exposure

It took a while for him to decide on a safe place to look at Angela's photos. After all, they were almost stolen property and not meant for his viewing, either. They were supposed to be evidence, or maybe just contain a few clues. But John could not shake the hunch that there were some answers about Dicky Dupree in those snapshots. Oddly enough, the safest place turned out to be his room in the barracks.

All he had to do was drop the shoebox into a grocery bag, stuff a sweater over the top, and walk casually down the hall to his door. Once inside, he turned the key in the lock and slipped the box out onto the table near the window. Before he turned on the lamp, he closed the blinds tightly.

The photos were standing on edge in several neatly divided packages. He pulled the rubber band off the first packet, fanning the pictures out on the metal tabletop.

"The parade."

He peered closely at each view, stopping to study the one she had snapped of Jeff across the street, in front of Sears. He was leaning against the Cherry Street side of the building, hands in pants pockets, his eyes turned toward the parade. A couple of kids sat on the Church Street curb, blocking the reflecting sunlight with upheld hands. The shot was too far to the left to see who else was close to the priest. Instead, there were just the cars parked on that side of Cherry Street and the sidewalk along beside them… and some father, carrying a sleeping child, probably back to one of those cars. The priest, himself, did not present a surly presence. "But then, that's why he gets away with it."

He set those aside and picked up the next banded stack. These were a series of shots of small children taken through, of all things, a chain-link fence. Each picture had one child in it, wearing a bathing suit. "But there is snow on the ground!" He looked more closely, then felt something in the pit of his stomach. Each one of the children was grasping and pulling on that fence and every one of them appeared to be crying.

"Oh, no…"

The next packet was more young children, mostly boys, all naked.

"Damned filthy scum, both of them." He thumbed through quickly, then banded the pictures back together. There were two more packages, which he hardly looked at, because they contained the same subject matter.

With a shaky hand, he opened the last stack, glancing quickly at a series of nude shots of what appeared to be all of the same teenaged girl, lying in some greenery… dried shrubs, or leaves, or grass. As he glimpsed the last one, he recognized her.

It was Sarah.

She appeared to be sleeping. John could feel the heat on his face as the indignation rose up within. "They must have drugged her." Quickly he shoved the little stack of photos together, put the rubber band around them, and laid them face-down on the table. "Oh no… oh no…. what did they do to her?" He sat there until he realized there were tears rolling down toward his chin.

"I can't let Tom know this." He wiped his face with his two hands. "I can't let anybody know this. The word would get out and Tom would know and her whole family would know." He reached for a handkerchief from his back pocket, but before he even finished wiping his nose, he realized the futility of it. Charges would have to be made and in the process, everybody would know about what happened to her. He shuddered to think what that may have been.

"Still, I think I need to talk to somebody. Somebody I can trust. Maybe there's a way we can keep things... bearable."

He put the packets back into the box and placed the lid on it, before sliding it under his cot. As he stood up, he suddenly felt tired. In a few minutes, he was slipping in and out of slumber, his body tossing about, trying to escape the pictures in his mind. In an attempt to get some control over those images, he forced himself to visually go back to the parade pictures. One-by-one, he went over and over those shots.

Suddenly he sat up straight in bed.

"The father carrying the sleeping child."

He drew the box back out and grabbed the first packet. It was the third one in line and he took it over under the lamp for a better look. The daddy was coming out of the back of the Sears store, where the loading dock and the employees' entrance were located. He was looking toward the parade, but was turning to his right as though to go away from the noise and the crowd. The young child was soundly asleep, its arms hanging loosely over its daddy's shoulders and the little head was tucked under the man's chin. John thought he could almost see the daddy's face, but it was too far away.

"I need this thing enlarged," he muttered. Then he remembered Bill Flannigan. "Yeah. I'll call Sarge."

Twenty minutes later, the two friends, dressed in civvies, were chatting over a beer in the Village of Essex Junction. John reached into his shirt pocket and pulled out a photo. "Hey, Sarge. I need a favor. You know all those guys in the photo lab, don'tcha?"

***

J. Canon Johnson was finally arrested that same April, on charges involving those two altar boys in South Burlington. It was dutifully reported in the *Burlington Free Press* on Saturday morning's edition, but placed discreetly on the bottom of page three, so as not to appear to embarrass the local Catholic Diocese. Unfortunately, the article was accompanied by a photo of this priest, taken last summer on the Ticonderoga cruise, capturing the man in the midst of adoring children. It had been great press for the church, at the time, but now it was about to bring the condemnation of the community — even Christians… for sitting on the lap of this predator, was a little boy whom the Chittenden County Sheriff's Department identified as the missing child, Richard "Dicky" Dupree.

Mrs. Ferndale, the downstairs housemother for the Big Girls, read the article while sitting in her rocker in the dayroom. She shook her paper in disgust, muttering something about tying somebody to a whipping post, before she turned the page.

Lisa Marie looked up from where she was playing with the paper dolls, wondering what that was all about, but there was no more grumbling and paper-rattling, so she went back to her quiet time, like the rest of the girls in the room.

It was Cee Cee who had been standing right behind the woman when the sudden snap of the newspaper page had occurred and it was she who peeked over the shoulder to see what was making Mrs. Ferndale blow a gasket. What she thought she saw made her hang quietly by until the woman folded up the paper and laid it on the window seat near the dayroom lockers. The girl waited until the coast was clear, then slipped the thing under her arm, and went to her sister.

"I think I found Dicky," she whispered.

"What?!" She saw the newspaper, half-concealed. "What are you doing with Mrs. Ferndale's paper? Give me that!"

Cee Cee did not let go. "You need to look."

Lisa could see there would be no fixing this, so she glanced around to see if anyone else was watching. "All right, all right." One more glance, before she pointed down the hall to the downstairs bathrooms. "Go in there. I'll be right in."

Cee Cee complied and Lisa followed a moment later, closing the door behind her. "Let me see that thing."

When they found the picture, Lisa Marie gasped, "That's Dicky, all right. It even says so."

"He was at the parade. I saw him."

"Of course he was. That's where somebody took him."

"No. I mean him." She pointed at the priest. Her sister's eyes went wide. "He was standing right behind us. I remember him from the boat ride."

The "boat ride" Cee Cee was referring to was a two-hour day cruise aboard one of the last side-paddle-wheeled passenger steam liners still operational in the United States. Built right there in Shelburne in 1906, the two-hundred-twenty-foot long beauty had plied the waters of Lake Champlain, carrying passengers and freight for over forty years and by the time the Dupree children got to enjoy its regal presence, the Ticonderoga had come far past its glory days. Maintenance and the rising cost of the coal which fueled the steam engines was driving the owners to the financial edge. Still, faithful devotees kept the vertical beam engine pounding away, driving her forward, her single smokestack streaming staunchly through the fresh-water air. It was this small group of dedicated folks who also kept up the charitable tradition of offering a free ride to the youngsters at the Children's Home and at St. Joseph's Orphanage, every summer. The two children's facilities shared the fun for the afternoon, running around, standing at the rail to watch the churning waters below, staring up at the captain's cabin, marveling at the gauges with shiny brass circular frames which were displayed in a horizontal row right near the huge tubular shaft beating a constant, thunderous rhythm. Indeed, it was quite an outing, with both the children and their chaperones, intermixed for the whole trip.

The Dupree sisters remembered all that and they also

remembered Father Jeff.

"He had candy," Cee Cee recalled.

"Yes, he did."

The two of them dashed out from the bathroom and down the hall, calling out, "Mrs. Ferndale! Mrs. Ferndale!"

The woman was headed back to her rocker when she turned toward the ruckus. She took one look at the sisters and the newspaper and gently bit her lip. "Oh, dear."

***

Sonny was still in bed when Doreen saw the picture in the morning paper. "A priest... a filthy, rotten priest." She stared at the picture of Dicky smiling on that man's lap. "My little boy. My little boy." But before the tears could start, the phone rang.

"Doreen, it's Ellen. I know you probably don't want to talk to me, but I wanted to warn you about this morning's paper."

"Too late. I already saw it."

"Oh." The former mother-in-law paused, demonstrating her own way of respect for a grieving mother. "Well, we don't really know who did it. Good grief, Doreen. A priest? That's hard to believe."

"Is it?"

"Of course it is. I mean, we all depend on these good men." She waited for an answer, but when it didn't come, she went on to the real purpose of the call: "I suppose we ought to let LeRoy know."

"I'm sure you can handle that very well," she said. Then she slammed the phone hard onto its cradle.

***

"What do you mean, you aren't ready to turn over those pictures yet? I didn't tell you to look at them, mister. I said to get your hands on them and then give them to me." Detective

118

Ed Smith was furious, his fist slamming into the palm of the other hand. "I tell you what... if it weren't for the fact that your father gave his life in the line of duty for this police department, I would toss you to the wolves right now, Johnny Courtney."

"I just need to check out some things. I need to know what was up between Jeff and Angela and... Sarah. I need to get it straight, sir. I need to know."

"No, you don't need to know. That's my job."

The young man raised a cautionary finger. "Actually, it's the job of the Chittenden County Sheriff's Department, sir. The Snoop Squad is only supposed to analyze the evidence and then report to them."

"The hell you say! I could turn you in for what you did to Martha Donaldson, do you realize that?"

"But that would only implicate you, sir. Surely, you don't want me to perjure myself on the witness stand."

The frustrated detective slumped against his parked car. Looking across the moonlit lake, he paused, then spoke slowly: "I could end up hating your guts, you know that?"

It was a moment of revelation: John suddenly realized the detective had a surprisingly thin skin. He decided to go for broke.

"Or, you could give me a little space here and eventually end up thinking I'm a damned good lawyer." He turned to walk away then stopped. "I think," he said, without looking back, "you are a damned good detective and you know how to figure out an accommodating solution for both of us." Then he stood perfectly still, staring at the sidewalk in front of him, waiting for the answer. It seemed to be a long time before it came.

"All right. I'm giving you three days. Do your thing and get over it. But have those Donaldson snapshots at this spot, in my hands, by six o'clock Sunday night." He heard the man take a deep breath. "Are you listening to me, Mister Damned-Good-Lawyer? I want all of them — do you hear me loud and clear? — every last one of them, in my possession by Sunday night."

John Courtney moved his head in a decisive acknowledgment of the plan, then moved on to where he had parked his car, at the edge of Battery Park. With great relief, he started up the engine and headed for Montpelier. He needed to talk to his uncle.

***

Antoinette "Tony" Dupree set a plate of steaming spaghetti down in front of her husband with such a slam the sauce-covered noodles nearly slipped off onto the table.

"That proves it," she said. "This stuff has been going on all the time and we knew it." She turned to fill a plate for Annie. "Mary was right and we should have listened to her."

"Sister Mary... Sister Mary Catherine, Mama." The girl shot a blue-eyed reprimand toward her mother.

Her blue-eyed papa gave her a visual slap. "Mind how you talk to your mama." He stuck his fork into the dripping noodles, pulling them up into the soup spoon he held in the other hand. "You're not in any position to correct your elders," he said, as he twisted the noodles around the fork. "Even if you think you know what you're talking about."

The feisty daughter pulled her forkful of noodles into the hollow of her own spoon, placed like a bowl under the fork's tip. As she wound the noodles into a neat, fat bite, she grinned. "I beat up a boy today."

"Anna Maria Dupree!" they exclaimed, as they always did — together — every time she came up with this stuff.

"What were you thinking?!!" Her mother's spaghetti tongs were suspended in midair.

"Mama! Listen, Mama! He's a real jerk." She stuffed the twisted morsel into her mouth. "I had to beat the crap out of him," she mumbled through the chewing process. "Because..." she swallowed and took a drink of her water...

"he said my cousin was eff-ed by a priest." The water glass was set down firmly. "Tell me what I should have done."

The two parents exchanged a knowing look before Tony served up a plate of dinner for herself. "Don't be talking like that," she said as she sat down. "You know better."

"We don't know what happened, Annie," Papa reminded her. "We really don't know if anything... even happened. After all, this was just a news photo, taken last year, right?" He leaned toward her. "We don't want to jump the gun on this, Annie. We don't want to get in the way of this investigation." He started to wind up his next bite. "And you need to take your defense of Dicky into a higher level... you need to give it to God. He will take care of it. He is the final Judge." He winked at his spunky daughter. "Okay, Annie?"

The girl squinted one eye back at her father. "I know God is in charge, but sometimes He wants us to kick a potty-mouthed jerk in the slats." The fork twirled and she stuffed in more spaghetti. When it was safely swallowed, she wiped her mouth with the back of her hand. "So, who wrote this story, anyway? The one in the paper, I mean."

"Somebody local, I'm sure," her papa answered. Seeing the look in her eye, he reached over to pick up the newspaper from the top of the beer barrel and handed it over to her. Annie turned to the third page.

"Eat your supper," her mama moaned. But the inquisitive one zeroed in on the article.

"Sophia Pizarro," she read. "Pizarro! That's Italian! She's one of ours, Mama!"

"Oh? And so what? We should fly the national flag of Italy off our front porch?"

"Um, no. Not that. But maybe you two should tell her what you know."

"Eat your supper, Annie," her mother moaned again.

Before she left for parochial school the next morning, Anna lied to her mother, but only a little. "I need to work on a special project after school," she said. "So, I could be kinda late."

"No fighting," Tony warned.

By three-thirty, the girl was standing inside the front door of the *Burlington Free Press*. The plaid skirt and white blouse gave her away, immediately. A man in a wrinkled blue dress shirt called out from his desk: "No school announcements, Missy... only on Wednesdays, remember?"

"I'm not here for that."

He moved away from his typewriter. "Okay, young lady. What do you need?"

She shifted her weight to one foot, put her hands authoritatively on her hips, and gave him an I-mean-business look. "I need to talk to somebody."

The man rose from his desk, vaguely amused. As he approached, he said, "Is that right? And just who do you need to talk to?"

The determined glint in those blue eyes brought him to a cautious stop as he approached her.

"Sophia Pizarro, that's who."

"Oh yeah?" He shoved his hands into his pants pockets. "And what do you want to see her about?"

"That's for me to know and for you to find out."

That answer was probably too sassy for the busy reporter, but the day was saved when a young woman slipped between the two of them. Her pudgy body was draped in a yellow cardigan and she smelled good.

"Hi there, young lady!" She grabbed Annie's arm and steered her back to a nearby desk, as she continued. "I'm Sophia and we can talk right over here."

As they sat down, she leaned over and whispered: "Hey-ee, kid, are you crazy?" She glanced toward the man in the wrinkled shirt. "You ticked off my boss. Watch your sassy mouth. Got that?"

"Hey-ee," she replied in the Italian lingo. "Don't worry, I know how to handle a bully."

The reporter leaned back and viewed her through narrowed eyelids. "Yee-ah? Or maybe you are too big for your britches. What do you think about that?"

Annie took a closer look at the round, golden-skinned face with the pale brown eyes and she suddenly liked this lady. "Uh… wait before you get the wrong idea, okay? I don't want to make anybody mad; I just want to talk about my missing cousin, Dicky Dupree."

Sophia's gaze moved slowly from the young girl's to a deliberate stop at the top of her desk. Her hands moved to the front edge of the desk pad, where ten fingers tapped gingerly in place. There was a brief pause, then the Italian reporter leaned back in her wobbly spring-loaded chair.

"Let me have your name and a phone number and I will get back to you later. Is that all right with you?" She waited for the girl to do that, folding the slip of paper and tucking it into her sweater pocket. "I will contact you, if I need you, but please don't ever contact me here at the *Free Press*… ever, ever again."

Annie was ticked. "So, you're writing me off, like a dumb little kid? Is that what you're doing?" She stood up, towering over the plump lady in the low desk chair.

The lady's brows pulled together over the fluttering eyelids. "Trust me, kid," she whispered, "I will get back to you… very soon."

Annie had no idea Sophia Pizarro was doing private research on child abuse in orphanages across the country and around the world. But then, neither did the *Burlington Free Press*.

CHAPTER TEN

Magnification

This time, the two of them were having a hotdog with their beer. Sergeant Bill Flannigan tugged at the front of his cotton shirt, fanning his chest and underarms. "I can't get used to the muggy weather in this place. It's only the end of May, for Pete's sake."

"You think Essex Junction is bad… go sit on a bench at City Park in Burlington," the captain replied. He wiped the mustard off his mouth with the flimsy paper napkin before he used it to swipe the sweat from his own brow. "We look like we've been in the shower."

"Oh well, it's pretty dark in here and we aren't looking for women."

They laughed together.

Outside, the sun was settling low in the sky. Soon it would begin to cool off and the big fan in the wall would start pumping some cooler air into the place. On the other side of the room, somebody dropped a coin into the jukebox. The velvety voice of Margaret Whiting started to sing a sad song of love, A Tree in the Meadow. A melancholy mood settled over the little bar.

"When are you shipping out?" the officer asked.

"No orders yet. We just know we're headed for Japan or thereabouts."

"Things are heating up in Korea, my friend," John said.

"That's probably what you'll be getting those planes ready for." He took a sip of the cold beer. "You'll be okay, man."

"I'll be okay. It's the wife and boys I worry about." He scraped a bit of relish off the table with a finger and wiped it on the edge of the paper plate. "Still don't know if they'll stay here or go back to Oregon."

"Oregon is closer to Japan, Sarge."

The handsome enlisted man nodded and finished the last draught of beer.

"Guess I'd better give you this before we both forget it," he whispered, as he handed a large manila envelope to his friend. "They said it was the best they could do; it's pretty fuzzy. But maybe it will still help."

"Thanks, buddy."

"Thanks for the hotdog."

The captain watched the man walk away, knowing they probably wouldn't be getting together like this again, for a long time. He thought about that aspect of military life as he finished his own beverage. Finally, Margaret's song was over. He pulled his damp shoulders away from the chair and headed for his car. Leaving the door open for both fresh air and the overhead light, he slipped the enlarged photograph from the unsealed envelope.

The boys in the lab were right; the man's face was still fuzzy. But there were a couple of other things that caught his attention: the subject was wearing a flat cap of some sort — the bill was too small for a newsboy style — and it appeared to be herringbone fabric. That was interesting, although there were probably still a lot of those old hats around. It could indicate the man's age, or his limited income, seeing as how this style was mostly a bygone thing. He wondered if it could be identified by a label.

The other interesting thing was what appeared to be a mole on the upper left cheek. "Now, that could be something important." Still, he had no intention of giving this to Detective Smith. That guy could enlarge his own photo. John reached into the envelope to retrieve the original snapshot before returning the enlarged one to that place of safety. The original went back into its spot in the packet of Angela's parade pictures. He put the lid back on the shoebox and set it on the floor behind the driver's seat. The enlarged photo got locked up in the glove box, where Detective Smith would not see it.

He was waiting back there in the dark of the trees, when John pulled in, turning off his lights before entering the area. Quickly, the young man reached for the shoebox and handed it to the guy.

"Everything here?" Ed Smith asked gruffly.

"Yes, sir."

"You share any of this with anybody?"

"Why would I do that?" He was not fond of lying, so he turned the answer into a question.

"Why wouldn't you?" The man took the lid off and pushed a couple of packets apart. "Where are the negatives?"

"There... weren't any." John was caught off guard. Seeing the suspicion in Smith's eyes, he tried to explain. "I was so put off by the pictures, I didn't even think about that." That, of course, was not true, because his uncle had asked him the same question and he had thought about it right then... so he was lying, after all. "Look, I've kept my promise. You have all of the photos. I need to get on with my own investigation. I am still looking for some answers."

The lid went back onto the box. "And just what, may I ask, did you learn from these pictures?"

"Some people are going to face serious charges: trafficking porn."

"And does that include your friend, Sarah?"

"She was a victim. See for yourself."

"I will do that," the detective said as he walked away. "I will certainly do that."

But even though he did that, nothing much happened. The

weeks dragged by.

***

It was sometime in the middle of May when Doreen Dupree finally began to seriously form her own theories concerning the disappearance of her son. She wondered why no one had checked to see if he was hidden someplace nearby, like a private home, or maybe not so private, like — did she dare suggest it? — that huge orphanage over there on North Avenue. She had heard about it from... somebody... she couldn't recall just who. The place had a lot of nooks and crannies, like closets and the scary, dark attic areas. She wondered if her Dicky was being held prisoner. It was a horrible scenario, so she tried to push it out of her head. When that didn't work, she tried to visualize other possibilities.

Then, on one late night, while turning over in her bed, she had a sudden, shocking thought: what if Ellen had been at the parade and what if she had talked her little grandson into going home with her? *"She's always disliked me. And now, she really hates me for kicking Roy out. She probably blames me for him being so sick. Why wouldn't she do this?"* She lay there and pondered the reality of such a thing. In fact, it stayed with her for days. Still, she didn't quite know how to do anything about it. "Maybe I should tell somebody. But who?"

Another idea beckoned. "I could go over there and pretend to make up for everything and take a look around, see if there is any evidence of Dicky being there." But after strategizing for a few days, she realized the woman would never even let her into the house. Again, she felt like she needed to tell someone. "But who?"

And still, the weeks dragged by.

***

Deputy Max Duncan was being interviewed on the *Joy in the Morning* program at the WJOY radio station. The candidate for Chittenden County Sheriff was in top form that sunny June morning.

"I can't tell you how great it is, Pete, to work with the fine men of the Burlington Police Department. They have been very supportive of the County Sheriff's Department and I think this kind of cooperation will get us closer to some answers concerning the Dupree case."

"Do you have anything new on that particular situation, Deputy?"

"Well, of course I am not at liberty to discuss the details, but I can tell you that I have personally been working with one of Burlington's finest, Detective Ed Smith, and we are hot on the trail."

"That's encouraging, sir."

"Let me reassure you and your listeners, Pete, we will continue to make every effort to solve this case. We have superb teamwork going here... and if the folks of Chittenden County want me to, I would be more than happy to lead the way."

"Only a few more months until the election, folks. You just heard from Deputy Maxwell Duncan, candidate for Chittenden County Sheriff. Thanks for dropping by, Deputy."

"My pleasure, Pete."

"And now let's hear from the Glenn Miller Band, with American Patrol!"

The thumping beat of this patriotic piece accompanied Max Duncan as he made the rounds of the little station, shaking hands and slapping backs. He winked at the secretary as he headed for the door.

The interview with WCAX radio took place across town, a half-hour later. It, too, was a rousing success. This time, the disk jockey ended the talk with Bing Crosby and Bob Hope singing If I Knew You Were Coming (I'd Have Baked a Cake). He couldn't wait to see whether Ed had heard the broadcasts; the guy had to be pretty happy with the compliments. The nearest private phone happened to be at Connie's Diner. Since it was a cop hang-out, the owner let them use the one right up there near the cash register, as long as the calls were "short and sweet."

He was surprised when somebody else answered the Snoop Squad's number.

"This is Deputy Max Duncan. I need to talk to Ed Smith."

"He's not here right now, Deputy."

"I need to touch base with him. Do you know where he is?"

"Yeah, sure. I guess he didn't tell you. I know he tried to call."

"Okay, I haven't checked back in with the office yet. So, where is he?"

"He's out at the Donaldson farm today. We finally got the paperwork and they're excavating that well, even as we speak."

"Right. Thanks."

Max did the math: the sheriff would already be out there. He would be depending on his deputies to cover the rest of the county's patrol. Max had been given permission to take a couple of hours to do the radio spots. After that, he was expected to get back on duty.

"I guess I had better check in and report that I have to interview Father Tom over there in Shelburne."

Father Tom, of course, was not home. Unbeknownst to the deputy, he had reported to his new assignment in Essex Junction on that morning. Max was not disappointed. Instead, he called in his location and let the dispatcher know he would be patrolling Highway 7, just south of Burlington, for a while. There were no calls for assistance in that area, so he signed off and headed for the Donaldson farm.

He was careful to look like he was cruising and monitoring

traffic, but his mind was on what they would find in that well and he wanted to be there when they brought up whatever — if anything.

A couple of miles south of the Children's Home he was nearly driven off the road by a car, careening toward him from the opposite side. A sharp turn of the steering wheel put him almost into the ditch and suddenly, all of his training kicked in.

The U-turn put him back on the highway and he pursued the car with a blaring siren and lights flashing. In the bright morning light, he spotted the screeching right turn onto Swift Street. Within seconds, he made the same turn, to see the cloud of dust where the car had come to a stop on the left side of the road. Before he could touch the brake, a woman had bolted from the car and was running into the wooded area. By the time he had come to a stop and scrambled out of his vehicle, she had disappeared down what looked like a pathway into a thicket of blackberry bushes.

The training continued to kick in and he called for back-up. Then he pulled his gun and started toward the footpath.

"I can do this," he said out loud. "It's broad daylight and it's a woman and she's headed in the general direction of the golf club."

He moved slowly, as quietly as he could, unhitching the occasional thorn from his shirt as he went. Twice he stopped to wipe the sweat from his face and to listen for any telling sounds up ahead. When he heard the sirens out on the highway, he breathed a hard sigh of relief and squatted down on his heels to wait for help.

They came up the path, weapons drawn, until they saw him. Immediately, they also dropped down, to listen.

"It's a woman. She seems desperate. Don't know if she's armed." He looked at the youngest of the deputies. "Go back and get a make on her car, then put in a call for the sheriff." The guy nodded. "And you," he said to the next one, "get over to the golf course and watch that she doesn't get out of here without being spotted."

He looked at the last one, Smitty, Ed's son. "You and I are going to move forward along this path, ten feet apart, with me leading. If she takes me down, you wait for her to feel safe enough to come out and then you get her." He wiped his brow. "Got that?"

Max went down low, moving slowly along the path. He paused to listen, here and there, then moved on. Smitty was back behind him, watching carefully for any sign from his buddy. And then Max lifted his hand to signal a stop. He crouched low, looking at the younger man, then cupped his hand around his ear as though to listen and pointed forward with his other hand.

There was the sound of soft sobbing.

Max could hear it more clearly than Smitty, but they exchanged a knowing look; the woman was crying.

Deputy Duncan signaled for Smitty to come forward, then reminded him that she could still be armed. "We need to see where she is hiding, or whatever," he whispered. "Be very, very quiet."

A few feet farther, they spotted what appeared to be a low-built shrub mound. The interwoven branches were quite dried out, but the structure seemed to be intact.

The sobbing was coming from inside.

A crackling from the path behind distracted their attention.

"You two okay?" the sheriff whispered.

Max put a silencing finger against his lips. "Listen, sir."

The senior lawman put it all together immediately. "She's suicidal." He jumped up and ran forward to peer into the ragged opening of the dried-out hut. It was not more than a few seconds before he gave the order.

"Get an ambulance out here. She's slashed her wrists."

Smitty dashed back down the path for the car radio even as the sheriff called out to the woman. "Don't do this, don't do this!" He stretched his arm carefully into the opening. "Let me help you, okay?"

"Get out!" she screeched. "Get out, or I'll cut off your fingers!"

"Okay, okay," he replied as he withdrew his arm. "But it doesn't have to be this way. We can work this out."

"Oh... no... we can't," she moaned.

"Please, give me a chance. Let me help you." He placed his face at the opening, where he could look at her.

"*Get out!!*" His eyes closed automatically against the dusty thrust of the knife into the dry soil, but he managed to grab her wrist and shake the weapon out of her grasp.

He opened his eyes too soon.

Even though the other handful of debris hit him with full force, he managed to draw the knife out of the hut and roll his body away from the entrance.

Deputy Duncan landed belly-down in front of the ragged doorway. "For god's sake, lady, we're trying to save your life, here!" He was careful to keep his face away from the entrance, as he waited for a reply.

Instead, he heard a scratching sound... then silence. He waited. Again, a scratching sound, followed by silence.

Suddenly, the sheriff stopped rubbing the dust out of his eyes.

"Fire!" he shouted. "She's setting that thing on fire!"

The details of how the two of them managed to rip that tinderbox construction up off the ground and pull the woman from self-incineration were reported in the local Vermont papers in various versions. One story said the men had stomped out the flames. Another said the fire never got started. Only one paper identified the woman as Angela Donaldson of Shelburne, Vermont, although she wasn't the main interest in the story. Nor were there any references to the type of activities taking place regularly at that particular location, or that Miss Donaldson knew exactly where it was. In fact, the gist of the news coverage magnified the heroic figures of the soon-retiring sheriff and his right-hand man,

Deputy Max Duncan.

So, the "partying place" was virtually overlooked in the big picture. Nobody wanted to shut it down. Even while the hut was temporarily unavailable, the location continued to service not only university students' secret social lives, but certain elements of the Burlington community. The situation was accepted as a normal part of the culture; the powers-that-be winked it away and everybody moved on. They had no idea about the demonic activity flourishing in the shadows of those thickets, nor the terrible, long line of consequences plaguing those who were foolish enough to participate in such activities. Indeed, more blackberry bushes were promptly woven into a new hut, but most folks didn't even notice. They continued to focus on the more popular take on this newspaper story: Maxwell Duncan appeared to be a shoe-in for the next Chittenden County Sheriff.

***

"So, what did they find in the well?" Father Tom asked.

John Courtney leaned back in the fireside chair. "A suitcase full of photographic negatives. About fifteen pounds of them." He paused, trying to pull forth the right words. "I'm guessing Sarah was trying to get them to the authorities."

"But how did she know about them? How did she know where they were, Johnny?"

"I'm only surmising, here... she must have spotted them the day we pretended to check out the old farmhouse for a wedding party site. You remember, we were 'looking for a place to have the dinner and to change clothes'?" The freckle-faced priest nodded, encouraging John to continue. "I figure she saw something, but it didn't register, until later that night. It must have hit her with full force, to make her go back on her own, to retrieve this evidence."

The priest leaned forward to look his friend in the face. "I guess you don't know about the darkroom."

"What?"

"Deputy Duncan told me about it." He sat upright, as though to get the facts straight. "They discovered it in one of the upstairs bedrooms in that old farmhouse, when they were first checking to see what Sarah was possibly carrying. They noticed there was a darkroom, but no photographs and no negatives." He took a soft breath. "That is not normal." He looked at his friend.

"Detective Smith must have known about this." John realized the man had not been cooperating as much as he appeared to be. "And no, that would not be normal. I'm even guessing there had to be photos in that suitcase, as well."

"You know, Johnny, those had to be some pretty unusual pictures and negatives, for Sarah to go back for them."

"Mmm..." The man did not want to comment.

"I can only think of one kind of photography meriting such a strong reaction on her part and I shudder to even think of such a thing."

"Well, we don't know for sure..." He decided to go to a different subject. "It is amazing how evil people can be, Tom. For instance, you were telling me about those things — demons, I think you called them. There was something you said that I can't get out of my head and that was how they can get into a human body." He laughed softly. "I can't fathom that, you know?"

"Ay-yuh, I hear you." He drew his right ankle up onto his left knee. "It is in the Bible, though, so we know it does happen. And... I have seen one manifest in a person, before. It's not a pretty sight."

"Not a pretty sight, huh?" The military man had some doubts. "For instance?"

"This guy's eyes rolled so far back into his head, all we could see were the whites. And the eyes, themselves, were twitching sideways in their sockets."

"Oh?" He had never seen that.

"The man was addicted to cocaine and I do mean

'addicted.' He had been in treatment off and on for years. He finally came to the Church for help. Told them he knew something was inside him. Said he could hear it talking. Said it screamed until he would do more of the drug." He let the right foot slip easily back down to the floor and leaned forward toward the fireplace. "He wasn't kidding, either, because the damnable thing started screeching at us during the exorcism."

"Really! What did it say?"

"Mostly foul language and filthy threats. The priest told it to shut up, in the Name of Jesus."

"Did it?"

"It did, but went to choking Jimmy's throat."

"Jimmy? You knew the guy?"

"Ay-yuh. Jimmy Turner. A nice guy, really. Got talked into doing something one night and it changed his life forever."

"So… did the demon kill him?"

"Not that time. The priest commanded the thing to come out, in the Name of Jesus and it had to, of course. Jimmy threw up a blob of something and it was gone."

John took a moment to think, then remembered. "What do you mean, 'Not that time'?"

"Well, Jimmy got his life together. He got married and he and his wife even adopted an Indian baby… a boy. It looked like things were going to be all right, for a while. But he slipped up during a visit with some of the sleazy characters he used to run with and he got hooked again. The demon came back in and brought more of them with it." He wiped something off his mouth. "Few weeks later, Jimmy slammed his car into a tree. Both he and his wife were killed. The little one went into, I think it was, the Children's Home."

"Oh my gosh, Tom. I know about that kid." He pointed at nothing in particular. "He was best buddies with Dicky Dupree."

They stared at each other, wondering what all that meant, until John had another thought.

"Wait a minute." He rubbed his bottom lip as though to help the right words to come forth. "Once these demons get kicked out, where do they go?"

"They... wander... seeking another body to inhabit."

"Could they go from one family member to another?"

"They can, but that doesn't mean they always do. Remember, they can only come in, if you open a door."

"And just how do you open a door?"

"Well, in Jimmy's case, he got high on drugs... lost control of his mind, spirit, and body." He felt a check in his gut. "Listen, Johnny, I'm not the expert on this subject. You probably need to talk to a real exorcist."

"Ri-i-ight. So then, how did you get to be in the room for this exorcism?"

"Jimmy went to school with my oldest brother and wanted him there. I got to go for two reasons: my brother said I could and the exorcist knew I wanted to be a priest. But there was the stipulation we brothers had to be absolutely quiet and stay on the other side of the room."

"Man! I never knew this about you! How come you never mentioned this?"

"You never asked."

Before they parted company, Father Tom jotted down the locations of a few Bible verses.

"This one talks about how demons go about looking for a 'house,' which means a body, of course. The next one shows how Jesus got rid of a demon, but there are more examples you can read if you want. Read the New Testament and you will see how prevalent this was back then... and it still is, today." He smiled at his friend. "In fact, just read the New Testament, period. Then, if you still have questions about demons, I'll introduce you to an exorcist, okay?"

Driving back to the base, John Courtney was glad he did not have to tell his friend about the pictures of Sarah.

Changing the subject to a discussion about demons had been the perfect ploy.

Nevertheless, the captain dusted off his service-issued New Testament that night.

He needed a closer look.

CHAPTER ELEVEN

Agents

With the discovery of child porn, the investigation took on a new dimension. Federal law enforcement agencies were now involved, which meant both the Burlington police and the Chittenden County Sheriff departments were reduced to the role of "local yokels." Communications between the two levels of government was clearly one-sided, with the hometowners supplying information wherever they could, while the "big boys" pretty much kept their stuff to themselves. Not much could be done about that. Most of the search for Dicky Dupree was filled with frustration. Still, Captain Courtney kept his quiet pursuit and Deputy Duncan continued to campaign on the premise that the local cops were working together, "day and night..." on the case. Both men were well aware it was already July.

It looked like it might be a long summer.

***

Like most of the general public, Doreen Dupree was not aware of the significance of the arrest and hospitalization of Angela Donaldson. She read the account in the *Burlington Free Press* praising the actions of the sheriff and his top sidekick, Deputy Max Duncan, without being particularly impressed.

After all, it had been a good eight months and they had not found her missing son. All she had to go on from them was a lot of talk. She looked out the window, checking the early morning sky. "Maybe we'll get some relief from this soggy heat today," she murmured out loud. "We might even get some news that would relieve a whole lot of other woes." She looked up, wearily. "God, where are you? It's been so long."

A shuffling figure made its way past her, into the bathroom. She recognized the faded blue chenille robe as that of the ill-mannered princess. Doreen did not look forward to another day of dueling with this teenaged tyrant. She leaned back into the overstuffed chair. "I hate this place," she whispered.

By the time the Royal Pain returned to bed at the back of the house, the newspaper was nicely folded and put in its place for the boss, whenever he was ready for it. He would, of course, not require breakfast — nor any other meal, for himself — but would grab the paper and be off to his job as manager of the local Fraternal Order of the Eagles. There was no appreciation for the difficulty of her job and even the card-party socials weren't making things easier. Under such deep personal desperation, the woman could see no hope for a future with this dysfunctional father-daughter relationship. Doreen did not belong there and neither did her children.

Besides, he already had a girlfriend.

She jumped in surprise at the ring of the phone on the stand beside her.

"That's probably Ellen," she muttered. "Forget it, lady. I already know the phony sheriff's department is grandstanding. I don't need to tell you to call Roy." But the ringing persisted and she finally picked up.

"Hey, Aunt Dory?"

She recognized the voice. "Annie? You're up early."

"Just making sure Sonny is outta bed. We're supposed to hike Mt. Mansfield today. Did he tell you?"

She sat up straight. "Oh-my-gosh! Yes, he did! I even made a lunch for him."

"So, I made sure they picked me and him up at your place, okay? I'll be over there in about twenty minutes." She chortled. "Don't worry, Aunt Dory, they aren't picking us up until eight o'clock. I like to make sure everybody's ready."

She was banging on the front door at seven-thirty. When Doreen opened the door to receive the traditional family hug, everything seemed to warm up. The blue eyes and fair skin of her father complemented the wavy black hair of her mother and the little niece brought the Dupree family thing tightly back together... for a moment.

She peered past her aunt, at the grinning face of her cousin. "Got your band-aids, Big Guy?" The twelve-year-old kid looked at his mother.

"I put them in there," she said, motioning to his borrowed backpack. "And some peanuts and a flashlight... and all the rest, like we packed it all last night. You're good, mister."

"Well, okay then," the girl said as she settled into the far end of the sofa. "I guess we're ready." She watched the other two take seats. "So, how's it going?"

"Well, school is over for this year." Her aunt preferred to talk about her niece.

"Yup, thank God. What a drag."

"You pass?" His voice was teetering between childhood and adolescence.

"Course I did," she smirked. "Nothing to it, really. I just don't do it when they want me to do it, because they think we should all do it when they think we should do it and that is not the way I play the game."

"Oh, honey," her aunt murmured. "Where does it say you get to make these decisions?"

She shrugged. "I didn't know I had to have permission!" Sonny was grinning again. "Like when I decided to go find that reporter who did the story on the priest who got arrested.

You know, the article that had the picture of Dicky sitting on his lap?" Sonny's grin disappeared. "I figured she might know something that might help. Gave her my name and number."

Aunt Dory's brows pulled together. "Annie, does your mama know about this?"

"Yup. She yelled in Italian for a few minutes, but she got over it." She looked up at the ceiling. "I've got to learn Italian so I can talk back."

The woman seemed to be getting something sorted out in her head before she asked the question slowly: "So... do you think this reporter could really help us find your cousin, Dicky?"

Annie leaned forward to waggle her hand in a Sicilian gesture. "Hey-y-yee, she's Italian! We hit it off right away. And," she lifted the same hand, palm out, toward her aunt, "she already called and we're meeting at our house next Monday night."

"Who's 'we'?"

"Mama and Papa, Sister Mary Catherine, me and the reporter."

"And... what do you all have in common, that you would have this meeting?"

"Let's just say, we're all going to share what we know about this 'Father Jeff' guy." Her eyes squinted. "We might come up with a bit of evidence, or a clue, or what they call in the movies, 'a lead.'"

"You know, it sounds like you have a pretty likely chance, with that group." Doreen pinched her lips together and then slipped them slowly into a pucker.

"Hey, Aunt Dory... if you wanna join us, it might give you some hope, you know?"

"Well, Monday *is* my day off."

The tiny living room barely held the six of them. Andy took the overstuffed chair with the doilies on the arms and back. Sister Mary Catherine — a younger version of her older sister, except for the nun's habit — shared the sofa with Annie and Tony. Doreen slipped quietly into the little rocker at the other end, while Sophia Pizarro held court from the kitchen chair placed in the center of the room.

"Where's Sonny?" Annie whispered.

"At the movies," his mother replied.

"Well, now that we've all been introduced, let me start by telling you a little about myself," the reporter said. "I work for the *Burlington Free Press* as, if the truth be known, just about every job there is in a newsroom. It's hectic, but overall, I enjoy it. And sometimes I come across information that helps me write my book." Five sets of eyes indicated the same question. "It happens to be a documentary, if you will, on child abuse in institutions across this country. I have been at it for nearly a year and it is beginning to take shape." Nobody even blinked. "I am following closely the search for this..." She turned abruptly toward Doreen, to make the correction. "Your little boy." Her hand smoothed out the page in the notebook on her lap. "Unfortunately, this situation is not all that uncommon." She surveyed the solemn faces, choosing her words carefully. "It is a scenario that seems to have been repeated for decades. I have heard many stories, but few can be verified and I've learned to take the time to dig, dig, dig, until I find the truth." She cleared her throat. "After talking to Tony on the phone last week, I feel you folks might help me to get this book done and maybe we can even get some answers about Dicky."

"So, you want to know how we, or... what we know about Father Jeff?" Andy queried.

"Feel free to share whatever you can think of."

"Okay. So, Tony and I used to volunteer over at the orphanage on holidays, for special skits and snacks and decorations, things like that. That guy was there quite a few times, hauling around a camera... his pockets full of candy. It got so the kids would swarm him when he showed up." He shrugged. "We thought he was a great guy. Who knew?"

"Well, I knew!" Sister Mary Catherine bristled. "I saw what he was doing, that sorry excuse for a priest." She folded her hands on her lap, waiting for permission to continue. Sophia nodded. "So, anyways, he had a camera, all right and he used it, all right... in the kids' dorms, at their bath time... jumping around and acting like it was all great fun. And I wasn't the only one who saw him. There were other nuns there and they thought he was comical. Yeah! They thought it was funny." She thumped the top of her knees with her folded hands. "I would get out of there, find something else needing to be done right away." The hands thumped a couple more times. "I suppose I should have said something right then, but I would have been the only one and those nuns have this thing about 'tattling' on each other. Better not to stir them up, if you know what I mean. So, I kept turning my back, until... I caught him and his sister teasing those little kids. It was just plain mean." She looked up, mournfully.

"That's all right, Sister, take your time," Miss Pizarro said, softly.

"I... don't know how they did it, but they got — I think it must have been a half-dozen of the little ones — they got them into bathing suits and soaked them down. I spotted them from the path where I was walking and saying the Rosary. They had chosen a spot where nobody could see them from the main building... but they never thought to hide from the path." She brought her hands up to her lips before she went on. "They were making those little tykes hold onto the chain-link fence... in the middle of winter. If the kid let go, she would slap the poor thing. I mean, that chain-link fence had to be freezing and these toddlers were soaking wet, with bare feet in the snow." Her shoulders heaved. "He was on the other side of the fence, crouching and moving around, taking pictures." She sniffed softly. "I took off up that path. All I wanted to do was to beat those two to a pulp. I was running, but there was no way to get to where they were, without going all the way around to the front of the building." She sniffed again. "By the time I got to that spot, they were all gone. No children, nothing. I don't know how they did it. I just can't figure out how they did it."

"Maybe they had some help," the reporter suggested.

"Ay-yuh," Andy growled. "They had to have help. Look at the logistics: Six wet, bawling kids in bathing suits and one woman getting them back inside, undetected? I mean, he was outside the fence; he probably jumped in a car and took off."

"Right," Annie agreed.

A silence filled the room.

"Had to be somebody else herding those kids back to get dried and dressed," Sister Mary Catherine mused. "Well, that's one theory."

"You said he was there with his sister? So, did you ever see him there with anybody else?" Sophia's brow wrinkled with the question.

"N-n-no, can't remember anybody else, ever."

"So, it may have been someone on the inside, helping for money... or for a favor," Andy concluded.

Tony cleared her throat to get her husband's attention. "We should mention about the bruises on the arms and legs. That was pretty common. And we should probably tell what he tried to do to Annie." She turned to her daughter. "If that's okay with you."

"Sure." She looked at her mother, then at Sophia. "Not that anything actually happened. He tried and we didn't buy it." She folded her arms. "Yeah, he tried to get a couple of us girls to help him 'find his dog.' This was on the way home from school."

"What made you suspicious?" the reporter asked.

She shrugged without unfolding those arms. "I'm not sure. I guess he just didn't look right. So, we told him we had to catch a bus and ran for it."

She scribbled a note before she spoke. "Okay, we have established that the man is a predator and was taking pictures of abused children. We also know his sister was helping him... and there is probably somebody over there that was helping... and that person could probably fill us in on more of this stuff, if we could pin them to a wall. Is there anything else?"

"What about my boy, Dicky?" Doreen's voice was almost too soft to hear. "Did this guy take my boy?"

"How well did he know Father Jeff, Doreen, do you know?"

"He was sitting on his lap in the picture."

"Yes, he was, but... we don't know if that was a one-time thing or not."

"Oh."

"Now, on the other hand, we do know your son was familiar with that guy's sister — the one who was helping him abuse those freezing children."

"We do?"

The reporter looked up at the surprise on those five faces. "Oh my goodness. I guess you didn't realize. She was arrested after a car chase and attempted suicide, this last week. Actually, she's Father Jeff's stepsister. Her name is Angela Donaldson, and for a couple of years, she was one of Dicky's housemothers at the Children's Home."

A collective murmur fluttered across the little living room.

So, Doreen Dupree left the meeting that night without much more hope than when she arrived. She and Sophia left together, the reporter having offered the distraught mother a ride home. As the door closed behind them, the folks inside exchanged woeful glances. Finally, Andy said it: "If that woman was helping do all that stuff over at St. Joe's, it seems reasonable she was doing something like that at the Home."

"Betcha fifty bucks she has a camera," Annie muttered.

It was getting dark as the car turned to move slowly down Church Street. Up until then, they had made idle talk, but as they passed the corner in front of Sears, Doreen choked up and cried out, "I just want my boy to come home."

"Of course you do, Doreen. And we all want to help find him." She pulled a tissue from a box on the dashboard and handed it to the woman. "Listen, is there anything else you can think of that would help solve this thing? Anybody else who might have been involved?"

She blew her nose gently, making a decision not to accuse Ellen, at least, not yet. "No. I've been over and over it and I can't think of anybody, or anything else. It's like a brick wall."

"I hear you. And I can tell you that is not unusual. But sometimes we get a glimpse, or have a dream or something and there it is."

It was quiet until they turned left onto Main Street and she pulled the car into the driveway. "Tell you what, Doreen: Here's a phone number." She fished a card out of her purse. "It's a special number for my dry cleaner. If you think of anything, just call and ask when your husband's shirts will be ready."

***

"Trafficking porn should be a federal offense," the sheriff informed his men. "Unfortunately, all we have is the Mann Act and that only covers prostitution across state lines. The wording isn't specific enough for anybody to get charged with a federal crime for selling disgusting pictures of innocent kids." He tossed the crumbled lunch bag into a wastepaper basket near his foot. "But the FBI seems to find a way to prosecute these guys, usually for something else. So, all we do now is to assist wherever the feds want us, which would be highly unusual, because they feel they have superior methods and equipment. I guess the main thing is we have them involved in the search for Dicky Dupree." He shifted his weight in the office chair. "Did I tell you there were a dozen shots of him in the suitcase?" He belched the onion from his take-out hamburger. "Also of his little friend, the Abnaki... uh, Joseph Turner. They figure the housemother contributed those. Anyway, the FBI is up to something, otherwise, they couldn't be involved in this whole matter."

"So, all we have is the priest and the housemother both in jail, but on unrelated charges," Smitty surmised.

"Right, but they are also suspects in the disappearance of the kid, because of those pictures found in their possession." Max looked at his boss for confirmation.

"Right." The sheriff glanced over at the dispatcher, who was taking a call, then came back to the conversation.

"And I would assume," Deputy Duncan continued, "that the Snoop Squad is also playing second fiddle to the feds."

"Mmmm," the sheriff hummed. "But of course, nobody will actually say that."

"Wouldn't it be something if the Chittenden County Sheriff's Department came up with something that would break the Dupree case?"

"Keep your shirt on, Max. We don't want to lose friends in the FBI," the older man cautioned.

Max grinned. "Just supposing, sir."

The crackling on the radio stopped and the dispatcher turned around. "Sir, we have a domestic violence in Shelburne."

"Let me see that address," the sheriff said.

Looking over the man's shoulder, Deputy Duncan emitted a slow whistle. "That's the Donaldson farm." He shot that look to his buddy. "Smitty and I can take this one, sir."

The newer farmhouse was located down near the dirt road that passed the Donaldson farm, having been built shortly after Arnie married Delores. He said he didn't want any memories of that old bag he'd been married to before. So, the two of them moved in to start a new life, each of them with a child. The honeymoon was interrupted, however, when the parents discovered what they termed "an unhealthy relationship" between the thirteen-year-old girl and her eighteen-year-old stepbrother. They solved the problem by allowing the young man to take over one of the upstairs bedrooms in the old farmhouse. As far as Arnie was concerned, that was the end of it and peace settled over the new household.

The two deputies approached the house without flashing lights or siren. They quietly stepped out into the sweltering heat of the August sundown. Max took the lead, then knocked gently on the door. There was a shuffle at the window, then steps toward them. They both moved to either side of the little porch and waited. The door cracked open slowly.

"What do you want?" a man's voice slurred.

Max introduced both himself and Smitty. "We got a call that there was a disturbance at this address?"

There was a deep breath. "You got the wrong house."

"Let them in, Arnie," the woman's plea came from the back of the house.

As he yelled, "Shut up!" the door cracked wider and Max shoved the toe of his boot between it and the doorjamb.

"Arnie. Arnie, it's me, Max Duncan. You remember me, don'tcha? I was here to help when the well collapsed."

"Let them in...!" Her voice was louder.

"Arnie, we can make this real simple and polite... or I will have to force my way in. Your choice." The law officer waited, listening for any furtive movements that might indicate the presence of a weapon. He nodded at his partner. Smitty stood ready, his nostrils flared, one hand on his holster.

Slowly, the door inched open.

Max had not thought about sundown being at his own back, until it bathed the disheveled man in the doorway. Arnie's hair was drooping down on each side of his head, held out upon the tops of his ears like two ebony wings and his red eyes glistened in the glaring light. "I don't mean any trouble," he whistled through his side teeth.

The deputies quickly saw there were no arms, just a pitiful

figure of a man who took a teetering step backward as they entered. Behind him, framed by the kitchen door, a woman stood, bleeding from the nose. Her eyes peered fearfully from their reddish-purple sockets.

Max gave Smitty the nod and the younger man moved, slowly, sympathetically toward the woman. "Ma'am... oh my goodness, ma'am. Let me help you." He moved in close and motioned to the kitchen. "Let's see what we can do about that bleeding."

As those two retreated, Deputy Max went into sympathetic mode, also. "Arnie... Arnie," he said softly, "what the heck happened here, man? This is not like you. You're not a violent person." He pointed over to the sofa. "C'mon and sit down. You need to get it together." The man obliged, his head hanging as he slid back on the cushion.

Careful to keep a safe distance between himself and the farmer, the deputy perched on the front edge of a wooden rocker's seat, keeping his feet steady, his elbows on his knees and proceeded with the questions: "Okay, so tell me what happened."

A half-hour later, Smitty and Delores appeared at the kitchen door. "You mind if we join you?" the young man asked.

"We were just saying, you two must have gotten lost," Max joked. "But come and join us." He stood up. "Mrs. Donaldson, would you mind having a seat beside Arnie?"

She looked at him. "Is that all right with you?" Her husband nodded and patted the seat beside him, so she sat down, carefully, beside him. When she got up close, he could see the injuries and his face went pale.

"Oh my god, Delores," he whispered. "Oh my god."

She reached out to touch his hand. "I can't really blame you, Arnie. You probably should have done worse than this... after what I've done." She was not able to wipe the tears from the painfully swollen lids. "I have ruined your reputation, your business, your future." The breath was involuntary, and it shot pain through her bruised chest. "It was the way I made money to survive, before I met you and then... you wanted to do all this... expand the farm income... the plans... the future... the retirement... so I kept on doing it." She touched a tissue gingerly under the pink of her running nose. "It just caught up with me. I couldn't get out of it." Her gaze moved slowly to his. "I have hurt so many kids... and my own son... and your Angela." She tried to blink but could not. "I should go to Hell, Arnie, I really should."

Arnold Donaldson sat still, before he finally spoke: "I don't know how we will ever 'fix' this. I really don't." He turned his hand over to clutch hers. "But I do know I never want to do to you again... what I have done... tonight."

A light went on in Max Duncan's mind. "You know what, Arnie? Delores?"

Hope lit up his face. "I think I know just what you need to do. I think you need to talk to this acquaintance of mine... oh, wait... maybe you remember him... Father Tom Ladue."

"That damned liar who pretended to do a wedding business here? You have to be kidding!"

She squeezed his hand. "No... wait. I think he needs to know some stuff, Arnie. I think we need to really consider this."

The two deputies got back into their vehicle before they compared notes. Neither one was surprised the other one had not taken any. They were all the way into Shelburne, so they pulled over for coffee at the Shelburne Inn. Before they went into the restaurant, they knew they needed to check in with dispatch.

"So, this is what our report will say... and it is the truth, okay?" Max stopped long enough to get it all straight in his head. "Okay," he said again, "we answered a call for domestic violence. The husband was grieving and out of control and the wife knew it and called for help for her husband. Injuries were sustained, but she refused to press charges. Officers recommended marriage counseling, to which both parties agreed. No citations were issued."

They found a secluded table, where Max got down to business: "So. What did we learn at this domestic call, Smitty?"

"Oh my god." He rechecked that he could not be heard, then went on in a heavy whisper: "That woman has been dealing in child porn ever since her boy was sixteen. She trained him to seduce and take pictures of little kids. Then she sold them, she said, mostly to somebody in New York City. I'm just guessing, but I'm thinking maybe it was the mob." He paused to see if Max was assessing the situation, too.

"Oh my god." He put his coffee cup down. "She has to be in over her head, Smitty. Almost a death sentence, if she didn't deliver, or told anybody. They must have her right where they want her."

"But now she has told somebody. Why do you think she did that?"

"Probably because Arnie was so out of control, he would have beaten her to death. Her back was up against the wall. And she knew he was in the living room with me, spilling the beans, anyway." His face was solemn. "I think we have a real problem, here, my friend, because now both of us know about this." The eyes scrunched. "If the mob is involved and they find out that we know."

The two men exchanged a confirming look.

"We have to tell the boss," Max said. "He can put out the word to the whole team."

"What good will that do?"

"Well, to shut us up, they would have to wipe out the whole damned Chittenden County Sheriff's Department. That would be too high-profile, even for the mob."

Smitty's face suddenly brightened. "Or... we could just tell the FBI."

Deputy Duncan responded with a laugh. "You know what? They probably already know somebody has to be selling that stuff to the mob."

"Oh... yeah. They probably do. But do they know it's Delores?" Deputy Smith looked hopeful. "That could get us a couple of brownie points with the feds."

"Don't count on that," Max replied.

CHAPTER TWELVE

Implosion

Suddenly it was September. Labor Day weekend came and went, the children clamored back to school and the investigation of the Dicky Dupree disappearance dragged on. Although details no longer made the news, there had been two arrests of individual suspects, albeit on unrelated charges. Delores Donaldson was indicted on tax charges, for interstate trade-related activities and had struck a deal for payment of those taxes upon the sale of the farm. The "For Sale" sign went up on the same day of the Donaldsons' sixth counseling session with Tom Ladue.

The sessions were held at the Ladue house in the Shelburne Bay area, even though the priest no longer lived there full time, having been officially a resident at the Holy Family Parish in Essex Junction for the last month or so. As they rose to leave, Delores tugged gently at Arnie's arm, stopping him from opening the door. "I can see this has been a rough one for you, Father Tom. This is not pleasant stuff to talk about... for any of us." Her countenance darkened. "But if it helps, try to remember that the things you learned today, I have been living with for — what? — twenty years?" Their eyes met. "I'm so sorry for what I have done to all those people and now, you. God should send me straight to Hell."

Arnie placed his hand over hers. "No, that's not the answer. Think back to what Tom shared with us last week...

about the demons, remember?" He patted that same hand. "We still have a lot to learn and a lot of fences to mend."

Tom waited for their car to move down the driveway before he closed the door. There, he turned and leaned wearily against it.

"Oh no... not our dear Sarah."

But he knew what he had to do.

"Thanks for the call," the Air Force captain said. "Muncy's Diner makes the best pie in Essex Junction, no doubt about it." He scraped the last of it onto the fork. "The banana cream is my favorite."

"Cherry with vanilla ice cream, for me," the priest declared, as he took one last sip of coffee. He looked around at the crowded restaurant. "You finished, John?"

"I am, after a little water." He spotted the concern on his friend's face. "Something on your mind?"

"We need to take a walk."

Outside, John put the Class-A Air Force captain's hat on his head, adjusting the shiny brim smartly in place. The pair made a handsome sight — the priest in black clericals, the captain in the Air Force uniform — as they started to the left, around the five-way traffic circle, an Essex Junction landmark. The duo turned left once again, onto Maple Street. They walked in silence for a ways, enjoying the crisp fall air. Finally, Father Tom spoke up: "I can't reveal my sources, but I wanted to let you know why Sarah went back to that place and took the suitcase."

"Okay."

"She was trying to destroy evidence. They were blackmailing her, with pictures... of her. Bad pictures, Johnny."

"Oh, hell, Tom." He stopped in his tracks. "I was *hoping* you never found out about those."

"You knew?" His mouth dropped open. "How did you find out about them?"

The lawyer still didn't like to lie, so he told a true fact. "I was helping the Snoop Squad for a while, there." The priest nodded his understanding. "But, I kinda got fired." He chuckled more as a diversion than a statement. Resuming the stroll, he attempted to change the subject. "But I appreciate that you let me know she was being blackmailed. Those two really were the team from Hell."

"They lured her to the blackberry patch and got her drunk. When she passed out, they... did their thing." He folded his hands behind him and bent forward into the walking. "So, what could she do? She was only fifteen then." He raised his head to glance at his friend. "I figure she must have finally found all those negatives and pictures while you two were searching for Dicky Dupree clues at the old farmhouse." His eyes went back to the sidewalk. "How long was she upstairs, do you remember?"

"Uh... quite a while. Maybe an hour. Yeah, that's probably when she found them. But then, Angela was coming up the walk."

"There was no way she could have gotten a fifteen-pound suitcase out of there, with Angela escorting you back to the sugarhouse."

John still wanted to change the subject. "So-o-o, now we know. And, in a way, she broke open that whole, dirty operation. She died a heroine, didn't she? I guess we should try to rest in that thought."

"I guess we should." Father stopped and turned around to head back. "But I don't think we need to tell her dad, or the rest of the family, any details about those pictures."

"Right." Then suddenly, it was the counselor being counseled: "It is enough that we all know she broke open a porn ring by securing that evidence, Tom. She died a heroine. We need to leave all the rest of it to God, every last one of us. That's it."

Back at the traffic circle, Father Tom headed north toward the Catholic Church and Captain John Courtney drove back to Ethan Allen Air Force Base.

As the car moved along, however, the man had one last question. He muttered it out loud: "What else did they make you do, Sarah? Did... did you know anything about that little boy?"

***

The first week of school seemed to be going well for the Home kids. Lisa Marie entered the sixth grade, which made her feel grown up. She was walking to school on that Friday morning, with her little sister.

"So, how do you like fourth grade, Cee Cee?"

"It's okay, I guess."

"What does that mean?"

"I don't like my seat in class." She wrinkled her nose. "I sit right behind Lester. He stinks."

"Oh yeah. I know who he is. He does stink. Probably nobody makes him take a bath."

"He smells like pee-pee." The little girl shuddered. "I even told my teacher."

"What did she say?"

"She said, 'Don't tell Lester because it would hurt his feelings.' Then she took this out of her desk drawer." She held up a pretty pink sachet. "Here," she said, as she handed the little pillow-shaped thing to Lisa Marie. "Smell it."

"Oo-oo-oo! That smells really nice. So, she gave it to you? Why?"

"She told me to keep it with me and when bad smells come, just hold it near my nose for a minute and that would help a lot."

"That was nice of her."

"Yeah, but I still don't like sitting behind Lester. And I don't like sitting next to Billy, either."

"What's wrong with Billy?"

"Mostly nothing. But the other day, he sneezed this loud

sneeze and there were big boogers hanging down, dripping on top of his paper and he couldn't get his handkerchief out of his pocket." One hand pressed against her stomach. "I almost throwed up."

Big sister couldn't help laughing, but she tried to make it right, immediately.

"He must have been really embarrassed."

A bundle of energy roared past them, interrupting the conversation. The boy was pretending to be a motorcyclist, his hands on the imaginary handlebars, piercing screeches coming from the back of his throat, as he wobbled fiercely in and out of the line of young walkers.

It was Little Joe Turner. A picture of Dicky flashed through Lisa's mind.

"He better slow down, before he hurts somebody," Cee Cee commented.

Lisa did not answer. She was thinking of how happy that little guy was lately. Somebody said it was because he was having home visits almost every Saturday. She felt a little tug inside. "Must be nice," she opined.

"What must be nice? He's being a pest."

"Okay, maybe he's a pest, but he's a happy one." That brought some pleasant news to mind. "By the way, Jenny gets to see her mother tomorrow."

"Jenny Roth has a mother?"

"Of course she does, Cee Cee." She was surprised the girl had never thought of that. "She's been sick for a long time, in Waterbury. But tomorrow somebody is taking her by bus down to White River Junction, for tests or something. The bus will make a stop at the terminal in Burlington — you know that place, right across from City Hall Park, where all the buses start and finish their rides?"

"Is that right next to the place with the orange doors?" She took a happy breath. "Where we go with Sonny, to buy doughnuts?"

"That's it. So anyway, Jenny will get to see her mother, for the first time in a couple of years, I think she said. She's so excited."

"Is she going home pretty soon, Lisa Marie?"

"I… don't know. I wish she could. She's been in the Home since she was five."

"How old is she?"

"She turned fifteen last week."

"Wow! That's…" Cee Cee did the math in her head. "That's ten years!" The little sister shot a woeful look toward the big one. "Are we gonna be in the Home that long?"

There was that tug again. "Course not."

They needed to part company at the school door.

The next morning, right after breakfast chores were done, the two sisters watched Jenny combing her long, dark hair. She was wearing a Sunday dress and her nails were polished red. There was even a light touch of pale pink on her lips. For a girl who wasn't very pretty, she looked really good.

They watched her walk down the half-circle driveway to the bus stop, where she boarded the Burlington transit bus and then they got busy with their own plans

Tomorrow, Mama was coming and Aunt Tony would be with her. It was a long time since they had seen Aunt Tony and Uncle Andy, or even Annie, for that matter. But tomorrow it was going to be just Mama and Aunt Tony. The girls were happy to settle for even that.

Meanwhile, they kept busy, waiting for Jenny to get back with the details of her visit with her mother. The Big Girls were enjoying small bowls of popcorn in the dayroom, under the supervision of the upstairs housemother, when the fifteen-year-old finally came in through the front door.

The hubbub died down to nothing, as the girls beheld her ashen face. She slipped off the light coat, folding it over her arm as she went to the door of Mrs. Ferndale's room. She knocked lightly. When it opened, she said something in a small, high-pitched voice, then slipped inside. The door closed.

"All right, girls," Mrs. Hays sang out in her cheery voice, "we have more popcorn. Anybody want seconds?"

Slowly, the whispering returned to normal volumes of conversation, but little eyes kept side-glancing toward the housemother's door.

"Sometime we should try cinnamon and sugar on our popcorn," suggested Mrs. Hays. "Instead of salt, I mean. Would you all like to try that?"

That got their attention.

"Maybe we could make it taste like choc'lit," Cee Cee suggested.

"Or pizza," another girl exclaimed.

"Or brown sugar and cinnamon. Like on oatmeal."

"No-no-no! We need the kind of cheese you shake on spaghetti. What is that called?"

"It's called 'cheese that you shake on spaghetti,'" a smart aleck answered.

The suggestions continued until they got ridiculous. The more ridiculous they got, the greater the laughter, moans, and yucks. Finally, someone offered the possibility of peanut butter and raw onion. A collective "Yuck!" rose from the munching crowd, just as Jenny stepped out into the dayroom. She paused, confused.

"Oh, Jenny," Mrs. Hays called out, "we were talking about bad toppings for popcorn. What do you think about peanut butter and...?"

The teenager walked slowly toward her housemates, knowing she would have to answer the question. When it was her friend who asked it, she was relieved.

"Did you get to see your mother, Jenny?" Lisa Marie asked softly.

"No," she answered, as she shook out the coat. "My bus got stuck behind a traffic accident. By the time I got to the terminal, her bus had come and gone." She laid the coat over her arm and raised her eyes... to see that knowing look, the look she had seen so many times in the last ten years. If they could have, every one of those girls would have hugged her tightly in this moment. But their own emotions stopped them. They just felt what she felt. There was nothing they could do about it, but empathize.

Finally, one of the younger girls spoke up: "You want some of my popcorn, Jenny?"

That night Lisa Marie pulled the sheet over her face and prayed her silent prayer: "God, why didn't you help Jenny to get a hug from her mother? What was wrong with that, will You tell me? She's so lonesome... she's been here for ten years. You've got to know that, because You are God." She lifted the sheet to grab a breath, then pulled it back down. "I know you are God and I can't fool You, so I'm just gonna say it: I'm scared. Yes, I am. I'm afraid. Are You going to make me and Cee Cee stay here, like You're doing with Jenny? Are You?" That painful tug rose up within her, again. "I need to know, Jesus. I need to know. Please tell me we don't have to grow up here, like Jenny. Please, God, please." She let a few tears slip down across her temples, because she was in private time with God and she would never, never cry in front of others... especially her mama. It was hard enough on Mama that the other three had done that every time there was a visit. So, she would be careful to be strong and help out and reassure her mama they would all get through this thing, whatever it was. Then Sonny went home and Dicky disappeared and leaving only herself and Cee Cee. And Cee Cee still cried every single time Mama visited.

Lisa Marie pulled the sheet off her face and rolled over onto her side. It was a long time before she finally went to sleep, because that painful tug just wouldn't go away.

The next morning, Lisa Marie prayed even more... that the buses that took them to and from the First Methodist Church in Burlington would not be hindered in any way, assuring they would all get back to the Children's Home in time for the one o'clock visit of Mama and Aunt Tony. The rule for family visits set the cut-off time at four o'clock, when the children needed to get back to chores in preparation for the evening meal. That meant this visit could last for a whole three hours. Maybe they could go for a ride, get some ice cream, look into their mama's lovely blue eyes, talk about where they would live, very soon. So many possibilities, so much hope. Finally, it was one o'clock.

Both girls took a place on the window seat to watch for their mama and Aunt Tony. Two sets of eyes kept vigil as the minute hand ticked on and on and on, but the car did not come. Slowly, the anxiety returned. Lisa tried not to upset her sister, but every minute that passed, was a minute they would not get to visit with their mama, or their aunt. Every precious minute was an incredible loss. The tug inside rose to an unprecedented height, as visions of Jenny showing up too late… too late… for just a hug. One little hug.

Cee Cee sucked up a sudden breath. "Is that them, Lisa Marie?" She was looking at a Beach Wagon which her older sister recognized immediately. As it moved slowly up the driveway, she noted the clock showed it was one-forty-five. A whole hour of their time together had passed. Passed, without the hugs, the touching, the sweet words. But she swallowed hard and ran for the picnic table and the two Adirondack chairs out there at the edge of the playground, where she would finally be with, at least, some of her family.

The 1939 Chevrolet Beach Wagon slowed to a stop just before reaching the carriage porch. Lisa recognized it as Uncle Andy's car, but Mama was driving it. She had pulled over as close to the edge as possible, to let any other cars get past, but opened the driver's door to check, anyway. She was wearing the bright red dress with the little white flowers all over it, again. When her brown-and-white saddle shoes hit the ground, the girls ran for the car. She was pulling on a white cardigan when they grabbed her around the waist. The arms wobbled into the sweater sleeves, then lowered down to return the hugs. It was a moment of pure joy for the girls. Mama was there, warm and alive and loving on them. During that blissful encounter, they paid no attention to the slamming of two other car doors. It was Aunt Tony's voice that brought them around.

"Hey-eee! Do I get a hug, or what?"

"Aunt Tony!" they squealed with delight. All arms extended for another massive hug.

"That's better," the woman said, as they drew back. "All right. So, look behind you. Somebody wants to say 'Hello.'"

The two girls could hardly believe their eyes. Annie stood there, hands forward, but elbows tight to the ribs, her feet spread apart like a quarterback ready to take a hit. The baggy sweatshirt drooped nearly down to the thighs of her dungarees and the high-top tennis shoes ground into the lawn as she rocked side to side. "So? Do I have cooties, or something? Where's my hug, huh?"

Once again, the hugging dance was performed. Then the little group moved back toward the outdoor visiting area. Mama and Aunt Tony eased into the lounge chairs, while the two older girls slipped onto the picnic table's benches. Cee Cee, however, squeezed in to sit with her mother.

"So, what have you girls been up to?" Doreen asked, as she scooted over to make room for her younger daughter.

The conversation went on, but Lisa wasn't much into it. She was watching their faces, hearing familiar voices, drinking in the experience of having family right there with her. She was remembering what Aunt Tony's kitchen was like and Uncle Andy's grin and how Grandma Dupree lived a few blocks down the street. Suddenly, Annie stood up.

"I've got a bat and a ball in the car. You want to hit a few?"

"Um. I would, but where can we do that?"

"Right out there," Annie pointed to the broad expanse of lawn between them and Shelburne Road.

"Oh. No, we can't. We aren't allowed to go out there."

Her cousin snickered. "You kids can't go out and play on your own lawn?"

"It kills the grass," she explained. "And they need to keep an eye on us. That's too far away."

"Even with your family with you?"

"Annie." Her mother gave her a look, then turned to Cee Cee. "What grade are you in now?"

Lisa watched her little sister, all snuggled up against her mother, so quiet and secure. The talking went on, but the older sister wasn't listening. Something was tugging inside of her, again. Looking at her mother's blue eyes was painful, because those eyes, that face, that mama would be gone again, in a little while. Watching and sealing memories were urgent tasks right then... no time for frivolous chatting.

"How about we go take a couple of swoops on those swings?" Annie was eyeing the playground.

"Company can't be on the playground."

"What? Why not?"

"They can't hang around the other children. Besides, they might get hurt and sue us."

She started to say something else, but caught that Italian mama look again. Instead, she surveyed the buildings for a few seconds. "So, that's where you live, huh? Where do you sleep?"

"Up there," she pointed to the second story windows.

Annie nodded. "What's that center building with the porch?"

"The dining room."

"You eat there?" She saw Lisa's confirming shake of the head. "Ever get to sit out there on that nice porch?" This time the child shook her head "no." Annie's gaze continued to the right. "So, I'm guessing that's where Sonny was."

"Yeah. But he got sick." She tried to look wise. "That's why he hardly ever comes here with Mama. He doesn't like this place."

Annie hummed a little acknowledgment, then dropped her

gaze to her own tennis shoes. "I'm on a girls' softball team. We had practice this morning."

"We go to church on Sunday mornings."

"Yeah. I guess you don't have early Mass like we do." She was re-tying one of her shoes. When that was done, there seemed to be nothing to do, but lean back and yawn. Then she had a thought. "Can you have comic books here?"

"Yup. We have a few."

"I've got a Captain Marvel in the car. I could leave it here with you, if you want."

"Sure."

"Let's go grab it. It's on the back seat."

As the two of them headed for the Chevy, Lisa Marie felt that fearful tug again. She stopped to look behind where her mother was sitting. "You go ahead," she said as she turned back. "I'll wait for you over there at the table." Settling on the bench, she felt a little better.

Annie took her time getting that comic book. She also took time to get a closer look at the outside of the main building, the carriage porch, the décor, the fence keeping the Little Kids safely corralled. That was pretty much all she could see, without getting spotted and told to get back into the visitors' area, but she killed a good fifteen minutes. When she handed the book to her cousin, she got a brief nod of thanks. "I'll read it later." Right now, Lisa was happily enjoying the attention of her mother.

"Your hair is getting so long, my girl. Do you like having braids?"

"It's okay, Mama."

"I think you're old enough now, to have a perm." She turned to her former sister-in-law. "Don't you think so, Tony?"

"Sure. Tell you what, Lisa Marie, one of these days you come over to my house and I'll give you a Toni Home Permanent." Everybody laughed, because of the name of the permanent company.

"Mama, could we go for a ride and get some ice cream?" Cee Cee's request brought an awkward silence. Doreen looked at her watch.

"Not this time, honey. We need to leave in a few minutes."

The tug came back, causing Lisa to suddenly sit up straight.

"What time is it, Doreen?" Aunt Tony looked concerned.

"Almost three."

"Oh, yeah. We should be going."

"But we have until four o'clock to visit," Lisa reminded her. In the corner of her eye, she saw Cee Cee pull her mother closer. "And we already lost forty-five minutes because you were so late."

The woman loosened Cee Cee's grip as she spoke. "Well! I didn't know we had a time schedule," she snapped.

The rebuff struck deeply. Her mama was mad at her, actually mad at her. That could not be happening. "I... I'm pretty sure you said 'one o'clock,' Mama." She swallowed hard. "We waited and waited..." She saw Cee Cee's eyes filling with tears. She would be crying again, in a minute. Doreen brushed her skirts with her hand and picked up her purse.

"I'm doing the best I can, young lady." Grabbing Cee Cee's hand, she headed for the car.

"I guess we should have been here earlier, honey," Aunt Tony said as she put a comforting arm around the girl. As they moved slowly forward, Annie came alongside.

"Listen, we have to pick up my papa from a fishing trip, down at the dock in Shelburne. My mama can't drive, so your mama had to drive the car. That's the reason she could even come today, okay?" She saw how white her cousin's face was and signaled her mother to stop. "You okay, kiddo?" She turned to her mama. "Her eyes don't look too good."

"Hey-ee, little girl... you need to bend over." She put her hand on the girl's waist and pushed on her back. "Bend. Bend. That's right." Annie retrieved the dropped comic book. "Stay like that for a minute." Tony turned to call out to Doreen, but the mother was busy trying to get Cee Cee to stop wailing. It was turning into a mess.

Suddenly, Mrs. Hays was there. "It'll be all right," she whispered. "She's just kept it all inside, for a long, long time. We've been expecting this little implosion. We've seen this kind of thing before." A glance toward the car revealed the director, Mrs. Bushey, was gently leading the crying little sister down the driveway toward the Big Girls' living quarters. The mother was getting into the car. "It's important this girl gets a loving goodbye from her mother, ladies."

"That's okay," Annie piped up. "She's not going anywhere without us. We'll walk her over there with you." She put her head down to speak to Lisa.

"Think you can stand up long enough to say goodbye to your mama?"

By the time they got her over to the car, however, she was looking pretty bad, again. The housemother signaled for the two to give hugs and get into the car, then asked Mrs. Dupree to roll down the window. The blue eyes were defiant, but she did get the window down.

"Lisa needs to know her mother loves her, no matter what," Mrs. Hays said quietly.

"She already knows that."

"I think she needs to hear that from you." She drew the girl over to the window.

"Mama, don't be mad at me." The voice was hard to hear. "Please don't be mad at me."

"I'm not mad at you! You need to think before you speak — telling me I showed up late and all that."

"But we... we..." The final tug released the torrent, right then and there. "Mama, we can't do this anymore!" She leaned her brow against the top of the window's opening, inches from her mother's face. Her normal Lisa Marie countenance twisted into something her mother did not recognize and the woman drew back in shock, as the words came spilling out: "We can't. We can't. We want to go home. We don't want to be here, anymore." The child's frantic eyes told the whole story. "We've been here almost five years. Five years, Mama."

"I'm doing the best I can!" The anger showed up again. "Why can't you understand that? Now, get yourself together, young lady. I can't be coming here, if you're going to act like this. I can't take this, either." She started the car up and reached over to roll up the window.

"No, Mama, no! Please don't leave us here." As glass filled the empty space, she pushed the twisted, wet face against the pane. "Mama!" she screamed against the barrier, "Mama... please... please don't leave us here..."

Mrs. Hays pulled her gently back from the moving car.

Out on the highway, Tony wiped her eyes. "Good gawd, Doreen. How can you stand it?"

Annie was leaning forward from the back seat, her head between the two of them. "Is it always like that?"

"Not... as bad as that, usually. Lisa Marie doesn't usually lose it like that."

"You've gotta get those girls outa there," Annie said.

"I'm doing the best I can!"

"Aw, jeez, Aunt Dory... haven't you ever heard of welfare?" She slid all the way into the back seat.

"Well, that's easy for you to say, Annie. You don't know what it's like to be looked down on and that's exactly what people do. I would be ashamed to be on welfare. I can work, even if I don't like my job. But I'll be damned if I'm going on welfare."

It was a few miles down the road before the girl spoke up. "All I can say is, it's amazing what excuses some people will come up with, so they don't have to take care of their own kids."

Tony turned swiftly in her seat. "Anna Maria Dupree! As soon as we stop this car, you are going to get such a swat!"

CHAPTER THIRTEEN

Lists

John Courtney paced the floor of his barracks room. Here it was, almost Halloween and nearly a year since the disappearance of Dicky Dupree. Even with the involvement of the sheriff's department and the FBI, no solution seemed to be in sight. The daily distractions of Air Force life, coupled with Sarah's sudden death, had hindered his investigation, as well.

"Enough with the frustration," he told himself. "Get it together, mister. Get the whole situation straight in your head and start over." Like the good lawyer he was, he picked up a legal pad and a pencil. "Oka-a-ay, pretend you're Sherlock Holmes, with the floppy hat and crooked pipe." For some reason, this thought amused him, so he stopped pacing and slipped into the Naugahyde recliner, tilting up the footrest with a healthy slam. That seemed to help.

"I need to make a list of people."

The first name on the list was easy: Joe Turner had been a suspicious character, right from the first, what with his lying to Detective Smith during the initial interview. John had not pursued this lead, having gotten sidetracked into the Donaldson farm fiasco. Perhaps he should have done this sooner. He checked his watch. It was still early. Mrs. Bushey would still be in her office. Quickly, he headed down the hallway toward the barracks phone. All he needed to know was whether Little Joe Turner's aunt and uncle would be picking the kid up this next Saturday.

Sure enough, the elder Turners showed up at the usual ten in the morning to pick up the young lad. Mrs. Bushey allowed Johnny to hang out in her office, as though he had some important business there. So, when the couple came into the building to pick up the boy, the lawyer could get a good look at them. It was entirely possible the uncle was the man in the enlarged photograph.

Sure enough, when they arrived, Joe Turner was wearing a flat hat made out of black-and-white hound's tooth fabric. Johnny could hardly believe his luck. As the couple stood outside the office door, waiting for Joe to come running down the hall to them, he sidled up to the doorway for a closer look. Working up his most charming smile, he offered a warm, "Good morning!"

They turned in surprise, automatically answering the greeting.

"A pretty cool one out there," he continued.

Mr. Turner nodded, as Ava said sweetly, "Yes, and it's only October."

"Hope that doesn't mean we're headed for a hard winter." He zeroed in on the little lady with the twinkling eyes. "I don't suppose you've come across any of those wooly caterpillars? You know, if the bands are wide, whatever?"

"It means a colder winter, I think." She was almost blushing.

"Here he comes," the older man muttered.

In a couple of minutes, the three of them were out the front door. Johnny leaned against the doorjamb, disappointed. Mrs. Bushey looked up from her desk.

"Well?" she asked.

"Guess not," he answered. He pulled his jacket together and waved a thank-you as he left.

Mr. Turner was wearing rimless glasses and there was no

---

mole on his left cheek.

***

The second name on the list was Doreen Dupree. While he had not met her, he was sure she was still in touch with the Burlington police and probably the two other law agencies, since she was the mother of the missing boy and they were sure to be keeping her up-to-speed. There was a chance she might furnish him with a lead.

He found out where she lived because a certain official at the Home wanted badly to find the boy who had gone missing while under their care. The man was careful to wait until the two youngsters in that household had left for school, then he knocked on the door. A lady with orange hair answered.

"Good morning, ma'am. I'm John Courtney and I'm looking for Doreen Dupree?"

"What do you want?"

"I want to help find her son."

"Oh?" The door opened enough for her to get a better look. "Who sent you?"

"Are you Mrs. Dupree?" He looked apologetic. "That's who I really need to talk to."

She acknowledged her identity with a suspicious gaze. "Who sent you?"

"I'm pretty much here on my own."

"Why?"

"I was originally hired by the Children's Home, but then the local lawmen and then the FBI got in on it and the folks at the Home thought they could do a better job, so they let me go." She didn't look all that convinced. "Well? Do you think they are doing a better job?" The shoulders shrugged. "Look, I have a friend who got killed trying to find your boy. Her name was Sarah Ladue. Have you ever heard of her?"

"N-n-no."

"Yeah, well, so there you are. Somebody should at least have told you that. At least you would have known people have been out there trying... just ordinary people, trying to find Dicky Dupree."

"Her name was Sarah?" The brows came together, thoughtfully. "Was it in the paper?"

"I don't think so."

"What do you mean, she died? What happened?"

"Mrs. Dupree, I think we need to sit down together and talk about some things. We might be able to justify the death of my sweet friend and maybe even find your son."

She served leftover coffee from her own breakfast, right there at the kitchen table. John noted the dishes were still in the sink, but that wasn't his concern. He started by telling the story of how Sarah had tried to get evidence off the Donaldson farm.

"I'm sorry, but if they didn't tell you about her death, I'm thinking they haven't told you about the shocking evidence either. Am I correct?" She shook her head. "No. That's what I thought. Well, this isn't going to be pretty, ma'am, but we need to get all our cards on the table so we can play with a full hand. No more pussy-footing around." He gave her a warning look. "I'm just going to tell it like it is."

Her head bent forward. "It's about the dirty pictures, right?"

"You know?" That stopped him in his tracks.

"I went to a meeting the other night," she whispered. "They talked about Father Jeff and his sister, over at the orphanage. I figured it out, after I got home."

Over the next half-hour, Doreen Dupree filled him in on the details of that meeting. John began to jot down names and notes, including Sister Mary Catherine's story about the chain-link fence.

"There had to be somebody on the inside," he remarked.

"Yeah. That's what we all figured… and it made me wonder about something else, after I got home."

He waited.

"If they can sneak a slick trick like that one, why couldn't they be hiding my boy over there in that crowd of kids? I mean, they could dye his hair, or something. And that is a really big building."

Again, he was speechless. He wondered immediately if any of those law agencies had thought of that possibility. "Did anybody at that meeting mention that?"

"Nope. I just thought of it after I got back home. I almost called Sophia, you know, to bring it to her attention."

"You have a private number for her?"

"Yup," she replied, as she reached for her apron pocket. "It's a number for her dry cleaners. I'm supposed to ask when my husband's shirts will be ready."

Johnny slipped into the driver's seat and closed the door. "Well, Detective Smith did say he had a lot of friends."

***

In order to get to the third person on the list, the lawyer had to check public records. It didn't take him long to see when Angela Donaldson would get out of jail. With no money for bail or to pay the fine, she had been locked up, bandaged wrists and all. According to this information, she would be released sometime next Tuesday. He made sure his Air Force duties were covered before he pulled his car to the curb, a block down from Martha's King Street apartment. It was a guess, but he figured Angela was broke and she wouldn't want anybody from the farm to come out to meet her.

Sure enough, he spotted her walking from the corner of Main and Church Streets, about eleven o'clock that morning. She turned right on King and headed straight for her mother's place.

He waited for fifteen minutes.

To his relief, it was Martha who answered the door. Quickly, he drew the brightly bagged bottle from behind his back. "I come bearing gifts," he whispered.

Martha slowly smirked. "You rascal. Come on in."

She took the pretty package and shuffled toward the kitchen. "Have a seat."

There was a rattling of paper and the clink of glassware. "Angela's here," she called out. "She's in the shower."

"Great!"

"She's been in jail."

"Oh, really? What happened?"

"Tried to outrun a cop car." She was scuffing carefully back into the living room, the open bottle in her right hand, three empty jelly glasses held together by three fingers of the left. He rose to help her. She let him take the three glasses.

"She crashed. Got cuts on both hands. But they're better now." She poured a little drink for herself and looked to see if he wanted one.

"I'll wait for Angela, thanks." He smiled. "So, how have you been, Martha? Behaving yourself?"

The hoarse laughter rolled forth. "Never mind about that. What can an old woman do, anyway? Maybe scare the neighborhood dog away from the rose bushes." She was lighting a cigarette. "So, what brings you by, anyways? It's the middle of the week. Don't you have to be at the base, or something?" He didn't have to answer the question, because she spotted Angela poking her towel-wrapped head around the edge of the bedroom door. "Get some clothes on. We've got company." The girl glared at John, then disappeared.

There was some light conversation as Martha puffed and sipped, then Angela came to join them. She was wearing gray sweats and her damp hair was held back with a wide red ribbon. Choosing the place closest to her mother, she pulled her bare feet up under her as she curled up on the opposite end of the sofa from him.

"What the hell are you doing here?"

"Brought you two a peace offering," he said as he motioned to the bottle. "I was waiting for you, like a gentleman."

She rose to pour the two glasses a third full. As she handed one to him, she asked, "A peace offering, huh? For what? Lying about having a wedding on the farm?" She took a deep sip and breathed out heavily. Her eyes closed for a couple of seconds. "Man, that sure tastes good. You don't get that in jail."

"Well, how are you doing, Angela? You gonna be okay?"

"Oh yeah. I just panicked." She snorted. "Like you really care." She glanced toward her mother, then back at him. "I don't want to talk about it."

He brought the glass to his mouth, but only wet his lips. She caught that.

"You gonna drink that stuff, or are you gonna fake that, too?"

"I have to go easy. Got OD duty at three this afternoon."

"What's that?"

"Officer of the Day."

"Eww, look at you... big old Officer of the Day."

They watched Martha pour another drink for herself.

"So, what does a OD actually do, hotshot?"

He took his time explaining, because there were other things he wanted to talk about, but figured it would be best to wait for Martha to get ready. He endured another twenty minutes of barbed-filled conversation with Angela. Finally, the older woman's head began to nod and he made his move.

"I saw the ad in the *Free Press*. Looks like your dad is selling the farm."

Marsha's head jerked upward, the eyes wide open. "He's selling that damned farm? I don't believe it." She peered into her daughter's face. "What happened?"

"They... uh... got into tax trouble, Mother."

175

He was struck by how well she lied, with just enough truth to make it believable. Even the story about a cop chase; it was true and yet it wasn't the real story. The lawyer watched, more than he listened, as she skirted all the details in further explanation, her mother nodding and taking it all in like it was the whole truth and nothing but the truth, "...so-help-me-god." This was better than any classroom illustration he had ever encountered in law school.

But it was more than that. He drew back mentally, for a little pause, and then he realized what he was witnessing was something deeper, much darker than he thought. It was something bad, something downright evil, coming forth from this woman's mouth.

"There's an agenda, here," he thought... *"a hidden agenda and I don't think even Angela recognizes it."* His attention was drawn to her mouth, which was moving in a half-smile, one side drooping slightly, then tightening, then drooping again. A lick of the tongue moistened the lips intermittently and the voice came forth as melodious and convincing... and chillingly masculine. *"That's not her own voice,"* he thought. *"My god, what am I hearing?"*

Suddenly, it got quiet. In the dim light of the apartment, he could see Martha's head bobbing again. Angela was sitting still, watching her mother.

"Is she asleep?" He ventured back into the connection with the talker, whoever that was.

"Yes. More likely, drunk." It was Angela's voice.

"Sorry. I won't bring any more of this stuff into this apartment."

"Not your fault. My mother is a big girl; she makes her own decisions."

"Yeah, true, but no need to be opening doors." Something clicked in the back of his mind, but he had more important things to do at the moment, so he continued. Leaning forward, he looked at the cracked linoleum floor. "Um, Angela, I have an eye-witness who can prove you and Jeff took some kiddy porn pictures over at St. Joe's."

She stiffened. "What are you talking about?"

"The shoebox pictures." He saw the alarm in her eyes. "I have seen them. All of them."

"How?"

"I conned your mother out of them. Told her I knew somebody who buys photo art for calendars." He shook his head. "She had no idea what was in that box, did she?"

The woman was incredulous. "You can't do this... not legally. You stole my private property, you cocky jackass!"

"Nope. It was given to me, for legitimate reasons." He was watching her hands. "You can't do a thing. You also can't get them back."

"Why not?" she snapped.

"They've been confiscated by the Burlington Police Department." Her face went hard. "Now, they may or may not give that information to the FBI. If they do, you can be charged with complicity in conducting interstate commerce without paying taxes. That's how they got Delores." He noted that she was listening. "On the other hand, if you come clean about some other stuff, the Burlington police might be inclined to step back."

"What kind of stuff?"

"Who helped you to take those pictures at St. Joe's?" She looked confused. "I mean the ones at the chain-link fence. We have a witness who says she saw the whole thing." There was a suspicious squint of the eyes. "One of the nuns saw you."

"Is that so? Well, I just bet I can tell you who she was."

"I'm waiting."

"That probably was Sister Mary Catherine." She smiled when he blinked twice, very quickly. "Okay, *Bingo*. Yeah, Jeff stiffed her on that one. Took off without paying her the hundred bucks." She let it sink in. "So much for your 'witness,' Mr. Lawyer." It was a mocking laugh. "That fat little piece of Italian crap sure isn't going to testify against herself."

"She doesn't have to. Those pictures came from your shoebox." He was watching her hands. "You and Jeff can still be charged with the tax thing. We simply wanted to know how you pulled off that sadistic camera shoot. Now we know."

"Big deal. Nobody's going to do anything about it."

"We'll see about that. Meantime, you have something bigger than that to worry about." Her head jerked to attention. "You and Jeff are number one on the list of suspects in the disappearance of Dicky Dupree."

She began to rub her knuckles, first one hand, then the other. "That's a waste of time. We got the pictures. That's all we were after. We had no reason to kidnap the kid."

"Wake up, Angela. Jeff is a predator. He had plenty of reason to grab that little guy." He decided to go for it. "In fact, we suspect you have the kid 'hidden in plain sight,' as they say."

"What does that mean?"

"You have Dicky Dupree hidden right there in the orphanage, that's what."

Her mouth dropped open, then shut and then she laughed. "Where did you get that idea? Are you kidding me? Nobody could do that; it's impossible."

"Not really. There are lots of places to keep him out of sight, as well. That is a huge facility. Jeff could have snatched him and taken him to that place while everybody else was at the parade."

"Well, he didn't... and neither did I."

"Prove it."

Now there were fists, tapping knuckles together. "Okay... okay." Suddenly she had it: "The parade pictures! They will prove Jeff was outside the Sears store the whole time period that the kid supposedly was taken. And since I was snapping the pictures of Jeff, so was I."

John remembered the clock in the jewelry store window behind where she had been standing... from one of the *Free*

Press photos. He placed a hand over his mouth, contemplating that situation. She certainly was out there and so was Jeff.

"Gottcha, hotshot!"

He stood up. "Guess you do, Angela. But things could change. Don't be too smug."

"I'll be whatever I damned well please," she snorted.

"That could lead you into some deep, dark places. Look how far you've dropped already, little lady."

That seemed to be the final straw. "I'm not your 'little lady,' mister! I've had it with you and your high-and-mighty attitude! Get your sorry butt out of here before I scratch your eyes out!"

"Oh, you're not going to scratch my eyes out," he said as he turned away and headed for the door. "You can't touch me, so don't even think about it."

A low rumbling growl made him turn quickly to look back at her.

Her face was gone. All that remained were two deeply set black eyes, in the midst of twisted, pulsating gray flesh.

***

"Sounds like you had a little run-in with a demon," Father Tom said. "You're lucky it didn't attack you."

"Attack me? I pulled an about-face out of there so fast, you could hear my butt suck air." The priest grinned; these military types had their own language.

John leaned back against the countertop in Holy Family's rectory kitchen. "I completely forgot to tell it to shut up, in the Name of Jesus."

"Probably a good thing you didn't try."

"But that's what you said, that's what you're supposed to do."

"It only works when you have the authority, John."

"I don't get it. I believe in Jesus. I know He's real."

"Even the demons know He's real. That isn't enough. That isn't where the power is and certainly not where the authority is." He poured a cup of coffee. "Only people who dedicate their lives to Jesus, who accept Him as their Savior, have that authority." He took a sip of the lukewarm brew. "If you're not there, those devils will definitely laugh and beat you up." He tilted his head to one side, then the other, relaxing his neck. "And even after you surrender your life to the Lord, they can still resist your command — even in the Name of Jesus — if they can smell one single ounce of fear in you."

"Rats. That thing got me on two counts, Tom."

"If you don't surrender to Jesus, you won't triumph over the devil, my friend. It's that simple and that complicated."

"Sort of like this Dicky Dupree case." He shifted his weight. "A kid disappears from a restroom and there are cops all over it within the hour. What happened there? How did it get so complicated?"

Father Tom answered with a question: "How's your list going... the one you told me about on the phone?"

"I'm not sure I'm even doing this right. I mean, I keep coming up with more rabbit trails."

"Who was first on the list?"

"Joe Turner, but that fell through. No mole on his cheek and he wears glasses." He tapped his fingers on the countertop. "The second one on the list was Dicky's mother. She thinks he may be hidden in the orphanage. I think the FBI would already be all over that one, myself."

"Who's the third one listed?"

"Angela."

"And was there a fourth one?"

"Oh, that got taken care of before I even got to her. I wanted to see what Ava Turner might have to say." He shook his head. "She died of a heart attack three days ago."

CHAPTER FOURTEEN

Shadowed

Detective Ed Smith shared an apartment with Sophia Pizarro over on Intervale Avenue. The rental included the whole second floor of what once had been a single home, located at the edge of the Italian community. It was a nice apartment, since covered stairs rose up the outside at the back of the clapboard building and two front windows looked out upon the interval below. The narrow strip of land on the other side of the road dropped off, a hidden cliff, to the spacious lowlands where the Winooski River snaked its way northwest. On this particular evening, the two of them were seated together on the sofa, enjoying the view.

"Nice night," the widower noted, as he pulled her into a sideways cuddle.

"Yeah, for sure." She lay her head backward onto his shoulder. "In a few minutes that sky is gonna be gorgeous."

"Ay-yuh, it will." He planted a little smooch on the top of her head. "So, what did you want to tell me? Must be important, if you made me wait 'til after supper."

"I wanted to have your full attention on this, mister. No misunderstandings, you know-whad-I-mean, here? We don't want any trouble in the family. We gotta stick together."

He broke out his spacey-toothed grin, because she couldn't see his face. *"She's doing her 'mafia talk.' Why do I love that?"* He gave her a gentle squeeze. "Right. We gotta stick together.

We're family."

Her head lifted and turned so she could look him in the eye. "Okay, maybe not in the eyes of The Church." She blinked slowly. "But in the eyes of God, I would certainly hope we are." Her body slipped toward the edge of the cushion, turning slowly as she spoke. "So! So, we need to talk." There was a big breath, followed by her hands cupping his face. "I need to go back to college. Back to UVM. I need to try for my Master's, Eddie. I need to do that. It's the only way I can apply for a grant. I need that grant money so I can do research for my book." The hands caressed his face for a few seconds before she drew them back and folded them in her lap, but her gaze did not disconnect from his.

Finally, he blinked. "Of course you do." He looked down, then back up into her light brown eyes. "I know how much this means to you and I agree, somebody has to expose all that crap." He touched the velvety bronze of her brow. "And I don't think anybody, including me, should stop you from doing this." He pulled her gently into his embrace. "Only promise me you won't be gone too long or too often. I'm a tough old codger, but — dammit, girl — I would miss you so much."

A telephone rang. It was the one in the bedroom, so it had to be answered.

Sophia rose and raced to pick up the receiver. "Northside Cleaners," she sang out.

There was a pause. "If you can wait a moment, I can check on that for you, right away." She turned to see Ed standing in the doorway, so she covered the mouthpiece with her hand. "It's John Courtney. Says he needs those shirts right now."

"Aw, hell." He stomped his foot. "No!" But the look on his face made her hesitate. She was right. "Aw, hell," he said again. "Tell him he can pick them up."

"Yessir, you can pick them up right away." Another pause. "Half an hour, sir? That would be fine."

Ed Smith decided to walk the six blocks or so to Battery Park. He needed time to figure out what Courtney might be up to. As he strode along, his mind was mostly on that subject, but years of detective work had also trained him to always be aware of certain signals in the area around him. At the third corner, he was sure he was being followed.

He kept his pace consistent as he crossed over onto North Street, but when he reached the sidewalk, he paused suddenly, looking up into the sky. The glory of that sunset was the perfect excuse for him to stand perfectly still, gazing heavenward.

The 1948 Ford sedan turned off to the left before it reached the park. Out of the corner of his eye, he noted the out-of-state license plate.

"Has to be the feds," he whispered to himself. Somehow, they may have tapped into his fake dry cleaner's phone. He should have seen it coming: The Burlington telephone operators could listen in on any conversation they wanted to. It was just a matter of flipping a switch. It happened all the time. His own Snoop Squad had used their assistance on many occasions... why wouldn't they do the same for the FBI?

He checked his watch. Courtney would be arriving any second, to park in the shade behind Colodny's Market. That was a half-block away. All he had to do was to get to that man's car before the Ford came back around the block.

A flash of sunlight on the entrance side of the storefront window just ahead of him signaled a need to duck out of sight. By the time the Ford sedan passed, the man was crouched low between the old brick buildings. He waited until the car turned left at the park, then slipped out and sprinted toward the spot where the lawyer was just pulling in.

He yanked the car door open and slipped in. "Don't turn off the engine. You need to back out, slowly."

"What?"

"For cry-sake, man, drive... out... slowly." As the driver

carefully obeyed, another vehicle crept to a stop at the north end of the park. It pulled over, but nobody got out. "Yeah, there they are," Ed Smith murmured. "Well, let's give them the scenic route." He tapped the driver's steering wheel. "Head out on your right, along North Avenue."

"What are we doing?" John Courtney asked.

"Giving the feds a fun evening," came the reply.

"Am I going to jail for this?"

"Nah… they won't ever admit they're even doing this… trust me."

A couple of minutes later, Ed Smith directed John to turn to the left, into the parking lot of a nursing home. "Pull into the space marked 'Visitors.'"

"What are we doing?"

"Visiting my cousin."

Inside, Ed scribbled in the guestbook and waved to the lady at the desk.

"Ten minutes until visiting hours are over," she reminded him.

He acknowledged her with a friendly wave, led John down the hall, and knocked gently on the first door on the left, before they entered the room.

An elderly man sat asleep in front of a large picture window, his recliner leaning halfway back. A TV murmured from across the room. The detective drew a kitchen chair toward the large window, placing it where he could see their car out in the parking lot. "Have a seat," he instructed John. He, himself, took his own place on the bottom corner of the old-timer's bed, in the same line-of-sight for the vehicle. Seeing the curiosity on Courtney's face, he motioned out the window. "Watch and learn," he whispered.

Outside, the sun had finally set and a dull gray dusk was settling over the area. In a few minutes, the lights would be on, illuminating the sparse line of cars in their parking spaces, but the professionals knew how to get in and out in a short period of time. It was only the shadow of a man passing behind their car, pausing for the briefest moment to bend out of sight, then rising to disappear into the dusk.

The parking lot lights went on.

John was impressed. "I've studied cases on this stuff before, but this is the first time I've ever seen it for real."

Ed stood up, motioning for the lawyer to follow him over to a small kitchen table. "Pick up that chair and come over here," he directed, as he took a seat on the other one.

The old man never stirred as Johnny complied.

"Alright, what did you want to see me about, mister?"

"Ay-yuh... I thought I should talk to you about a couple of things." He had to collect his thoughts. "I... talked with Dicky Dupree's mother, for one thing. She had some interesting questions." He glanced over at the sleeping man, to be sure it was safe to go on. "For instance, she wondered whether her boy might be hidden over there at the orphanage...'in plain sight,' as she put it. That's a big building, as you probably well know. Now... I'm thinking it's more like somebody could be keeping him comfortable, but isolated, if you get my drift." He glanced at the man, again. "She also made me aware that you and Sophia Pizarro are in cahoots with this phony dry cleaner contact." He noted Ed's slight frown. "I figure she must be the lady who answers the phone... and maybe you can fill me in on that."

"Doesn't matter anymore," Ed declared. "The feds obviously know all about it. But listen, they also know us local cops have contacts like this all the time. Hey! So do they. It's all part of the game." He sat up straighter in the small chair. "They also know that Sophia and I are... involved. We live together. We support each other. She's writing a book about child abuse in these institutions all over the world. I'm only a local cop, doing what I can, in my own territory."

The young lawyer bowed his head for a moment. "Well, sir," he said, as he raised his gaze to meet that of the detective, "I certainly respect that." Ed Smith nodded a thank-you. "Sooo," John continued, "did your friend, Sophia, fill you in on the meeting they held over at the Andrew Dupree residence?"

"She did."

"Did she tell you that they suspect somebody on the inside helped Jeff and Angela to get those pictures of the kids at the chain-link fence?"

"She did."

"And did she also tell you this critical evidence was witnessed by a nun, one Sister Mary Catherine?" He noted the affirmation from the detective. "Well, there is more to it than that." He shook his head. "You may not believe this, but I also talked with Angela Donaldson, the day she got out of jail. It was an interesting conversation, let me tell you. Not only did she prove that neither she nor Jeff could have snatched the boy, but she fingered Sister Mary Catherine as the insider who helped the two of them to pull off the chain-link fence photo shoot." He was watching Ed's face closely. "Jeff didn't pay up the hundred-dollar fee he promised that little nun, so, Angela claims, the Sister turned them in, while swearing that she, herself, was trying to stop the whole thing."

"Aw, crap." He stood up. "You probably need to talk to Sophia. We should leave."

Ed scribbled a sign-out time at the desk register before the two of them left. As they reached the car, he signaled John to get in while he, himself, made a quick visit to the back bumper of the vehicle. In a flash, he was slipping into the passenger seat next to John. "Pull out and head back toward the park. Sophia is home right now, so let's head there."

As they pulled onto Intervale Avenue, the young lawyer was curious. "So, did you get rid of that thing on the back bumper?"

"I made sure you ran over it, as you pulled out of the parking space," Ed said, with a chuckle.

"Is that going to make a problem?"

"Not really. For all they know, it wasn't properly secured."

"Well, that's a help," John Courtney murmured, as he pulled his car around to the back of Ed and Sophia's rental.

"Ay-yuh," the detective replied. "But, of course you probably realize, that the feds have your license and address and probably the size of your undershorts, by now."

"No big deal. The Air Force already has all that *and* my fingerprints."

Amicable laughter accompanied their ascent of the back stairs. They were back on the same page again.

***

"Hey, if you're going to live here with me, you're going to have to get a job," Martha Donaldson notified her daughter.

"Might be a little difficult, Mother. I now have a jail record, remember?"

"So do a lot of people. We know a few of those folks, ourselves." She drew smoke into her lungs, tilted her head back, and blew it toward the ceiling. "I bet you could get a kitchen job, or a waitress job, if you wanted. All you have to do is get your snooty nose out of the air and take whatever you can get."

"Don't get your snuggies in a bind. I'm working on something, even as we speak."

"What do you mean?"

"There's an opening for kitchen help over at St. Joe's. I have someone on the inside who can probably get me in." She pushed back a strand of black hair from her face.

"Are you kidding me?" The woman flicked ashes into the metal tray on the table next to her chair. "They would hire an ex-jailbird cop-dodger at a Roman Catholic place like that?"

"The Church is big on rehabilitation programs, Mother. I'm a prime candidate." She smirked as she sat down on the end of the sofa, next to her. "I probably have a real good chance at getting this job."

"I certainly hope so. I'm damned sick and tired of being poor. Some more money would sure come in handy. When do you think you'll know?"

"Probably by the end of this week."

It took a little longer than that, but Angela Donaldson reported for work at St. Joseph's Orphanage the week of Halloween, 1949. Having a paycheck was a good thing; keeping Sister Mary Catherine her obedient little partner-in-crime was even better.

***

It was that same Halloween that things began to come together for the Dupree sisters at the Children's Home. As UVM volunteers decorated the dining room with black and orange crepe paper streamers, electrified black cats with green eyes, and silhouetted witches flying across melon-colored moons, Mrs. Hays brought the two girls upstairs to her room. They sat obediently at the foot of her rocker and waited.

"Well now," she smiled, "I have some wonderful news for you." The hope in those eyes touched her deeply. "Your mama is taking you both out of here tomorrow morning. You will have your very own home together, all three of you children and your mama."

It was almost too much to believe. A godly wisdom kept the housemother quiet, letting the information settle in, until the little one turned to her older sister. "Are we going home, Lisa Marie?"

"I... think... so." The blue eyes conveyed suspicion toward Mrs. Hays. "Are we?"

"Yes, Lisa Marie. Your mama has found a way to do this. You're really going home."

The two gasped and hugged. They hopped up and down and turned to hug Mrs. Hays. Then they flew down the big staircase to the Halloween party.

The festivities began, bobbing for apples on strings, relay games, cupcakes with black and orange sprinkles, and the long fun walk around the block. At last, they were brushing their teeth and telling Jenny, "We'll come to see you, write to you. Tell us when you get to go home. We'll never forget you."

The next morning was the last time they ever saw her. The excitement and adventure of a new life took them far away from the girl with the long, black hair. Still, the specter of her lonely spirit followed them for a long, long time.

***

Election Day came right on the heels of Halloween, the first week of November. At the end of the day, Max Duncan was the new sheriff of Chittenden County. No one was terribly surprised and there was a celebration at Connie's Diner, in his honor. Ed Smith and his son were there, sitting at the usual back table, where they could talk more privately. As the guests began to leave, the waitress brought around a fresh pot of coffee. She waited for Captain Courtney to take a seat with these gentlemen, then poured a cup for him, as well. The uniformed man had just picked it up when Max Duncan pulled up another chair.

"What's up?" the new sheriff inquired.

"Thought this would be a good opportunity to talk to you guys, while I can catch you all together," John said. "I was hoping Sophia could make it." He looked up to see her coming through the front door. "Oh, good." He waited until she was settled.

"I just wanted to run a couple of things by you, here." He glanced around, then plunged right in. "It's been almost a year and we still haven't found that kid. Now, I don't know what the feds are doing, but I sure can see what our so-called county and city law officers' cooperative efforts have done... or better yet, not done. Now, don't get me wrong... I know we have all been trying, but we seem to be at a dead end, here." He looked up into cold stares. "Again, I'm just the amateur in this bunch. I'm not here to judge anybody. But I did think if I could give you what little I have, maybe it would strike a note with one of you, or some of you. So, would you just hear me out?"

"Sure, John," Sophia said quietly.

"Thanks." He cleared his throat. "Now, when I first came in on this, there were three main suspects: Jeff, Angela, and Joe Turner. Maybe some of you had more than that, I don't know. Well, Jeff and Angela have photographic evidence that they were both on the street watching the parade at the time of the kidnapping. That leaves Joe Turner, who appears to have lied about knowing the kid quite well and then maybe one more guy... a John Doe. Ed, you have a shot of that guy in Angela's pictures... the man carrying a sleeping child... or maybe a dead one. This guy has a mole on his left cheek and wears a hound's tooth cap with a small brim." They were all listening carefully, but he couldn't tell whether they already knew all that. He went on, anyway. "There are a couple of others, but they're probably what you guys call 'a long shot.'"

"Go for it," the sheriff muttered.

"Sophia, I know you thought this couldn't be right, when we talked the other night, but we have to consider the possibility of the nun."

"What nun?" Smitty leaned forward.

"Sister Mary Catherine," Sophia answered. "Angela has fingered her as the insider at the orphanage. But I find that hard to believe. She just doesn't fit the role of someone who would allow child abuse. Sorry," she said to John.

"I understand. Just wanted to get that out there. And then we probably need to check out Delores Donaldson... although she seems to have regretted the porn thing and is trying to make things right. Still, kidnapping and maybe even murder, well, that might not be so easy to admit to, no matter how many regrets you have."

"The feds have checked her out pretty thoroughly, Johnny," Ed spoke carefully. "The way I see it, we probably still have three suspects: Joe Turner, Sister Mary Catherine, or John Doe." He looked around the table. "Anybody have anything to add?" There were no takers, so he turned back to the captain. "Any conclusions to all this?"

"Wish I could say 'Yes,' but I can't. I'm stumped."

"Welcome to the club," the sheriff said, as he rose to leave. The rest of them followed, trailing him out the door.

Outside, John turned to Ed for one last comment. "I wish the feds would cooperate. They might learn something from us, for Pete's sake."

The slight tilt of Ed's head to his right told the whole story. "They probably just did."

The two of them watched a paneled delivery truck slowly pull away from the curb, right there in front of the diner.

CHAPTER FIFTEEN

Emancipation

The colonel had not been happy. Having one of his officers under FBI surveillance was not something he wanted to deal with. The "anonymous" phone call had sent him into a purple panic, so his words to Captain Courtney were short and to the point: "Drop this investigation or get out of the Air Force." It was as though Providence made the decision for him. The truth was, he was ready to return to civilian life, and he wanted to know what happened to Dicky Dupree. That was it. Fortunately, his uncle would be most happy to have Johnny on board in Montpelier.

Before all that became official, he decided to have another visit with Mrs. Bushey. She received him in her office, as usual.

"Well, at least you can pursue this case without looking over your shoulder for the Air Police," she remarked, after hearing the news. "I hope you'll keep in touch with me as you make progress."

"Of course."

She folded her arms. "I told you about Ava Turner's passing, didn't I?"

"Ay-yuh. I was sorry to hear that. Wanted to talk to her, but of course, it's actually too bad about the kid. What's going to happen to him, now that she's gone?"

She broke into a gentle smile. "Well, that was a very

pleasant surprise. Joe Turner offered to take him home, for good. Said it was because there was no longer the issue of Ava's health."

"Really...?"

"I guess that will keep them both from being lonely. These things seem to work themselves out sometimes."

"I believe that. Look at how I'm finally leaving the Air Force."

"Exactly. And look how Dicky's three siblings are now living with their mother. That probably wouldn't have happened if the kidnapping hadn't brought her back to Burlington."

"That's sad, but there's a whole lot of truth in that." Suddenly he had a thought. "Say, didn't they know the Turners when Dicky was only a toddler?"

She frowned thoughtfully. "Why yes, I believe they did. As a matter of fact, Ava told me they had lived right next door over there in South Burlington."

His question was one of forced nonchalance. "You wouldn't happen to know where that happy little family is living, would you?"

"Near the Village of Essex Junction... at a Colchester Road address, I think."

"I need to make sure I keep them up-to-date. I'm sure they feel abandoned by the authorities right about now." He stood up. "I know you probably can't disclose personal information, but maybe you could tell me if they have a phone."

"I think they probably do," she said, as she scribbled the number on a slip of paper. With one short sweep of her hand, the scrap fell to the floor. "Oh-oh, I think you dropped something, John."

***

Tony Dupree and her sister, Mary, shared a special skill. Because their papa was stone deaf, they learned sign language before they learned to walk. However, due to the mixture of Sicilian and American cultures, their version of "signing" was quite unique. More than once, the young girls had signaled secret insults about people in the same room, even tucking in a swear word, here and there. They loved it.

So, when Sister Mary Catherine stepped into her sister's kitchen for her usual Friday visit, it wasn't too surprising when she started to talk with her hands. What was unusual was that she was also talking with her mouth... about something else.

"Hey-eee!" she said. "*Be careful. Someone could be listening,*" she signaled.

Tony's eyes widened, but she returned the greeting. "Hey-ee!"

Mary's hand fluttered again: "*Just talk normal.* Wow! I walked all the way. Missed the bus."

"It's getting too cold for that, Sister." She pulled out a kitchen chair. "Here, sit down."

"Thanks. My dogs are barking, as Mama used to say."

"Rest in peace," Tony said, drawing out a chair for herself. "I'm making grilled cheese for us today."

"Smells good."

"*You in trouble?*"

The nun nodded "Yes," but continued her normal conversation. "Did you put mustard on them this time?"

"Yup." She looked around. "What do you want to drink?"

Sister laughed loudly. "You have to ask, right?" She peered at the barrel. "Is it ready for consumption?"

Tony drew two glasses from the foaming barrel, wiping them on a dish towel before setting them on the table. She took a sip before turning the sandwiches onto small plates.

Oral conversation continued until Sister Mary Catherine came up with a great idea. "Let's have a little music while we eat! How about Peggy Lee? Or maybe Bing Crosby? No, how about you put a stack of records on and let it go to town. We might even get a little dance in this morning!"

"Hey-ee! Now you're talking. Let's warm up our cold November buns."

As soon as the music started, the nun's hands once more flew into action.

"*I am in big trouble. I did something bad, bad, bad. I lied about the kids at the chain-link fence.*" Her eyes moistened as she continued. "*I am so sorry. You trusted me. I was lying. It was me. I helped them take the pictures. Father Jeff promised me one hundred dollars to help them. He lied. He left but did not pay me. I was mad. I told on them.*"

"*Why did you help them?*"

"*I needed the money.*"

"*What for?*"

"*I want to leave. I don't want to be a nun anymore. These women are mean. I am desperate to escape.*"

"*You could just leave.*"

"*No. I know too much.*"

"*What does that mean?*"

"*Andrea called me. Told me she needed a kitchen job. She knows I am on that committee. Told me... if I don't hire her, she tells on me. Told me FBI is watching and listening. Told me that's how they caught Jeff. Told me I have no choice. I am bad. I can be arrested. I absolutely want to leave the*" — she finger-spelled the word, "*o-r-d-e-r. I don't see God in this place. I am asking God to take me... swoop me into purgatory... clean me up for Heaven. I feel trapped. There is no hope. I said she could have the job. Now she is there, in the kitchen. She is watching me.*"

Peggy Lee finished her last jungle beat. Tony spoke up cheerfully: "I love that song. And nobody sings it like she does."

"You got that right. Who's next?"

"Der Bingle!" The older sister waited for the crooner to get into the song, then continued the motion-conversation: "*Listen to me. Andrea is a liar. Jeff arrested for touching boys. FBI watches for murderers. You are not a murderer. You are a victim of lies. Yes, poor choices. But a good person. God will let you make up for it. But* be careful. Big government can swoop over you."

"What can I do? I have my part, my share, in the guilt. I was stupid. Turned into a monster. Shame to my family." The tears were moving down. Fearfully, Mary covered her face with both hands, holding back the sobs.

Tony wrapped her arms around her sister and hummed along with the Mr. Crosby's Irish Lullaby. By the end of the song, both women were back under control. "Here comes Ella Fitzgerald! And are you ready for a bit of a refill?"

"Sure. Just a little."

But Tony sat up straight in her chair, ignoring the barrel of brew. She leaned forward, a gleam in her eye.

"I have an idea. We can get you out of this mess. It will be hard. Maybe not see each other ever again. We will grieve. But we will see each other in Heaven, God willing."

At the usual departure time, Tony walked Sister Mary Catherine to the bus stop at the North Entrance of Battery Park. As soon as the bus left, Tony walked back toward her home, but stopped at the little red door of her father's house, right across the fence from hers. She found her papa in the garden. He'd felt her slam the door and greeted her with a soft smile. When the elderly man saw her face, however, he stood taller. He had been tapping the freshly filled bowl of a little round pipe. Quickly, her papa stopped, to point the pipe's stem toward a wooden porch swing located a few feet away. She obeyed his direction and took a seat. He shuffled over, sat down, and scratched a stick match along the thigh of his pants. As the flame burst forth, he lifted it to the tobacco, took a couple of draws to get it lit, then lifted his gaze to hear what she had to "say."

"Papa, you told me some people in the old country owed you a favor," she signaled. "I'm thinking now is the time to collect on it." She looked deeply into his eyes. "Mary needs you. She is in big trouble..."

The following Friday's visit occurred at the usual time, with Italian sausage on a roll for lunch and then they decided to take a walk. As the two ambled along, they made quite the pair, one in her nun's habit, the other in a simple tan coat and a green kerchief to keep her head warm. She carried a green canvas shopping bag that almost matched it. They chatted softly as they headed downtown, crossing the snowy streets carefully, keeping inside the shoveled areas as much as possible. It was when they reached the bus terminal on St. Paul Street, that they got a yen for a fresh doughnut and coffee. Inside the orange doors of The Harvest, they found a small spot toward the back and quietly consumed the special treat. Once the green kerchief tilted toward the door to identify the man who had been following a ways behind. The nun nodded. "You should probably use the restroom before we head back," she suggested.

By the time the man had taken his order from the counter to a table, the nun was sitting alone. He lifted the coffee cup to his mouth, the eyes moving back and forth between his target and the ladies restroom door. After a couple of minutes, he saw the nun, herself, go into that same bathroom. He waited, squirming as the minutes went by.

Suddenly, he hurried over to the waitress behind the counter and murmured into her ear.

"Oh, really?" she said. "Let me go and check."

She was back in a few seconds. "Actually, there's nobody in there... but the window was open." She shivered. "It's too damned cold for a window to be opened."

A Greyhound bus was just pulling out, headed south. The man stood on the sidewalk and swore quietly to himself. Sister Mary Catherine was probably on that bus. He turned to hurry two doors down to the bus terminal so he could find out where that bus was headed, but as he reached the door, he spotted her.

She was crossing the street, black robes flapping as she ran for City Hall Park.

"Gotcha!" he muttered gleefully.

He let her get a few hundred steps away, then crossed over at the north corner of the park, making sure she didn't get out of his sight again.

And she didn't. Instead, she moved steadily along, all the way back to the house where the two sisters had had their Italian sausage lunch. There she unlocked the door and went in.

He moved carefully to the van parked on the street. Slipping into the passenger seat, he wagged his head. "Almost lost her," he muttered.

His partner looked back along the street. "So, where's her sister?"

"Not my problem. Last time I saw her, she went into The Harvest with the nun. I figured she was in the restroom..." Suddenly, it was quiet in the car.

"Aw, hell... they must have been wearing each other's clothes all along. Sister Mary Catherine is probably on that damned bus."

But the bus had made a stop in Shelburne, where the lady in the green kerchief disembarked, walked around a corner, and slipped into a nondescript, black sedan.

A week later, Tony brought lasagna over to her papa. As she placed it on the kitchen shelf, her anxious eyes asked the question. He gave her a nod and then they hugged, weeping quiet tears of relief.

CHAPTER SIXTEEN

Moves

By Christmas, John Courtney was out of the Air Force and scheduled to start with his uncle's law firm right after New Year's Day. Meanwhile, he chose to spend the holiday with his mother right there in Burlington. After all, he would not be dropping in as often, what with living in Montpelier. There was also the business of keeping contacts with certain law enforcement personalities in the area, a necessity if he was to continue his own search for Dicky Dupree. For this reason, he invited Ed Smith and Sophia Pizarro for a quiet dinner at Riverbend, a posh Burlington restaurant overlooking the Winooski River. They were having dessert when he finally broached the real question.

"Anything new on the kid?"

"Not that I know of," Ed answered. He cut another bite of the pecan pie. "It's come to the point that most of us are thinking he's probably... gone. I mean, it's been over a year, you know?" The fork was halfway to his mouth before he got the disclaimer out. "Unless somebody just loved him enough to grab him and take him home out in the middle of Kansas, or something."

"That would be a really good thing. Have you seen where his mother and siblings are living?" Sophia washed a bite of chocolate mousse down with the last of her red wine.

"Actually, I have. I've been there. Left my card for the

mother, in case she stumbles over any leads." John pushed the empty sherbet glass away. "It's an honest-to-goodness 'shack by the railroad track.' In fact, there are three of them, right in a row, each with three or four small rooms... walls as thin as cardboard." He sipped the cold coffee. "They're on welfare. Still..." He shrugged his shoulders. "...those kids are so happy to be a family again."

"It's a whole, different perspective, I can tell ya." She brushed the crumbs off her ample bosom. "I've heard so many stories about, and even from, institutionalized children and I can tell you that the most common denominator in their lives is a deep, deep, desperate loneliness. It permeates their whole existence. Everything they see and hear in the world is related to the hope of what things will be like when they are 'home' at last. Every pretty yard, a bicycle leaning against the garage, the ash tray in the dentist's office... all these kinds of things are pictures of what they will have when they get into a home of their own. It's not even realistic, because most of them will end up like the Dupree kids. But that piercing longing is still there. If you ask them about it, they don't even know how to express it. But you can see it on their faces and hear it — oh, my God — how you can hear it in their voices."

"I can see why you are pursuing your education and your book project." He leaned forward on his elbows. "How is all that coming along?"

"She starts classes in January." Ed's face beamed proudly.

"So... will you be including the Dicky Dupree story in this... documentary?"

"It sure fits right in," she admitted. "But I would hate to have no definite ending, you know? I'm hoping we have some answers by the time we are ready to publish this thing."

"So," he said again, "do we have anything new? Anything at all?"

The couple exchanged a look.

"Okay." John glanced around before he laid it all out. "I know that our list of suspects has been reduced even further.

Joe Turner turns out to be an actual 'good guy,' taking his namesake to live with him after Ava died. That leaves a John Doe, and well, I still am wondering about Delores Donaldson, and yes, about Sister Mary Catherine."

"I can tell you Delores Donaldson can't even go to the grocery store without being tailed. If she did anything to that boy, she would have given it away by now." The detective's brain shifted into work mode. "I can tell you, she shows not one smitch of evidence of having done anything like that. And I can tell you that she would have turned in Angela, if she knew anything about that one. There is no love lost between those two."

"I believe it was established that both Angela and Jeff were photographed at curbside during the actual kidnapping, as well." Sophia was thoughtfully folding her napkin as she spoke. "On the other hand, we now know that the nun, Sister Mary Catherine, has left the Order and disappeared off the face of the earth, so to speak."

John nodded, but waited. He wanted to hear it from her.

"We think we know what that was about," Ed murmured.

"Oh, I know what that was all about. I'm Sicilian, for god's sake." She took a breath. "The Family was involved. She's not dead, but she might as well be, as far as the feds are concerned."

"How can you be sure about all that?" The lawyer let her walk it through.

"Well, for one thing, she's not a good liar. There were a couple of pieces of her story about the chain-link fence photo session." She laid the napkin neatly beside her plate. "She never told us why she didn't go to check out the bathrooms after those kids were brought back inside. Surely, she would have caught somebody drying them off and dressing them." She leaned back in her chair. "And one more thing: All of those children were wet. Their little hands were wet when they grabbed that freezing-cold fence. She could have identified them by the skin tears resulting from pulling those little fingers off a metal fence." The anger arose in her voice. "How could injuries like those have gone unnoticed by a whole damned orphanage full of nuns?!"

The two men sat in awed silence.

"Nah, she didn't kidnap or kill anybody... not sharp enough. In fact, such a klutz that she had to be whisked away, to keep her out of jail for helping take porn pictures." Her eyes narrowed. "But being a klutz doesn't excuse her."

The gentlemen waited for her to finish.

"Let me tell you something, John... Even if there is a John Doe kidnapper, even if she didn't harm or hide that kid, herself... she is as rotten as the rest of those phony Christian 'handmaidens of God.' She may be even worse, because she pretended to be their champion, while letting such atrocities happen to them." She stood to her feet, reaching for her winter coat. "I really owe you an apology, sir, because I defended her, although it looks we're both wrong about that woman."

As he drove carefully down the icy streets to his mother's house, John Courtney added it all up. Delores and Joe Turner were off the list; Sister Mary Catherine was probably not a suspect. That left only John Doe.

***

Angela Donaldson was furious to learn that Sister Mary Catherine had resigned from the Order and was nowhere to be found. The other kitchen help kept their distance as she slammed her way through the morning meal preparations, muttering and growling under her breath. When her break time finally came, she retreated to a corner of the backyard, lit the cigarette she had stolen from her mother, and started to figure it all out.

"People don't just 'disappear' like that... unless it had something to do with the mob. I wonder if she was as involved with those people as Jeff and Delores and me." She snorted. "It must have been them who snatched her. I wonder what she did."

A sudden raspy scream blasted at the back of her neck. Terrified, she froze, unable to breathe. When the raven flapped out from behind her, it was still screeching. She watched in shock as it alighted on a nearby evergreen. Sucking in air, she fought to calm the pounding in her chest. So intense were her efforts that she did not notice the deep rumbling rattle of those breaths, nor the creeping flesh on her countenance. After a moment, things settled down. Then she realized she had dropped the cigarette. It was sizzling on the ice near her foot. As she stepped to kill the flame, the thought crossed her mind that what had happened to the nun might even happen to herself. "What if they're after me, too? Or Jeff?" The scenario grew worse as she continued to think about it.

Somebody called her back to work. She hurried into the building, but her plan was being birthed before she even shed her coat.

That night, back in the apartment on King Street, Angela pulled a letter out from her dresser drawer. She had received a note from Jeff only a couple of weeks before.

It informed her that after months of negotiations and delays and more negotiations, a settlement had been reached where he would not have to serve time, if he agreed to enter therapy to "take care of" his problem. He was living in a group home in the middle of Boston and that was all he could tell her. In fact, the purpose of the letter was to let her know he could no longer have any contact with her, or Delores, or even Arnie Donaldson, his stepfather. The letter contained an apology for everything he had involved her in and wished her well. It was mailed, sure enough, from the city of Boston, Massachusetts.

"But that doesn't mean Jeff is really there. It could be a ploy to throw me off the scent. They could very well make him 'disappear' like Sister Mary Catherine and if so, they could come after me next... if they are needing a cover-up of some sort." The next thought yanked her into yet another direction. "But if they're doing some kind of cover-up, they would have to include Delores... and then my dad, because he knows and so do all of the law officers in Chittenden County and the feds, besides..."

So, that didn't add up.

"The most likely answer is that it's the feds who are hiding her... probably from the mob. She must have become an informer, working for the government, that sleazy Sicilian." Still, there was no real proof that Jeff was actually in Boston, nor that he, himself, might not also be in on some FBI plot to hang the Mafia. The more she thought about it, the tighter the circle became. At last, she settled on the original plan hatched early that morning in St. Joe's kitchen.

She, herself, had to disappear.

***

On December thirtieth, John Courtney packed up the last of his belongings and headed for Montpelier. Before he left, however, he made a short detour to Essex Junction to take care of a couple matters. His first stop was to see Father Tom at the rectory. They sat once again in the little kitchen, having coffee.

"Word has it, the feds are mad as hell. They know Tony Dupree helped her sister get away." John was speaking softly. "But they have nothing to charge Tony with."

"There has to be more to it, don't you think?" The priest rotated his cup a bit. "I'd be willing to bet it's a scuffle between the FBI and the Mafia and the Mafia just won this last round." He rotated the cup a little more. "And, knowing there's kiddie porn involved, I'd have to guess that's what the scuffle is about."

"Well, if things run true-to-form, Sister Mary Catherine has a new identity and probably a new hair color, by now. And, even if our government finds her, Heaven and Earth will have to move before they can get her back into the States."

"My question is, what is it she knows that would make The Family whisk her away like that? Or... was it strictly an Italian family matter, meant to get her away from the garbage she had stumbled into? I mean, those two girls have strong family ties to the old country."

"I don't know, John. We may never know the whole story. All I do know for sure is Delores, Jeff, and Angela still have connections to all that garbage. If Sister Mary Catherine's disappearance is tied directly to kiddie porn, then those other three are probably at risk, also."

"Okay, but Delores is under constant watch. I think they are hoping somebody will make a move and she can finger them, or something like that. Jeff is in treatment someplace in New England and very much under guard. That leaves only Angela out there."

"Angela. Yes. That one worries me, regardless of the feds or The Family. She's already under siege, with that demonic presence."

"You're the priest. You tell me. Will she ever get rid of that thing?"

"I certainly hope so. Otherwise, it will continue to grow in power and eventually will take over. It will torment her until she dies. That is how those things work."

"I can't help but wonder... doesn't it make sense that Jeff would have a similar spirit? I mean, he was involved in that stuff a lot longer than her."

"He probably does. And unless he gets the right treatment, the same fate awaits him."

The lawyer sighed. "My god, man... can't somebody do something?"

"Well, we can pray, John. But remember, it has to do with the doctrine of *free will*. Each man is entitled to choose what road he will travel. God will not interfere with our free will." He was quick to add a caveat: "Of course, He will listen to other's prayers on behalf of Angela and Jeff. He doesn't want any of us to suffer at the hands of Satan's workers." He smiled softly. "So, there is hope, my friend."

"Ay-yuh." Johnny stood to leave. "But with all that evil and all the damage those three did, we know they did not kidnap Dicky Dupree. And you know what else? I don't think Sister Mary Catherine did, either. She didn't have the strength or the brains to do it."

"So, that leaves...?"

"John Doe... whoever he is."

The last stop was at the Dupree home, located not quite a mile north of the Village of Essex Junction. Colchester Road was covered with a light dusting of snow, but he pulled into the bumpy driveway without any trouble.

Three small shacks stood in a row, across the road from the railroad tracks running north and south between Colchester and Essex Junction. The shed-like buildings were located at the bottom of a short slope. Behind, a barbed-wire fence separated them from Indian Brook and a cow pasture rising to the top of a wooded hill. The Duprees lived in the dwelling at the north end of the row. He got out of the car and knocked gently on the door.

A skinny red-haired boy answered the door. When John introduced himself, the kid turned and called to his mother. "It's John Somebody!"

"Oh, come on in!" She was wiping her hands on a dish towel as she motioned him toward a faded sofa. There was a small Christmas tree beside it and something smelled good in the pot sitting on the tiny stove. The three children sat politely while John and Doreen talked.

"I'm happy to say I'm now out of the Air Force and working with my uncle's law firm, so I hope to have more time to work on your case. Of course, we are still in the search mode, but I hope we can get some answers before too long and I hope they will be good news."

"We've been praying," Lisa Marie said.

The little sister nodded her head in agreement, then added her own version of encouragement. "And we keep up our spirits by doing what Mrs. Hays told us to do."

"What's that?" he asked.

"Remember the popcorn," she said with a timid smile.

"It means to try and think about the good things that happened... before." Lisa Marie was using her teacher voice.

"Oh, I see." The lawyer was quietly impressed. "That's probably a really good thing to do." He checked his watch; it was time to get going. "So, I wanted to leave one of my cards, with the new contact number and address. If you happen to come across *anything*, you can contact me right away."

He handed one to Doreen.

"Could I have one of those, please?" It was Lisa Marie again.

"Of course." He handed one to her, then, seeing the faces of the other two, slipped a card into each of their hands. "We'll all work on this together, okay, gang?"

As he pulled the car back onto the highway, he spotted the three young faces peering at him through the one front window.

"Oh, God," he prayed, "help us to find that boy."

CHAPTER SEVENTEEN

Snow

Suddenly, it was 1950 and winter was hitting with a vengeance. The snow descended in silent, stealthy fallings, eradicating the edges of roadways and the lines where buildings met the ground. Footprints made in one hour were invisible the next and the frenzied swirl of the storm into the face of the hiker transformed the rhythm of his stride into a drunken wobble. Such were the travels of the three Dupree children on their daily walks to school in the village and the return trips in those gray January afternoons. They stayed close to each other as they traversed the partly plowed road and turned at last into what was their driveway, now under snow so deep it nearly plugged the tops of their boots. Inside the little home, they pulled off the scarves and mittens their mama had knitted for them for Christmas, shaking the snow onto the towels she had spread in front of the door.

On one particular afternoon, the trio settled down at the table to sip on hot tea, which had been brewing most of the afternoon: one tea bag in the aluminum pot perched on top of the little oil burner heater. It had sat next to the covered pan of peeled potatoes which had been placed there in the morning, to slowly cook for supper, as the heater warmed the house. It was one of the ways Doreen had managed to make things work financially... like the curtains covering the windows to keep the heat from escaping through the cracks of their frames. These window coverings were made from extra dish towels, hemmed by hand, and stretched across the glass on strings which were held in place by tacks on each end. They were, of course, kept closed to keep the heat in and so the lack of curtain rods was of little concern.

At the moment, the little family was huddled down, talking about the day at school and anticipating the mashed potatoes and white gravy that would warm their bellies before it was time to crawl into bed.

"Homework first," Lisa Marie reminded herself out loud.

As soon as that was done, Doreen turned on the little electric stove and quickly made the flour and milk mixture into gravy, adding just enough salt and pepper to make it interesting. She turned the burner off just before it was finished, letting the residual heat finish the job. Then she mashed the potatoes in their own steaming drizzle of pan water.

"Ready?"

Three plates were held up close for her to fill. But before she did that, she reached to the side and poked a fork into quarter-sized peach slices and slid them onto the cracked dishes.

"Ooo!" the children exclaimed. "Peaches!"

"Okay, but only a quarter of a peach, kids. That way, we can have the other quarter on our oatmeal in the morning, okay?"

While they were enjoying their store-bought canned peaches and mounds of mashed potatoes, she had another little announcement: She was now doing ironing for the lady across the tracks — "The one who works in Burlington at a department store" — and so there would be a little more money every week.

"That's good, Mama." Lisa's eyes were bright. "And next April, I'll be old enough to babysit, so I can buy my own clothes and maybe some groceries, too!"

"Uh-huh," her mama replied. "And maybe we can get a

car." She raised her eyebrows, reminding the girl there were bigger priorities than clothes.

The dishes were washed up in cold water and Ivory soap. Then the sink was wiped out. "Let me have them," the mother called out. Each child went into a bedroom and got into warm pajamas, then brought out their underwear and socks. A metal scrub board and the hand soap were brought to the cold water and each one washed out their own items, squeezed them dry, then hung them in front of the oil heater on the back of a chair. By morning, they would have fresh underclothes to wear.

There was time enough to listen to a half-hour radio show and then there was the brushing of teeth with baking soda and salt and slipping into bed. Sonny had his own sleeping bag on the floor of a tiny room which he called his own. The girls used a twin mattress on the floor of the room they shared with their mother, sleeping foot-to-foot, their heads at opposite ends of the bed. They whispered prayers before snuggling under the tattered, but warm, quilts.

Doreen pulled out the washed potato pan and filled it with water. Carefully, she poured old-fashioned oatmeal into it. Before she stirred it, she added a pinch of salt. Then she put the cover on it and placed it on the back of the oil heater. By morning, it would be piping hot and ready for breakfast.

At last, she pulled the string on the overhead light of the living area and slipped into the room she shared with her girls. The single cot was lumpy and it took a while before she felt the relief of real warmth. At length, she heaved a heavy sigh.

Across the room, two little girls did the same.

Despite the near-poverty lifestyle and the hovering memory of a missing child, a strong, comforting peace settled over the household.

***

The same crippling snowstorm was buffeting the city of Burlington, just eight miles away. Struggling city plows lost the race about three o'clock that afternoon, leaving the transit buses on their own to complete their routes. By the time Angela left the orphanage after the supper hour, there were no more buses running. It was about six-thirty when she stepped out into the drifting banks along the sides of North Avenue. She moved slowly from one streetlight to another, until she disappeared into the darkness.

The Mafia would blame the feds and the feds would forever suspect The Family, but the fact remained... she would never be seen again.

***

"So, how do you catch a John Doe?"

"You go fishing." Sheriff Max Duncan grinned at Johnny Courtney's question. He had come to Montpelier on business, gotten snowed in by the swirling storm and forced to do a layover. After a cold sandwich in the motel, he had called the lawyer and arranged a meeting. They sat in Courtney's office, sharing a hot pot of coffee and leftover maple-glazed doughnuts.

"And just what does that mean?"

"It's done all the time. You put out some kind of public announcement to make the suspect spring into action... or a reaction, if you will." He wiped the frosting off his mouth with the back of his hand. "For instance, you imply that there is new evidence and you are closing in on a person of interest." He shrugged his shoulders. "It may not get a response, but it sure makes John Doe uncomfortable. Imagine the questions that come up in his mind: 'Did they find this? Or did they talk to somebody? Or did I foul up somewhere?'"

"Okay, I can see how that might work."

"It doesn't always get results. Some criminals are more laid back and don't take the bait... but, hey, we are at a stand-still, here. And," he gave John a knowing look, "I have campaign promises to keep... and this one was a big one."

"Right." John leaned back in his chair. "So, just what do you plan to do?"

"Your friend, Sophia, is still on a part-time employment status with the *Burlington Free Press*... a 'contributing reporter,' I believe. Do you think she would help us out with this?"

He felt the confirmation, deep down. "Actually, I think she would be very interested. She's writing a book on child abuse, you know."

"That's what I heard." He took a sip of coffee. "Also heard she's a damned good writer. I think she could pull this off." His eyes asked the question. "You think she could?"

"Ay-yuh... no doubt about it."

"Then I need for you to make the phone call that gets me that interview."

"No problem."

Sophia met with the sheriff the very next Thursday. They decided her home on Intervale Avenue would provide the most privacy. Detective Smith was there, but not officially included in the conversation.

"I want you to know," she whispered to Max, "that I still think Sister Mary Catherine was somehow removed by The Family. Are we clear on that?"

He nodded, knowing they were probably being recorded by the government. But his words came out clearly, to mislead any secret listeners: "This has nothing to do with Sister Mary Catherine. She is not part of this investigation any longer. Her participation is too far-fetched. She could not have kidnapped or murdered that boy. The fact that she has quit the Order and left town has nothing to do with this case."

"So... where has this investigation led you?"

"I have to be careful here, Mizz Pizzaro." A brief pause. "But I can say, we are hot on the trail."

"Really?"

"Really." He lowered his voice. "But we should start with putting out a call to the general public, asking for any additional information from anyone standing on that particular corner of Church Street during the time of the kidnapping. Just say we are looking for more confirmation of a new lead."

"Which is…?"

"We are not ready to disclose that information at this time. All we need is to hear from folks who were present at the scene. There could very well have been somebody who saw or heard something. We need them to come forward. So, give them this phone number and let's see what happens."

"If my boss approves the story, it should be in tomorrow's edition."

By Saturday, there were seven telephone calls to the Chittenden County Sheriff's Department, with "tips" about the kidnapping. The next day, the Sunday local news section featured another article about the "great response" the sheriff's department had received from the faithful readers of the *Burlington Free Press*. "We are getting closer," Max was quoted.

The following Monday, John called the sheriff. "What's happening?"

"We snowed 'em," Max gleefully announced. "It should be just a matter of time."

***

Lisa and Cee Cee were really thinking their mama had settled down. The cigarettes were gone and there were no more card parties. The girls kind of figured it was probably because the little family was now attending the First Methodist Church on Main Street in the village. A car picked them up every Sunday. Sometimes Mama went and sometimes just the three children. There was no Sunday school in the tiny congregation, but lots of hymn singing and the minister was funny and encouraging and it was a chance for lots of good company with other families, not to mention the sweets and hot drinks. And they always had a ride home, even though they probably could have walked. Indeed, Doreen seemed to have found some sort of peace.

But then, there was the funeral in February that changed everything.

Mrs. Tanner had lived in a rambling farmhouse across Hinesburg Road from the Duprees and the Turners, out there in South Burlington. When this dear friend passed away, Doreen made a special effort to attend the Mass at St. John Vianney. Mr. Wilson loaned her his car and the four of them arrived for the one o'clock service, slipping into one of the back pews. The children enjoyed the drama and the stained-glass windows, even though Mrs. Tanner lay stiff and pale in a shiny black coffin right up there in front of everybody. Finally, the chanting and perfumed smoke stopped and everybody moved slowly past the gleaming casket, filing at last into the reception hall. For a moment, the pale light of a February afternoon fell across the room; then the children felt a sudden warmth.

Long tables draped in white cloths were decorated with small vases of red berries from the shrubs surrounding the Tanner farmhouse, itself. Along one wall, the potluck was spread out in aromatic splendor. Ceramic casseroles displayed golden macaroni and cheese, tuna and noodles sprinkled with paprika, garlic mashed potatoes with crushed, crispy bacon sprinkled on top, and one extra-large one with luscious, fragrant spaghetti sauce seeping slowly into the slender noodles below. Large flat pans held such delights as scalloped potatoes and ham, homemade lasagna and even a hamburger pie, topped with thick brown biscuits. Before the children got to the desserts, they spooned up some home-baked beans that had shiny slabs of salt pork peeking out from the center.

"That's enough," Doreen cautioned them. "Save room for dessert."

The four of them settled into a corner table to enjoy the feast. At length, Lisa Marie looked up and surveyed the room. "Mama, do we know any of these people?"

"Well, you were all kind of young, but maybe you and Sonny will remember some of them." She pointed her fork toward a lady two tables away. "Do you recognize that person? That's Lenore, Mrs. Tanner's daughter."

The light went on. "Hey! I do remember her." She looked more closely. "And she's even prettier than I remember." Her eyes went back to her mother. "Would it be alright if I go talk to her for a minute?"

"I... guess it would be alright. Just be kind. Her mama is... in Heaven and I'm sure she is very sad, right now."

The almost twelve-year-old approached the table politely, waiting for Lenore to notice her. Someone stood up and gave the daughter a hug, then walked slowly away, leaving the grieving lady alone. Lisa moved in a bit closer to get her attention. When the woman's sad eyes beheld the girl, she tilted her head slightly. "I think maybe I know you. Is that right?"

She nodded vigorously. "I sure remember you, Lenore!"

"Okay... and why is that?" She was trying to match those familiar blue eyes to a face, but it wasn't working.

"You and your mama were really nice to me. I got to wear your dress and shoes and veil for my First Communion. Remember me? I'm Lisa Marie, from across the street!"

She reached for the girl. "Oh, my goodness... oh, my goodness, little Lisa Marie." She kissed her brow and hugged her again. "I can't believe it... little, skinny Lisa Marie. The shoes were too big and the dress was too big... oh, my!"

"But when I put on that veil, I felt beautiful. I really did.

And that day, I got married to Jesus, just like the nuns." She slipped into the chair beside Lenore. "At least, I felt like I did."

The young woman laughed softly, shaking her large, blonde curls. "It's amazing Mama kept those clothes; after all, I was almost eighteen when they got used for your First Communion!" She looked down at the red berries in the tumbler. "But then, that was my mama."

"I remember something else about you, too."

"Yeah?"

"I remember when we had the earthquake. In my house, we watched the dishes fall from the cupboards and break on the floor. We were so scared. But the next day, you and your mama came over to see if we needed to have some dishes to replace the broken ones." She peered at Lenore. "Do you remember that?"

"I do remember the earthquake, but just barely. What I actually remember was the lightning strike on the old oak tree between your house and the Turners. I thought it was the end of the world. Do you remember it? I mean, how could you not?"

"Oh, my gosh! Yes, of course I do! It was like the whole neighborhood had exploded." She blinked. "And there was a fire, wasn't there?"

"Yes. Oh my goodness, yes. It burned for a long time. We all thought it was the end of that historic old tree. But it survived, anyway, remember?"

"Yeah, I guess." She smiled shyly. "A lot happened after that. We moved. We ended up in the Children's Home."

There was brief silence at the table, before Lisa brightened. "I remember the time those four soldiers showed up in a Jeep to take you to the USO dance at Fort Ethan Allen." She closed her eyes for a second. "You had your blonde hair caught up in a net at the back of your neck, swinging back and forth in the breeze as you drove away with them. And you had on bright red fingernail polish and you were smiling as the Jeep bounced away." Her young girlish imagination revived that magical moment. "You were so beautiful." She opened her eyes. "I wanted to be just like you."

"Oh, honey," the young woman said, as she touched the girl's hand, "be careful how you see things… they are not as romantic as you may think."

"What are you talking about?"

"I… I married one of those guys, Lisa Marie." She gave her a stern look. "He died in battle only three months later." The grim smile on her face told the rest of the story. "We don't have a whole lot of control over the things of this world." The lips went tight, again. "All we can do is trust in God and try to remember the good times, right?"

Somebody came along to express their condolences and Lisa watched the mask once again cover the grieving daughter's face. It was time to return to her own table. She was halfway, when she recognized the young boy sitting there, talking to Cee Cee and Sonny. Young Joe Turner had grown taller and somehow softer in appearance, but the straight, black hair still stood out on his head like a clothes brush. Her steps slowed down as she recalled how this fellow had been Dicky's "blood brother" and accomplice in their many misadventures at the Home.

The deep brown eyes turned to greet her. "Hi, Lisa Marie. Remember me?"

"Yup. Yup, I do. What are you doing here?"

"Mrs. Tanner lived across the street from me and my uncle." He motioned to a man who was sitting across the table, deep in conversation with Doreen. "I've been living with him since my Aunt Ava died."

"He don't live in the Home anymore," Sonny informed her. "Anyways, things are going to be a lot different in that place." He turned to Joe for the rest of the story.

"Yeah, they are changing from a Home and putting all the kids in group homes or in froster care," the Abenaki lad mispronounced proudly. "Somebody told Uncle Joe that they're going to tear down the whole place. It has termites." He bent forward into the circle of young faces. "But Uncle Joe thinks it all started with what happened to Dicky." He glanced over at the two conversing adults. "They might even get sued by your mom and dad."

"So much for the Children's Home. I ain't gonna miss that place." Sonny was thoroughly satisfied.

But Lisa wanted to learn more. She slid her chair closer to Doreen and Joe Turner, with a loud scraping noise. The man, whose back had been toward her, suddenly turned around, coming almost face-to-face with her. In that moment, his pale eyes changed from curiosity to a strange, distant look. She stared back at him.

"So, you're Joe's uncle. I never knew that was you. You used to live next door to us. Do you remember us kids?"

The answer came through quivering lips. "I… do." He glanced at her mama. "So, we were all there at the Home, many times and never realized it, Dory."

"Yes," she replied sweetly. "Imagine that. It's a small world, for sure."

"So, they're closing down the Home, huh?" He glanced at his nephew, then affirmed it with a nod. "How come?" the girl asked.

"Just… changing from institutional life… to a more normal home life for the kids… I imagine." He pressed one hand close over his bottom lip, as if to control something.

"Too bad they didn't do it before they lost our little brother."

"Lisa Marie." Doreen lifted a calming hand, but it was too late. Mr. Turner arose from his chair as he signaled his nephew. He turned to bow his head politely to Doreen before he spoke: "Nice seeing you again, Dory."

"You bet, Joe. Take care."

The two Joe Turners headed for the exit, but before the door closed behind them, the older man turned and stared at Lisa. It was just a couple of seconds, but they were filled with a dreadful chill. She shivered.

"Mama, I'm cold," she said.

"Well, it's February and there's a whole lot of snow on the ground. Of course you're cold."

CHAPTER EIGHTEEN

Blackouts

On the way back down the road from the church, Lisa called out from the back seat "Mama, go slow past our old house, so we can see it." Doreen obliged and three sets of young eyes peered first to the right for a quick glance at the Tanner farmhouse, then left to their little place. A tired white picket fence separated it from the road.

"Same fence," Sonny murmured.

"We had flowers there, didn't we, Mama?"

"Ah-yuh, tulips in the spring and then purple irises in the summer."

"There's the big barn Daddy built." The boy was proud of it, even though the building seemed much smaller than he remembered. Still, it stood taller than the one-story house in front of it.

"We had a swing, right beside it. Daddy built that, too." Big sister glanced quickly to see if Cee Cee recognized any of this.

"That's our old house?" The little sister stretched across in front of her mother.

"Sit back, Cee Cee, before you fall. I can't see to drive." The child reluctantly obeyed.

Sonny leaned forward, peering intensely past Lisa. "We had a garden in the back and woods where we hid so we could eat the cookies we stole from the jar in the kitchen." He grinned at his mother's surprised eyes in the rearview mirror. "We snuck 'em into our pockets, whenever we had a blackout."

"What's a blackout?" Cee Cee poked her head over the back of her front seat, waiting for the answer.

"Turn around and sit down, young lady. You're going to fall, if you don't stop kneeling on that seat."

"Oh, look! It's Mrs. Turner's house," Lisa exclaimed, as they passed the brick structure. "I liked her."

"But what's a blackout?" the voice from the front seat persisted.

"It was during the war," her mother explained. "People had to turn off their lights and pull down their window shades at night, in case the bad people were coming in airplanes to drop bombs on us." The brown eyes were suddenly fixed on the Mama. "It was called an 'air raid.' They usually would come in the dark, so we turned off all the lights, so they couldn't see us. We needed to hide in the dark."

"Were we afraid?"

"Not really, because it never happened, but we practiced a lot, just in case."

The eight-year-old took a moment to put the picture together, then asked softly, "Have you ever seen a bomb, Mama?"

"Only in the movies, honey."

"So, just exactly what does a bomb do, anyways?"

"It's a big bullet that drops on you and kills you," the brother blurted out.

"Tsk... Sonny, that's enough."

The boy grinned again, then started his nose-picking ritual, to Lisa's great disgust.

Cee Cee slid over closer to her mother. The engine hummed as the car moved through the snow on its way back to Essex Junction.

Lisa laid her head back and thought about Mrs. Turner, standing there in her cozy little kitchen, while she, herself sat quietly enthralled by the fragile harmony of that place. Everything in the room seemed to be making music. More than once she had marveled at this strange, melodious phenomenon: A clock on a shelf above the kitchen table struck cadence with its pendulum, ticking along with Mrs. Turner's whispery-whistled melody. As she pressed clothes on the old, wooden-legged ironing board, the thudding slide of the small flat iron stroked a rhythmic accompaniment. Nearby, a pet canary's piccolo-tweets, interspersed with gentle bell-ringing, completed the magical ensemble. Lisa would listen for a long while, until, under the spell of this lullaby, she would slip into a peaceful nap, right there in the rocking chair.

Back in Essex after that long day, she lulled herself to sleep with this melodious memory.

But the next night, she moved from the comforting concert at the Turner home, to the inharmonious atmosphere of the Dupree dwelling next door. Again, it was not so much a dream as it was a hazy memory, coming on the edge of falling asleep. The first thing she remembered about the place was her parents' double bed was located in the living room, surrounded by two overstuffed chairs and a table with a sewing machine on it. She was sure there were other items in the room which she wasn't recalling, but that didn't seem to matter. In her mind, she saw the bed and then she felt herself moving toward the door into the kitchen. As she moved closer, sunlight glowed through a window over the kitchen sink attached to the back wall of the house.

Then she was in the narrow kitchen. To her right, a small table and chairs were pushed close to that wall, barely leaving room at the end of the sink for a back door. She was enclosed on her left by a small stove and refrigerator behind her and some cupboards in front of her. Between them, a door stood halfway opened, revealing darkness beyond.

She stood there, looking at the shadows inside the doorway. *"That's our bedroom,"* she finally thought. *"There's a double bed on the left, where us three older kids sleep and then a crib at the foot of it, against that wall, where Dicky's crib is and then there's some kind of dresser and then there's a door on the back wall of the house… what is that?":* She saw herself standing in front of it, looking at the doorknob with the keyhole underneath. *"Oh yeah… there's a toilet seat in there… that's all. No sink. No window."*

Suddenly, she remembered something else to her right, on that same back wall of the house. The toy box.

It was located behind the opened door of the little bedroom. She didn't recall any of the toys inside, but she could clearly picture the lid that closed down over the top of the large box and that was an unsettling memory. Still, she stood there, looking at it, waiting for something. It took a few minutes.

"It was night. We were all in our beds… but I woke up. I was afraid, because I knew there was a bad thing, a bogeyman, in the house. I sat up and listened and pretty soon, I knew that it was in the kitchen. I could hear it breathing, coming toward the closed door of our bedroom. I knew we had to hide, but I couldn't tell the other kids, because the monster would hear us… so, I crept across the space between the bed and the toy box and quietly crawled into that wooden shelter, pulling the cover down to protect me.'

"But I could hear it still coming. I could feel it slowly opening the door, then stopping and listening and looking. And then it slowly, slowly opened the lid on the toy box."

She cried out in stark fear.

"What's the matter?" she heard her mother ask from across the small bedroom.

"I… I just… have to go to the bathroom."

"Well, all right, but just don't be so darned noisy about it."

Unfortunately, the next night brought very much the same memory, except this time the creature came and Lisa Marie tried to hide behind the opened door and the monster paused, then slowly pushed the door closed to reveal her hiding place. She squealed in horror.

"What in the world is all that noise?" Both Cee Cee and her mother were awakened.

"Bad dream." She turned over and fluffed the pillow. "Sorry."

"Hmph," her mama grunted.

The hazy memory came for a third time the very next night. She had tried to think of something else, to fall asleep peacefully, but the images of that nightmare kept appearing. This time, she heard the dreadful thing coming out there in the kitchen, so she dropped down and rolled all the way under the bed until she pressed against the wall. To her horror, she saw the bottom of the door opening and stealthy feet coming to a stop.

Suddenly, the monster dropped down and peeked under the bed.

She screamed, pressing hard against the wall.

Doreen was shaking her. "What are you screaming about?"

"It's coming to get me... I was hiding under the bed, but it found me."

"Who's coming to get you?"

"I don't know."

"Well, nobody's in here but us three girls. You go get a drink of water and then you come back to bed."

The next morning, Doreen sat down beside Lisa Marie as they ate their oatmeal. "I remembered something this morning." She stirred the milk into her cereal. "When we lived over there on Hinesburg Road, I had to go pull you out from under the bed that one time."

"You did, Mama?"

"I did. And you were screaming your head off that time, too. Never did find out what was bothering you. I... don't suppose you have any idea what's so scary inside your head like that...?"

"No, I don't," came the soft reply.

Cee Cee, who had been listening from across the table, licked her spoon and made a suggestion. "Maybe you should ask God to show you."

Her big brother snorted. "It's just a nightmare."

"But I wasn't asleep yet," she objected. "I just keep seeing the same thing... something is trying to get me."

"Or maybe it's trying to talk to you, or something." The dark brown eyes were hopeful. "I still think you should ask God to show you."

Mama put her arm around Lisa Marie. "It sure wouldn't hurt, my girl. And it might not even be something scary. Try not to be afraid, okay? Let's give it a try. We can't have this happening every single night, for goodness sake."

So, they all prayed, right there at the table and the girl went off to school with a good bit of hope. In fact, she prayed several times that day, whenever she thought to do it and by the time she hung her undies on the back of the chair to dry, she was ready to get into bed and wait for God to tell her... whatever it was.

Slowly, she relaxed into the place of drowsy scenarios... the kitchen, the bedroom, the horrifying knowledge of something dreadful on the other side of the door. But this time, she stood right in front of the doorway and waited for it to open. It was not a long wait. She could feel something pausing on the other side, even though she could not hear the breathing because her heart was pounding too loudly. Her own breath froze in the back of her throat, as the door started to open, ever so slowly and quietly.

She closed her eyes, afraid to look. Then she felt the edge of the door pass within inches of her nose... and she knew it was open. *"I can't look,"* she thought.

It was like something blew air into her face. Automatically, she cringed, then opened her eyes to protect herself. Her hands were shielding her face as she let out a fearful whimper.

But nothing happened.

Slowly, she moved her hands apart and looked.

A tall, iridescent figure was standing all the way back into the kitchen, up close to the table and chairs. It stretched out a shimmering arm and pushed the back door open, then motioned for her to come forward and go through this rear exit from the little house.

"What is it going to do to me?" she thought. Then, as though on cue, the specter slipped out of the house, leaving the door wide open. "Shut the door and lock it," she instructed herself. Quickly, she moved to do just that, but when she reached the doorway, she took time to peek out to see if the ghostly thing was still hovering about.

There was an early morning light breaking over the garden, but the mysterious visitor was nowhere to be seen. Still, something drew her through the open door and there was an atmospheric shift; the hazy memory morphed into a full-blown dream:

Now she was in the garden and the sun had come up and it was hot. The dirt on the path between the rows was burning her bare feet, so she ran toward the chicken house where there was some shade. There she stood for a bit, cooling her warm soles and looking around. The chicken coop was actually no longer a chicken coop. She remembered that, for a little while, there, her parents had had an idea how to make some more money: Turn the chicken coop into a nice little dwelling and then rent out their — technically — one bedroom house. So, the two Dupree brothers, Andy and LeRoy, had made it into a pretty nice place, even though it had a three-holer way in the back, for a bathroom. It was actually larger than the house and was heated by a wood stove, which was installed, stovepipe and all, by the two men. Lisa recalled her mother wallpapering the living room and how her little brother was disciplined by sitting in the corner of that living room, where the irrepressible lad spent his time maneuvering a tiny bug in circles with his pointer finger blocking its way. But more than anything, she also remembered her mama dragging all four of them out of that structure as a chimney fire blew into full force. They had had to move back into the house, leaving their chicken coop "second home." Right now, in the haze of her renewed memories, the place was only a charred skeleton, with the offending stovepipe still hanging off a black beam. Behind it was the Turners' property, where a small barn sheltered a workshop and some chickens of their own and a cow.

A cow. A milk cow.

Suddenly, she was standing just inside the barn. It was like a theater curtain had been drawn open. A ray of sunshine beamed down from a window, causing the straw on the barn floor to glisten. There was the pinging sound of milk rhythmically hitting the metal pail. Mr. Turner was milking the cow with one hand, while embracing Cee Cee with the other, only this *hand was up under the three-year-old's little skirt.*

The nightmare stopped, as Lisa Marie finally clearly remembered… watching… helplessly. Now, no longer in dreamland, she was overwhelmed by the dreadful realization that — only minutes before Mr. Turner did that to Cee Cee — he had done the very same thing to her.

"It's true. It happened. I remember. I remember."

This time, she lay there silently, tears filling the twisted crevices of her face. The fury was great, but the shame was far greater.

She decided not to tell her mother.

But the next morning, she did remember that Little Joe Turner was living there, all alone with Mr. Turner and she wondered what was happening there.

CHAPTER NINETEEN

Pursuits

It was getting well into March. The Cakewalk Festival at UVM was over and so was the Vermont sugaring-off season. It was "mud vacation" for most schools in Chittenden County and there had been no significant leads developed by the sheriff's department concerning the disappearance of Dicky Dupree. The new sheriff decided to renew a few more contacts. If nothing else, he could continue the narrative that he was "hot on the trail." What he needed, right now, was a huge diversion... to fool both the public and the mysterious John Doe. He had to get things stirred up, but in a legitimate and professional manner. Of most importance he concluded, was the contact with *The Burlington Free Press* and that connection could be best accomplished by being a tiny bit controversial.

He decided to challenge the Roman Catholic Diocese of Burlington, which of course, involved the whole state of Vermont. All he had to do was to ask about the connection between the errant priest (whom he knew was now defrocked) and the missing child, Dicky Dupree (whom he knew was not really connected to that priest) and there would be a storyline that could go on for a few weeks... maybe a couple of months. It would be something he would lose, but it would keep his name in the news and that was what counted. So, on an early spring afternoon, he presented the idea to

Sophia Pizzaro.

"Oh, my gawd!" She shot a look to her sweetie. "This could actually work, Ed, don't you think?"

He leaned forward. "You know you could destroy your career, right? I mean, who wants to believe a county sheriff who makes wild accusations like that?"

"Oh, I won't actually accuse anybody of anything. I will only ask a lot of questions they can't answer and the dialogue should go on for a while. In the end, I will say our department is grateful for their cooperation and that we will be considering all options." He grinned. "It's called 'politics,' sir."

"So, you're really just buying time...?" The detective leaned back. "I guess that does work; I've seen it done before." He reached out to take Sophia's hand. "Listen, I don't want this lady to get in the line of fire, if you know what I mean. She has a book to write."

"Wait, this may fit right in with what I'm planning to write about St. Joe's," she smiled.

The sheriff's ears perked up. "You got something to write about the orphanage?" He licked his lips. "What do you have?"

"Listen, I don't care what anybody says... Sister Mary Catherine was in on something over there and so was Angela Donaldson."

"Like what?"

"I'm not sure of the details, Sheriff. But I do know both of them were in on the kiddie porn and both of them are now... missing, if you know what I mean."

"So, how can you write about something that has no ending?"

She smiled at the lawman, again. "You don't have to have a conclusion... only a set of facts that lead the reader to ask intelligent questions." She shook her shoulders in satisfaction. "There was a whole building of nuns — and probably priests

— who had to see the torn skin on the hands of those little ones and nobody… *nobody*… reported it." She pointed at Ed. "Not one, not one report, right, Ed?" She turned back to Max. "That is going to be in my book, in as much detail as possible… the photographic evidence, the convictions of the Donaldsons, the disappearances of Angela Donaldson and Sister Mary Catherine. Those are all facts. They are bona fide occurrences surrounding this whole situation and I intend to use them all. Who knows? Maybe they will bring something to light… some kind of justice."

"Um…" the sheriff wanted to make it perfectly clear, "my part in this story?"

She smiled again. "So, the story of the Chittenden County Sheriff Department's encounter, however unsuccessful, with the Roman Catholic Diocese of Vermont… well, that will make the story a lot more believable." Her eyebrows raised. "And so it should."

Within a half-hour, Miss Pizzaro had the next press release ready to drop off at the paper that evening. It was published the next day and the carefully orchestrated plan began to unfold.

***

It was the last Friday in March. Mud vacation was officially over, but the three Dupree children came from school to their front door, stomping mud off their feet before entering. Lisa reached up to push another loose shingle back into the siding of the house. The winter had been hard on the flimsy structure.

"I'm hungry," Sonny told his mother, who was rummaging around in her bedroom.

"There are hot dogs and beans." The reply seemed to come from under the cot, or someplace like that, so Lisa Marie poked her head into the room to see what her mother was doing. She opened her mouth to speak, but no words came out. Her mother was all dressed up in that red-and-white dress, only this time, there were high heels, instead of white socks and saddle shoes. Doreen was brushing the dust off the dress-up shoes. As she stood up, Lisa saw the powdered face and the red lipstick.

Cee Cee entered and gasped. "Mama! You look beautiful! Where are you going? Can we come, too?"

"No, no... you three will be on your own for a little while." She shook her carefully curled hair. "I have a date." Her blue eyes fixed on her older daughter. "Lisa, do you still have that little bottle of perfume you got for Christmas while you were in the Home?"

She was suddenly happy to see the hope in her mother's eyes. "Yeah, I do. I do have that, Mama." She drew it from the bottom drawer of the old dresser. "It will be perfect, Mama." She smiled. "You look so nice. Are you going to the movies?"

"No, just out to dinner." She tugged at her waistline. "Do I really look good, Lisa Marie?"

Again, the warmth of her mother's happiness touched the young girl's heart. "You are gorgeous!"

Cee Cee flew out to the other room. "Mama has a boyfriend!" she announced to her brother, who was sniffing the pan of beans and hot dogs. "Hey, stop that! That's for supper. Get your snotty nose out of there."

Inside the bedroom, the conversation continued.

"Just a dab, Mama. That's what Mrs. Hays told me. Too much is too strong." She stood back and watched as Doreen touched a little of the fragrance behind each ear. "Wow... you really look good."

The mother reached out to touch her daughter's shoulders. "Okay, this is the first time you kids will be on your own. Remember, I am trusting you to take care of things, Lisa Marie. I really need to know I can trust you."

"It's okay, Mama. We'll be fine. It's not like you're going to be gone all night. I'm ready to babysit. I'm almost twelve. You don't have anything to worry about."

She hugged the girl, then turned for one last look in the small wall mirror.

"So-o-oh..." the child asked with a girly-girl smile, "...who's the lucky guy?"

"Somebody I've known for a long time." She centered the locket at her throat. "We met again at the funeral last month."

"Oh yeah? Did I meet him?"

"Of course. You talked to him, in fact. You remember Mr. Turner."

A cold chill fell.

"Well," Doreen continued, "he called me this week and asked me out to dinner." She turned a big smile toward the girl.

"Stop it, Sonny! I'm telling Mama. That's not funny." His taunting laugh filled the living area. "Mama! Mama! Sonny is sticking his finger in his nose and sticking it in the beans!"

"Am not," the boy declared.

"Put the cover back on. Just put the cover back on." Cee Cee was desperate. "Mama-ah!" she wailed.

Doreen came out from the bedroom. "Sonny! Stop it right now!"

Astounded by the glamorous woman in front of him, the boy froze, his mouth wide open.

"I will not put up with this kind of behavior, do you understand?" the sweet-smelling goddess demanded. She moved closer. "Do you understand me, mister?"

He could only nod in acquiescence.

"Good," she murmured. Then, in a twinkling, she realized what had just happened. She tilted her head to one side, to let him know that she knew. "You're growing up, Sonny. You need to start acting like it."

The knock on the door brought things back to reality. As Doreen went to answer it, Sonny and Cee Cee sat down politely to greet the new boyfriend. Lisa Marie remained in the bedroom.

There was some chatter and murmuring as introductions were made, then the mother came into the bedroom for a final word with the daughter.

"Aren't you going to say hello to Joe?"

"No... I don't want to do that."

"Why not?"

She took a big breath before she said it. "You don't want to go out with Joe Turner, Mama. He's a dirty old man."

"Lisa Marie, how can you lie like that... just to keep me from finally having a date? I deserve a little fun and I'm going to have it, whether you like it or not."

At eleven o'clock, Doreen opened the door. She had walked all the way from the village, in a blowing March rain. Her hair was flat and wet, and makeup streaked her sad face. Only Lisa Marie saw all that, for the other two had gone to bed an hour before.

Mother and daughter quietly prepared for bed, with no conversation. In fact, the events of that evening would never be discussed in that little household. The sordid details would serve no constructive purpose.

But the girl began to really worry about Little Joe being alone with his uncle.

***

On a calm April morning, John Courtney pulled his day-old *Burlington Free Press* from the mailbox and started unrolling it before he even reached the door of his apartment, a few blocks from the state capitol building. By the time he settled into a comfortable chair, he had already scanned the headlines. Even though most of the news was already several days old, the paper provided a crucial link with the general happenings in the Queen City. Today's edition held a good example of that — a short piece on the latest developments in the Dicky Dupree disappearance. It seemed Sheriff Max Duncan was now suggesting the possible involvement of the local Roman Catholic Diocese.

"There have been some very concerning developments within that sphere, including the disappearance of a certain individual who knew the boy before he was taken, then was employed at St. Joseph's Orphanage, just before going missing, themselves." The article went on to remind the reader that it was eighteen months since the boy was last seen at a Thanksgiving parade. Then it went back to the sheriff. "I want to thank all of your readers who responded to our plea for any information on this tragedy. These tips have been incredibly helpful and we are greatly encouraged, but we do need to check out any possible information which the Burlington Diocese may have. I am grateful for their cooperation. I'm sure we will get to the bottom of this, before too much longer."

John noted that the article failed to mention Sister Mary Catherine's disappearance. "Probably saving that one for the next snow job," he murmured.

He answered the jangling phone next to his chair. It was his uncle.

"Do I want to go to Chicago for two weeks?" He laughed out loud. "Does a cat have four paws?" He listened for a bit. "A seminar? On what?" He smiled. "That sounds great. Sign me up." He tilted his head to listen more carefully. "Really? They would put me up? Wow! No hotels, then." He was liking this better by the minute. "Oh, so they won't be there. Well, that's fine. I would be happy to hold the fort while they're gone. So, when do I leave?"

***

Doreen was shocked to hear Roy's voice over the phone.

"Ma is real sick. I'm here in town. Andy called me and I took the bus. Got here in twelve hours. I thought you might want to know."

She sat down slowly on the battered sofa of her Essex home. "What's wrong with her? Is she in the hospital?"

"Ay-yuh. At Bishop Degoesbriand. They're saying it's pneumonia."

"Okay… okay. Why are you even calling me about this? She hates me."

There was a brief pause. "I guess I thought you would want to know."

"Well, yes, but I don't know… just what I can do about it."

Another pause. "Well," he said softly, "I just wanted to call and let you know."

"Okay," she said yet again. The realization he was actually back in town finally hit her. "How long do you think you'll have to stay? Any word from the doctor?"

"He didn't say. But if I stay too long, I'll lose my job, for sure."

"Uh-huh." She was stalling for time. This situation needed to be thought through, although she wasn't quite sure why. "Um, tell you what. I need to think about this situation. Can I call you back, say, tomorrow?"

"I would appreciate that, Dory. Call me back in the evening, because I will spend most of the day at the hospital."

By the next day, she had a plan. All she had to do was to get into that house and see if her suspicions were right. If they were, Roy would have heard something or seen something revealing the presence of their son. She decided to go visit Roy that evening, in person. Surely, he would not stop her from entering the house.

It was six o'clock when she arrived. He was standing on the tiny porch. She was struck by how much healthier he looked this time… even handsome. She was glad the orange color in her hair was finally gone, although she wasn't quite sure why that thought was even crossing her mind. After all, she was on a mission to check out the house. That woman could have Dicky all set up in the attic, for all she knew.

He opened the door to let her enter first and she just kept going. He stood there, bewildered, as she yanked the door to the attic stairway wide open. She was halfway up before he found his voice: "Wh-what's this all about?" When she didn't answer, he climbed only high enough to turn around and watch her pulling open the storage area doors along the sides of the attic. "You trying to find something?" She didn't answer until she had slammed the last door shut and was motioning for him to get out of the way so she could descend.

"I need to check out a couple of things, Roy."

"Like what?" He stepped down into the living room. She brushed by him, heading for the basement stairway. He followed her. "Maybe I could help you, if you would..." She was already at the bottom of the stairs and moving quickly.

He stood at the top, listening to her pulling boxes and moving things around. When she got back to the foot of the stairs, the look on her face brought a twinge of worry.

"Dory? Dory, what's wrong?"

By the time she reached the top, her face was white and she was breathing hard. He reached to steady her, but she pushed him back into the kitchen. Her eyes were focused on the gardening shed that was visible through the back door window. She glared at him. "Where's the key to the shed?"

He shrugged in acquiescence. "Right behind you on that hook." As she turned to lift it off, he made one more try. "Doreen, exactly what is it you're looking for?"

The answer came from someone he hardly recognized. "For your son, that's what!"

Before she had made it all the way back to the shed, Roy had reached Tony on the phone. "Doreen's having some kind of breakdown. Can you get right over here?"

Tony almost ran the whole five blocks. She found him watching Doreen throw things around in the shed. Inside, the woman was shrieking. "Dicky! Dicky! Answer me! Answer me, right now!"

"You need to get her out of there," Tony said. "There are sharp objects in that place."

"Now that you're here, I will. I don't want anybody to think I was hurting her."

"You're not hurting her, Roy. Just get her out of there and into the house. I'll lock it up and be right in."

Although still not the bulky young man he had been when he married her, LeRoy Dupree was still a lot stronger than Doreen, so he swooped her up and carried her across the grass like she was a wiggling child. He entered the open back door and moved into the living room. By the time he laid her gently on the sofa, she was crying behind her hands. "Dicky... Dicky..."

He bent close. "He's not here, Dory."

"She took him. She's hiding him. I know it."

"No, that's not true. He's not here. Ma doesn't have Dicky."

"How do you know that?" Her hands came down to reveal a wild glare. "You don't even know your own mother. This is exactly what she would do. She's hateful and vicious."

"I don't believe that, either."

She sat up. "He's around here, someplace."

"Lie down, lie down." He pushed her shoulders gently back to the sofa.

She tried to sit up again, but he was holding those shoulders flat. "C'mon, just lie down for a little while, hon."

The woman lay there stiffly, for a few seconds before she exploded again. "Don't you dare call me 'hon.' Don't you dare call me that."

"So, what do you want him to call ya, Dory?" It was Tony and she was pouring something into a small glass. "How about 'Barbara Stanwyck'? I mean, this is quite the performance, I must say."

"What...?" The tear-filled eyes revealed a sudden

confusion.

"You don't really think Ma took Dicky. That doesn't even make sense. How did you come to that conclusion?"

"I... I figured it out. Nobody would ever suspect the grandmother." She sniffed. "She probably talked him into coming home with her, from the parade. He would have done that. Of course, he would have done that."

"Okay then. So did you find him?" She was stirring something into the glass.

"Not... yet. But he's got to be here, someplace."

"Hey-ee," Tony murmured as she waved LeRoy out of the way. "I bet I can prove to you that your boy is not here... not at all." She slipped her little round tush onto the sofa beside Doreen. "Here, you can sit up now." She was looking thoughtfully into the glass as she made an offer she knew Dory wouldn't refuse. "I can prove positively that Dicky is not here. I know that would put your heart at ease. But here's the deal." She took a tiny sip. "First you need to drink this all the way down."

"What is it?"

"Something that will settle you down and help you to think a little better."

"I... don't know," came the suspicious reply.

"So, do — whad-ever-ya-want." The Italian lady took another small sip. "I don't tell you what I know, until you chug this down."

"Uh, alright, I guess." After all, Tony had taken two sips and she seemed to be just fine. The drink went down in two tries, then Doreen wanted her answer.

"It's really very simple. If Dicky was anywhere in this household, somebody would have heard him. He couldn't eat or snore, or flush a toilet, or even pee in a pot, without somebody hearing him. Am I right?"

The mother nodded.

"Ma, herself, was sick and had to go to the hospital, so there would have been no way she could have hidden him somewhere else, either. Whad-do-ya think?"

"Ay-yuh, I guess that part is right." She felt the warmth in her tummy as she waited for the rest of the offer.

"The only other person who might have heard him, for the last three days is…?" The two women looked at Roy. He shrugged his shoulders and nodded his head. "Didn't hear anything, right, Roy?"

"If I heard my son's voice, or anything moving around, or whatever, why, I would have checked it out in a hurry, I can tell ya."

"Hmmph! This wouldn't be the first time you lied to me, LeRoy."

"Hey-ee! Give the guy a break. Don't you think he wants to find Dicky, too?" She addressed the man: "You want to find your own kid, don'tcha, Roy?"

"Damned right," came the solid answer.

A few minutes later, he helped a woozy Doreen into his mother's car and drove her to the dilapidated home she shared with their three kids. When he got her inside, he admonished the youngsters. "Your mama has had a bad day. She should probably go to bed."

He helped Lisa Marie guide the woman into the bedroom, where she lay down, sighed, and closed her eyes for a good night's sleep.

He spent an hour catching up with his children, then left before they prepared for bed. A short way down the road toward the village, he pulled over, sitting quietly in the car.

"They don't even have beds," he whispered.

***

The seminar was in May. Upon arrival, John Courtney tipped the cab driver and hauled his suitcase up the stairs to the front door of a handsome brownstone row house. It reminded him of New York's Bronx neighborhood, with the line of stairs edging both sides of the narrow street. Above, windows rose in broken columns, posted like lookouts in the sandstone wall of an expansive fortress. Here and there, flowers tumbled over the edges of a window box. He pulled the key from his pocket, noting the planters near this little porch landing were still empty. But then, it was still early for all that.

Inside, he noted the steep stairway leading to the upstairs bedrooms. Below, the narrow living room and kitchen of the first floor were pleasant, the décor being definitely of African background. Oil paintings on the walls depicted elaborate renditions of elephants, lions, antelope, and other wildlife, wrapped in primitive versions of greenery found in that region. A bowl sculpted with colorful fruit around its exterior was centered on the large kitchen table.

"Whoa," he commented. "This is like being in a museum."

As he hauled the suitcase up the stairs, he noted more paintings... these all being portraits of people of golden and deep brown color, garbed in native dress. At the top landing, the young lawyer surmised with a smile that these folks were probably Negroes and wealthy ones at that.

"Hosted by successful Negro Americans." He smiled even wider. "Cool...!" Suddenly, he had a new respect for his Vermonter-uncle, who had friends in high places and they weren't just run-of-the-mill politicians. They were special... a quiet planting of things yet to materialize in American government.

He chose the room looking out on the street and carefully unpacked. Before he turned in that night, he scanned the seminar schedule. Registration check-in wasn't until four the next afternoon.

There would be a little time to check out the park the cab had passed as they approached the townhouse. "Maybe I can get into some real running," he whispered.

The young man would be running, alright... into a real surprise.

"No, wait. You haven't even finished your first classes. You don't get a grant that fast. What happened?"

"I didn't say I had a grant, Ed. I only said I'm going to England in July."

She reached over to pat his hand. "Gosh, I didn't think you would be so shocked."

"Well, we... we have a thing going, here, you and me." He looked away, then back. "I thought we had more time."

"So did I. At least until yesterday, I thought we had at least six more months to be together." Sophia's lips pinched together and released quickly. "It just happened so fast."

"You gonna let me in on the details?"

She snuggled up to him on the sofa. "I would have told you sooner, but I honestly didn't think it would actually happen." The lovely head moved gently to his shoulder. "It's almost like a fairytale: I'm sitting in the library and one of my profs spots me and makes a beeline right over to the chair beside me. 'Miss Pizzaro,' he says, 'just the gal I need to see.' So, then he tells me about this couple he knows, who are interested in my book project. It seems they lost a nephew who was abused at an institution in England. Murdered by a housemaster, or something. My prof had told them what I was doing and they immediately requested a meeting with me." She laughed softly. "Imagine that, bambino. Somebody requested a meeting with this chubby Italian reporter."

"Stop that," he muttered as he kissed her on the crown of her head.

"Anyway, we met a few days later. They seem to be quite nice, but suffering from a lot of guilt, because they could have taken the boy into their home but chose not to... and the poor kid gets killed. You can imagine. Or maybe we really can't. But they asked a lot of questions, then told me they would get back to me. I sorta figured that was the end of it, you-know-whad-I-mean?" The mob talk slipped out once again, reminding him of how much he loved that.

"Sure. So, how long before you heard from them?"

"Don't really remember, because I shoved it out of my mind. We do that, don't we?" She lifted her hands to ask it: "Why do we do that, Ed?"

"Don't know, hon."

"So, anyway, it was a phone call. I met with them and they told me they would like to sponsor me while I do research in England. Sponsor me! Who does that, bambino? I'm telling you, you coulda knocked me over with a feather, you-know-whad-I-mean?" She turned for confirmation, her eyes wide over the flushed cheeks. The excitement lit up her whole face. He thought he had never seen her so beautiful.

"Okay, but what does that mean? What is a sponsorship? How do you live over there? You need a place to rent and money for food and whatever else…?"

She sat straight up, numbering things off on her fingers. "I will be staying in a caretaker's cottage on the grounds of a manor belonging to one of their friends. The caretaker married a woman with four kids and moved into a nearby hamlet or something, so the cottage is open. It has two bedrooms and a fireplace, and it's made of stone and has flowers around it in the summertime. This couple, the Taylors, will be providing me with a monthly stipend for a year so I can eat and buy a bicycle or whad-ever I need to get to interviews or whad-ever and I only need to do two things: Report to them on a monthly basis and pay half of my fare to get there. I guess they figure if I put a little of my own sweat into it, I'll be pretty faithful to come across with some good work. At the end of the year, I get an evaluation and we will go from there." She looked at him. "Whad-do-ya-think?"

The sigh escaped before he could stifle it. "I think you need to have me do some checking on these people. If they are genuine, then you have truly been blessed, Sophia. You can't pass this up."

She hugged him. "Thank you, thank you, thank you. How long before you can clear them?"

"I need your professor's name. We'll start there. But we should know in a week or so." He grinned. "After all, I *am* a detective."

The Taylors checked out. Not only could they do all that, they could have done it for a dozen other writers and still had enough in the bank to buy half of Burlington. When Ed delivered the news to her, Sophia began to tear up. "So, I'm really going."

He couldn't even reply. Instead, he reached for her, holding on as though he had received a death sentence.

***

The little park turned out to be a rudimentary ballpark. When he arrived, an early morning game was in progress, apparently part of a community outreach to some rather young boys. He stood there in his running clothes, surveying the two teams' "benches" — which were dilapidated wooden church pews with the backrests knocked off — and assessed the situation. The boys were probably six-to-ten years old, mostly Negro and dressed in T-shirt uniforms, one team in white, the other in black. They wiggled in anticipation at every pitch, reacting with screeches and taunts, being as much like their favorite professional as they could be.

"Hey, whitey-whitey-whitey!" they teased the batter. John looked more closely at that one and sure enough, it was a white kid, bent over and determined to send that laced-up orb flying to the treetops. The pitcher made the throw.

"Stee-rike one!" the elderly female umpire croaked.

He looked around at the attending crowd, where a few folks were sitting on blankets or folding chairs. Again, the onlookers were mostly colored, but he did notice a few Asians and whites, as well. The field, itself, barely made the grade.

The bases and home plate were marked by tin pie pans buried face-down at their proper sites around the dirt path of the baseball diamond. The pitcher's mound was an elevated heap of beaten-down soil. The ballpark fence simply did not exist.

Still, the youngsters were having a great time. "Hey, boy! Hey, Red! What happened to your 'do'?" The ball went whizzing past the befuddled batter.

"Stee-rike two!" The umpire held up her hand to stop the pitcher, then waddled over to the home plate, pulled a tired whisk broom from her belt and proceeded to sweep the pie plate clean. It glistened in the morning sun as she laboriously returned to her position behind the catcher. Immediately, the redheaded kid stepped forward for the final pitch.

"Ooo-oo-oo! You gonna hit that pretty little ball, Paleface?" The laughter rang out. "You gonna hit it, or not?" The pitch came and the batter swung with all his might.

The ball went into a high, backward fly, hidden in the morning sun's rays, out of sight to the white lady on the blanket, who did not know to move out of the way. It came down hard and she fell to one side.

People rose and ran to help her, so John turned his attention to the shocked kid at the batters' plate. He ran over to comfort him. "Hey, kid! Hey! Hey!" He laid his hands on the frozen shoulders. "It was an accident, buddy. It was an accident." He bent down to look into the kid's pale blue gaze. "It wasn't your fault." The eyes seemed frozen and the mouth did not move. John looked around, trying to spot the youngster's coach, but most of the people were gathering around the wounded woman's blanket. He decided to keep trying to help, right where he was.

"Hey! Hey, young man. What's your name?" No response. "You need to tell me your name, mister." The light blue eyes blinked. "That's right. That's good. You can do this." He cupped the boy's face in his hands. "So, tell me your name."

"Richard," came the weak reply.

"Okay, Richard. My name is John." He let that sink in. "So,

you need to talk to me, Richard. You need to tell me what my name is."

The bluish eyes blinked.

"What's my name, Richard?"

"J-John."

"Good. Good job, Richard." He took a breath. "So, there's been a little accident here, right?" The boy nodded. "But it wasn't your fault. These things happen when we play sports, Richard. These things happen and we do what we have to do." He glanced over toward the crowd around the woman. People looked worried. "So, you and I are going to go over to that lady and see what we can do for her, okay?"

"Wait," the boy said. "She's... my aunt. That's my Aunt Kate."

"Oh, God, no."

A sudden tap on his shoulder was accompanied by a deep male voice. "Who are you?"

John looked up into the face of a deeply-colored man. He noticed the man had the same black T-shirt Richard was wearing. "Are you Richard's coach?" The man nodded, suspiciously. "Good. He needs you. I understand the ball hit his aunt." The coach nodded again. "How is she?"

"Unconscious and..." He shook his head slowly.

"Maybe I can help. I have some first aid training."

"Get yourself over there. She needs to breathe. I'll take care of the boy."

He pushed quickly through the crowd. "I know first aid." They parted and he knelt down beside the wounded woman. Her hat had been knocked off. Beneath waves of auburn curls, a purple lump was visible on her forehead. He paused, thinking she looked familiar, but she wasn't breathing and he needed to do something about that. Quickly, he opened her mouth and cleared everything he could from within. Then he pinched the nostrils closed and put his mouth over hers. Tilting her chin upward, he blew strongly, as deeply as he could, to reach her lungs, twice. With a swift shift in his weight, he pushed several times on the breastbone. The folks around watched as he repeated this procedure twice more. He did not notice the older folks urging the others to back off, declaring the woman needed air. Nor did he notice the tug in the back of his mind, as he worked, but on the third try, her chest convulsed and she took a breath on her own.

John stayed close — only inches away — and watched as her eyelids fluttered and then opened, revealing the beautiful golden-brown eyes.

The picture was suddenly complete.

"Sarah...?" he whispered.

CHAPTER TWENTY

Disclosure

They were having spaghetti again. Annie was dawdling over the meal.

"So, what's the matter with you tonight?" Tony waggled her fork at her girl.

Annie shrugged. The woman gave her husband that look.

"Cat got your tongue?" He took a sip of his beer.

"Just thinking."

"'Bout what?" He wiped the foam off his upper lip.

"Sister Mary Catherine."

"What about her? I mean, we know she's fine."

The girl dropped her fork into the noodles. "How do we know that?"

"Trust me, we know." He shot that look back to his wife. She leaned back in her chair before taking up the gauntlet.

"Don't drop your fork into the sauce like that. How many times do I have to tell you this?" She reached over and pulled the messy utensil out of the tangle. "Look at that mess." She continued the reprimand as she rose to lift a clean fork out of the rubber dish drainer near the sink. "Let me tell you something else, young lady: You don't have to know everything about this family. Not yet. Some day we may have more to say to you." She stuck the tines into the heap on Annie's plate. "But not yet." She bent close to the child's pout. "Not yet. You understand?"

"I'm not a baby, you know. I'm a teenager, for Pete's sake. You could at least give me credit for having a real, working brain."

He was smiling. "Oh, is that what you call it?" There was a quick nod to Tony. "So, there, Mama. Now we know."

"It's not nice to tease your children, Papa." She was pleased to put her father in his place.

He winked at her. "Especially your favorite ones, right?"

He had her, for a couple of seconds, there. But then she pulled the "frustration tactic." The fists came tightly up under her chin and the face scrunched into a ball of fury. The groan grew into a growl, which in turn, grew into a rant.

"You don't trust me. I don't think you will ev-ver trust me. I can't even get a straight answer from my own mama and papa. I might as well be talking to a couple of tree stumps. No, to a couple of bricks. No, to a couple of... of..." Now came the tears, gushing forth right on cue, to usher in a slimy nose-dribble, which plopped into the dinner plate.

Andy Dupree lifted his distraught daughter's head from over the tainted spaghetti and pulled her gently to the living room couch. "Okay, Annie, get it together," he crooned as he sat down beside her. "It will all be clear one of these days. You have to give it some time." He leaned in to murmur the plea. "You just have to trust us, honey. That's the key. Just trust us. We know what's best for you, believe me."

That was how Anna Maria Dupree confirmed that her parents had a secret... a deep, dark secret. And it had something to do with Sister Mary Catherine, for sure.

It was all she needed for leverage, something which would most certainly be required to tip the scales in her favor, for she had a plan.

Music Festival was coming to Burlington in a couple of weeks. The annual festivities always took place in May, and while it mostly featured concerts and theater presentations by high schools from all over the state of Vermont, the biggest event seemed to be the Music Festival Parade. In reality, however, the "in" thing for that whole week was attending private parties all over the city. That was the part of her plan which Annie figured would be the most difficult: She wanted to have a pajama party at her house the night before the parade... and she wanted to make sure the beer barrel would still be left in the kitchen. What with the successful histrionics at the dinner table, she was now reasonably sure she could accomplish this double goal.

She waited a few days before making her first move. This time they were having green salad and pizza. Andy had picked up the pepperoni delight from Bove's Restaurant on his way home from work. Tony added more mozzarella and popped it into the oven for a couple of minutes, then they sat down. Annie waited for her folks to each pull a slice, then reached for her own.

"It's Music Festival in a couple of weeks." She lifted the point of the slice to her mouth. "Not even two weeks, in fact." She bit into the cheesy goo.

"So. That is so nice. All that music. Maybe we can go to a concert this year. Whad-do-ya-think, Andy?"

"What kind of a concert?"

Her mouth was full, but like a true Italian, she answered around the edges. "Uh, I don' know... mebbee opera?"

"Uh-uh, Mama. They don't have opera. These are high school kids. What do they know about opera?"

Mama swallowed. "Well, they should. They should know what good music really is."

"What kind of music do they have?" He wasn't going to be hooked into an hour of drab droning, not even for Tony.

"Almost everything else and usually mixed in together in each concert. Like, they have a little jazz, a little classic, a little marching music."

"Marching music, eh?" He looked hopeful. "Do they have concerts with only marching music?"

"That probably won't happen. If you want all marching music, you should just go to the parade, Papa."

"Well then, let's just do that," he suggested.

Tony's face fell. "Or we can wait and check the schedule in the paper. They do have a schedule in the *Free Press*, don't they, Annie?"

"Ay-yuh," she replied lightly. But her lightning mind took the cue dropped by her father. "So, if we do just go to the parade, Papa, don't you think it would be nice to take Lisa Marie and Cee Cee and Sonny with us?"

"Oh my... I would think twice about that, Annie." Her mother was expressing concern. "Remember, it was at a parade that Dicky disappeared."

"Yeah, that's right. Your Aunt Dory may not want to go along with that."

"But Papa, those kids can't stop being kids. That's not fair." She reached for a second slice, but her mother pushed her hand away.

"Eat your salad, so you don't get pimples."

Annie never quite got the reasoning behind that statement, but this was no time to argue. Instead, she jabbed into the leafy dish. "Could I have more olive oil, please?" While Mama poured the oil, the wily daughter moved into the next part of her plan. "Well, how about this: We have them stay overnight with us, the night before the parade and that would give Aunt Dory some time to herself and maybe things would not be so scary for her. I have lots of space in my room."

She listened to herself chew as the parents thought it through in a moment of silence. "But not for Sonny. He's too big for that." Papa was serious.

"Oh... I hadn't thought of that," she lied. She chewed a little longer, before putting on her fake surprised face. "I know, Papa! You could take Sonny fishing up at the cabin." The gleam in his eye encouraged her. "I realize, it would mean you'd have to miss the parade."

Now, if there was one thing Andy Dupree loved, almost more than his wife, it was fishing. He dropped bait into water all year 'round, even ice fishing on Lake Champlain's frozen winter surface. Evidence of this addiction was stacked around all three walls of the Duprees' garage. The family albums were filled with photos of him fishing in Vermont, New Hampshire, and Maine. There were even a couple of locations in upstate New York. He was the quintessential piscatorial expert and he didn't mind that everybody knew it. So, why wouldn't he pass on a mere music festival parade? But he was careful about it. "You know, Annie, you may have something there. That poor kid hasn't had a papa around for quite some time. A trip to the cabin might be a really good thing. What do you think, Tony?"

"I know, Mama! You and Aunt Dory could go to a movie together that night and then us girls can all go to the parade together in the morning."

"I don't mind going to a movie, but I'm not leaving you three girls alone in the house."

There it was... the leverage spot. She took a breath and let it fly. "I am old enough to watch the other two. What? Don't you trust me?" They stared at her. "I turned thirteen in March. I'm old enough to babysit, for Pete's sake. Don't you trust me with Lisa Marie and Cee Cee? Or is it that I have to trust you, but you don't have to trust me?" They were still staring. "I can understand that you don't want to trust me with what happened to Sister Mary Catherine... but I can't understand why you won't even trust me to babysit my own cousins!" Then, just for good measure, she let her bottom lip tremble.

"You and Dory would only be gone a couple of hours, Tony."

"Yeah, I guess that's right."

On the Friday night before the parade, Uncle Andy picked up the Duprees from Essex Junction, dropped Doreen and the girls at his own house and left on the fishing trip with Sonny. Annie was disappointed that her big plan for a pajama party had fizzled into a mere overnighter with her cousins — other mothers refused to let their girls attend an unchaperoned event — but she still felt a burst of freedom. It was still a party and she was still the hostess.

The cousins were delighted to see the cheese and sausage platter prepared by their Aunt Tony. "There are cans of pop in the fridge, popcorn in the bowl, and ice cream in the freezer," she informed them. "And remember, no cooking." Then she seemed to have another thought. "We're going to make the nine o'clock show, so we expect you will all be in bed and asleep when we get back."

The young girls got into their pajamas and started a board game on the floor of Annie's bedroom. By eight o'clock, the women donned light jackets and headed out the door. "Remember, we are trusting you to behave and be sure you keep the door locked." Then the three girls watched the ladies walk down the long driveway to Monroe Street.

"Count to twenty," Anna Maria Dupree instructed her cousins.

"Why?" the other two chorused.

"They'll be down around the corner and we can really party."

Neither Lisa Marie nor Cee Cee even liked the taste of beer. They opted for the canned pop and the food and the board games. Annie only got to sip half a glass before she finally fell into the double bed with the other two. It was time to get some shut-eye. All that conniving for the last few days had truly worn her out. When Tony and Doreen returned home from the movies, all three girls were fast asleep.

The next morning, they arose late. The Saturday morning parade was scheduled to start at eleven o'clock. After a rushed walk, all five of the Dupree ladies found themselves standing on the corner in front of Abernathy's department store, at the head of Church Street. It was one block north of where Dicky had disappeared, only on the opposite side of the street... an unfortunate thing for Doreen, but necessary, since they had arrived late and there was no time to get a more neutral location.

Any apprehension she may have felt was soon washed away, as the festive banners and bands started the musical event. Flags furled, batons twirled, and snare drums rattled a happy staccato that stirred her weary heart. Sweat beaded the brows of the young bass drummers as they whacked the basic rhythm of the marchers, while hundreds of white tennis shoes stomped in obedience to the rhythmic beat. It was while the Enosburg Falls High School band was strutting past, that she felt the tug on her arm.

"Mama," Cee Cee yanked at the sleeve. "Can I have a balloon? There's a guy down there selling balloons."

"No, honey. We don't have money for balloons."

"Hey, I know that guy," Aunt Tony said. "The money goes for charity." She reached for her purse and pulled out three one-dollar bills. "Let the girls have a balloon, Dory. It's for a good cause."

A few minutes later, Doreen and the three girls were choosing what colors they wanted for their balloons.

"Hey, Lisa Marie!"

It was young Joe Turner. He was dressed in a frilly shirt, with a sleek red scarf tucked into the open collar. Lisa noted his hair was now slicked down, taming the clothes-brush tufts that had always been there before.

"Joe! What's going on? You come for the parade?"

"Of course. I wouldn't miss it."

Her mother was purchasing the balloons, so she pressed the conversation. "So, you here with your uncle?"

"Heck no, he had a bad time at the last one we went to... He grinned. "No, he didn't want to come today. He let me come with some buddies."

"Really? He didn't want to come?"

"Aw, it's kinda funny. Last time we came to a parade, he went to get ice cream cones for Aunt Ava and me, but walked into the edge of a door. Broke his glasses and cut his face. Aunt Ava had to wipe a big blob of blood off." He laughed. "I remember, she spit on a handkerchief like a mommy would get the chocolate off her baby. And he had to drive back to South Burlington without his glasses."

"Oh." She glanced around to make sure nobody could hear. "How are you doing, living with your uncle?"

"Good." The almost eight-year-old seemed surprised by the question.

She moved in closer. "Joe, um, we used to know him when we lived next door. Some things happened… in that barn of his."

The fear in his eyes distracted her. She didn't notice her cousin sauntering toward them.

"He was… touching us kids." She saw that he knew what she was talking about. "I… hope… that's not happening to you."

"Nah, that ain't happening." He wasn't looking at her any longer. With a twist of his shoulders he turned to leave. "See ya."

"I heard that," Annie muttered. "You need to turn that pervert in. In fact, if you don't, I will."

***

The cabbie was doing his best to get to the emergency room at the hospital. Even though he knew she was seriously hurt, John Courtney was in no real hurry. He cradled her head carefully in the hollow of his shoulder and whispered into her ear. "Sarah, I know it's you. Tell me you know me."

"I'm being watched," she whispered back.

"Not right now. Please talk to me."

"The less you know, the better."

He helped her to adjust the ice pack on her brow, while his lawyer mindset kicked into gear. "Why? Are you a federal witness or something?" She turned to get closer to his ear, but the pain stopped her. "Nobody can hear you right now. Please tell me what happened. At least tell me what happened at the well."

"I fell in and passed out. Somebody yelled and I came to, but I couldn't answer. After a while, they were removing wood up at the top. I had only one loose arm to protect myself from falling debris." She paused to get it right. "So... a guy was lowered head-first to a few inches above me. He told me they were going to get me out, but it would be very painful. Asked me if I would object to taking a shot that would make me unconscious." She tried to laugh. "I couldn't say no to that, 'cause I was already in pain." Another pause. "Next thing I remember was waking up in a strange hotel room."

"How did they... how could they snatch you like that?"

"They must have wrapped me in that bag. I saw it in the room."

"A body bag," he concluded. "Of course. You were out cold. They could have had somebody identify your face, then closed it up quickly." He looked down at her. "Want me to hold that thing for you?" She let him hold the ice to her head, immediately rubbing her warm hand over the cold one. "I guess that explains why they had a closed casket funeral. You weren't in there."

"They must have told my dad that he didn't want to see... whatever." She stiffened. "I miss my dad. How is he?"

"Tom gets over to see him pretty often. He still grieves, of course."

"Aw, dammit. I'm so sorry to have done that to him."

"Well, can't change that. Life is not easy for any of us." He was still curious. "So, you woke up in a strange hotel room and...?"

"I'm only telling you this part, understand?" He grunted. "Anyway, that's when those two men started telling me I was going to jail for helping Jeff and Angela. They told me about Mrs. Donaldson, too. I didn't know about her. I didn't know half of what they told me. But the more they talked, the more scared I got." She shivered. "Then they told me that I wouldn't be prosecuted if I would be a witness for the government, whenever they got the case ready to go to court."

"The case against whom?"

"They wouldn't say. They just said I had a choice to make, right then and there. I had to pretend to be dead... lose my identity... be someone else for the rest of my life... because, even after the trial, the people I would testify against would come after me." She reached up to his hand to give it one gentle stroke. "I didn't want to leave my family — or you, for that matter — but I didn't want to go to jail, either. So... I agreed."

"So, they have you living with a family here in Chicago?"

"Oh, I imagine they will move me again; I have attracted too much attention."

"Okay, that probably will happen. So how can we keep in touch?"

"We can't."

"Sure we can. There must be some way."

"No, Johnny." Gently, she pulled his hand down and looked at him. He was shocked to see her eyes were bloodshot, but he could not look away. She was serious. "They would have to kill you. They told me if anybody ever found me, they would have to be eliminated, for the safety of everyone else involved in this project."

"There are others?"

"This is a lot bigger than it looks."

"Of course." He felt somewhat foolish. He was a lawyer. He should have figured that one out, when she first started talking.

"Alright, I have told you enough, Johnny. Now promise me you'll never tell any of this. If they can't trust me, they will eliminate me."

"But I don't want to lose you again, Sarah."

"You already have, my handsome friend." She laid her head back into the comfort of his shoulder.

Within minutes, the cab drew up to the door of the ER. The driver hurried around to open the door. John slid out and helped Sarah to move slowly across the seat and out onto the pavement.

"Kate! Kate!"

He turned to see a couple rushing toward them. The woman wrapped her arms carefully around Sarah. "Oh my gosh, kiddo!"

"Let's get her inside," the man said. He glanced at John. "Thanks, fella."

"Of course. You would have done the same thing, I'm sure."

He dropped down into the back seat and closed the door.

"Where we goin'?" The driver was looking at him in the rearview mirror.

He started to give the address, then felt a check in his spirit. "Back to the park, please."

"If anybody questions this cabbie, they won't be getting any addresses... or names of house guests."

Suddenly, he realized that he, *himself*, would have to be very, very careful from now on.

CHAPTER TWENTY-ONE

Spirals

John Courtney was back in his Montpelier office by the first Monday in June. The secretary at the front desk had several notes for him, concerning long-distance calls from a Lisa Marie Dupree, all of them "collect." He knew these had to be important, but his own desk was loaded with catch-up work, and he had a nine o'clock morning meeting with his uncle concerning the Chicago seminar. It was something he would get to as soon as he could.

She beat him to it. The call came in at noon and he accepted the charges.

"Hello! Lisa Marie?"

"Hey, Mr. Courtney. I hate to bother you, but you said I should call if anything came up."

"Of course, young lady. What can I do for you?"

"My cousin, Annie, said I should turn that pervert in, or she would do it, herself."

"Okay. So, who are we talking about?"

"That Joe Turner who used to live next door to us in South Burlington."

He sat straight up in the chair. "Okay," he repeated, reaching for a pad and pencil. "Has something happened?"

"Yes."

He signaled the secretary to alert his uncle. *"It might be wise to have someone else hear this,"* he thought quickly. He went into stalling mode. "Are you at school, Lisa?"

"Yes. On my lunch hour."

"Is there anybody else there with you?"

"Nope. I'm in the phone booth near the bus terminal."

"The Essex Junction terminal, right?" He heard the light click of his uncle's office phone being lifted. "Well, Lisa Marie Dupree, thank you for calling me. Now, I want you to just relax and take your time. Tell me why you have called."

At the end of the conversation the man had a page full of notes. He looked up at his office door as his uncle poked a concerned face around it.

"Lots of accusations, but no hard evidence. Somebody needs to put the screws to this guy."

"I know just the man who can do that," Johnny smiled. He had Sheriff Max Duncan on the line within the hour. The lawman was all too happy to comply.

Two things happened on the following Wednesday morning: There was another short article in the *Free Press*, featuring a claim that the law officer had narrowed down his search for the John Doe suspect and an arrest was imminent. "We should have this case wrapped up in a few weeks," the sheriff was quoted.

The other thing was the arrival of Chittenden County Sheriff's Department vehicles moving slowly up and down Hinesburg Road, one at a time, every two or three hours. They moved stealthily along until reaching the Catholic church, then made a U-turn and slowly moved back down to Williston Road, where they turned left and disappeared in traffic. By the time there had been three passes, the folks on Hinesburg Road were getting quite curious.

Finally, Lenore called from the farmhouse.

"Hey, Joe! What's going on, with all the sheriff traffic up and down the road? Have you noticed?"

"Ay-yuh, Lenore. You're the third one to call. I think we're all wondering, but we'll probably find out soon enough."

When he hung up, he walked into the living room where he could see the road clearly. He removed the morning paper from the chair before sitting down to stare out the window. Before long, the news story about John Doe was being tapped nervously upon one knee.

***

Ed Smith was surprised. "Yeah, I read the news article, but I thought Sheriff Duncan was blowing smoke again. So did Sophia. In fact, we both laughed about it. It looks like he's spooking the guy, to get him to slip up, or whatever."

John looked at Ed. "Meanwhile, it looks like Turner may have snatched the kid while pretending to go for ice cream cones. We think the boy was a handful and there was a struggle and the guy killed him by mistake, then had to cover it all up. You remember the photo of the father carrying the sleeping child? I believe it shows Turner without his glasses. And the mole on his cheek? I think that was a drop of blood."

The detective nodded, then turned his attention to Father Tom. "And how do you fit into all this, sir? I thought you were working with the Donaldsons."

"I was, but they are well on the road to recovery, if they keep their heads on straight and their hearts on Jesus." He wasn't smiling. "No, I am here to watch over the younger Joe, who lives with this man. I want to make sure he doesn't end up over at that orphanage."

"You can do that?" Ed wondered.

"I have a few connections. I believe I can find him a good home."

The three men were seated comfortably in Ed and Sophia's living room. Ed rose to gaze out the window at the flats of the interval below. "Yeah. That's good, Father. In the end, it's about the kids, isn't it?" He turned back to the other two. "You know, that's where we missed it. That's where we missed it in this whole case." The listeners waited.

"We never thought to interview the children. Never wanted to scare the kids, I guess. But if we had, we'd have known about the broken glasses and the molestation and who knows what else?" He shook his head. "We would have solved this whole thing in just a few weeks."

"Right," John agreed. "All we'd have needed to do is exactly what we're doing right now: get hard evidence." He touched his chin lightly. "Which reminds me, Ed. This is privileged information, strictly off-the-record. I trust the Burlington Police Department isn't taking Duncan seriously, either. We don't want them interfering with a premature move, or something."

"Hell, no. They think Max is being a clown." He nodded a reassurance. "That's the stand I take in the office and that's the only stand I will take in that workplace."

"Thanks, Ed. I knew I could count on you."

"Yeah, well, things are changing for me, anyway. I'm applying for early retirement."

John was shocked. "What? Are you kidding me? My dad loved working with you, Ed. You're a pillar in that whole Snoop Squad. What in the world are you thinking?"

"I'm thinking that in a month or so, Sophia will be in England, in a little cottage on some baron's estate, or something." He shoved his hands into his pants pockets and stared at the floor. "I can't really afford to follow her all over the world, but I would like to give it a shot. I have some savings. Honestly, I don't think I can even stand to stay in this apartment, once she's gone."

John suddenly thought of Sarah. "Mmm-mm," he hummed softly. "I hear ya."

"She has a couple who are willing to sponsor her as she researches for her book on child abuse." He went on to explain the situation to Father Tom.

"So… are you thinking of going with her… as her husband, I mean?" The priest's query brought an awkward silence. He broke it by answering his own question. "Surely, her sponsors would not take lightly to supporting both her and her boyfriend, would they? But they probably would accept a husband, don't you think?"

The wheels were turning, but he let the words come out, anyway. "Well, see, Sophia and I have this understanding. We love each other, but we don't want to hold each other back. She has her book and I have... to help people solve cases." He cleared his throat. "We love each other, but we don't want to get in the way of our goals."

The priest nodded. "I see... but then I also see something else." His brows raised politely. "May I point out something ironic?" The lawman shrugged an "okay." Father Thomas Ladue smiled brightly. "Don't you see it? Sophia is investigating and you are a — what? A detective!" His hands went out palms-up. "Where is the conflict in your goals, my friend?" He slapped his hands together. "You two are a great team!" He clapped again. "Stop fighting it! In fact, just marry this woman you can't stand to be without, would you?"

Ed was speechless.

John was grinning.

A simple wedding would be scheduled for the last week of June. Father Tom would officiate and John Courtney would be Best Man. It looked like something pretty close to a fairytale ending.

That night, John slipped into bed at his mother's house in Burlington. He would have to get back to Montpelier by nine in the morning, but he couldn't settle down. With another punch at the pillow, he laid his head down one more time.

It was Sarah. In the park, in the taxi. In a government protection program. In Chicago. In the role of Aunt Kate to a redheaded kid. A kid named "Richard." Richard. What a formal name, like Richard the Lion Heart, or Richard the Third. Who would hang a name like that on a little kid? No wonder they had nicknames, like Richey and Ricky and Dicky.

It hit like lightning.

He threw the covers back and jumped to his feet. "Oh my God, my God, no!" He took a breath. "No, Sarah, no. No... you don't have that boy."

And he knew he couldn't do one single thing about it.

***

By Saturday, the movement of sheriff's vehicles changed to passing by, turning around and then parking a couple of hundred feet away from the Turner residence... always on the opposite side of the street. The parked observers would watch for the approach of curious neighbors, then pull back out onto the road and continue slowly past the brick house, disappearing onto Williston Road.

An hour or two later, another vehicle would pull over, this time a few hundred feet past the house, again avoiding contact with any of the neighbors. It continued on Sunday.

On Monday morning, Joe Turner was pretending to work on the shrubs along the front of his house, where he hoped to get a better look at what was happening. Lenore and the rest of the local folks had noticed him out there and were keeping watch from behind curtains and venetian blinds. His body went rigid when one of the department's pickup trucks suddenly pulled into Lenore's driveway.

The woman, herself, was shocked as the vehicle pulled in, but she brushed her blonde curls back and quickly answered the knock on the door. Deputy Smith introduced himself and got right to the point.

"I'm sure you folks have noticed our surveillance of the neighborhood over the last few days, ma'am."

"Yes, indeed. What's that all about?"

"We've received reports of suspicious activity. I don't suppose you've heard we have been staking out the

263

neighborhood at night...?"

"Why, no!" The surprise was what he wanted to hear, because the department had not been doing any such thing. Just bringing up the subject and then denying it... that would do the job.

"Well, we haven't been doing that, let me reassure you."

"Oh... of course not." Her eyes revealed her doubts about that.

"What I'm really here for is to ask for your cooperation for a couple of days."

"Oh my goodness! What do you need from me?"

"We need permission to park in your driveway... for a couple of days."

"What for, Deputy?"

"We need to make some observations. I'm sorry, but I can't discuss any part of our investigation. This is a good location from which we can make some observations. That's all I can tell you."

"Well, I guess I could still get my car out, if you park over to one side." She looked worried. "Will you be here just during the day, then?"

"I am not sure. But whatever time we are here, we'll be sure to leave room for you to get in and out." He stood up to leave. "By the way, you're not expecting any company, or a whole bunch of people over the next few days, are you? We'll need to have a clear view of the neighborhood down that way." He purposely pointed in the direction of the Turner residence. "Don't need a whole bunch of cars blocking our view, if you know what I mean."

"Oh, of course, Deputy. That's no problem. I'll make sure nobody parks anywhere that would block your view."

Deputy Smith had not been gone two minutes before the first phone call came. Within the next half-hour, everybody knew the sheriff's department was zeroing in on something around Joe Turner's place and they had been spying on the folks on Hinesburg Road even at night... of all things.

The next morning, Joe Turner called Lenore. "I have a big favor to ask." His voice was unusually weak. "I hope you don't mind. It's just that things are getting pretty weird around here and the whole neighborhood is aware of things going on." She waited politely. "I hope you don't mind, Lenore, but I'm worried about what all this is doing to Little Joe."

"Of course."

"Ay-yuh." His tone reflected a sense of relief. "He's been having bad dreams and coming up with really off-the-wall questions and..." He seemed to choke up a bit. "I just don't want him to get hurt." Another choking swallow came softly across the phone line. "This would break Ava's heart. It really would."

"Oh, Joe, this will be over before we know it. Those cops will find what they need before too much longer. We only have to be patient... and pray, Joe."

"Oh yes! I know that's true. God help us, right?"

"Right."

"And that's exactly why I called you, Lenore. I know you are a woman of faith, for sure. And that's why I know I can trust your judgment."

She smiled. "Why, thank you, Joe."

"So, that's why I'm asking for a favor, Lenore." He cleared his throat. "I... I really need to get Little Joe away from the nonsense happening near my property. He shouldn't have to go through all that scrutinizing or whatever. He's just a kid, Lenore. He shouldn't be scared like this. Right?"

"Of course, Joe." She began to see what was coming.

"Oh, thank God, because I was wondering... I guess I was more like, *hoping* you might take him for a few days or maybe a couple of weeks and help him to settle down." He took a quick breath. "Of course, it wouldn't be on a permanent basis. He needs to get away from being under the magnifying glass. After all, he's just a kid."

"Isn't this a little too close? I mean, he can still see what's going on, even if he's not actually in your house." She offered another suggestion. "Maybe there's somebody in Burlington or Colchester, or even Williston…?"

"Aww, nuts. I know I'm being kinda selfish, here, but I need to be able to… give him a hug. You know, let him know I haven't abandoned him." There was a quick sniff. "He's had enough of that in his life already."

"Mmm. Ay-yuh. I see what you mean." She did a mental double-check. "So, it would only be for a little while. He will get to go back to you as soon as all this nonsense is over."

"I promise you. I don't want to lose my nephew. After all, he's all I have left for family."

Young Joe Turner moved in with Mrs. Lenore Tanning Curtis the very next day.

CHAPTER TWENTY-TWO

Splat

The knock on the door came sooner than Joe had expected. He opened it to the authoritative presence of Sheriff Max Duncan. As the early morning sun glinted off the brass of his badge and uniform embellishments, he flashed an official smile.

"Good morning, sir. Are you Mr. Joseph Turner?"

The interview was also a lot longer than Joe had expected. It made him nervous, even though the lawman assured him this was strictly informal and no notes would be kept. Mr. Turner was only being helpful in an ongoing investigation, which of course, could not be revealed to the public at this time. The questions seemed to be endless: "How long have you lived here? Who have your neighbors been all that time? Do your neighbors have any relatives in Rutland? How about Island Pond? Have you ever had a traffic ticket?"

"You should know that, Sheriff."

"Of course. You'd be surprised how many people we catch lying about that... and that tells us a lot about the reliability of the rest of their answers. You understand that, I'm sure. Yeah, you're a pretty sharp individual, Mr. Turner." He leaned into the next question as though it was a great confidentiality. "By the way, sir, have you noticed any unusual nighttime activities in the neighborhood?"

Joe was being extremely cautious. "What do you mean? I'm usually in bed pretty early, myself."

"Right. Well, this would involve very little noise, I'm sure. But I need to ask, in case you might have seen or heard something unusual."

"Nah, can't say that I have. Maybe you should ask the rest of the folks."

"That's an excellent idea, Mr. Turner." He rose to leave. "In fact, we will be doing that in the next few days." He adjusted the holster on his hip. "We intend to get to the bottom of the disappearance of Dicky Dupree and we won't stop until we do." He tipped his hat, then turned to go out the door. "Oh, Joe... I trust that you won't let that information go any further. You're a pretty sharp individual..." He grinned. "I'm sure you've already figured that one out, right?"

The older man faked a comradery laugh. "Yup, got that one figured out, Sheriff!" In the back of his mind, he was wondering if he should get a lawyer... which he couldn't afford and which would surely reveal his awful, terrible fear.

At the door, Max surveyed the neatly kept lawn. "Mr. Turner, let me compliment you on your front yard. All the shrubs and neat trimming along your cement sidewalk up to this porch. Not all people put that much effort to their lawns. I bet it is a real asset to the neighborhood." He took a step forward. "So, what do you call that shrub right there by the porch step? I think that would look real good in my backyard."

Joe couldn't remember, but promised to let him know.

"I appreciate that, sir." Sheriff Duncan stood still for a few seconds, seemingly to take in the peaceful setting. Then he took a few steps toward the street, before suddenly stopping. Slowly he turned and caught the eye of his victim. "By the way, Mr. Turner, do you own a cow?"

Less than a week later, Joe Turner suffered a stroke, while working in his yard. He was transferred to the hospital and then to a nursing home out there on North Avenue.

***

He was counting up all the people who had seen him last month. It was a challenge, but he thought he could remember all of those who had talked to him on the day Sarah had been hit by the baseball.

"The coach got a good look at me, for sure and all those people watching me doing first aid and then the ones who got the ice pack and the cab. And of course, the cabbie, himself. And what about the couple who rushed her into the emergency room? If they were trained agents, they took a mental snapshot of me, the cabbie, and even the name of the cab company… and probably the number of the cab itself. Those people know what they're doing."

Montpelier was simmering in the July sunshine, but John Courtney stepped up the pace, just the same. He had a one o'clock hearing that would not be kept waiting. All the homework had been done and he was ready, but even under the pressure of legal duties, the man just could not seem to let loose of this thing about Sarah.

"Lord, how did she get in so damned deep?" But the larger question was how he, himself, could ever do anything about this situation. "That kid needs to get back home to his family."

His uncle shouted from across the street, waving for him to catch up. As the two men entered the building, John pushed the problem back into its deep, dark hole. He would get back to it, soon enough.

***

"Well, she let go of the suspicion that your ma kidnapped Dicky, but now she's sure he's being held in a secret part of St. Joe's." Tony was crawling into bed.

"Mmm," her husband replied. He watched her pull the covers up over her nightgown's lacey bodice, before making the comment, "I think Dory is going through some kind of shell shock, like the guys coming back from the war."

"Think so?" She thought about that. "So, what about LeRoy? Think your brother is going through that, too?"

"Nah. He went through that when she kicked him out into a completely foreign working world. Poor guy had never done anything but farming. It was whatcha call 'culture shock' for him. That's what happened and now it looks like maybe he's come out the other end of the tunnel, you know?"

"So-oh, you think Dory can do the same thing?"

He snuggled up to wrap his arms around her. "Don't know. Right now, don't care." He was nuzzling her ear.

"Wade-a-minute." She drew back. "I'm really concerned, here."

"Do we have to talk about it, right this very second?" He nuzzled again.

She turned to face him, nose-to-nose. "Tell me when you and me are ever alone any more... except in bed." He pecked a kiss on the end of her nose. "I'm serious. No. Stop." His mouth was inches away, grabbing little kisses between her sentences. "We have a smart kid. Stop that. Nothing gets by her, I swear." She drew back to make her point. "Wade-a-minute, will ya? Just tell me, in private, do you think Dory is really losing it, or will she come out of it? What if they never find the boy?"

This time, he drew back. "She will come out of it, whether he makes it home again, or not."

"How do you know that?"

"Because you and I and Annie and a whole lot of other people are going to be there to help her, that's why."

"Oh yeah? You think so? You wouldn't be lying to me, would ya?"

"Tony, Tony, Tony... the only thing I lie to you about, is my fishing."

She smiled. "Yeah, that's true. You do lie about your fishing."

He pulled her close again. "Problem solved," he murmured as he snuggled into the velvet folds under her chin.

"Not really. What about the investigation?" She opened her arms only enough to release a scent of great possibilities. "They should have found him by now. Stop that. Don't think you can do me like this and not finish this little talk, mister." But this time she moved with his caress. "I mean it, Andy. Don't think you can brush off this whole conversation." He made another move. "And don't think you're gonna get... away... with... it... right... now..."

He got away with it.

***

Mrs. Bushey was on the phone with John Courtney's mother. There was news for her old friend on this warm summer afternoon.

"I tell you, girl, it was a shock. I mean, I suspected it was going in this direction, but the reality hit me right between the eyes at the meeting yesterday morning: the Children's Home will be a thing of the past within a couple of years. Yes, it will take that long. We have to slowly phase it out..." She closed her eyes to get the right answer to the next question. "It's mostly because they want to find the right home for the right kid, I think. But you know, that's the part that concerns me... the exposure to households that don't hold to the godly standards we have always had, here at the Home. Ay-yuh. Ay-yuh. Well, it's one thing to talk about letting go, but quite another to actually do that. I will remember these children for the rest of my life. Oh, thank you for the compliment." She smiled at the phone. "Of course! I'll see you on the first hole, the minute we get this whole thing done." She listened for a few minutes before she brought up the other subject.

"But there's more news. I guess they have Joe Turner as the number one suspect in the disappearance of Dicky Dupree. Oh, you already heard, huh? Yes, he is. It's a pretty nice nursing home, actually." Leona Bushey looked surprised. "Who, Johnny? He isn't? I don't understand. I thought he would be over-the-top about this." Her eyebrows went up. "Well, he's right about that. They don't have a body, alive or dead. Yes, he's right. Maybe we should all pull back and wait." She nodded in agreement. "Let's hope we get the little guy back, safe and sound. Umm, I think he would be about eight years old, by now... Yes. Yes, it is. Has been, for everybody. But you can be proud of your boy, my friend. He sure gave it his best shot." She smiled. "Really? Not giving up, huh? That's our Johnny!"

***

Detective Ed Smith was sitting in the Snoop Squad office, finishing up the paperwork for his early retirement. If all went well, he would join his new wife in England by the end of August. Somebody yelled to him from the other room.

"Hey, short-timer! You got a phone call."

He picked it up and immediately recognized Sheriff Max Duncan's voice.

"Got to ask you a favor, my friend." There was a short pause. "Just got word that Joe Turner is not doing well. That puts a whole new twist on our plans. We need to get a deathbed confession, to put it bluntly."

"It's that bad?"

"It's that bad."

"Well, I guess we'd better go for it then." There was a sudden thought. "Just you and me, right?"

"If we slip in and out before the big boys get a clue."

The two men showed up at the front desk, showing their badges even though the sheriff was in uniform. It made things seem more urgent. The facility director came whizzing out of his office and ushered them to room 104.

"We need to have the other gentleman leave the room for a few minutes," the officer said soberly.

When the door was closed and they were alone, the detective leaned close to the jaundiced face. "Mr. Turner, you have visitors." He waited for a response, then tried again. "Mr. Turner, you need to wake up and talk to your company." Again, there was no response. "Okay, Mr. Turner, you need to open your eyes and talk to us. We are the police."

The yellow lids flickered open. Pure fear shown from the pale eyes as they tried to focus. "You've had a stroke, remember? It's alright if you can't see us very well. We need to ask you some questions." He nodded toward Max. "This is Sheriff Duncan and my name is Detective Ed Smith. Do you understand this, so far?" The terrified man looked toward the ceiling and uttered a feeble grunt. "Good. Well, Mr. Turner, I think you know you are pretty sick, here, so we're not going to stay long or bother you any more than we have to. Do you understand that, also?"

A second acknowledgment puffed gently from the drooping mouth, so Max leaned in closer and spoke in a quiet voice. "We know there's a priest waiting down the hall. He's coming to give you Last Rites. You know what that means, don't you, sir?"

A quick breath shook the fragile chest and the man closed his eyes again.

"We're real sorry to have to bother you, but we also know that you wouldn't want to go… without getting that terrible thing off your chest, off your heart, off your soul. Am I right, sir?" Ed knew he was walking on thin ice, but the suspect was at death's door. It was now or never.

The sagging mouth drew back and a soft wail escaped. The two men waited until the tears started to emerge at the edge of the lids.

"Aw crap, Joe. You don't want to burn forever, do ya?"

Max was suddenly the man's buddy. "You need to leave with a clean slate, man. You really do."

"Joe," Ed begged gently. "Tell us what you did with the boy. Please, Joe. Think of Doreen. Think of the kids."

"It's a chance for you to leave on an honorable basis. No more lies, no more fear. Let it all out, let it all go. You have nothing to lose, Joe." Max reached over to lay his hand on the old man's limp, useless one. "Please, Joe."

The shriek came at the same time the other boney hand flew across the bed to slam into Max's shoulder. The sheriff knew instantly that it had been meant for his face. He rose up in fury. "You lousy 'perv'! We know you took that kid." He pinned the man's shoulders to the bed and yelled into his face. "Where is he?" He started to shake the man. "What did you do to him, huh? Huh? Huh?"

Ed was pulling the lawman off Joe Turner when the door flew open and the director came rushing in. "What's going on here?" Ed quickly gave him a reassuring scrunch of the nose.

"I've got this, sir." He pretended to comfort the officer. "You're letting this situation really get to you, Max. You know better. You're a professional." He turned to the nervous director. "Our sheriff has such a heart for the children. I trust you can see that." He leaned over the dying patient. "I hope you will forgive us for disturbing you." The growl that rolled out from deep down in the old man's throat was chilling. Ed was stopped cold in his charade. All he could do was stand there and stare. Max caught the same thing and froze, as well.

Then, the pale eyes focused, moving slowly until the look rested directly on Maxwell Duncan. It was glaring, icy hatred.

"You need to leave," the director murmured.

"Yes. Of course. Thank you for your cooperation." Ed was following Max out of the room, when he had a sudden idea. He turned around and asked the question boldly: "Joe Turner, did you kill Dicky Dupree?!"

As another low growl rumbled forth, the good hand turned palm-up and the middle finger jutted repeatedly into the air.

The following afternoon, the Snoop Squad gathered in Ed's office. "Joe Turner died early this morning. We believe he kidnapped and killed Dicky Dupree. However, we have no hard evidence. No body. No deathbed confession." He sighed. "Also, no other suspects." He looked around at the glum faces. "I am so sorry, gentlemen. I am so sorry. But... we have an unsolved case, here." His nostrils flared. "Helluva disappointment for all you hardworking Snoops and a helluva way to end my career."

***

John Courtney was relieved. He was sure Joe Turner had not taken that boy. The guy was a pervert, for sure, but he most likely had not been guilty of the disappearance of Dicky Dupree. After all, most of the evidence was questionable, when one got right down to it, because it was mostly coming from impressionable children. He recalled someone making the point in law school that children were excellent listeners, but they were very poor interpreters. A lot of damage had been done in divorce cases because children testified innocently, but erroneously. Besides, right now, this lawyer was pretty confident Richard "Dicky" Dupree was alive and well and probably living in Chicago... at least for a little while longer.

The problem was, he needed to find a way to establish that fact, without exposing Sarah or himself to any harm. *"And anybody else, for that matter,"* he thoughtfully reminded himself. If this thing was "a lot bigger" than he knew, he could end up sentencing a whole bunch of people to... elimination.

He drew back, mentally, to ponder that: *"What gave such powers to certain government agencies or even to organizations like the Mafia? Who or what had the authority to make such things happen? Whatever or whoever they are, they are very, very evil,"* he concluded. So, he knew he had to proceed with great care, if he wanted to get this boy back home. It would have to be a meticulously constructed case, with no possible loopholes. He would have to prove, absolutely, that there had been no murder... only a kidnapping. It followed that he would have to prove the boy was still alive. So, there had to be, first, the proof of identity. Was that young baseball player actually the missing child?

The evidence was overwhelming: the boy was eight-ish, had red hair, and identified Sarah as his "Aunt Kate." He had to know she wasn't really his Aunt Kate. He had to know that. The boy was also at a strange loss of words and confused about what to do, when the accident had happened. "He was so scared, he could hardly remember his own name," John murmured into the mirror where he was shaving. That fact had been bothering him for weeks. Why was the kid so damned scared? That wasn't normal. He didn't even cry. He just froze.

"*And his name was Richard.*" He revisited that thought, hoping to get a new insight. "*There is a nickname for Richard... Dicky. Everybody knows that.*" He wiped his chin with the hand towel. "*But there are still other nicknames. And he didn't actually identify himself as 'Dicky'... for whatever reason.*"

John pulled out the toothpaste and squeezed a white strip along the top of the brush. "Maybe he really *didn't* know who he was. So, what if the kid had been taken by somebody, if he had bumped his head and gotten amnesia? What if they had taken him to Chicago and left him in a bus station and he got into the social service system and they put him into a home? What if he was shocked into recall, from this accident and remembered who he was? And how does Sarah fit in with that scenario?

John realized he was supposed to be brushing his teeth. As he slowly began the ritual of front-to-back and repeat on the other side, the routine struck him as being very much like the repetitive reasoning involved in trying to solve the Dupree mystery. The only difference was, at the end of this task, his teeth were clean, while all that effort to solve the Dicky problem was never completed. He rinsed the toothbrush and hung it back in the holder.

"So, with the first task, I started with actual teeth and toothpaste." He looked himself in the eye in the mirror. "What do you really have to start with in performing the task of solving the Dicky Dupree problem?"

The answer was sobering.

"I don't even have an actual Dicky Dupree." So, he was right back to the proof of identity thing. He sighed. "Guess that's where I need to start. No sense in getting into the problem of 'eliminating threats' before I even know for sure that's really our missing kid."

"Hey, Ed! You all packed and ready to go?"

"Not yet, John. I don't leave until I get all the paperwork okayed."

"We need to get together before you go. When would be a good time?"

"Whatcha doing right now? Are you in Burlington?"

"I do have to be at the courthouse this afternoon."

"Come on over. I'll have a cold one in the icebox, just for you."

"Um… would you mind if I came over a little earlier? I have something you need to take with you when you leave and the sooner the better."

He was sitting on the sofa across from the detective, less than an hour later. After a bit of small talk, Johnny looked meaningfully at his friend. "Say, before it gets too hot out there, we ought to take a walk, for old time's sake. What do you say?"

Ed took the cue and the two of them descended the back stairs before striking out along Intervale Avenue, toward the Winooski Bridge. It was the ideal route for spotting walkers or vehicles that might be tuning in on this private conversation.

"So, this might be a bit of a surprise, Ed. It's important you don't stop dead in your tracks, just in case we are being watched." He glanced sideways to make sure the man got the message. He cleared his throat. "I think I may have found Dicky Dupree." He let it sink in for a few seconds. "Can't give you much more than that. But I need to make sure it's him. I need somebody to help me get a sketch of what the kid would look like right now, today. It's been — what? — two years?"

"Something like that, I guess. Too long." The detective shot a warning glance. "You in trouble, man?"

"Could be, if this gets out."

"Crap! You don't know who you're messing with, mister."

"Got a pretty damned good idea."

"Yeah, well." He asked the question, anyway. "What is it you need?"

"A police sketch artist who doesn't have a clue about this kidnapping."

"No such animal in all of New England."

"What do you suggest? Should I go to another part of the country? I thought these things were on record... you know, 'in the system'?"

"That's correct. The whole country is familiar with this particular case. No, you won't find what you're looking for. They would all know what you were doing and the word would get out, I guarantee you." He got a little smile on his face. "But I know a guy."

The relief was reflected in John's voice. "Aw, I knew you would find somebody. Who is he?" He watched his friend's mouth widen into a spacey grin.

"You're looking at him."

"What?" He came to a stop.

"Don't stop in your tracks." He pulled John forward by the elbow. "I started out as a sketcher on the force. Still got my art supplies. All I need is a photo and there is one in the files at the Snoops office. I can get my hands on that, at least temporarily." He motioned a right hand turn at the next intersection. "We should head back."

"How soon can we do this?"

"I can get the photo right away, this morning. Can you meet me at my place right after your courthouse appointment?"

John called in his report to the Montpelier office before leaving the courthouse. He arrived at Ed's apartment at three that afternoon. The art supplies were laid out neatly on the kitchen table. Ed reached over and turned on the radio.

The talk show was loud and funny, covering the whispered conversation of the two men. "We'll need to have this in color," John mouthed the words softly. Ed nodded and went to work.

Before heading back to the law office, John made a stop at the Dupree home out there on Colchester Road. The three children sat on the sofa, waiting to see what he wanted to talk to their mother about. She asked if they should leave the room, but the gentleman needed their help, as well.

"I have here a drawing of Dicky. It could be a big help if we knew what he might look like nowadays," he said, as casually as he could. As he carefully drew the portrait out of its folder, he attempted to soften what could be a bit of a shock to the four of them. "Now, this is only a drawing. It may not be all that accurate." In his heart, though, he was positive it was a true-to-life rendition of the baseball player in the Chicago park. He held it by the two top corners and turned it around for them to see. Their faces went somber. He waited.

"That ain't him," Sonny muttered. "That ain't my brother."

Cee Cee was troubled. "His eyes aren't right."

Doreen and Lisa Marie were nodding in agreement.

"What's not right? Can you be more specific?"

"Not the right color." Sonny was sure of that.

"Yeah," the three ladies chorused.

Doreen looked straight at the man. "Dicky has the very same color eyes as me."

John looked closely. Her eyes were a deep bright blue. He looked at the drawing. Those eyes, though accurately recording what he had seen in that park, were a very pale blue.

"Um… if, if these eyes were painted in a deeper blue, like yours, Doreen, would this still be a picture of Dicky?"

Lisa was shaking her head "no" before he finished talking. "The nose is too pointy. Dicky has a little pug nose. Even if he has grown up, it would still look like Mama's pug nose. They look a lot alike."

John drove back to Montpelier in a deep funk. "Bright blue eyes, pug nose… I would not have forgotten that, for sure."

It looked like this crime, whatever that was, was being laid right back on Joe Turner, and of course, he was dead. Indeed, there was nowhere else to go on this case and sadly, no happy gift of closure for Ed Smith, before he went off to England.

The tires hummed along the highway as the sun began to set on this late July evening. A cooling wind streamed in through the vehicle's open windows, bringing with it a calming sense of satisfaction. "At least I tried. We all tried. I only wish I could find one, single good thing to come out of all this."

It came to him like the soothing breeze across his brow: "Sarah didn't take the boy, after all." She was not guilty of that. Oh, she was on the run, probably for the rest of her life, but she certainly didn't have the boy. "Thank God."

But he wondered where she was.

CHAPTER TWENTY-THREE

Ripples

Time appeared to pass more rapidly after August 1950. Doreen and the children seemed to move on, although they held onto the hope of finding the lost boy. Things were better at home, especially since LeRoy furnished them with real beds. The girls loved the stacked bunks, while Doreen and Sonny each had their own real twin-sized beds. Those rooms, though a bit more crowded, were a real source of comfort in yet another aspect: LeRoy was actually taking care of his family. When he found work across the tracks at the Wilson Dairy Farm, there was a surge of hope in the three children that maybe, just maybe, they might have a daddy around again. LeRoy was back in his element, doing farm work and the Wilsons even provided room and board for him. In the evenings, after the milking was done, he would walk over and have a little time with the four of them. Slowly, Doreen began to look forward to these visits, even putting a little lipstick on before he got there. Sonny followed his dad around like a puppy with a new owner. But Lisa Marie and Cee Cee had their own little thing going. They were huddled out behind the house, looking down on Indian Brook, on this particular Saturday afternoon.

"I'm not doing Halloween this year," Lisa was saying. "I don't think witches and goblins and all that stuff is fun. It isn't. It's scary and I don't want scary things in my life anymore." Cee Cee rolled those eyes upward to watch her sister's face. "I found out there's another name for that celebration. It's called 'All Saints' Day.' Did you know that?"

"Nope. What does it mean?"

"Well," Lisa spoke slowly, "I talked with our minister about it. He says us First Methodists celebrate this day by being thankful to God for all the good people who have died for Him. He said we should be thankful for the ones we don't even know about." She inserted her own take on that. "I'm thinking we don't know about Dicky. I'm thinking we should be remembering Dicky on All Saints' Day."

"Oh-h-ho," Cee Cee said, sadly. "But isn't Mr. Courtney still looking for him? I thought he was still trying to find him."

"Well yeah, he is. I guess he is. We haven't seen him in a long time. Since the time he showed us that picture, remember?"

"Uh-huh. It didn't look much like Dicky."

"Right. I think Mr. Courtney was disappointed. Maybe he saw somebody and thought it was Dicky… I don't know."

"I don't know, either." Cee Cee shifted her weight on the old wooden plank separating their bottoms from the damp ground. "I don't like to thank God for Dicky dying, though. Maybe he's not even dead. It makes my belly feel funny."

"Maybe we should get back to doing what Mrs. Hays told us to do. Do you remember what she said?"

"Um, no. That was a long time ago."

Lisa shifted to the other cheek in order to look directly at her little sister. "How could you forget something like that? We were so mad at Mama, remember? She was sitting on that man's lap and she made us go to the bathroom and told us if we cried we wouldn't be able to come and visit her anymore." She waited for it to sink in. "When we told Mrs. Hays we didn't like Mama anymore, she told us we would always love her because she was our mother and we would have to forget and forgive. Remember?" She caught the glimmer of recall in those dark eyes, so she went on. "She told us to just remember the good stuff. That's what she said. 'Remember the...'?"

There was a quick breath. "Popcorn! Remember the popcorn."

"Exactly." The twelve-year-old sat back, quite satisfied with herself. "And that's what we need to do with Dicky. We need to remember the good stuff."

"But we still hope he'll come back home, Lisa Marie."

"Yup. But in the meantime, we need to remember... what?"

"The good stuff."

"Right. And so, I'm not doing Halloween anymore. I'm doing All Saints' Day."

"Okay." Cee Cee shook her dark hair decisively. "Me, too."

***

Before Christmas of that year, Joseph Turner's estate was settled. It was handled by John Courtney's uncle's firm, with John, himself, appointed as trustee. By January, the Turner home on Hinesburg Road became a rental and young Joe continued to live with Lenore. In addition, Father Tom, with the blessing of the local parish priest, kept a friendly eye on Joe's spiritual welfare. These two men often made their visits with Joe on the same day, taking those opportunities to keep their own friendship well-bonded. By the time another year had passed, the three were like family, with Lenore bustling around them like the proverbial mother hen. In the fall of 1952, Joe Turner turned nine. The two men enjoyed birthday cake in the middle of a dozen overactive young fellows, each and every one of which was armed with a water gun. John was still brushing droplets off his sleeves as he drove Father Tom back to Essex Junction. The mood was mellow inside the car as it moved along that hazy September afternoon.

"Well, they all had a good time," the priest murmured.

"They certainly did, and I have the wet shirt to prove it."

He glanced at his friend. "I think you wore clericals on purpose, so they wouldn't go after you so much. I mean, who wants to sin against a priest, for cryin' out loud?"

Tom grinned and looked out the window. After a couple of minutes, he remembered something. "You know what? Little Dicky Dupree would have been nine this year, too."

"Ay-yuh, I believe that's right." He waggled his head as he realized it. "It's hard to believe three years have gone by." He tapped a finger against the steering wheel. "And it still doesn't feel right, you know?"

"No, it doesn't, if you're looking for justice. After all, the old man died before we could charge him with anything. In fact, if he were still alive today, we still couldn't charge him."

"We don't have a body."

"Exactly. And that's what it would take."

"It really ticks me off, Tom. Not getting justice, I mean. You certainly hit the nail on the head. The reason why it doesn't feel right is because we have not seen justice served. And look what it's done to all those people involved. Especially the Dupree family."

"Have you visited them lately?"

"Nah, now that the father is back in the picture, I try to keep my distance." He shrugged. "Anyway, what do I say any more? I don't have a single clue more this year than I had last year." He snorted in disgust. "It's a big, ugly mess that sticks in my gut. I get so mad sometimes. It's like fighting an invisible, hideous monster. That thing is so real, I can almost smell it."

"I hear ya," the priest commiserated. "Did you know that evil actually has an odor?" The driver gave him a surprised look. "It's downright putrid, I can tell ya."

"I take it you've experienced this, firsthand...?"

He was nodding. "I have. It smells a lot like sulfur... or rotten eggs... more like a combination of those two." He laughed. "If it wasn't so evil, it would be funny to watch people scatter in all directions, to get away from it."

"Are we talking about demons, here?"

"Yes, indeed. Demons are the embodiment of evil, my friend, and they really do stink." He offered a small caveat: "But they don't always smell. Just now and then. I think they do that if they want to scare us more than usual."

"Man, you are forever surprising me! So, tell me about that. How did it happen?"

"There have been a couple of times. Once, it was that one occasion that Jimmy was getting delivered. You remember, he was young Joe's adopted father." John acknowledged this with a blink. "Well, when that thing was coming out of him, with all the swearing and filthy talk, this sickening smell filled the room."

"You didn't run from it?"

Father Tom laughed. "Nope. The exorcist didn't run, so us guys didn't run." He laughed again. "It was like we were all playing 'chicken.'" His voice went high, like a young boy. "I'm not running unless somebody else starts running first."

John's amusement subsided with a sobering observation. "Okay, that's one more piece of evidence that those things exist. I think you're making a believer out of me, Father Tom."

"I hope so, Johnny, because we are up against evil every single day of our lives. Those things are at work all over the place and all of the time. The atmosphere is full of them. You only need to look around you. In our case, we just need to look at Mr. Joe Turner." He looked out the window. "That man definitely had spirits of lust." He turned to speak to his friend. "I say 'spirits' because he was so deeply into perversion, there had to be more than just one. That guy was totally under their control." He cupped his hand to cover the small cough. "You have to wonder how he even opened that door, in the first place."

"Oh yeah, the 'opening the door' thing. How does that happen again?"

"Mmm. It's different for different people, but usually starts with some form of obsession. For some folks, it might be jealousy, or greed, or — here's a big one: hate. For others, it might be taking that first cigarette, or drink. It isn't taking that first cigarette, so much as becoming obsessed with smoking. Now, hard drugs are different, John, you know that. What you and I are referring to is, folks thinking about and doing what should be ordinary things... in excess. Obsessing about something. That is a wide open door."

"So, Joe Turner was obsessed with... little kids."

"The professional world calls it 'pedophilia.'" Tom shifted in his seat. "We Christians call it 'sin' and we know all sin comes from Lucifer and his demons."

"Wait a minute." He checked to see if the guy was kidding. "Are you telling me there is a real, in-your-face devil?"

"I am. You can find him in the real in-your-face Bible."

"Oh, I know. But I always thought it was just a figure of speech... like Hell and all that stuff." He shrugged. "I mean, if there is a real devil, then there would have to be a real Hell, right?" When his friend nodded confirmation, he went for the nitty-gritty of the thing: "Na-ah, Tom! You can't be serious. That stuff isn't for real."

"Do you believe Jesus Christ is real?"

"Of course I do."

"Well, in the Bible, Jesus talked more about Hell than He did about Heaven. I would say that's pretty good evidence of an in-your-face Hell."

The car came to a stop in front of the rectory in Essex Junction. Father Tom sat still for a moment, before turning back to his best friend. "Pretty scary stuff, huh?"

"I'm beginning to think so."

"But the good news is, you belong to Jesus, Johnny. Your name is, as they say, 'written down in Heaven.' Your ticket is punched." He took a big breath. "But now, perhaps it's time to start fighting all this damnable evil... like what happened to Dicky Dupree... but fighting it God's way, instead of man's way."

"And that would be...?"

"Recognize who you are, as a child of God and what power Jesus has provided for you to use against these rotten spirits. It's in the Book, my friend. Study it like you're taking another bar exam."

"Really?"

"Really. Because then and only then, will you finally find true justice."

"Is there such a thing, Tom?"

"Not by man's standards. The only true justice is God's justice."

"Do you think God will show us true justice concerning this Dicky Dupree thing? I'd like to know the answer to that one."

"He could, if it would help anything. But that's up to Him. Our job is to trust Him and try to see whatever good there may be in this whole situation."

"Good? Good? Is there anything good that can come out of something so bad?" The man wanted an answer.

"We can ask. And then give Him the chance to pull it all together. After all, God knows everything. He knows where that body is. And he knows what lies ahead for the killer."

"If that's true — and I want to believe it is — He also knows whether the kid is still alive." He sighed quietly. "I guess we just have to trust and wait."

"It might be easier, if you tried to get to know Him better. Why don't you give it a try, Johnny?"

That marked the moment Johnny Courtney decided to study the Bible. It wasn't seminary, but it was fine, because this time, he was absolutely serious.

***

Four months later, sometime toward the end of January 1953, the whole neighborhood out there on Hinesburg Road was surprised by another news article in the *Free Press*. Some real estate developer had purchased the old Dupree house and the land behind it — all the way back, to include the woods. Plans were being made to turn this area into a new street which would stretch toward the wooded area, where it would become a cul-de-sac. The real estate company was proposing the construction of five new homes and an updated sewer line that would benefit the whole surrounding community.

"Well, there goes the nice little neighborhood," somebody remarked across a backyard fence. "Taxes will go sky-high."

"Not to mention, the increase in traffic. We already have enough noise around here." The neighbor whined on: "I suppose we'll have more kids in our school, too. So, we'll need to make that building bigger and then who do you think is going to pay for that?"

And so, the murmuring continued. In March, another article indicated that the developer had finally purchased the land and paperwork was in process that would enable the project to move forward. Oddly, the public hearing was attended by only a couple of representatives from the Hinesburg Road community. They were sent home with a political hug and patriotic pat on the back. In April, the renters in the old Dupree place loaded their possessions into a couple of small pickups and left.

It was like the death knell.

But then, there was Sheriff Max Duncan, who was running for re-election that year. He approached the situation with his usual free-wheeling, charismatic jargon, not committing to one side or the other, but convincing a fair majority of those citizens that he would make sure things stayed safe and sane, no matter what life tried to shove down their throats. He was their man; he would handle it and he would handle it well.

Not too many people were remembering how unsuccessfully he had handled the disappearance of Dicky Dupree, because they were more caught up in this present crisis. For the ambitious lawman, this was the ideal opportunity to get back his reputation as an All-American hero.

So, the sheriff made careful plans for the months ahead. He made sure he would be present whenever he was needed during this whole transition, even offering assistance whenever there were traffic control issues during the road construction. Indeed, he progressed to a first-name basis with the developers, the construction workers, and the residents of the affected dwellings. Finally, he made sure to have an inside source at the *Free Press*, who would alert him whenever the reporters would be on site.

And then he waited.

The big equipment showed up in the middle of June. The old-time residents had been watching the surveyors and the flagging and the men with paperwork on clipboards, for a couple of months, but when the big trailers arrived, loaded with huge demolition equipment, they knew it was all over.

In the early morning hour, Lenore wrapped her arm around her foster son. "Don't worry, Joseph, they aren't going to take your house. It's not one of the buildings they'll be destroying."

The boy leaned into her embrace. "Yeah, but I would still feel better if Mr. Courtney could be here, just in case."

She was feeling a bit apprehensive, herself. All that noise across the street was not pleasant. "I... guess I could give him a call, if you want."

"So, they will be demolishing the old Dupree house, barn and... I think... a chicken coop or something. That's what I have, Lenore."

"Okay, but he's awfully scared, for some reason."

"Um..." the lawyer was thinking it through. "Okay, there could be more to this than we think. Tell you what... keep him away while they demolish that one house. It's the only one, according to my information. So, just get him into the car and go someplace, okay?"

She was beginning to panic, herself. "I… can't, John. The street is blocked both ways. I… we… can't get out of here."

"Oh, damn." She heard him breathing. "All right. All right. Where is he?"

"Out front, watching them move the, the big crushers, or whatever they are called, off the trailers."

"No-no-no. You need to get him inside the house." He was thinking quickly. "Listen, Lenore, go out there and tell him to come inside so he can talk to me on the phone."

"Yeah?"

"Yeah." When she didn't respond, he gave the order like the Air Force captain he had been. "Get out there, missy, and get that boy back here on the phone with me. And do it now!"

Very early the next day, both John and Father Tom arrived at Lenore's house. A call to the realtor the day before had put them on alert that there would be even more demolition than had occurred the day of Lenore's phone call. They stood on her lawn and surveyed what was left of the Dupree residence.

"Wow." The lawyer couldn't believe the change. "It's like there was never anything there. How did they get all that stuff out of there? It looks like a flat piece of ground."

"So, what are they supposed to demolish today?" Father Tom waited for the answer to his question.

"It's not so much a demolition, as it is a removal. They need to remove that old oak tree. The roots are in the way of the new sewer system and the widening of the new street entrance."

The old oak tree was, after all, a historic piece of that little community, so *The Burlington Free Press* sent a reporter to cover the story. This did not get past the Chittenden County Sheriff. He was there before the press even showed up.

"Hey!" he yelled to the two men on Lenore's lawn. "You're up before breakfast." He ambled over to do the handshake thing, then went into the politician prattle. He had not gone far, however, before Lenore came out to join them.

"Hey, Lenore." Father Tom was relieved to see her. "Sorry, but we wanted to get here as early as we could." He looked across the street. "So, looks like you folks are going to lose an important part of your local history."

"Ay-yuh." She watched the trucks pulling up at the base of the tree. "It sure didn't take them long to get to it. Look at that. They'll probably have it completely erased from history by the end of the day."

Another car came to a stop, right in front of the group on the lawn. It was identified as an official press car. Max Duncan moved toward it.

"Good morning, young lady. I am Sheriff Duncan and I am here to assist you in any way I can."

"I am here to cover the sad ending of a local historical site, Sheriff. I may need your help in clearing the way for some important historical photographs."

"Of course. I understand." He approached her and tipped his hat. "Let me start by introducing you to some of the tree disposal experts."

They had trimmed the uppermost part of the tree by the time young Joe Turner joined the others out on the lawn. He hugged the two men, gave a nod to the sheriff, then turned to view the scene.

"Wow," he said, as he sat down on the grass.

"Yes. Quite a production." The sheriff was very pleased with the situation.

"Kinda sad, though." The young boy's comment was nearly lost in the roaring rattle of the saws high above. He shielded his eyes from the morning sun. "How many of them are up there?"

"Only two," Father Tom replied. He turned to observe the boy. "Did you have something to eat this morning?"

The youngster lowered his head. "Nah. Not hungry."

"I tried to tell him," Lenore explained, weakly.

John Courtney stood to his feet. "Well, I don't know about

you, young man, but I am hungry as a bear. I need something to eat." He bent down to address the lad. "And I would appreciate some company."

"I could fix you some eggs," Lenore suggested.

"That sounds good." He addressed the boy again. "You need to keep your strength up, or I could lose my job." He gave Joe a meaningful look. "If I lose my job, I won't be able to come and visit anymore." His eyebrows pulled together. "That would be a real shame, Joe, wouldn't it?"

By the time the two returned out front, tummies full, the larger upper limbs had been removed. Workers on the ground were feverishly sawing them into manageable sizes, to be hauled away at the end of the day. Suddenly, somebody gave the signal and it was time for a break. The sheriff took advantage of the moment.

"Hey, Melvin!" he called to the project manager. "Come join us. We have lots of chairs and lots of water." The young man gave a couple of directions to his workers, then moved slowly over to slide wearily into one of the folding chairs.

"You're doing a great job out there," Max said. "So, what's next?"

Melvin wiped his brow with a dirty white handkerchief. "Well, we'll have to start chipping the wood from around the cement reinforcement at the damaged part of the tree." He smiled as he accepted the ice water from Lenore. "It may be a problem, because it doesn't appear to be a professional job." He took a long sip of the cool water. "Any idea who did that repair?"

"Oh, that would be Joe Turner." She paused to get the facts straight. "Yes, he did that at the same time he put in the cement walk on the front lawn." She laughed softly. "We were all watching, because it was so cold and we all thought that the cement wouldn't set right. But," she smiled brightly, "it did." She seemed satisfied. "In fact, we all thought it looked real nice."

The sheriff's eyes went wide. "Joe Turner put in that sidewalk?" She nodded. "When did he do that?"

"Ummm, all I remember was the cold weather. Maybe it was in November. It couldn't have been in December. Yes... yes... it must have been in November."

The sheriff pressed in. "He put it in all by himself?"

"As far as I know." She was curious. "Why? Was that illegal or something?"

"Or... something." Max Duncan caught the eye of the other two men. "Oh, my g..." He could see they were following his train of thought. "Yeah. Yeah."

Melvin got up to get back to work. "Thanks for the cool drink."

The three men stood there, all thinking the same thing. Finally, Max said it out loud. "That's where he hid it. That's where the body is... in the damned sidewalk." He stomped and swore at the same time. "Under the damned sidewalk!"

He turned to John. "I need permission to take up... the whole thing, if necessary. Can I depend on your permission to do that as soon as possible?"

"Of course. No problem. It's covered by law. We can get this done by late tomorrow."

But the lawman wasn't satisfied with that. He wanted to go over to take a closer look at the area. He telegraphed the message with one look, to the lawyer.

"Yeah," John said. "The tenants are not there. They elected to be gone when all this stuff would take place. We won't be bothering anybody." They were walking over to the Turner house as he spoke.

"Wait for me!" Father Tom was catching up, after sending Joe back into the house with Lenore.

The three men came to a stop at the edge of the walk touching the porch step. Max remembered the bush he liked, but Mr. Turner could not identify. "I think we should start here," he said. "In fact, let's just check the soil under this shrub, as long as we're standing here."

From there, they inspected the soil along the edges of the cement sidewalk, inch-by-inch, until their backs and knees began to ache.

Suddenly, Melvin was standing at the edge of the renters' lawn. His face was pale as he spoke.

"Sheriff, you need to come and check something."

"Okay, Melvin. What is it?"

"We chipped the wood away from the cement, and well, we saw something. You need to come look at this."

"Look at what, Melvin?"

The young man swallowed hard. "There's some little feet sticking up from the inside of the hollow that was cemented shut. Looks like it might be a small kid."

He had their attention.

"Yeah, it was a miracle we didn't just start smashing through the cement. We never would have noticed if it wasn't for the red socks."

***

Ed Smith watched his wife coming up the flower-lined walk to the cottage where they had been living for the last few years. He pulled the door open before she was even there.

"Hey, honey!" She was beaming. "I have some good news!"

He couldn't hold it back. "So have I. You won't believe it…" He moved quickly to his familiar chair, eager to share.

"I won't?" She dropped the heavy briefcase at the foot of his chair and gave him a light kiss on the top of his head, before looking around the small room. "Any tea, love?"

"What?" He wasn't even thinking about tea. "No. No, I didn't, I completely…" He started over. "I got an air mail letter today." Seeing he had her attention, he continued: "From John Courtney, the lawyer." He leaned forward, holding the envelope out for her to see. "They finally found Dicky Dupree and they know who the kidnapper was and that he…"

"Who was it?"

"Old man Turner, that's who!"

"Wow! All right, Ed!" She went into writer-mode immediately. "So, now you need to document the whole thing and that will wrap up that particular chapter in the book." She smiled. "What a lucky break!" She turned to find the little teapot. "You want a cup-pa?"

He really didn't like that she had adapted to the local lingo. He missed the lady who spouted "mob talk," back there in Burlington, Vermont. He missed being his own Snoop Squad person, right in the middle of the action. Nowadays, he spent more time tagging along, than leading. The discovery of Dicky Dupree's body was big news… really big news… and she just brushed it off as a finishing touch to one of her chapters. Like he never had anything to do with it.

Instead, she was telling him her big news: "…and as he was talking, I realized he was referring to that one orphanage over in the Dublin area." She pulled a cup from the shelf over the stove. "It was the perfect opening. I just asked if I could investigate that situation and he was all over it and I mean all over it. He couldn't wait for me to start." She wiped the cup with a tea towel. "So, I called the Taylors and they were thrilled at the opportunity." She turned, beaming at him. "We're leaving for Ireland, just ten days from now!"

He still couldn't believe it. Here, he had had the most important news in his whole Snoop Squad career and all she was thrilled about was another chance for a piece for her documentary. Her documentary. Her book.

His face fell and he leaned back into the chair.

A spirit of rejection descended over his soul, hovering about for the next few days. By the time he and Sophia moved into their apartment in Dublin, it had evolved into a dark cloud of resentment. Although he made a feeble effort to resist the overwhelming depression, the man eventually withdrew from it all by frequenting a local pub, where, on the very first night, he met a lady with a lilting laugh. Almost immediately, her hauntingly sweet presence controlled his every thought. The enchantment went on for days, seductively knocking at the very core of his being. Finally, one late night in a Dublin Park, he opened the door...

CHAPTER TWENTY-FOUR

Losses

"I know this is going to sound crazy," the priest said, "but I think Sarah may still be alive."

John Courtney froze in his chair, the coffee cup suspended in front of his face. His friend across the table took note of that, then continued.

"Just hear me out." Father Tom tugged at his clerical collar. "What do we really know? Who identified the body? How come it was a closed casket?"

The lawyer slowly lowered the cup to the saucer and cleared his throat. "I... I'm afraid I can't answer those questions, Tom."

"Of course not, man, but there must be somebody who can." He shrugged. "What about the guy who was sheriff before Max Duncan?"

John did not answer.

"What about the fact that they had some new guys doing the excavation of that well? Do you remember that?"

"Um... yes, I believe you're right." He squirmed in the chair. "But, are you sure about this? What makes you think she's alive?"

There was silence in the rectory kitchen as Father Tom collected his thoughts. Finally, he leaned forward. "For the last three years, I've been getting a card on or around my birthday. They weren't signed, but they were postmarked out of Chicago, Illinois." Seeing his friend's face pale, he sat back, watching the knowing look in those eyes. "What?" He tilted his head. "What? I know that look, my friend." He leaned forward again. "What do you know about this?"

"I don't know anything about any birthday cards, Tom."

"Fine. But you've been to Chicago, so what do you know?"

"I don't know a lot, but what I do know is that you could be getting in over your head."

"Like how?"

John stood to his feet. "I don't really know — but hey, how do you know those cards are even from Sarah?"

"What was her favorite color?"

"Um… aqua, I think. Yeah, it was aqua."

Father Tom reached inside his jacket to draw out two cards, both in opened envelopes. "I tossed the first one, so I only have two to show you. Here," he said, handing them over to the doubter, "see for yourself."

The Shelburne address to Fr. Thomas Ladue was neatly typed, but there was no return address. John slipped the cards out, one at a time. Both of them were mostly aqua in color. He looked at the priest. "That doesn't necessarily mean…" But Tom held the questioning gaze into his friend's eyes; he knew there was more.

"Mind if I keep these for you?" John asked.

"What for?"

"I'd like to keep them in my safe deposit box."

"I have one of those."

"I'm sure you do… but you don't want to keep anything like this in your own personal possession." He took a big breath, buying time to think this through. "We don't know what we're… or would be… might be, dealing with, here." The look in Tom's eyes intensified and the barrister knew the jig was up; he was going to have to get his friend involved, just to keep him from getting too involved. "Damn," he muttered. "Damn."

Although Johnny Courtney felt there was probably little cause to think someone might be listening, he asked his friend to accompany him on a short walk, where they could speak in private. By the time they had reached the top end of Prospect Street, he had filled the clergyman in on the details of his encounter with Sarah, almost three years ago. They strolled slowly back down the hill to the rectory in silence. As John headed for his car, he could only shake his head in resignation.

"We don't want to get anybody... eliminated, Tom."

"Nope, we don't." Before he turned at the start of the sidewalk to the front door, Father Thomas Ladue made one observation: "Sadly, her daddy — my brother — passed last year. Too bad you didn't at least let her own father know. It would have been a little easier on him, don't you think?"

"I would have put his life in danger."

"I think he would have happily taken that risk. But, that's water under the bridge. Right now, I'd just like to get Sarah back."

"We probably can't get her back, Tom. We need to deal with that. After all, we're up against some pretty big entities, here, spiritually and otherwise."

"Yeah, that's true, but the Bible tells me my God is bigger... lots bigger."

***

John was still thinking about the conversation with Tom, as he pulled into a parking spot in front of Strong's Hardware. One of the Burlington transit buses was moving out from the stop on the corner of Main and Church Streets, leaving a dark cloud of diesel smoke close to the sidewalk. A man waved it aside as he prepared to cross the street toward City Hall. Johnny recognized him immediately.

"Ed! Hey, wait up!" He slipped out of the car and waved.

The man stopped, grinned, and waved back.

"What the heck are you doing back in Burlington, man?" John asked as they shook hands.

"Aw, it's a long story." He was still grinning, but it was not genuine. "How've you been, John? Still with your uncle up there in Montpelier?"

"Yup, yup. Still doing the lawyer thing. How about you?"

"Back on board at the precinct... but as a consultant... I'm still officially retired."

"Back from England?"

Ed Smith nodded. "Ay-yuh. Like I said... a long story." He glanced at his watch. "I'm due to check in, but," he said, thoughtfully, "we should get together. How long are you in town?"

"Having lunch with my mother at Hotel Vermont, but I could get together after that. How about two o'clock?"

"Connie's Diner?"

"Great!" He slapped the detective on the shoulder. "Nice to see you, man!"

After a pleasant lunch with his mother, John decided to walk all the way up Church Street for his meeting with Ed Smith. "*Church Street*," he thought. "*Aptly named.*" The bright September sun reflected off glass storefronts to illuminate a traffic-filled aisle which ended, appropriately, at the foot of the Unitarian Church's cross-topped steeple. Amid the swirl of fall leaves, he made the right turn around the corner of Abernathy's ground floor and entered through the chromed door of the little diner. He spotted Ed in the back booth.

"Just coffee," he told the waitress, as he slipped into the seat.

In the next few minutes, he heard the whole story: Ed's disappointment with his wife, his infidelity, the decision to go their separate ways. At the end of it, the older man sat staring into the traffic passing by outside the windows. "So," he muttered, "we had — what? — a few years over there. That's all it took." He looked back at his friend. "We should'a stayed right here in Burlington. We'da been a whole lot better off."

"Hey, maybe it's not over yet. I mean, time heals all wounds, right?"

"Maybe so. Maybe so." He took a sip of coffee. "But not always, Johnny." His chin jutted out in determination. "Meanwhile, I'm back with the Snoop Squad and feeling appreciated. That's something."

"You living here in the city?"

"Ay-yuh... funny thing about that: I got back into our old place over there on Intervale Avenue." The forced grin came back. "Kinda weird, huh? Like living with a ghost."

"A ghost?"

"Yup. The Sophia who lived there with me no longer exists. It's like she died over there in Ireland." The grieving eyes glistened. "I had to get back here... before I died, too."

***

He left Connie's Diner with a heavy heart. Father Tom had talked them into getting hitched and now it was a marriage in shambles. Johnny didn't want to pass that information on to Tom, for sure. It would eventually come out, but he wasn't going to be in any hurry about it.

"He'll want to fix it; get the marriage back. Just like he wants to get Sarah back... and that's not going to happen." He was wondering just how many more losses this faithful man-of-God could take. A cloud front moved to darken the bright sunlight, just as he reached the end of the first block back down Church Street. He stood still a moment, adjusting to the sudden shadows and then he found himself staring across the traffic at the Sears and Roebuck store.

"Another loss," he said aloud, remembering the little boy who had gone missing and was not found alive. "Not to mention the loss to the whole Dupree family." He stood still. "And what about all that loss of innocence, at the hands of that old letch, Joe Turner? And the hands of the pedophile priest and his accomplices, Angela and Delores Donaldson, and yes, even Sister Mary Catherine?" He shoved his hands into his pants pockets. "Not one of them got punished for any of it," he muttered. "Where is the justice in all of that?" He shook his head in disbelief. "Where is God in all of that?"

He was getting back into his car when he suddenly remembered Angela's mother, Martha Donaldson. Just for the heck of it, he drove around the block to King Street, where he parked across from her apartment. A quick look revealed the tattered drapes were still hanging in the window. He decided on the spur of the moment to check up on her. It had been several years, but he was sure the old woman would still welcome him. He was already knocking on the door when he remembered he had no brandy.

"Yes?" The man needed a shave and he smelled like bleach.

"Uh... I'm looking for Martha Donaldson...?"

The black eyebrows moved above the glower. "You family?"

"Uh, no. Just a friend."

"Okay then. I'll just say it right out: they took her away to the nursing home just this morning." He wiped his hands on a gray towel hanging from the waist of his pants. "They had to do something; she was living in swill."

"So... who took her?"

"Social workers."

"Well, is she allowed to have visitors?"

"Won't do no good. She won't know you. She don't recognize nobody." He wiped his hand over the towel. "Probably just as well. She wasn't eating or washing herself, you know. Truth is, she was drinking herself to death, that one." He passed the other hand over the towel this time. "Really went downhill when she lost her daughter, you know?"

***

For the next three weeks, John Courtney did not sleep well. On that third Thursday, he found himself in his uncle's office in less than pleasant circumstances.

"I can't believe you lost this case," his uncle was saying. "What's up with you, mister?"

"I… don't really know." He shrugged. "Haven't been sleeping like I should."

"So… you got a girlfriend, or something?"

"Nope. Just got stuff on my mind."

"What kind of stuff?"

"I… guess you might say… moral issues, Uncle Doug."

"Sure you don't have a girlfriend?"

This time he laughed quietly. "No girlfriend. Just not seeing a whole lot of justice in this world."

"Oh hell, son, that's why we have lawyers." He had a sudden thought. "Is that what happened to you in court this morning?" His forehead furrowed. "You had everything you needed and still, you lost. I can't believe it."

"I can't believe it, either." His eyes telegraphed the regret. "I just don't know what happened. We need to give our client another chance."

"That's exactly what we're going to do, Johnny. We are going for a retrial and I am giving this case to somebody else." He pressed his lips into a reluctant smile. "I'm sure you understand."

"Of course. That's what should happen, here. I understand completely."

"Meanwhile, we need to see that this doesn't happen again."

"Yes, sir."

"You're a damned good lawyer, John, and I want you to get back in the game. But it looks like you need to take some time off." He tried to be cheerful. "Take a month off. Get some rest. Go on a vacation. Read a good book." He managed a real smile. "Maybe you *should* find yourself a girlfriend, huh?"

A few days later, Father Tom drove John to the airport out there in South Burlington. As they took the luggage inside, the two friends gave each other last-minute instructions.

"There's an extra car key on the holder in my apartment's kitchen. You may want to keep it at the rectory, just in case."

"Check. And don't forget, any phone calls have to be in code; those Burlington operators keep tabs on things that go on, especially with politics and church circles. We can't take any chances." The priest stopped and looked his friend in the eye. "For God's sake and for both our sakes, Johnny, be sure to pray all the way through this. Promise me."

"No question about it, Tom. We need all the help we can get."

"And all the protection."

Fifteen minutes later, Father Thomas looked up at his friend's face, tightly framed in the plane's window. He crossed himself, then signaled a holy kiss toward the lawyer. Then the plane took off for LaGuardia in New York, where John Courtney transferred to a flight headed for Chicago, Illinois.

He had one month to find Sarah… and maybe a girlfriend, at the same time.

CHAPTER TWENTY-FIVE

Chicago

This time, his house hosts were at home. The ebony-skinned couple welcomed John with open arms. "Your uncle saved our son from prison," they explained over a dinner of smoked fish and fresh fruit.

"Oh-my-gosh! He never told me that."

"Of course not," the lovely hostess replied. "Your uncle is a very noble man."

"Careful, Ariana," her husband cautioned, "we don't want to make gods out of nice people." He flashed a white smile. "What can we do with these romantic women, John? They make too much of just plain good folks."

"But he came all the way to Liberia, my darling."

Johnny noted the term of endearment, then addressed yet another surprise: "My Uncle Doug went to Liberia? What are you saying? That he knows international law?"

"Well, perhaps that may be an exaggeration." Steven Kamara cut carefully into an apple. "Let's just say, he got an idea that blew the case into oblivion."

"Alright! Would you care to fill me in?"

The couple smiled at each other. "We can't," they said together.

The gentleman sought to soothe John's disappointment. "But, let me say that we are so pleased you would come back to Chicago for nothing more than a vacation. Your uncle's phone call was pretty funny, though. He wants you to find a girlfriend."

They laughed together, before Johnny smoothed it over. "I guess what I actually need is to do some sight-seeing and a lot of running."

"You're a runner, John?" she asked, suddenly alert.

"I am. Big time, Mrs. Kamara."

"Oh, please call me Ariana, John." She raised an eyebrow toward her husband. "I think Steven may have a word for you on that subject."

He held up a wait-a-minute finger as he finished chewing and swallowing that bite of apple. "Uh… yeah. About that…" He poked the knife into the fruit for another slice. "We've been having some changes in the neighborhood, John. It's quite different from when you were last here." He held the slice up on the tip of the knife. "Got some bad elements slipping into the whole area… in fact, into the whole city of Chicago." He put the slice down on the colorful African-style plate. "Mind you, the political scene in this city has many blotches on its character… but now, we have these groups… these — I can't call them anything else — gangs of thugs and they are cropping up everywhere." He gave his houseguest a hard look. "It's not all that safe out there, especially in this neighborhood and especially if you are white." He picked up the apple wedge. "I am so sorry to tell you that, but I would be remiss if I did not."

The white man took a moment to think about that.

"So, I couldn't even go visit the little park just down the street? They used to have local baseball for the neighborhood kids." He looked first at Steven, then Ariana. Their solemn visages told him he was right. "But I was… looking forward to reconnecting with… a couple of… kids… that I met."

"They probably aren't even there anymore." Steven reached over to give a sympathetic tap on the younger man's arm. "Sorry, son."

Ariana perked up, trying to save the pleasantries of this

special visit. "Oh well, just never mind all that. Listen, you are here and we are here and we have a lovely chance to make a beautiful memory. In fact, a chance to thank your uncle, by giving you a vacation you will never forget!" She smiled hopefully at her guest. "What do you say, John Courtney? Shall we make a little bit of happy history?"

He nodded politely. "Of course," he said.

But he held little hope of even looking for Sarah, let alone, finding her.

***

The three of them were in a taxi, on the way to Wrigley Field, when he began to realize who he was staying with on his vacation. Although the two of them were today decked out in Cubs shirts and hats, the Kamaras' conversation over the last few days had revealed a much more cosmopolitan lifestyle. At first, it was just a word dropped here and there, then those words began to add up and pretty soon, the nephew of Doug Courtney began to put two-and-two together: the Kamaras were on the staff of the Ambassador to Liberia.

"That explains why they are out of town so often," he surmised. But even as they took their box seats, he had some unsettling thoughts; He didn't know if they were familiar with the secret workings of the United States government. In fact, he wondered if they even knew about the battle between the FBI and the Mafia, or about the horrendous sale of child pornography in America… or even its connection to the rest of the world.

It was a long game, but at the end of the sixth inning, he managed to get away for a phone call to his friend back in Vermont. The operator asked for change to cover the first three minutes of the long-distance call. Johnny was grateful to hear Father Tom answer the rectory phone.

"Hi, Tom! Just checking in with you. I got here a few days ago, but my hosts have kept me pretty busy."

"Great to hear from you, Johnny. How's the running going? You getting the stress out of those muscles?"

"Not really. My hosts are determined to make memories. I have hardly a minute to myself." He quickly got to the code. "But I am sorry to say there are gangs all over this city. Probably were here before, but now things are a lot more widespread. Its evil expanded, you know what I'm saying? That whole neighborhood changed since I was here last time."

"Oh, man, I'm sorry to hear that." There was a brief pause. "I guess your social life will be pretty limited. So much for finding a girlfriend, buddy."

The lawyer laughed. "Don't sell me short, my friend. My social life is *running*, until I get all the kinks out. Finding the perfect running partner would be a bonus, right? And sometimes I even get what I want."

"Well then, just get out there and run. Your dream girl could be just around the next corner. Be careful, though."

"I'll keep you posted, Tom."

Fifty feet away, somebody was watching John Courtney make that call. The youngster peered carefully as the man walked past him, apparently on his way back to a seat in the bleachers. There was a small hesitation, then the boy began to follow at a brisk pace. By the time John sat down beside the Kamaras, the lad was right beside him.

"'scuse me, mister."

The three of them turned to listen.

"Is... is your name 'John'?"

The boy was a little older, but John recognized him immediately. Shock numbed both his brain and his mouth, but Ariana saved the day.

"Richard! What a surprise!"

The redhead smiled a crooked-toothed greeting. "Hey, Mrs. Kamara." He gave a short wave to Steven. "Sir!"

Ariana turned to explain: "Richard is our paperboy, John."

Steven spoke up. "You two know each other?"

John nodded, but it was the boy who answered. "I'm pretty sure this is the man who kept me from making a mess of my life." The blue eyes fixed on the man's face. "You are him, ain'tcha? You sure look like the guy in the park when I hurt my Aunt Kate."

"I am." He cleared his throat. "How are you, son?"

"Pretty good. I come here and help pass out programs, so I get in free." The crooked smile flashed again. "Pretty good deal, huh?" He lowered his head. "Anyways, I just wanted to say thanks."

The conversation was interrupted by a home run. At the end of the jubilant roar of the crowd, the boy indicated he had to leave, in order to catch a transit bus back home.

"No, no, Richard. Come and sit down. You need to see the end of the game. Why don't you just ride home with us?" Steven was insistent, so the boy acquiesced. He went on to strike up a conversation with John, in between baseball maneuvers. The Kamaras listened quietly, but kept their eyes on the ball field.

"Yeah, I was pretty shook up, when that happened. Had to go to counseling for quite a while."

"It's good you did that, Richard." Suddenly, the lawyer decided to cautiously approach the witness. "Can you tell me how I helped?"

"Yeah." The lad lowered his voice. "My counselor kept pointing out that you sure did the right thing by talking to me like that. It helped a lot. That's why I wanted to say thanks, John."

"I'm glad I was there for you, Richard." Mr. Courtney asked the next question carefully. "And your aunt? How did she do? I left her there at the hospital with... I'm guessing it was your mom and dad."

"She couldn't remember things for a while, but it passed... I guess. I haven't seen much of her since then."

"Oh? Well, I hope she is well."

"Yeah," the boy said again, "she seems to be okay."

On the ride home the Kamaras gently pressed John and Richard about the details of the high fly that nearly killed Aunt Kate. Richard related all the details accurately, having been over them so many times while under treatment. The lawyer, however, seemed rather subdued, mostly nodding in agreement. As they dropped the boy off in front of his home, the couple observed that Johnny Courtney was taking careful mental note of the address.

The evening was growing late, but there was always time for one more cup of "red" tea, so Ariana's bright tray of the seething brew was welcomed by the two men.

"This has been a great treat, today," John told his hosts. "Watching the Cubs and then running into Richard, like that."

Ariana curled her feet under her, leaning back into the deep cushions of the sofa. "We enjoyed hearing his story on the way home. Seems he thinks your stepping up and keeping him grounded at that shocking moment... was a special thing." She held the small cup carefully on the saucer. "He said the counselor kept pointing out that those words — 'These things happen all the time in sports,' gave him a basic reference point during the months of counseling that followed."

"Ay-yuh. You never know when you might be doing something special for somebody, you know?" He blew gently over the top of his own cup. "The poor kid was paralyzed with shock, but fortunately, I had seen this before, in the Air Force... so I just did what I needed to do."

"He said you stayed right there with him, until his coach came along and took him home." She took a gentle sip, watching the man nod in agreement. "So, then what did you do?"

"Uh... I went over and gave his aunt mouth-to-mouth until

she started to breathe again."

"Oh my goodness! She wasn't breathing?"

"No."

"You saved her life, John!" She glanced at her husband, then turned back to the lawyer. "That was brave, sir, but could be very risky. People get sued for doing things like that... especially around here. Do you know how lucky you were? If she had been..." As she stopped to steady the teacup in its saucer, her husband came to her rescue.

"So, then what happened?"

"There was a cab parked right there. Somebody brought us a towel filled with ice cubes, so I grabbed it and held it on her forehead as the taxi got us to the emergency room at the nearest hospital — I forget the name of it. By the time we got there, that couple came running toward us. They thanked me and took her inside." He hoped that would cover the details, so he wouldn't have to lie about knowing it was Sarah and especially that he would not have to reveal the details of that painful, final conversation.

The warm living room was filled with the fragrance of the tea, even though a breeze softly billowed the lacey gauze window coverings.

"And this 'Aunt Kate,' Johnny," Steven asked softly, "what do you know about her?"

"I... I can't tell you much, Steven." At least he wasn't lying.

"Well, at least tell us... was she pretty?"

"Absolutely... even with the lump on her forehead." He felt a little warmth touch his neck.

"Your Uncle Doug said he wanted you to find a girlfriend out here..."

She was interrupted by her husband: "Or anywhere, for that matter." He laughed, knowingly. "You know what, John? I think he needs you to settle down and be more dependable. What do you think of that?"

"Uh... I'm thinking that will take a major miracle."

"Careful, careful, careful, John Courtney." She smiled at

Steven. "We are what you call, dyed-in-the-wool optimists!" Her beautiful eyebrows rose. "Meeting that lady under better circumstances just might be rather interesting."

John took a couple of seconds to put together the appropriate answer. "I hope that means you have special supernatural connections, my friends."

"In our line of work, that is a prerequisite," the handsome black man said.

"So..." She slipped her legs out from under and placed her sandaled feet upon the boldly patterned area rug. "You should know that we are somewhat acquainted with Richard's family." She quickly qualified that. "Nothing intimate, but you do get to know your paperboy's folks... what with days that Dad has to do the route because Junior has the flu... you know how that goes." She wiggled her toes, as she took another sip.

"What are you up to, Madame Matchmaker?" He grinned at his wife.

"I'm thinking Aunt Kate just might want to thank John... in person."

***

Steven had to make a quick trip to Washington, D.C. that same week. With Ariana scheduled to attend a ladies' luncheon on the day her husband left, John found himself finally alone.

It was the perfect time to get in a run, even though it meant he would have to throw caution to the winds.

Eagerly, he chose to head for the familiar little park where the accident had happened. He recalled there was room to circle the whole area three or four times, providing ample exercise. Before long, he was making the first round, taking in the surrounding view as he jogged along. The grounds had definitely deteriorated in the last few years; trash was scattered over what used to be the humble baseball field.

Weeds replaced the tin markers for all the bases and there were no more benches for the fans. The playground at the north end had no working swings; the posts stood slightly tilted over yellow grass.

"Doesn't look like they even play here, anymore," he thought.

At the end of his first round, the memories began to come back. Little details he had forgotten suddenly popped up in vivid reality: the shock in Richard's eyes, the mouth-to-mouth, the realization this injured woman was actually Sarah, the ride to the hospital, and then, the abrupt ending of that special encounter.

As he began the second round, his attention turned to the walkway in front of him. His feet pounded into the hard dirt path that lay ahead, all the way to the corner, where he would once again turn left to continue the run around the parameters of the park... only this time, his gaze traveled farther ahead, toward the next block. He could almost see the block after that and then there was the block after that one, where Richard lived. He wondered for just a couple of seconds what would happen if he just kept going straight and made a casual jog past that house, but turned, instead, to follow the pathway at that end of the playground.

But by the time he was headed for the third turn at that corner, he had convinced himself it would be perfectly fine for him to jog on past the next couple of blocks and even past that house... after all, there was sidewalk all that way and it was probably a safer run than padding along a weed-infested dirt path.

He made it past the first two blocks, then crossed over to the next. His eyes were focused on the dwellings ahead, so much so that he never noticed the three young black boys leaning against a chain-link fence across the street.

He tried not to stare at the place where Sarah probably no longer lived, but did slow down a bit. Just to make it all look legitimate, he went another two blocks before he turned around and headed back, for another look. In fact, he stopped in front of the place and bent down to retie a perfectly good shoelace, glancing sideways at the door, the windows, the driveway. *"I wonder if she's in there right now, maybe visiting for a couple of days?"*

Jeering laughter disturbed the daydream. He looked up to see the group of young Negro boys, now numbering five, instead of three.

"Hey, man! You forget how to tie your shoe?" The rest of them laughed as their leader began the taunt. As they moved toward him, the teenager continued: "We need to show you how to make a pretty bow? Huh?"

John suddenly realized he had wandered into some gang's territory. "Aw, damn." He felt like a fool.

The ringleader sauntered toward him, swinging a chain as he walked. "You get lost, mister? Well, ain't that a fricking shame." More laughter. "I guess we just might have to teach you how to be more careful."

The former Air Force captain, only five-foot-eight, himself, sized up the arrogant leader. *"About the same build, but never trained for combat. I can probably take him."* He strode confidently toward the kid, gently grinding one fist into the palm of the other hand.

"Us military types don't get lost very often," he said as he came to a stop in front of the leader, "but when we do, we know exactly how to get back on track." He smiled at his challenger. "I'm sure you already know that and I do apologize for straying over into your territory."

The youngster eyed him suspiciously. "What'd you say? You're sorry? Is that what you're saying?"

John continued to smile, but kept gently moving the fist inside the palm. "No offense intended," he said lightly.

The boy turned to his followers, laughing. He wiggled his shoulders and spoke in a high, female voice: "Ooo, no offense intended! No offense intended, sweetie!" Then he turned back toward John. "Too bad, sucker. I am offended and my friends are offended…"

"BEUFORT BRADLEY PORTER!" A golden-brown lady stood up from behind the shrub where she had been weeding. She glared at the brash troublemaker. "I... know... your... mother," she announced, slowly and ominously. While the boy was still standing there with his mouth open, she nodded to John to move on out of there. As the relieved jogger passed around the little gang, he heard her growl, "What's the matter whit-chew? You all get on home now and don't let me see you hanging around this corner again, you hear?"

John Courtney was through with the jogging; he would do the stairs in the Kamara home from now on. He climbed them and got into a hot shower. "Oh, my gosh," he muttered, "rescued by a beautiful, powerful neighborhood angel. Who would have ever thought...? Somebody must have been praying."

CHAPTER TWENTY-SIX

War

A few days earlier, Father Thomas had hung up the phone and retreated to his room. He needed to sort out the message he had just received from John.

"Alright," he whispered, "what did he actually say?"

He refreshed his memory. "The code word for anybody or anything watching him was 'evil.'" John had pointed out that he was surrounded by "evil expanded," so that meant he was in danger, even before beginning any investigation. The priest remembered the code word for "investigation" was "running," so he felt confident that he had the gist of the message, anyway. After a few minutes, he finally put it all together.

John had stumbled into complications on two fronts: well-meaning hosts and increased street-danger were keeping him from trying to find Sarah. So, the original threat of government surveillance, exposure, and 'elimination' — as bad as that was — had become a whole lot more involved.

For the next two days, he spent late afternoons in his room, praying for protection and guidance, not for himself, but for his friend. On this particular afternoon, his face was burrowed into the coverlet on his bed.

A knock at the door brought him up off his knees. Father Joe stood quietly on the other side of the threshold. The younger priest opened the door all the way and stepped back.

As he entered, the older man kept his focus on the floor and then he spoke: "I don't know what this is all about, my son, but I do know that I need to be here with you. I came here to your room as soon as I realized we were to do this." He motioned toward the prayer cushion on the floor. "Mind you, there is probably much more to this prayer vigil than you might think."

The younger priest looked puzzled.

"Ah, well, you will see it soon enough," he said.

The two men knelt and prayed together, until it was time for vespers. They continued this intensive prayer for three more days, between three and six in the afternoon, before things finally began to happen. On that night, the heavens above Essex Junction, Vermont, were filled with spiritual warfare.

It was about three o'clock in the morning when Father Tom was awakened by a deep, rattling noise. He opened his eyes, looking for someone, perhaps a drunken intruder who had fallen asleep right next to him, in his own bed. His extended arm swiped across the empty space beside him, before he rapidly withdrew it, because of the vibrating bedclothes.

"Why are the sheets moving?" he muttered. No sooner had he uttered those words, than the rattling increased, increased, increased, to a thunderous cadence. Suddenly, he was caught up in a swirling, dizzying foreign dimension, where he floundered helplessly, until something snapped him around, pinning his back tightly against a hard surface.

There, inches away, a dark entity writhed in intense hatred. The stench of its breath was overwhelming as it roared furiously into Tom's face. Suddenly, its clawed hands clasped and the thing whirled them around like a shot-putter.

The shot-blow into his face brought a stark-white fear.

"What...?" He took a breath.

The second blow came with even more force and he could hear the bones in his nose cracking.

There was only time for a short breath through his mouth before the third blow slammed his front teeth out of their sockets.

He sucked the next breath through blood.

"Jesu—"

The grasp on his hair yanked his head so fiercely upward that the spine was violently pulled apart at the neck and then the horrific shaking, shaking, shaking that led to shafts of searing lightning and then — abruptly a deep, putrid, flood of darkness.

"Back off in the Name of *Jesus! Back off* and leave this place!"

The shaking stopped and Tom fell back into his pillow. Father Joe laid his hands on the man's face.

"Healed in the Name of *Jesus!* Healed by the Blood of the Lamb!"

Suddenly, it was quiet in the room.

Tom was trembling all over, but he still opened his eyes. "Is it... is it gone, Father?"

"Oh, yes. Of course it is."

"Am I bleeding?" He was wiping the moisture from his face.

"Only in that other dimension."

Looking at his moist, but bloodless hands, he began to relax. "How did you know it was happening?"

"The Holy Spirit pulled me straight up out of bed and I landed right here." Father Joe seemed quite pleased.

"So… what just happened, here?"

"I don't know. You're the one who was on the other side of the veil, not me."

He tried to describe the horror of the attack, but there was no way to relate the intensity of such hatred. He apologized for the inadequacy of his words. "I guess you had to be there."

"And I probably have. I've been in spiritual warfare for many years. These things happen. All you have to remember is that demonic beings don't really have any power over you, unless you give it to them."

"I don't think I even had time to think about it, sir."

"That's how they like to work."

"I wish I could have kept my wits about me and done it right." He was still trying to get his wind back. "I guess I'm not a real good example of priestly wisdom." He took another breath as the thought hit him: "This has to have something to do with our prayers for Johnny, don't you think?" He sat up, but his head was bent forward. "I guess that sounds kind of dumb."

"More accurately, the dumb part was remembering to pray for protection and guidance for your friend and not remembering to do the same for yourself. That's a golden rule in spiritual warfare."

"So, that's why I was attacked?"

"I think so."

"Oh my gosh. I thought I was going to die. I really thought I was finished. That was so bad." He wiped the sweat off his forehead. "Aw, it's not like anybody else would believe any of this, anyway."

"Oh, they might. You'd be surprised."

"Would I?" The younger priest really wanted to know. "Why would anybody else believe what just happened?"

"Probably when it happens to them." Father Joseph smiled. "That's the way is usually goes."

The young priest would not figure it out for a couple more weeks, but it eventually became evident this brutal attack was in direct retaliation for the angelic protection of a certain jogger out on a noontime run, just fourteen hours earlier, all the way over there in Chicago. Father Thomas Ladue was learning yet one more facet of what it meant to "war in the spirit."

"They're calling it some kind of witness protection, but who knows?" Steven whispered to his wife. They lay in bed, nose-to-nose, the sheet pulled up over their mouths, just in case. "I had no idea what we would be getting into, checking up on that woman."

It had been only five days after Ariana had suggested that John and Kate might enjoy meeting again. Out of respect for the man's Uncle Doug, Steven had flown to the nation's capital and made some discreet inquiries about Richard's Aunt Kate, meeting with a special friend from the "inner circle." What he found out made him more curious about John, himself.

"He's the genuine article, but we already knew that, because of Doug. But it also stands to reason that he probably knew her — I'm guessing — back in Vermont.

My friend didn't tell me she was from there, nor did he tell me her real name, but you and I both see the way John looks, whenever we talk about her."

"Yes," she murmured, "there's no doubt about that."

"We also don't know what she testified about, but all of that is over, according to my friend. She's just under protection, for the rest of her life." He paused before he addressed the heavier information. "It has to be some kind of contest between the government and organized crime... maybe an outright battle."

"Oh dear... this young man is playing with fire."

"I agree, because he has to know about the protection thing. Look how evasive he was when we asked what he knew about her." He touched the end of her nose. "He has to know, and he has to know he's in danger." He moved his finger to smooth her eyebrow. "Thing is, he mustn't know that we know all this."

"I think you have a plan, Mister Kamara."

"I do."

"What would that be, sir?"

He pushed a soft puff of hair back from her cheek. "We need to discourage him."

"And how do we do that?"

"Tell him she's married."

"But he can and probably will check on that."

"Let him. He will find out that it's true."

"She's really married?"

"Yes, ma'am. Married the emergency room doctor."

She laughed out loud. "Oh, my heavens! And does that doctor/husband know about all this protection stuff?"

"Doesn't have a clue." He kissed her lightly on the brow. "And as far as anybody else knows, neither do you and I."

***

The Kamaras waited until Friday evening to make their next move. That was when Richard came to collect for the paper. The three of them were sitting in the living room when he knocked on the door.

"Can you come in for a minute, Richard?" Steven beckoned him to a chair.

"Sure." He greeted the three, sat down, and laid his collection bag flat on top of his knees.

"Let me just go get your money," Adriana said, as she left for the kitchen.

"Sorry to keep you waiting, son."

"Oh, that's okay, Mr. Kamara. I have to tell you something, anyways. I'm not going to do this route anymore. We're moving."

"You are?!" the gentleman exclaimed. "What happened?"

"Just need to get into a different neighborhood. Too much gang stuff going on. My folks don't want me out like this, all alone."

"Are you selling your place?"

"Already sold it... to a Negro family. They should be okay."

Steven slumped in his chair. "Of course. They should be okay."

John spoke up. "I assume your Aunt Kate will be going with you?"

"Oh no, sir. She hasn't lived with us since she got married."

The lawyer stared. "Oh, I see."

"Yeah, they got married a couple years ago, I think. Anyways, they have twins now."

"Twins..."

Ariana came back with some paper money in hand. "Who has twins?"

"Richard's Aunt Kate and her husband, dear. Isn't that nice?"

"Oh my goodness! How delightful." She paused to count out the money into the boy's hand. "And do they live with you folks?"

"Nope. They're somewhere in Europe, I think. My dad says Aunt Kate needed to go to some special clinic over there."

"Clinic?" Ariana tried to be polite.

"Yeah." The crooked-toothed smile went wide. "My dad said she had to lose some weight. I guess she's about thirty-five pounds overweight right now." He chuckled. "My dad calls her Roly-Poly 'cause she looks like a basketball."

Steven interrupted. "Richard's family is moving, darling. We are losing an excellent paperboy."

Mrs. Kamara murmured a melancholy objection, as the boy rose to leave. All three managed to wish him well, with friend-hugs all around. When the door closed, Ariana turned to John. "Oh my. There goes my grand plan for a face-to-face meeting. Oh, darn. That could have been so nice."

Steven moved to the sofa. "Just goes to show we never know what'll happen next." He looked to his wife with this question. "Shall we?"

She sat down beside him. "I guess this is as good a time as

any."

"We're also moving," Steven informed the man. "Have to take an apartment in D.C., since we'll be spending a lot more time in Liberia. At least, it's looking that way."

"It's just a matter of cutting down on travel time," she added.

"Of course. Who wants to live on an airplane?" John understood. "So, when do you two plan to make the transition?"

"Two weeks from today." She looked around the room. "So, we have already scheduled the mover."

The situation was crystal clear; the weary lawyer rose to the moment.

"You folks have been terrific hosts and I will never forget this trip. But I think it would be best if I get out of your way as soon as possible. I should be able to get a flight sometime this weekend, don't you think?"

Within an hour, he had a flight booked for seven forty-five the very next evening. As soon as that was accomplished, he said goodnight to his hosts and went to his room, managing to pack within fifteen minutes. He looked around to make sure he had everything except what he would need in the morning. Then he climbed into bed. The minute his head hit the pillow, he began to chuckle.

"Thirty-five pounds on a five-foot body?" The chuckle became a soft laugh. "No wonder he was calling her Roly-Poly." The picture in his mind was too funny and he began to laugh loud enough that he had to muffle it with his pillow. He laughed and laughed and laughed, until the tears moved in multiple rivulets down across the thirty-something wrinkles of his cheeks.

His Sarah was really gone.

***

John returned to Vermont early on that Sunday morning. He took a cab and stayed overnight with his mother. The next day, he joined his friend for a late lunch at the Lincoln Inn. Neither one of them was hungry, dawdling over the food, looking for the right words.

"Well, at least we know she's alive and well. Married and twins, huh?"

"Yup and probably done with the testifying, if she's actually in Europe."

"Hmmm. I guess we'll never know all the facts."

"And does that really matter?" John put his fork down. "I mean, she did what she needed to do. She's exonerated from the terrible harm she did, I think, what with helping to hinder all that child abuse... in whatever way she was able." He wanted to say so much more, but it came out in just a few words: "I honestly hope it goes well for her from now on."

"Ay-yuh, she's tried to make it right, even given up her identity." Tom wiped his mouth with the paper napkin. "Time to let it go, Johnny."

"I guess we could say the same for..." He caught himself, but it was too late, so he finished the sentence: "...for the Smiths. They have lost their marriage in pursuit of justice on behalf of all those poor little kids."

The priest brightened. "Not exactly. He got a call from her last week. The book is done and she wants to come home."

"Oh, you knew." He was relieved. "Well, that's excellent news."

"Sure. Counseling will be done, but those two truly love each other and I think they'll be ready to let the bad stuff eventually fade off into the sunset."

"I wish the same thing could be said about this hideous abuse of innocent children." John's shoulders hunched forward as he emphasized the point. "And to the power of organizations tearing society apart at its tender roots."

"So do I, Johnny, but the reality of it all is those organizations, or even world governments allowing it, will not be changing anytime soon, nor will sin disappear from the face of the earth in the foreseeable future." He looked sympathetically at his friend. "The fact is we are in this thing until Jesus comes back... and we don't know when that will happen, either." He bit his lip, ever so lightly. "That's when we'll see real justice, my friend."

"Try telling that to people who are suffering right now. I doubt they would even get it." He pushed the half-empty plate away. "So, what do you tell them, Father Tom, when they come to you for an answer?"

The priest cleared his throat. "Depends on the age and the circumstances, but if it happened to be a grown man, like yourself, I would make it clear: crap happens, because God will not violate the principle of *free will*. He does not want robots. He wants real children of God, who have been through fiery trials and come forth as His glorious, joyful family." He folded his hands on the edge of the table. "We don't understand that and that's why it seems so unjust, Johnny. But it's not actually God's choice; it's my choice as to whether I will follow Him or not and the same rule applies to every single person on this earth. The bottom line is, if we don't choose to dwell in the cleft of the rock — our Father's covering — we choose to fall into whatever chasm lies in front of us... we have no protection."

"Ay-yuh. I know that's the truth... but still, it seems so..." The word would not come forth.

The two men left their lunch money on the table for the waitress and ambled slowly out to the five-way traffic circle. A chilly breeze caught them by surprise and they quickly turned their collars up against it. Winter was definitely just around the corner. They walked along together for a few yards, then John stopped suddenly.

"Listen. I just had a thought. It's not entirely hopeless. Just listen to this." His friend turned around to face him. "God is helping people to stand up to all this garbage. There is resistance, whether in the earthly realm, or the heavenlies. And we have seen it, in this whole situation: we have books and testimonies championing institutionalized children; we have folks who give up their identities for the sake of innocent little ones; we have praying saints who plead for supernatural justice, and then we have the little soldiers, like that housemother, Mrs. Hays… all of whom encourage us, who remind us…"

"Now you're talking, Johnny. I think you get it."

"Yeah, well, I probably got it all along; just been too overwhelmed to get it down on paper, if you know what I mean." There was a wry smile. "We all, sooner or later, have to go through some pretty rough stuff, my friend, including those precious little ones in those pictures. When the trauma happens, each life is transformed forever. There is no going back." He pulled his jacket closer. "We can't restore that innocence, Tom. We can only encourage them to move forward."

"Exactly. They just need an encouraging word."

"Which is…?"

"Trust God that there is something uplifting in every trial. Don't stop loving; don't stop hoping."

"Right," the lawyer said, as he stepped forward. "Like Mrs. Hays told the girls."

The priest hastened to follow. "And what was that?"

"Remember the popcorn."

THE END

Also from L. E. Fleury's *Junctions Murder Mystery Series*:

Book Two: HAUNTED

Book Three: PORTALS

Book Four: CHAMELEONS

Book Five: DAMAGED

Stay tuned for more to come!

Made in United States
Troutdale, OR
05/12/2024

19679299R00206